FATAL
FAMILY TIES

ALSO BY S. C. PERKINS

Lineage Most Lethal

Murder Once Removed

FATAL
FAMILY TIES

S. C. PERKINS

MINOTAUR BOOKS

NEW YORK

First published in the United States by Minotaur Books,
an imprint of St. Martin's Publishing Group

FATAL FAMILY TIES. Copyright © 2021 by Stephanie C. Perkins.
All rights reserved. Printed in the United States of America. For information,
address St. Martin's Publishing Group, 120 Broadway, New York, NY 10271.

www.minotaurbooks.com

Library of Congress Cataloging-in-Publication Data

Names: Perkins, S. C. (Stephanie C.) author.
Title: Fatal family ties / S.C. Perkins.
Description: First Edition. | New York : Minotaur Books, 2021. |
    Series: Ancestry detective ; 3
Identifiers: LCCN 2021002110 | ISBN 9781250789648 (hardcover) |
    ISBN 9781250789655 (ebook)
Classification: LCC PS3616.E7469 F38 2021 | DDC 813/.6—dc23
LC record available at https://lccn.loc.gov/2021002110d

Our books may be purchased in bulk for promotional, educational, or business
use. Please contact your local bookseller or the Macmillan Corporate and
Premium Sales Department at 1-800-221-7945, extension 5442, or by email at
MacmillanSpecialMarkets@macmillan.com.

First Edition: 2021

10 9 8 7 6 5 4 3 2 1

For my godmother, Barbara Kazen

and

in memory of Don Morris, my godfather

and still my favorite artist

(Confederate.)

B | **5** | **TEXAS.**

Charles E. Braithwaite

Pvt., Co. **A**, 5 Reg't Texas Infantry.

Appears on

Company Muster Roll

of the organization named above,

for September + October 1862.

Enlisted:

When August 2, 1861.

Where Houston, Tex. Harris Co.

By whom W.B. Botts

Period War

Last paid:

By whom Maj. Ambler

To what time June 30, 1862.

Present or absent

Remarks: Deserted
After Manassas

Book mark:

C. McEntire

(642)   Copyist

FATAL
FAMILY TIES

ONE

I was angling my taco toward my mouth with the speed of the ravenous when a voice made me nearly fall off my barstool.

"Lucy, you have to help me!"

My taco hit my cheek instead, and juicy pork carnitas began dribbling down the left side of my face. At the same time, several thinly sliced radishes spilled out of the corn tortilla and back into the woven-plastic basket where my second taco lay waiting.

A paper napkin appeared, and then another. I snatched them and tried to mop myself up before anything dripped onto my white silk blouse.

"You have cilantro on your chin." Another napkin fluttered in front of my face.

Removing the offending herb, I finally turned with narrowed eyes and then felt them pop open in surprise. There, sitting next to me at the counter at Big Flaco's Tacos, was Camilla Braithwaite, one of my three least-favorite former coworkers.

"Camilla?" I sputtered. "What are you doing here? How did you even find me?"

In answer, she pulled a magazine from her purse and dropped it down on the counter. It landed on the edge of my bowl of queso, sending precarious ripples through the warm, spicy cheese dip. Hastily, I moved the dish away as she jabbed her index finger at the magazine. The cover and several pages had been turned back so it was open to an article near the middle. Camilla's striking light brown eyes were intense, almost as much as the scent of her perfume.

"I took a chance and went to your office, even though it's Saturday. Josephine—she's British, right? She was speaking Italian on the phone when she let me in, but when we talked she sounded like the Duchess of Cambridge. Anyway, she said you were here. I've come to see you, about this."

With one more jab of her finger for emphasis, I looked down.

THE BATTLE OF JUST PLAIN BULL
THE INFLATED LIFE AND CONTINUED LIES
OF AMERICA'S LAST CIVIL WAR SOLDIER

Picking up the magazine, I said, "Hey, I saw this headline a few days ago." I flipped to the cover to be sure. Yep, it was *Chronology,* a national publication put out by one of the biggest and best museums in the country, known for making articles about history so interesting, they inspired many a social media discussion, and even a few movies. "I get the digital version now, but it's on my list of articles to read." Glancing at some of the photos, the history-loving side of me was thrilled. Despite myself, I smiled. Dang my naturally sunny disposition! It came out at the worst times.

Camilla didn't return my smile. "So you haven't read it yet."

"Nope," I said, handing back the magazine with my left hand while picking up my fork with my right to spear some of the fallen carnitas and radishes. Adding a squirt of lime to my forkful, I savored it, wishing Camilla and her flowery perfume would go away so I could enjoy my lunch in peace. I was finishing up a client's genealogy project today, and if I didn't lollygag at Flaco's like I normally did, I could complete it by early afternoon, leaving my Saturday evening open for much better things. Glancing out the taqueria's glass doors, where March had brought sunshine and springtime weather, I felt my spirits lifting at the thought of the romantic plans I had in store for tonight with—

"Read it now," Camilla said, interrupting my daydream and turning the article back around. My eyebrow arched. "Please," she added.

With a stiff toss of her head, her thick, russet-colored hair obediently swished from her collarbone to behind her shoulders. It'd been nearly four years since I'd last seen Camilla. Yet during the sixteen months I'd worked at the Howland University library in Houston, where I'd been a staff genealogist and she one of three research librarians, I'd come to recognize she did that particular move with her hair only when she was stressed. When she was relaxed, she brushed it back with her hand.

In truth, Camilla Braithwaite was normally fairly even-keeled and, of the three research librarians, I'd liked Camilla the most. She'd been easygoing and had a good sense of humor . . . when she and I were alone, that was. When the other two research librarians—Roxie Iverson and Patrice Alvarez—were around, however, and push came to shove in the library's social pecking order, Camilla had been a lemming. She'd followed the mean-spirited direction of the other two, treating me as if my niceness and generally happy personality were irritating traits rather than worthy of appreciation. In appeasing the small-mindedness of our coworkers, Camilla had helped me feel like a permanent outsider. So, she'd become my third least favorite.

"Why is it so important I read this?" I asked, holding up the magazine with one hand. With the other, I scooped up a hefty bite of my fallen carnitas, just succeeding in delivering them to my mouth without incident as she replied.

"Because I need you to prove it's not true."

TWO

❧

My curiosity grappled with my perhaps saner instinct to get up and walk out the door.

"Why me?" I asked. "You're a researcher, and a very good one. Why can't you do it?"

"Because it involves the type of research genealogists normally do, and that's not my forte. Nor Roxie's or Patrice's, you know that."

Darn right I did.

"Then why haven't you asked Ginger?" I said. "She's an incredible genealogist, and right there, in-house, working with you."

When I'd worked at Howland University, Ginger Liening had been my direct manager, a senior genealogist, and taught the university's genealogy studies courses. I'd adored working alongside her—when I got the chance to, at least. As an entry-level staff genealogist, I'd often been tasked with helping the research librarians as much as helping Ginger. Roxie had claimed they needed my assistance, but what they really wanted was someone to do their grunt work. Since I'd needed the job, both for the experience and the money, I hadn't been in a position to do anything but say yes to every project.

"Ginger retired and moved to Arizona with her husband six months ago," Camilla said.

"Dang it, that's right. I sent her flowers and everything. I don't know where my mind was." Scooping up another bite of carnitas, I said, "Though surely y'all have hired a replacement since then. Why not ask her or him?"

"Him, actually," she said. "Trent—that's his name. He does a decent job, yes, but I want someone who does what you do."

Camilla's cheeks turned a bit pink, which I'd never seen happen to her before.

"Which is?" I asked, though I suspected I knew what she meant.

She cleared her throat. "Look . . . back when we worked together, you . . . *cared*."

"You say that like it's a bad thing," I grumbled, but Camilla went on regardless.

"I saw it when people came in, wanting help with their ancestry," she said. "You understood how the past could affect a person or their family. That's what I need, someone who cares when things are sensitive."

I blinked. That wasn't what I expected.

"Not because I . . . you know . . . helped solve a couple of mysteries late last year?"

"A couple?" she said, the furrows in her brow deepening. "I only heard about the one with the senator."

I wanted to kick myself. At my request, the FBI and the Austin Police Department had worked to withhold from the press my name and assistance in uncovering a murderous hotel front-desk manager's attempts to take out the descendants of eight World War II spies, one of whom was me. Instead, all the kudos had gone to Detective Maurice Dupart and his team at the APD, and I'd been relieved to remain out of the spotlight.

"Never mind," I said hastily. Taking the magazine from her, I flipped through the article's pages. "You'd better order something," I said. "This puppy is six pages long and I don't speed-read."

Ana, Flaco's best waitress, seemed to have heard me, and offered Camilla a menu before placing a small bowl of freshly made guacamole in front of me with a grin.

"Flaco me dijo que necesitas esto," she said.

I grinned back at her. Yeah, Flaco was likely right. I probably did look like I needed some guacamole.

As usual, I could see Flaco multitasking at his grill, wielding tongs in one hand and a ladle in the other, all while glancing over his beefy shoulders from time to time, keeping an eye on his customers, and especially on me. Julio "Big Flaco" Medrano already treated me like his fourth child, but after my genealogical projects and general nosiness had gotten me into some hot water last year, he'd become extra protective, watching over me like a huge guard dog with a handlebar mustache.

Camilla ordered a Dr Pepper and eyed my guacamole as I used a tortilla chip to scoop up the gently mashed avocado spiked with fresh lime juice and mixed with chopped red onions, cilantro, jalapeños, and tomatoes. She then asked for an order with tortilla chips for herself as I began reading.

> His name was Charles Edward Braithwaite, and he was
> a coward, a deserter, and a charlatan.

I blinked up at Camilla. She had a smattering of freckles across her nose and full lips, which were pressed together in dismay. I turned back to the article.

After that explosive first sentence, the article about the life of Corporal Charles Braithwaite of Houston, Texas, who had the distinction of being the longest-lived soldier who'd fought in the Civil War, was interesting enough that I was able to block out the crunching noises Camilla was making as she plowed through her guacamole.

I read that Charles Braithwaite was born in Houston in 1842 to a family so poor, he and his siblings rarely had shoes. As a youth, he often stole food to feed his brothers and sisters, but was known for being able to slip away before anyone noticed, and thus never got caught. He intermittently worked for farmers in the area, picking raspberries, pears, and cotton, but never held steady employment.

However, in August 1861, at age nineteen, Charles was finally caught trying to make off with several heads of cabbage, but escaped incarceration by enlisting with the Fifth Texas Infantry Regiment as they prepared to fight in the war between the states. The Fifth Texas became part of Hood's Texas Brigade and fought in many well-known campaigns under General Robert E. Lee in Northern Virginia, from Seven Pines all the way to the Battle of Appomattox Court House, where Lee eventually surrendered to General Ulysses S. Grant, beginning the end of the Civil War.

Charles Braithwaite, on the other hand, stuck around for only a couple of those battles. According to the article, he deserted his regiment on September 1, 1862, after the bloody campaign at Manassas, Virginia, which came to be known as the Second Battle of Bull Run.

I read on. The article claimed to have evidence that instead of going home to Houston after deserting, Charles made his way south to a small town in Louisiana, where he hid until the war's end. After finally returning to Houston in 1865, he soon found no one had heard of his desertion, mainly because his regiment had been decimated at Antietam and subsequent battles. It turned out that Charles Braithwaite had few cohorts, if any, to check his past.

For years thereafter, Braithwaite lived quietly. He married, had three children, and worked at a lumber mill, rising up to the post of foreman. He eventually retired, having been known for being a fair boss and for hiring and promoting men based on their merit instead of on their race or color. He'd also provided enough food on the table that his children never had to steal themselves.

There were two short paragraphs that read favorably toward Charles. The reporter wrote that Charles "dabbled as an artist," occasionally submitting illustrations to local Houston newspapers of the time. He even returned home from his hideout in Louisiana in time to be in the crowd at the famous Texas Emancipation Day announcement on June 19, 1865, when Major General Gordon Granger of the Union Army stood on the balcony of Ashton Villa in Galveston, Texas, and announced the freeing of all enslaved people under General Orders, No. 3. A photo in the middle of the article showed Charles's drawing of what he saw that day. He'd beautifully captured the jubilation of the Black residents at hearing the news of their freedom at what would later become known as the first Juneteenth celebration. While the *Chronology* reporter called most of his other drawings "generally simplistic," it was admitted that Charles had a talent for drawing people.

The next paragraph then briefly laid out Charles's well-documented support of the Black population in Houston and throughout Texas, including working with the Freedmen's Bureau, stumping for political candidates who supported the rights of Black people, and, later, vocally opposing racial segregation laws. His children, Nathaniel, Edward, and Henrietta, and later their children, often accompanied him, and followed in his footsteps as adults. It was also mentioned that Charles gave to the poor, supported women's suffrage, and was adamant that education and medical services be a high priority for everyone.

Yet that was as close as the reporter went in a positive direction. In 1920, the article stated, when Charles was seventy-eight years old—having already outlived most people born in the mid-1800s—he recognized his golden opportunity. He began to embellish his history, especially his time in the war, for his own profit, giving his rank as corporal instead of what it actually was: private.

Still spry and healthy, Charles began taking speaking engagements, first in Houston, then in other parts of Texas, and began eventually traveling throughout parts of the South. As his fame for being a surviving Civil War soldier grew, parades were given in his honor and he was feted at nearly every turn. In his hometown of Houston, a park was named for him, as was Braithwaite Elementary. Later, as the Second World War drew nearer, two scholarships were set up in his name for underprivileged students looking to go into the armed forces.

Overall, the *Chronology* reporter had thoroughly denigrated Charles for seeking to make money off his time as a Confederate soldier. Nevertheless, they had still conceded that Charles refused to glorify the war and the aims of the Confederacy in his popular talks, often rebuking anyone who attempted to encourage him to do so. Instead, he spoke of his fellow soldiers' hardships, the suffering he and his comrades endured, and watching his friends die in battle. Records of his talks proved Charles also exalted the bravery of all soldiers—Confederate and Union alike—during the course of the war. And audiences ate it up.

I paused in my reading. The article was indeed an exposé, but it had been well-written thus far, walking the line between giving the hard facts and being downright accusatory, and tempering it all with a bit of praise here and there. I flipped through the last two pages, which contained several photos and a couple of fairly inflammatory pull quotes, including one that read *"Braithwaite went so far as to invent a fellow soldier named*

Powers in his journal, writing about him as if this young private had been his friend, though no such soldier existed." I could see why Camilla was upset, sure, but I was beginning to feel like she was being overly dramatic about insisting the article's allegations be debunked.

After taking in a photo of Corporal Braithwaite as a handsome young man and noting he'd passed his high forehead and cleft chin down to his descendant sitting next to me, I glanced back at the first page to check the reporter's name.

"Camilla," I said, "it sounds like this Savannah Lundstrom did her research. I sympathize with you on what she says about your ancestor, I really do, but I have to say, I'm not seeing anything in here that warrants being proven untrue."

I ran my fingers over the photo of Charles Braithwaite in his full-dress uniform, then met Camilla's eyes. "It's a shame he deserted his regiment, yes, but we don't know why he did. It could have been post-traumatic stress disorder, for instance. PTSD is hardly a recent phenomenon, you know. They had different names for the symptoms back then, calling it everything from 'feeble will' to 'mania.' In fact, the heart palpitations of panic attacks were often called 'soldier's heart' and were chalked up to practically everything other than true psychological conditions. War is hell for everyone involved, and Charles could have been suffering so much mental anguish that he just ran." I softened my voice. "It's possible he wanted to go back to his regiment, but feared being shot on sight for desertion. I think judging him solely on that one act when we can never know all the facts is a little harsh, especially when we know he went on to be an upstanding man in most every other respect."

Pointing to a paragraph on page two, I said, "Case in point, Ms. Lundstrom even acknowledges your ancestor spoke out on behalf of Black people and their welfare long before he became famous. And in his job at the lumber mill, he was known for being one of the few to hire and promote men irrespective of their race or color. She even admits that while he made his fortune off recounting tales of being in the Civil War, he spoke about what it was like being a soldier, not to glorify the Confederacy."

To this, Camilla nodded, saying with pride, "Yes, my ancestor's antiracist views are well documented, and my family upholds those views to this day." Then she fell back into a strained silence, and I picked up the baton again.

"All right, then. Despite his one questionable act of leaving his regiment, I say you should be proud of him, the person he was, and what he accomplished on the whole." I went to close the magazine. "Camilla, I'm sorry, but I don't think I can help you with this, and I really need to get back to my office. I've got a project to finish up and I really don't want to work late tonight. I have—"

"Keep going until the end," she cut in, before I could finish with the words *a date tonight with my boyfriend*. What I wouldn't have added, but really wanted to shout from the mountaintops, was that my boyfriend was a handsome FBI agent who'd just come home after a long undercover assignment and had a whole week off to spend time with me.

I gave Camilla a look of undiluted exasperation and felt a little proud of myself for that small act. When I'd worked with Camilla, Roxie, and Patrice at the Howland library, I'd reined in any feelings or actions that weren't friendly or helpful. I had to, for the sake of both keeping my job and maintaining a peaceful work environment.

Now, though? I was my own boss, and I owed Camilla nothing. Or next to nothing. I had no desire to be rude or disrespectful to her, especially for reasons as silly as office-hierarchy pettiness. To me, the better way to do things was to live well and happily, without giving consequence to the unworthy people in one's past.

That's not to say it's always easy when one of those people is staring you in the face and practically demanding your help.

"Please," Camilla said again, with a pleading note in her voice. "Keep reading until the end."

I felt myself relenting. Darn it if I weren't a nice person who was willing to keep giving people chances! I scowled and went back to the article, though it didn't take much longer for my grumpy expression to change to one of astonishment at what I read.

Before they knew it, Charles Braithwaite and his family were earning money hand over fist, and his children and grand-children were suddenly being welcomed at the best houses and social events in Texas and beyond. The formerly poor Braithwaites had moved on up to houses in the finest area in Houston, and they didn't let anyone forget it.

At the time of Private Braithwaite's death in 1945, it is estimated that he and his family had earned around $75,000—the equivalent of over a million dollars today—for his appearances as a Civil War veteran. Braithwaite made no bones about his appearance fees, either, and he didn't care from whom he took money. In 1925, Zacharias Gaynor spent a month's wages to have Braithwaite come to his house for dinner, a regular custom throughout history that often served to increase the host's social standing. It did nothing for the Gaynor family, however, and Zacharias, after spending all his family's money, was later sentenced to eight weeks in prison for failure to pay his debts, losing his job as a result. We can only guess at the hell his family endured during that time and afterward. But did Braithwaite care, or return the man's money? Of course not, and he only continued to milk his fame even when he became feeble, deaf, and nearly blind from cataracts.

Such was the delight at having a real-life Civil War "hero" in their midst that some local companies even spent a bundle just to have Braithwaite, who was semi-bedridden by this time, show up for one parade or another to wave listlessly from the back seat of a car, shilling for some company he no doubt couldn't even name.

Oh, but his children and subsequent generations were smart with the money Braithwaite gained. The three clans stemming from Charles and his wife, Violet, spread out over Texas and the United States, no longer the descendants of a man who stole as a youth and deserted his regiment as a soldier. No, the families continue to live off the image their ancestor so carefully cultivated from his lies. They still speak of Charles Braithwaite's valor, hard work, open-mindedness, and honesty whenever they can, holding him up as a paragon of the greatest kind of American, not caring that the legacy upon which their livelihoods were founded was hardly that of a great man, but instead the most selfish of cowards.

It seems that even today, escaping the truth is a well-honed Braithwaite skill.

THREE

Slowly, I closed the magazine. While I'd known *Chronology* to publish articles that contained harsh truths about historical figures, I'd never seen one take such a pointed and vitriolic aim at its subject's descendants.

"Do you see what I mean now?" Camilla asked.

"I sure do," I said. "Wow. And I have to say, I'd heard of *the* Braithwaite family in Houston, of course, but I didn't know you were related to them. I don't think we ever talked about it when you and I worked together."

That was actually an understatement. I'd been open about my life and background to my coworkers, but Roxie, Camilla, and Patrice had given me very few details about themselves in return. The most I knew about Camilla was that she had two teenage sons and that she'd gone back to her maiden name after getting divorced. There were times I'd wondered about her background, but my few attempts at engaging her in talking about anything personal during the sixteen months we'd worked together had always been met with a return to her standoffish demeanor and a segue in conversation.

"I don't care to talk about it with most people," Camilla told me. "Roxie and Patrice come from more humble beginnings, and when I started at the library six years ago, I had to work hard to convince them I wasn't some rich snob. My branch of the Braithwaite family has done well, but my parents were both college professors. We were comfortable, yes, but we certainly lived a lot less extravagantly than my cousins. Still, I've never felt like I need to explain myself to others."

And there we were again. I had been an "other" instead of a friendly coworker.

"How did you even see this article?" I asked, determined not to feel slighted. "I mean, I know we had a subscription to *Chronology* at the library, but I don't recall ever seeing you read it." As soon as the words came out of my mouth, I felt terrible for how rude I must have sounded. Camilla, however, didn't seem to notice.

"I don't normally," she said on a sigh, staring through the pass-through at Flaco, watching him flip sizzling slabs of meat while instructing his sous-chef, Juan, to chop some more vegetables. "One of the college students was reading it while I was looking up some information for her. She noticed the name Braithwaite and asked if I was related to Charles. When I said yes, she handed me the article and told me I'd better read it."

I decided it would be best to circle back to why Camilla had so unceremoniously interrupted my pleasant lunch in the first place.

"So, what is it exactly that you want me to prove? That your ancestor was telling the truth about staying in the war and receiving his corporal's stripes?" When she focused on me again, I asked, "Do *you* believe your ancestor was telling the truth?"

Her nod was vehement. "I do. We've always known he fought in the war and earned his promotion to corporal. There was never any hint that he was a deserter."

With most of my clients, I was careful in my replies to their long-held family notions. I understood all too well how important it was to believe your family—believe *in* your family—even the people you had never met and those who had passed away decades or more before you were even born. It wasn't rational by any means, but it didn't stop any of us from feeling it and wanting the positive stories we'd known about our ancestors to be true.

However, Camilla wasn't a client, not yet. I also didn't want to take on a fruitless endeavor that would put me at the beck and call of someone who had already proven herself unworthy of my trust.

"What proof do you have?" I asked. It was a bit blunt, but Camilla gave me only the merest of side glances before answering.

"Beyond all the family stories, we have a few other things, including Charles's journal and a photo with him in his corporal's uniform. We also have a letter from Charles to his father detailing the Battle of Seven Pines, after which he earned his promotion to corporal. He wrote about the horrors of war and the bravery of his fellow soldiers even then." Camilla's eyes registered earnest belief. "It's a very moving letter. I can show it to you, if you like."

All I could think was, *And every bit of that could have been forged or re-created after the war to suit his purposes.* Still, I said, "Yes, I'd love to see it. Did you bring the materials with you from Houston?"

Camilla shook her head. "No, everything is already here in Austin. My family gave all of it to the Harry Alden Texas History Museum when it opened in 2003. They have it on display in their Civil War section." Then she frowned. "Well, they do for now. A friend of mine who works for another museum told me the curator will most likely be obliged to take the exhibit of my ancestor down until they can confirm the truth."

I laced my fingers together. "Camilla, I don't know the curator of the Alden museum, but I do know the assistant curator. He's a good guy, and if he has to investigate, he'll do so thoroughly and with respect. In fact, he also has researchers for things like this who are just as good, if not better, than me. I can give you his phone number and email right now." I opened up my phone to go to my contacts. "Why don't you call him, explain the situation up front, and let him and his team do the work for you? Not only will you get high-quality research but you'll also get it for free. With me, you'd not only have to hire me, you'd unfortunately have to pay me a premium to fit you in between the three upcoming projects I have on tap. I'd have to push one or more of them back to work on this, and they may go to another genealogist once they've been notified I can't start their project on time."

I wasn't bluffing. On my website was a clear notice that anyone who wanted a rush job would be charged extra. If one of my other clients opted to go to a competitor because I had to push their job back a little, I wanted to make sure I could still pay my bills.

Camilla was shaking her head. "No, I want you to handle this. I want it done with discretion and . . . and by somebody who cares, like I said. I'll pay you your rate plus the premium."

To my surprise, she reached into her purse and pulled out a checkbook, then looked at me with solemn determination. "What do I owe you as a retainer for now? Or would you rather me transfer the money electronically? Either is fine."

"Hold on," I said, gently putting my hand over the check before she could start writing. Even if she could afford it, I didn't think it was fair to take her money without fleshing out a good reason for it first. "You're rushing into this, Camilla, and I have to know. Why is this so important to you?"

"Does it really matter why?" she said, sitting back when I'd taken my hand away.

"It does," I said. "I mean, I get that you wouldn't want your relative's legacy to be tarnished, but, if you'll forgive me, who is really going to care that much, outside of your family and maybe a handful of others, like the museum curator?"

"I've no doubt there will be an article in the *Houston Chronicle* and pieces on all the local news stations, too," she said darkly.

"Probably, yes," I said. "I agree that it wouldn't be fun to have such an article written about an ancestor of mine. Still, with the way the media and people's memories move on in the blink of an eye, whatever scandal that comes from this would be forgotten in a couple of days, at most."

She was quiet, like she was really hearing me, so I continued to press my point.

"Also, while Charles Braithwaite did take money for appearances, he hardly stole it. Nor did he present himself as some sort of hero. He merely pushed himself up one rank, to corporal, which sounds more prestigious than 'private,' yes, though not by much. I really don't think that now, over seventy-five years after his death and over a hundred and fifty-five years after the Civil War, anyone is really going to care that Charles Braithwaite deserted his regiment and then sought a little bit of fame from outliving his fellow soldiers."

"He wasn't a deserter," Camilla snapped, her voice growing louder and a flash of anger bringing out more bright spots in her cheeks. A few patrons sitting by us at the bar turned to stare. "Look, Charles fought for the Confederacy, yes, though his speeches thankfully confirm that he had no interest in glorifying its aims for the war. Nevertheless, when it came to his rank, he fought, and fought bravely, and he was promoted for it. He earned his corporal's stripes, Lucy."

I opened my mouth to give a hopefully soothing reply, but Camilla wasn't done.

"But you're right, preserving that part of his legacy isn't the only thing that's bothering me. There's also someone who's claiming Charles ruined their family," she said. "And another person is starting a petition to have the park and elementary school renamed." She held up the magazine and shook it. "People are starting to use these claims to disparage my family."

FOUR

I gave the evil eye to the one guy still gawking at Camilla and he hastily went back to his basket of tacos.

"Are you serious?" I asked. "Who's claiming your ancestor ruined their family?"

Camilla pulled the magazine toward her and found the last page of the article again. She pointed to the section mentioning Zacharias Gaynor, the man who'd ended up in prison for failing to settle his debts after paying Charles Braithwaite to come for dinner.

"The descendant of this guy, that's who," Camilla explained. "His name is Neil Gaynor, and he's a PhD candidate at Howland University. He knows me because he's always in the library doing research and I've helped him a bunch." She sat up a little straighter on her barstool. "I've become quite known for being a go-to research librarian, but I still don't do the kind of in-depth genealogical and historical research you do. Believe me, if I could do this all myself and keep it quiet, I would."

"I think there's a compliment in there somewhere," I said dryly. Camilla's eyes cut to me in surprise, but before she could feign contrition, I said, "So what does Mr. Gaynor want from you?"

"It's ridiculous—he claims his family began a downward spiral into poverty after his great-great-grandfather spent all his money having Charles to dinner in 1925. He says Zacharias's children went hungry, and one died from malnutrition. Apparently Neil's great-great-grandmother went to Charles to ask for their money back, and Charles refused. Zacharias died not long after and the family has continued to live at poverty level since then." Camilla huffed out a breath. "Whether or not it's true that Charles refused to refund them, Neil says he's already spoken to a lawyer and he's planning on suing our family for reimbursement of their family's monies, with interest."

"How much money would that be today?" I asked.

"It's not a huge amount until you add interest over the decades," she replied. "Then it comes to a bit over ten thousand dollars."

I interpreted the look of misery and frustration on her face. "Which is a good chunk for a lot of people, but not for a family like yours—and it would probably cost at least half that just to pay for lawyers to counter any suit, so it might be easier to just pay him." When she nodded with a sigh, I added, "But you're also probably thinking that if one guy gets that kind of money from your family so easily by threatening a frivolous suit, then others could come out of the historical woodwork and do the same."

"With how litigious our society is these days, it's a possibility," she said.

I had to admit, she had a point.

"And who wants Braithwaite Park and Braithwaite Elementary to be renamed?"

Camilla's face radiated annoyance. "A woman running for city council. She contacted me as well, telling me she didn't think it was right for a park and an elementary school to be named after—and I quote—'a lying, greedy man.'" Camilla's look turned doleful. "Then she added in stuff about how no public entity should have ties to the Confederacy. As an educated person, I can't say I disagree with her. My extended family discussed it back in January, in fact. We're already in touch with the city to remove his name from the park and school, and I told the woman as much."

"How did she respond?" I asked. "Will she drop the petition?"

"She said she'll drop it when the name change is announced, though she said we were doing the right thing, and we are. My family understands that you can be proud to be from Texas and from the South while still recognizing and hating the fact that the South's pro-slavery history, including the Confederacy and the Civil War, caused so much pain—and it still reverberates today. My relatives and I believe in being open to a change that will no longer put the Confederacy front and center. Yet we also don't agree with erasing or destroying history or historical artifacts. Instead, my family believes Civil War history—just like all history—should be properly studied, discussed, and learned from, and any relevant artifacts should be displayed in places like museums for educational purposes."

I smiled broadly at her. "Camilla, I feel the exact same way."

I knew my reaction had pleased her when, this time, she used her hand to brush her thick hair behind her shoulders. Then she picked up the issue of *Chronology*.

"I want to be clear, Lucy. I don't love it that this reporter called out Charles for cashing in on his time as a Civil War soldier, but she nevertheless reported the truth when it came to the nature of his talks. She correctly states that Charles spoke mostly about what it was like to be a soldier in the war. She also admitted to the good things Charles did afterward, like championing education and a woman's right to vote." Camilla shook the magazine so the pages shimmied, her voice becoming impassioned. "What I can't stand is that she ensconced the truth in this overall cloak of ridiculous inaccuracies about Charles being a deserter who later lied about his life for profit. And then she says his descendants, all the way down to my present-day relatives and me, have perpetuated and continued to profit from Charles's so-called fraudulent claims. I mean, we're not perfect—what family is? But to imply that we make our livelihoods out of 'escaping the truth'? What the hell is she playing at?"

I had to admit, I was thinking along those lines as well. Camilla, taking my silence for consent, slid the issue of *Chronology* toward me again, snapping me out of my contemplation. "So you'll look into this for me?"

I didn't move to take the magazine. "I appreciate your reasonings, of course, but I'm still not sure. *Chronology* is a respected publication." I tapped the name of the reporter at the top of the article. "If this Savannah Lundstrom found evidence that Charles Braithwaite deserted his regiment and never ascended to corporal, I'll likely find the same thing."

"Isn't it enough that I'm happy to pay you to try?" she asked.

My eyebrows rose even as, inwardly, I sighed. The old Camilla I knew—distant and unwilling to offer up a measure of friendship—was back, her expression impassive.

I thought about my three upcoming projects. One of the clients had been clear that they weren't in a rush, and I hadn't yet confirmed a start date for the other two. Nevertheless, I'd been planning on doing some preliminary work on all three during the upcoming week, mostly on the days Ben had meetings. Otherwise, I'd deliberately left the upcoming week light so I could spend as much time with him as possible.

After all, Ben and I had enjoyed only a couple of weeks together in early January before he was sent off on another undercover assignment. When he'd resurfaced a couple of days ago, hearing the sound of his voice on the phone had made me all kinds of happy. He was still in Washington, DC, for some meetings, but he'd be back in Austin tonight. Even better, after a week of rain, today had been gorgeous, and it was forecasted to be in the low sixties and sunny for the next couple of days. I couldn't think of better circumstances to enjoy getting reacquainted with my relatively new boyfriend, and I really didn't want to be working on a project for Camilla Braithwaite in the meantime.

However, as a self-employed person, I could always use the money, and I did need to keep busy while Ben was in his occasional meetings. Plus, I was already thinking that proving the article's truth would probably be as easy as pie. I'd just have to look up Charles Braithwaite's compiled military service record, or CMSR, and that would likely tell me most of what I needed to know. I might not even have to spend more than a couple of days on the project, so why not take it?

"I think you know I'd do my best to get clear proof either way," I began, "but what if I find that the reporter discovered the truth? Will you be all right with that?"

Camilla hesitated, but answered, "Not really, but if that's what it comes to, then that's the breaks." She shook her hair back once more, half with her stressed-out twitch and half brushing it back with her hand, making me believe she was trying her best to believe what she'd just said.

I nodded. I wasn't going to try to talk her out of it again. I'd done what I could and I wouldn't feel guilty about taking her money for the rush job.

"All right, Camilla," I said. "That's all I can ask for, and I'm happy to take the project." I told her my retainer price for a rush job and that an electronic money transfer would be better, and she didn't even blink. Moments later, my phone pinged with a deposit to my work account.

"Are you going back to Houston, then?" I asked, after we discussed contract terms and I forwarded her a copy of the agreement from my iPad. She also gave me her copy of *Chronology* so I could read the article again.

Camilla slid off her barstool and slipped money for her bill under a bottle of Flaco's special homemade hot sauce. "Not until Tuesday afternoon. I'm taking a couple of vacation days. My boys are with their father, and I'm here to see friends and to visit my great-uncle, who's in his mid-eighties and not doing so well lately."

I dunked a tortilla chip into my queso. "I'm sorry to hear that. Is your great-uncle from the Braithwaite side?"

"Yes, though he descends from Charles's eldest son, while I descend from the younger son. Trent, the new in-house genealogist, showed me a relationship chart. Technically, my great-uncle and I are something like third cousins, a couple of times removed," she said. "Anyway, he's always been really tight with my side of the family, so I grew up calling him Uncle Charlie."

"Well, it is exhausting and a little weird to say 'my third cousin, twice removed Charlie' all the time," I deadpanned. Camilla stared at me for a moment like she'd never heard me be funny before, then her lips quirked up briefly.

I popped the chip in my mouth, only to find the queso had gone stone cold. I pushed the dish away, switching back to my guacamole. "I think I'll go see your ancestor's things at the Alden museum on Monday. Would you like to meet me there in case I have any questions?"

Camilla looked a little hesitant at the thought of spending time with me in a semi-social situation, but she nevertheless agreed. We discussed times and settled on ten o'clock on Monday at the museum's entrance.

Picking up her purse, she said, "Anything else before I go?"

I pursed my lips in thought, then asked, "Are there any other artifacts of Charles's history that aren't in the museum?"

"Just a couple. One is a copy of *Oliver Twist* that Charles kept on his bedside throughout most his life. It's not a first edition or anything, and it's in rough shape, if I recall. My uncle Charlie has it on his bookshelf. It was given to Charles by his wife, Violet, my however-many-times-great-grandmother . . ." She raised her eyebrows in question at me.

"If you and Charlie are third cousins, twice removed, then Charles and Violet are your fourth great-grandparents and Charlie's second," I answered. "For people our age, in their thirties, our ancestors who married and had babies around the Civil War years are generally either our fourth or fifth great-grandparents, but it all depends on how early or late they had children." I pulled another tortilla chip from the basket. "Any other family artifacts?"

"There's just one more thing, and the Alden museum didn't want it," Camilla said. "Charles made a three-paneled painting of a battle scene at some point after the war ended. It's a pretty big painting when the panels are side by side." She held out her arms to their full extent, saying, "About six feet long by three feet high. Charles designed it so his three children would each have a third."

"He painted the battle scene as a triptych?" I said. "How cool."

"I think so, too," Camilla said. "Though it's not really a triptych anymore because one panel, the left one, went missing. It originally went to Charles's daughter and it was last seen around 1988, which is the year the last whole-family reunion happened. That piece presumably bounced around to various members in that branch of the family since then, and no one knows where it ended up."

"Do you know any of your cousins from that side of the family?" I asked.

She shook her head. "No, I don't. The branches descending

from Charles's two sons stayed in touch because so many of us remained in Houston, or at least in the southern half of Texas, but the branch descending from Charles's daughter scattered a long time ago."

"Well, it's not surprising in any family when you go back that far," I said. "In six generations, your family tree has branched a minimum of . . ." I gazed off at the huge velvet painting of Flaco dressed like Elvis in *Blue Hawaii* (but holding a cast-iron skillet instead of a ukulele), while I did some mental genealogy gymnastics in my mind. "Oh, at least sixteen times since 1865, and likely much more if some of the branches had multiple children, which it sounds like they did. You're likely one of anywhere between a hundred and fifty to well over two hundred of Charles's great-great-great-great-grandchildren. You can easily lose track of distant cousins when there's that many."

Camilla's eyes widened. "Sheesh. Are you serious? I have that many cousins?"

Entertained, I used a tortilla chip to point at her. "And that's from only your Braithwaite line. You have thirty-two couples who make up your fourth great-grandparents. So, think on those numbers of cousins."

Now she gaped at me, and I had to admit, it felt kind of nice to impress her with my knowledge.

Camilla gave her head a little shake, as if to clear away the numbers I'd put in her mind. "Like I said, all I know is that the third panel was last seen at the family reunion in 1988, when the triptych was put back together for the day."

Despite myself, I smiled at the hint of mystery. "That's a neat story in and of itself," I told her. "I'd love to know what happened to that left panel."

Camilla shrugged. "So would I, but no one else in the family really seems to care, except for Uncle Charlie, who has the center panel, and me. I have the right panel and I barely saved it from my younger brother after my dad passed. My brother—he's Charles Braithwaite the Fourteenth, if you can believe it. Every relative of mine wanted to name a kid after Charles." She gave an indulgent eye roll. "We've always called him Tor, though. It's short for *quatorze*, French for 'fourteen.' Anyway, Tor was about to sell our painting for ten bucks at a garage sale, and I grabbed it literally seconds before some guy handed over the money."

My look of scandalized horror mixed with dramatic relief actually earned me one of Camilla's rare smiles, softening her face and warming her eyes.

I asked, "Do you know why the Alden museum didn't want the painting?"

She hitched her shoulders again. "Charles often made sketches and doodles—you'll see that in his journal in the museum—and he was really good at drawing people, like in the drawing he did for the Texas Emancipation Day celebration. But the triptych is . . . something different entirely. It looks a bit more like folk art, with the soldiers painted somewhat crudely and the clouds looking like white blobs, but I still like it. Anyway, with the museum, I think it was a combination of Charles using an unusual style and the fact that one of the three panels was missing. They told my family that they found our painting interesting, but it had more sentimental than historic value."

We both heard a *ding* and she reached into her purse to check a text.

"I've got to go," she said. "My friend Sarah is waiting for me." She hesitated, then gave me a nod. "Thank you, Lucy, for looking into this for me."

"You're welcome," I said.

She began walking away, then turned back. "Monday, after we go to the museum, would you like to see Uncle Charlie's third of the triptych?"

"That would be fun," I said with a smile. There was a closeted art historian inside me who longed to get out, and I indulged her whenever I could.

Camilla was watching me, though, her eyes becoming narrower and narrower as I lifted another guacamole-laden tortilla chip to my mouth.

"Lucy, are you really this nice?"

"Huh?" I said, so surprised I didn't have an intelligent response.

"Never mind," Camilla said hastily, another uncharacteristic flush rising up on her cheeks. "I'll see you Monday at the museum." She was out the door before I could even blink.

FIVE

W hat's wrong with being nice?" I said.

"Absolutely nothing, love."

"Maaaaybe you could stick up for yourself a little more with some people, though."

"Yes, but was Camilla *trying* to be snarky to me?"

"Surely not."

"Eh, I'd put it at fifty-fifty."

"Good grief. Do *y'all* think I'm too nice?"

"Darling, of course we don't."

"Certainly we do, but we love you anyway."

I looked between my two best friends, which meant whipping my head from one side to the other, since I was sitting in between them. We were out on the little balcony of our shared office space, which was on the third floor of the historic downtown building known as the Old Printing Office. We were sipping on our first glasses of rosé of the season while lounging in our deck chairs and watching cars navigate the Saturday-afternoon traffic on Congress Avenue. As usual, it was like listening to the sweet angel with an English accent that was Josephine on one shoulder and the naughty-but-lovable devil with a slight Texas drawl that was Serena on the other.

"Y'all are only semi-helping, you know."

"It's what we do best, my friend," Serena said, clinking her wineglass to mine. Her phone was buzzing and she got up, answering the call as she headed back into the quiet of the office. Josephine and I could hear her saying, "Hasana, thanks for calling me back. I've got more dresses on hold for you than will fit in five dressing rooms and I think you'll love every one of them. Can you meet me in an hour?"

I lifted an eyebrow. "I didn't think she was taking on any more personal-shopping clients. Her *Shopping with Serena* blog has gotten so big, she barely has time for rosé on the balcony."

"Ahh, but Hasana Pritzger isn't just any client, darling," Josephine said.

Using my wineglass to point back into the office, I whispered. "*The* Hasana Pritzger? The host of *Making a House a Home*?"

Josephine nodded, her dark curls bouncing in time, and we both squealed like the fangirls we were. *Making a House a Home* was our favorite lifestyle show, and Hasana Pritzger, her husband, Milo, and their three wavy-haired children were the best thing on television right now.

"How come I didn't know?" I asked.

"It just happened yesterday, when you were out on an errand," Jo replied. "I was on a conference call with a client in Spain and one of my clients here in Austin when Hasana walked in. I was so gobsmacked, I nearly switched from Spanish to Portuguese. All I can say is, it was a good thing I wasn't translating anything important. Had she arrived two minutes later, I might have told my Spanish client the Austin company had called their hand-blown glassware *esquisito* instead of *exquisito*."

Since I spoke only one other language—Spanish—compared

with Josephine's six, I looked blank as to the difference. "*Exquisito* means 'exquisite' in Spanish," she said, "but *esquisito* is Portuguese for 'weird' or 'strange.'"

I grinned. "That so? Interesting. I'm thinking we should petition to change our city's slogan from 'Keep Austin Weird' to 'Keep Austin Esquisito.' It has a nice ring to it."

Josephine gave a throaty laugh and held up her wineglass. "Cheers to that."

We drank, then she held out a hand, resting it on my arm. "Darling, I'm terribly sorry I told Camilla you were at Flaco's earlier. When she showed up here looking for you, I was the only one in the office. She introduced herself as one of your former coworkers, but I thought she was one from your time at the Hamilton Center. I had no idea she was one of *those three* until Serena explained later."

"You weren't to know," I assured her. "Camilla, Roxie, and Patrice—or '*those three*,' as you called them—were out of my life and forgotten within hours of my last day at the Howland library, which was months before I moved from Houston to Austin and Serena and I met you." I took a sip of my rosé, adding, "Plus, it was no big deal in the end, really. Camilla was willing to pay the rush premium, and it should make for a quick project for me to work on this coming week during the times Ben has to be in meetings."

The smile on my friend's face went full-on Cheshire cat, and she used one of her long legs to give mine a knowing nudge. "You mean in between times you're having your way with Special Agent Turner."

I grinned, even as my cheeks battled with the potted azaleas on our balcony for brightest pink. "Maybe."

"It's about time, love."

"You're darn right it's about time," Serena said as she took her deck chair again. "Go ahead, tell us all the ways you plan to ravish him. Inquiring minds want to know."

"Yes, we do, so do tell," Josephine said.

"You two are shamelessly proud of your gutter minds," I said.

"Absolutely," Jo said, then used her wineglass to indicate all three of us. "That's the rules with our little triumvirate—details on all the really fun parts of our love lives, and the naughtier the details, the better."

Laughing, I held my hands up in surrender. "Hey, I'm all for giving up the juicy details, you know that. But until very recently, all I've been able to do is listen to y'all. I decided to think of it as research."

Serena pointed her finger over my shoulder. "Well, as much as we'd like to know your research findings, Luce, I bet *he'd* like to know them more."

I spun around in my chair. Ben was standing behind me, grinning, hands in the pockets of his jeans, and a totally adorable flush coloring his cheeks.

"Hi," he said.

The speed at which I jumped into his arms and kissed him earned me appreciative whistles from my rosé-drinking, gutter-minded best friends.

Ben and I sat at my kitchen island and caught up over take-out sushi and wine, then took bowls of butter pecan ice cream over to my sofa, where I sat with both my legs hooked over one of his as we enjoyed our dessert.

The scruff on his face was the same it'd been the last time I'd seen him, but while weeks ago his hair was long enough to curl over his collar (and run my fingers through over and over), now it was quite short and textured. Very Harrison Ford in *Blade Runner,* actually, so really sexy indeed. A cut over his right eyebrow deep enough to need two stitches further added to the sense that he could be a cop from the gritty future, sent to hunt down rogue bioengineered human replicants.

Gently, I touched the wound. "I really want to know what your undercover job was that caused you to get this, but I know you can't tell me, so I won't ask."

He took my other hand and laced his fingers through mine, rubbing his thumb over the back of my hand. "You're right, I can't tell you about the job, but I can tell you that what got me this cut was when a cocker spaniel I was playing with while tailing a suspect at the park jumped up to lick my face and inadvertently slammed my sunglasses into my forehead. The glass broke and caused the gash, which wasn't very pretty at the time."

"Oh, ouch," I said, though it was hard to keep from smiling, especially since Ben was already doing the same. "Did the suspect see you get conked by the cocker?"

He shook his head. "Not at the time, thank goodness, but we were able to arrest the guy about an hour later. Turns out that dog did us a favor when he beaned me, too."

"Really?" I said.

"Yeah, evidently this seriously dangerous guy has a major aversion to open wounds. He saw my cut and started dry-heaving so violently that we were able to nab him with almost no resistance. If only it could always be that easy," he added with a sigh, and I saw tiredness begin to creep into his smiling eyes—blue, with a bit of green around the pupils.

Then, all of a sudden, they sharpened again as a two-beat *thunk-thunk* noise sounded out on my balcony, followed by a long, guttural sound. Ben's hand tightened on mine and he made a move to shield me with his body.

SIX

I put a calming hand on his chest.

"It's okay, it's just NPH," I said. "Jumping down onto my balcony from the tree."

The guttural sound came again, a deep yowl, and we looked out the French doors to see a fluffy orange tabby cat who was bigger than most small dogs. His white chest practically glowed in the dark as he stretched up on his hind legs and pawed at the door handles.

I got up and opened the door. NPH walked in lazily, fluffy tail aloft, like he was the king of the place. Which he sort of was, even though he actually reigned over Jackson Brickell, my condo manager, who was his official human.

"Sometimes I feel like he expects to be formally announced when he walks in like this," I said. When greenish-yellow eyes blinked up at me as if to concur, I stood at attention and said in clipped tones, "May I present the Honorable Neil Patrick House-cat of Travis Heights, SoCo, and untold acres of Little Stacy Park."

NPH erupted in a loud purr that sounded like a motorboat on idle and gave my legs a brief rub. He approved.

"Hey, buddy, long time no see," Ben said. He patted the space I'd just vacated and NPH leaped up, butting his head against Ben's outstretched hand, clearly remembering him even though he hadn't seen Ben in two months. Within seconds, NPH had curled up next to Ben and was enjoying a good scratch.

Just like that, I was second fiddle—but it was so cute, I couldn't do anything but melt. I copied NPH, but on the other side of Ben, and without the scratching.

"So, tell me about this project you're going to be doing," Ben said. He winked, adding, "During the hours you're not ravishing me, of course."

"Naturally," I agreed, returning his wink, then told him about Camilla and how she'd interrupted my lunch at Flaco's to beg me to look into her ancestor's Civil War service. "Or 'the Late Unpleasantness,' as my maternal great-grandmother used to call the war."

"Not the 'War of Northern Aggression'?" Ben asked.

I let my Southern accent deepen and thicken. "Darlin', my great-grandmother Peggy was one of the most celebrated Southern belles in Atlanta, Georgia, and she, like nearly all the belles she knew, preferred not to give any extra credence to the war at all if she could help it. It was the Late Unpleasantness, or she'd act like she didn't know what in tarnation you were talkin' about. I only met her a few times as a child, but that part I remember clear as day."

Ben, tired as he was, was staring at me with his mouth slightly open. "I've never heard you go all Southern belle. Wow . . ." He cleared his throat, then said, "Ow," when NPH, who'd been getting lovely scratches from Ben's hand, gave him a little nip for stopping momentarily. "So, ah, this Camilla. Did she and the other two . . . What were their names . . . ?"

"Roxie and Patrice," I said.

"Right. Did they mean-girl you or something?"

"Yes and no," I said. "They certainly made me feel like I would never fit into their group, but the term 'mean-girl' makes me feel like a victim, and I certainly wasn't that, either, if that makes any sense."

He nodded. "It does."

I gave him a quick kiss at seeing the understanding in his eyes. He got me. "Anyway, Camilla was the nicest of the three and was generally cool to me when we were alone, but I'm hardly expecting that we'll become best buds through this project. All I'm hoping for is that we have a good working relationship and she doesn't get too upset when I confirm the article's findings."

"You think the article was right, then?"

I got up, padded over to my kitchen island, and found the issue of *Chronology* in my tote, then went back to Ben's warmth on my sofa.

He took the magazine and flipped to the marked article. "Yeah, *Chronology* is unlikely to publish something they couldn't verify, I give you that."

"That's what I was thinking," I said. "I'm going to contact the reporter, though, just to be thorough. I'll ask her for her source citations while I'm at it, too."

Ben was peering at the name on the article. "Savannah Lundstrom," he read out, squinting a little since he wasn't wearing his glasses. "I know her, actually."

"You do?"

He shrugged. "A little, at least, assuming it's the same person. Remember me telling you that, when I was in school, I once came to UT for a summer to take some master's-level courses? Well, she was in a couple of my classes. We were on the same team for a project once, that sort of thing."

I reached for my phone on the coffee table. After Camilla left Big Flaco's Tacos, I'd run a quick search on Savannah Lundstrom.

"Is this she?" I asked, showing him the headshot of an attractive woman around my age with curly, dark blond hair and almond-shaped green eyes. She gazed into the camera with a closed-lip smile.

"Yep, that's Savannah," he said as he scratched NPH under the chin. For his part, NPH couldn't care less about Savannah Lundstrom, so long as he kept getting attention. "I want to say I've seen her name in the last year somewhere, though . . . Oof, ow. Dude, NPH, you're not exactly a lightweight."

NPH, who was easily twenty pounds of healthy feline, had seemed to suddenly remember I was there, and stood directly on Ben's stomach to get a few scratches from me. I complied with a grin.

"Really?" Ben inquired of the cat, whose purr ramped up to that of a rumbling Harley-Davidson in response before curling back up at Ben's side. When I giggled, Ben pulled me in for a kiss. Doing so smushed my phone between us and made the screen light up again with the reporter's profile. Ben snapped his fingers.

"Now I remember. Savannah came back to UT last fall and spoke at a luncheon about being a historical journalist. I didn't attend, but I remember seeing her name and photo in the email." His lips curved into a teasing grin. "You know, it was when I was filling in as a professor for Dr. Millerton."

"You mean when you went by Dr. Benjamin Anders and you wouldn't help me in my research into Texas history? Until I wore you down with my charm and prowess as a genealogist, that is."

A measure of challenge met the humor in his eyes. When we'd finally made the leap and become a couple, I'd quickly discovered that grumpy, insufferable, by-the-book Special Agent Ben Turner turned out to have a melty marshmallow center underneath it all. It made me all kinds of giddy to know it—and that I brought it out in him—but I also loved our banter, and being able to tease him and having him tease me in return was something important for me to retain in our relationship. I wanted his sharp mind just as much as the sweetness underneath his admittedly well-muscled, hot exterior, and now he didn't disappoint, even though his day had been a long one and I could see he was rapidly veering toward exhaustion.

He swiped open his phone, tapping around with his thumb, and pretended to read off his screen. "I don't remember anything about *charm*, but . . . ah, yes, good. Merriam-Webster agreed to my request that the word 'genealogist' be redefined as 'someone who completely disregards advice, is thoroughly stubborn, nearly outs an FBI agent in the course of his secondary job, and sasses said agent within an inch of his life.' And look, they've added a visual."

He turned his phone around, and there was a photo of me from New Year's Eve at the Hotel Sutton. I was in my sparkly dress with Ben's tuxedo coat keeping me warm, and I was grinning like a fool because it had actually been snowing in Austin.

"Can you print out that definition for me?" I said. "I'd like to frame it and hang it next to my diploma and accreditations."

Laughing, he pulled me to him, cupping my face with his free hand. "I've missed your mouth—both physically and verbally, Ms. Lancaster." Then he kissed me soundly.

Only NPH meowing at both of us like a disapproving chaperone made Ben and me split apart and get back on the subject of my research into Camilla's ancestor.

"I hope you'll let me know what you find out on him," Ben said, after riffling through the magazine and all its photos again.

I beamed. Call me a geek, but the history-loving side of Ben made him even more attractive. "I'll probably talk your ear off about it."

"I look forward to it," he said.

I told him about meeting Camilla on Monday, and how I'd be going to see one piece of the triptych that Charles Braithwaite, Camilla's ancestor, had painted. Ben's tired eyes briefly brightened. "That sounds cool," he said, trying valiantly to stifle a yawn.

I smiled, got up, and pulled him up with me. "Come on, Agent Turner. You're so tired, you can hardly keep your eyes open. We can talk about this again at breakfast."

He whispered, "I like the sound of that," and gave me another long, lovely kiss that spoke clearly of his desire to want to wake up again, but the exhaustion in him was taking over. I told him I was going to stay up to do a little preliminary research and clean up, but I'd join him soon. I pushed him toward my bedroom and he moved like a zombie, pulling his shirt over his head to expose some really nice back muscles.

I heard him brushing his teeth; five minutes later, I peeked into my room and he was already in a deep sleep. NPH and I, however, stayed up another hour while I began my search into Charles Braithwaite.

I knew there wouldn't be any pension files for Charles either at the Texas State Library and Archives Commission or the Fort Worth, Texas, facility of the National Archives because he hadn't needed to apply for one. Charles had flourished after the war, first as a worker in a lumber mill, then, later, as a sought-after public speaker. Plus, like most Southern states, Texas had little money to give to their Civil War veterans, so pensions were approved only for soldiers or their widows in cases of extreme poverty or disability. That meant the place I needed to start my research was Charles's CMSR.

Back at the beginning of the twentieth century, the War Department created CMSRs in order to help process claims for military pensions and benefits for those soldiers who fought in the Civil War. They created a file for each soldier and gave a history of that soldier's service by copying word for word from the original muster and hospital rolls, as well as other documents such as regimental returns, which were a listing of soldiers, commanding officers, artillery, and other assets that helped to determine the "strength" of the regiment at a given time during the war. Because of the known accuracy of the War Department in creating these military service documents, I knew I could trust the CMSRs I would find online as being faithful to the original records.

That is, if Charles Braithwaite's CMSR had good information to begin with. If not, I would have to do a whole lot of cross-referencing and shifting of puzzle pieces to come to a good conclusion on him.

Scratching NPH under the chin, I told him, "I'd love nothing more than to take a quick trip up to Fort Worth to get a look at his CMSR in person, but for now, seeing his records on one of my online databases will have to do." NPH purred and I got to work.

As I'd had many clients with ancestors in the Civil War, I already had bookmarked links that would take me straight to the microfilmed CMSR abstracts. Charles Braithwaite had been a member of the Fifth Texas Infantry Regiment, and I found him easily on the muster rolls for Company A. Their nickname was the Bayou City Guards because they came from Harris County—basically, the Houston area, which is called the Bayou City to this day. His enlistment date was recorded as August 2, 1861, and he was officially enlisted in Houston by Captain W. B. Botts. At the bottom of the record, Charles was recorded as being present at his enlistment.

Earlier, when Ben had been on a work call, I'd done some quick research on Hood's Texas Brigade and found that the Fifth Texas Infantry Regiment, along with the First and Fourth Texas regiments, made up the brigade and fought in almost every battle waged in Northern Virginia. They lost nearly half their regiment at Gettysburg in July 1863, and by the time they surrendered at the Appomattox Court House on April 9, 1865, the Fifth Texas Infantry had been whittled down to a mere twelve officers and a hundred and forty-nine enlisted men.

I thought about this. As the soldiers from the Fifth Texas Infantry originally came from eleven counties from all over the eastern half of Texas, if each county had an equal number of men who survived the war, that meant that only thirteen men *per county* returned home to their wives and loved ones. Though I knew the numbers wouldn't have been equal per county, it didn't make that much of a difference in Charles's case.

"He was from Harris County, which is about seventeen hundred square miles," I murmured to NPH, thinking out loud. "That's a lot of territory. So if around thirteen men returned to Harris County and, let's say that Charles Braithwaite *had* deserted his regiment, the chances that he could have gone unnoticed by any surviving soldiers are pretty darn high."

NPH responded to this by rolling over on his back and batting at my hand. I complied with his wishes for more under-chin scratching as I began scrolling through the lists of names comprising the Fifth Texas Infantry.

As for CMSRs, the number of records per file varied fairly widely. Some soldiers had one document with simply their name, rank, and what company they were in within their regiment. Others might have a few records, most being muster rolls listing them present or absent within a particular two-month period. Still others had over twenty pages in their files, and a few had nearly forty.

As many siblings fought together in the war, it wasn't surprising to find more than one instance of the same surname in the Fifth Texas Infantry. Several of them had similar first names as well, especially if only their first and middle initials were given, which was a very common practice.

For instance, at one point I saw a J. A. Hattendorf right before a K. A. Hattendorf. Several pages on, I noticed a P. B. Robertson followed by an S. B. Robertson. When I looked through their records, though, it turned out that the two Robertsons were the same man—the former file having only a reference envelope that informed the reader that all records for "P. B. Robertson" were filed under "S. B. Robertson." The reason for this became clear in two documents, however, as it turned out that the capital letters "P" and "S" looked remarkably alike in the particular cursive script of the writer.

When it came to the Hattendorfs, however, both had enlisted in the town of Columbus, Texas, within days of each other and, thus, were likely either brothers or cousins, or possibly father and son.

As for Charles Braithwaite, there was only one of him. In fact, the next nearest soldiers with the name Braithwaite were found in Virginia, Georgia, and Arkansas.

I emitted a small sigh. As much as I liked the hunt, I also wanted this job with Camilla to be over as quickly as possible. Nevertheless, I settled back into my chair and started slowly going through the ten photographed pages of Charles's CMSR.

Per the notations, he was accidentally wounded in the thigh and spent a few days in a hospital in Richmond, Virginia, just after his regiment's first engagement at Eltham's Landing in early May 1862. He was absent, with leave, for ten days in mid-June, but was listed as present at the next muster roll. Two more muster records also listed him as present. He was then ill once again, and this time was transferred to a hospital, where he stayed for three weeks. This was not unusual. With the conditions and rampant illnesses of the time, the men seemed to be listed as sick with some ailment or another as often as they were recorded as present.

"Here we go," I muttered with the next abstract. Another muster roll listed him as absent, this time without leave. The date was just after the Second Battle of Bull Run. In a whisper, I tried making out the three words giving additional information. The first word looked like an abbreviation, starting with a lowercase "t." The second word was "to," and the third word was a proper noun and looked to begin with either an uppercase "T" or an "F." There seemed to be an "h" in the word as well.

I looked at NPH, who was blinking sleepily at me. "Dang it, I can't read the words."

NPH was unmoved by this pronouncement and promptly closed his eyes.

The website I was on had a handy tool for increasing or decreasing the contrast and brightness of the document, but neither helped. I could also invert the color scheme so the white page looked black and the black writing stood out as white. I tried that, but I still couldn't make out the words.

With the next muster roll, however, my breath caught. It was for September and October 1862, and Charles Braithwaite was listed as *Deserted*. A very readable notation underneath, which I knew was copied verbatim from the original document, read *After Manassas*.

There was nothing else in Charles's CMSR. I did notice there were three other men either named Charles or with the first initial "C" in the Fifth Texas Infantry, and I checked all their records on the off chance something was misfiled. After another half hour, by which time I was worn out, too, I gave up.

Before I shut down my laptop, however, I took a few minutes to further investigate Savannah Lundstrom, and found that the reporter had a long string of historical publications to her name. She grew up in Dallas, Texas, and traveled all around for her job, her bio read, and loved learning new things from the people she interviewed. She also wrote frequently on topics dealing with the South and Southwest.

I skimmed a couple of her articles, but none had the exposé feel of the one from *Chronology*. Yawning, I closed the lid on my laptop. For now, I was too tired to look any further.

Gathering a purring NPH in my arms, I walked to my front door and let him out. Fluffy tail held high, he trotted downstairs toward the lit-up condo that belonged to Jackson, and I knew he'd be safely home with his human before long.

SEVEN

Sunday was a perfectly blissful day, with neither Ben nor I mentioning our respective jobs even once.

Well, that's not entirely true. After lunch, we drove the half hour up to Austin's pretty St. Edward's Park and went for a leisurely three-mile hike along trails that seemed to have exploded with bluebonnets just for us. Much of our afternoon was spent talking about various conflicts throughout American history, including the Civil War, but Ben seemed to make a concerted effort to skirt the direct topic of Camilla's ancestor, and so did I. Otherwise, we thought of nothing but enjoying each other.

Monday morning came all too soon, and so did my meeting with Camilla at the Harry Alden Texas History Museum. Ben dropped me off on his way into the office for meetings, though as he and I spent an inordinately long and blissful amount of time saying goodbye, it took a car honking at us for me to finally hop out of his SUV. Nevertheless, it was ten more minutes before I saw Camilla coming toward me outside the museum's entrance.

Her eyebrows rose slowly but steadily when she saw me, and surprised humor brightened her eyes.

What gives? I thought. Then I remembered Flaco's and Ana's expressions had been much the same when Ben and I had turned up at the taqueria for a very, very late breakfast. They'd teased us mercilessly in turn—both in English and in Spanish, I might add. I guess I just had that happy, new-romance glow. *And darn it if I don't deserve it, too.* Still, I was already blushed out for the day, so I didn't respond to her smirk.

"Ready?" I asked, holding the door open for her.

"Are *you*? Sure you don't need a nap? Or a cigarette?"

I didn't respond to that, either, and merely continued on past her, holding out my phone so my online ticket could be scanned. Camilla hadn't bought a ticket in advance, so I walked in by myself, then stopped in my tracks when I caught sight of myself in a reflective piece of plexiglass shielding a poster announcing an upcoming exhibit.

"Oh, lordy," I whispered, then scrabbled to send Ben a quick text.

> Mayday! Check face for lipstick before going into work.

I got a text back almost immediately.

> Too late.
> Worth it.

I giggled as I made myself look presentable again, taking a tissue to my smudged lips and smoothing down my mussed hair before I trotted to catch up with Camilla, who was now asking a docent for directions.

A few minutes later, we stood side by side in front of a large exhibit dedicated solely to the life and service of Charles

Braithwaite. Today, his descendant's perfume was applied lightly, thank goodness, and it smelled quite nice. Like magnolias, with a hint of something fruity underneath.

"Well, the curator either hasn't read the *Chronology* article or is giving us the benefit of the doubt for now, so I guess that's a good thing," Camilla said.

"The curator hasn't seen it," I said, gazing up at the nearly life-size photo of Charles Braithwaite. "After you hired me on Saturday, I decided to text my friend who's the assistant curator here to see if his boss had read it. She hadn't, and my friend owed me a favor, so he pulled the magazine from his boss's stack of reading material. He said that should buy us about five business days before his boss notices."

"What if something starts trending on social media?" Camilla asked. "Or what if someone tweets the museum about the exhibit?" She gave me a look as if she were just now remembering how *Chronology* articles were known for sparking viral discussions.

"My friend is also the gatekeeper of social media for his boss," I said as my eyes roamed over Charles's journal, which was small and leather bound, with a thin leather lace encircling its middle twice before tying in a so-called monk's knot. "He told me she never looks at their feeds unless something blows up big-time." I glanced at Camilla. "But if that happens, he has his job to do and we're out of luck." When I saw the concern in her eyes, I added, "He doesn't expect anything to happen, though."

After a moment thinking about this, she nodded. "Okay. Thank you."

"Now, I'll want to go over all this with a fine-tooth comb in a minute," I said, "but there's a lot to look at here, so point out the things you think are important for me to see."

I faced Camilla, hoping my objectivity in the matter was showing. I'd decided that to do my best work and feel like I earned my fee, I needed to look at the problem of Charles Braithwaite without thinking he was either guilty or innocent.

Camilla, though, wasn't looking back at me, but instead was pointing to two small sheets of paper that had at one time been folded in half. The narrow, slanting script was so small and cramped, the museum had helpfully included a transcription next to it. "There. That's one of his letters back home to his father, where he details being in battle at Antietam."

"In September of 1862," I said, having done a bit of research on the various battles in which Texas troops had been involved. "That was just after the Second Battle of Bull Run. Antietam was a rough one, too, for both sides."

"Yes, it was," Camilla said. Still, there was a bit of triumph in her eyes at being able to produce a document written by her ancestor about that conflict. I had to admit, it was hard not to see it and be swayed a bit in Charles's favor. Then I reminded myself that Antietam had been well reported, meaning Charles could have read up on the battle and fabricated the events in his letter at any point after the war.

"Was the envelope saved?"

She pointed off to the side. An envelope addressed to Mr. Josiah Braithwaite in Houston, Texas, was there, but only a portion of it. The part where the envelope would have been postmarked, usually with a large circular stamp listing the name of the major city it had passed through and the date of receipt by the post office, was missing. The bottom edge of a blue-toned postage stamp, curling up with age, was still visible. I could just make out that the stamp had been for five cents.

I bit the inside of my cheek to stop myself from overthinking the convenience of an envelope torn just right to conceal a missing postmark. I was determined to remain neutral until I had all the facts.

Camilla then pointed to an enlarged photo next to Charles's

journal. It was a very detailed pencil sketch of a young, kneeling soldier who was pointing his rifle at something off the page. At the bottom of the page was another drawing, of a soldier lying dead on the ground, his rifle still in hand and blood oozing from the side of his head. From the wispy goatee and curling hair on both figures, it was clear the two subjects—the kneeling one and the dead one—were the same young soldier. Between the two sketches, Charles had written a few lines of text that made my heart catch.

> *I knew him, this brave boy, not yet seventeen. He was beside me one moment, smiling through battle, knowing all would be well. The next, he was gone from this Earth, half his skull gone. I have taken his rucksack to return to his poor mother. Farewell, young Powers.*

When I read the surname "Powers," I felt another little swoop of disappointment. In Savannah Lundstrom's article, she'd mentioned Charles writing about a young soldier named Powers, though she emphasized there had been no soldiers in his regiment with that last name. It was one of a couple of ways she'd illustrated to the readers that Charles had likely fabricated his war service.

It seemed Camilla had glossed over that bit of the article or was choosing to forget it. "And here's his uniform," she went on, "with one of the buttons missing. In his journal, he mentions losing the button after the war ended, when he was making his way back home."

"Did you or the museum curator scan the entire journal?" I asked.

"The museum did," she said. "It's available online through their website."

Now excitement coursed through me, like it always did when

I found journals or letters from my clients' ancestors and got to delve into the thoughts of someone who actually lived in that time. Serena used to tease me about being a voyeur into other people's lives, and I guess she was right, but I was always careful to treat what I read with the respect it deserved.

"There," Camilla said again, pointing to a yellowed sheet of paper with *Confederate States of America* printed in block letters above a logo bearing the image of Confederate president Jefferson Davis between the American flag and the Confederate flag. "That's Charles's discharge paper."

I nodded, looking at it with interest even as I wondered how easy it would have been for Charles to forge a discharge paper after the war. "Your family kept all of this, and it's just amazing from a historical and genealogical standpoint. I'm so glad."

Camilla gave me a brief, bright smile and we continued to look awhile longer before Camilla went down the hall to see a couple of other exhibits, leaving me alone to study the Charles Braithwaite artifacts in more detail. I took lots of photos and read the transcribed letter again, along with some of his journal entries that eloquently described the horrors of what he'd experienced out on the battlefield. Even so, the whole time I was vacillating between wanting desperately to believe in Charles Braithwaite's story and feeling like the chances he had been telling the truth were becoming slimmer and slimmer.

EIGHT

A half hour later, we were in Camilla's car on I-35, heading north, when we hit Austin traffic and a major stall in our conversation at the same time.

Finally I broke the awkwardness by asking her about her uncle Charlie. "Or your third cousin, twice removed, whom you refer to as your great-uncle, but call Uncle Charlie," I said with a grin.

When Camilla changed lanes but didn't reply, I'm afraid I started rambling.

"Speaking of family-relationship terms and uncles, did you know that, back before the fifteenth century, the word 'avunculus' was used to mean specifically your uncle on your mother's side? For instance, you might have said, 'My avunculus sold his best plow horse last week, the bloody fool'—or Middle English to that effect, naturally—and back before 1400, I would know, without a doubt, that you weren't referring to your uncle on your dad's side. No way, no how. You were being clear that it was your *mom's* brother who went and sold his best plow horse like a dunderhead."

Throughout this, Camilla had been slowly hiking her eyebrow, but eventually her lips quirked upward.

"Uncle Charlie never married," she said finally, "and he was always like an extra grandfather to me—to make the description of our relationship even more confusing. He was in Vietnam and came back with a leg injury that left him needing to walk with a cane, but it's never stopped him from traveling the world and being really active. Otherwise, he's been a wine merchant his whole career and never drinks except to taste the wine he sells." Camilla frowned, but kept her eyes on the road. "He might have been long retired by now if it hadn't been for his former business partner. The guy stole all Uncle Charlie's money. Ran off with everything, oh, nearly forty years ago now and Uncle Charlie never recovered a cent of it."

"That's terrible," I said. "Is he still working full-time? You said he was in his eighties, right?"

Camilla nodded. "Eighty-four, in fact, but he's not full-time anymore. He only works a couple days a week, hosting wine tastings throughout Austin and the Hill Country."

I blinked, a memory resurfacing. "You know, I think I've taken a class from him. Just over a year ago now. I signed up last minute with Nick, a guy I was in a serious relationship with at the time. It was the night Nick told me he'd met someone else."

"Wow, that sucks," Camilla said as she changed lanes again.

I waved it off. "Oh, it's water under the bridge, and I'm so glad I'm not with Nick anymore, but he dropped this bombshell on me just before the class started, so you could say it overshadowed the night. However, I do remember our class was taught by a handsome older gentleman who walked with a cane." I grinned, thinking back. "He could see that Nick had upset me and refused to acknowledge him any time Nick raised his hand with a question. And at least twice, he made sure Nick got the dregs of the bottle we were tasting. It was pretty darn funny, actually."

I laughed at the memory, and this time Camilla laughed with me.

"Yeah, that sounds like something Uncle Charlie would do," she said. "He was always my champion. My ex-husband and I are on decent terms now, thankfully, but when we first divorced, Uncle Charlie wouldn't give Gareth the time of day—and they'd been good friends up until that point."

"Does he speak to Gareth now that y'all are friendly again?" I asked. Camilla was already divorced when I'd worked with her, so I'd never met her ex-husband. Heck, she'd been so close-mouthed about her private life, I hadn't even known his name until now, nor did I recall ever seeing photos of her two boys, though I'd spoken to them a couple of times on the phone when they'd called the library's main line to speak with their mom.

"Oh, sure, they're back to being buds, like they were before," Camilla said, though without much enthusiasm. I decided not to push the subject further. It wasn't until we exited the freeway and made a few turns into an older suburb of small but well-kept homes that Camilla spoke up again.

"I'm worried about Uncle Charlie, actually," she said quietly.

"You told me he hasn't been well. Are you afraid it may be serious?"

She nodded, her eyes fixed on the road. "He hasn't seen a doctor yet, but he's allowing me to take him this afternoon, after I drive you home."

"Does he have any other help, or someone to watch out for him when you're not here?" I asked.

Camilla's lips thinned as we drove down a street named Fairview Drive. "Until recently, he's been healthy as a horse and has never needed any help, despite his age and a permanent limp.

The only person he's ever let do anything for him is Elaine, the woman who lives next door, but she's not my biggest fan, and vice versa." Camilla's hands grasped the steering wheel even tighter. "Though as much as I'd like to, I can't blame her for not alerting me that Charlie's condition has deteriorated. She's been out of town for the past two weeks, and Charlie never let on to me that he was feeling off." Camilla shook her head in consternation. "I didn't realize how poorly he was until I saw him on Saturday. I should have come sooner."

She came to a stop in front of a small house with sage-blue lap siding and white accents. On the front porch were two rocking chairs, and flats of spring flowers in four-inch pots were crowding the steps. At the foot of the steps were several bags of potting soil stacked in a haphazard pile. Uncle Charlie clearly liked a riot of color. The flower beds fronting his porch were abloom with a mixture of snapdragons, pansies, dianthus, and chrysanthemums, all in varying bright hues. The rest of the beds had been given fresh, dark soil, and were ready for planting.

The path to the front door was lined with pavers in a herringbone pattern, and as we walked up, I could see dirt spilling out across the bricks from one of the brown paper bags of potting soil with the name Soils from Heaven across the front in a swirly font. Almost the moment we stepped onto the porch, the front door opened and I found myself looking at an elegant woman in her seventies with a steel-gray pixie haircut.

"Camilla, you're finally back. Charlie has been asking after you." Her eyes were a deep forest green and watched Camilla reprovingly until they slid my way. "Does he know you've invited a friend?" Before Camilla could answer, the woman gave me a tight smile and held out her hand. "I'm Elaine Trudeau, Charlie's neighbor."

"Elaine, this is my friend Lucy Lancaster." Camilla's tone was cordial, if tinged with a hint of frost. "Lucy's the genealogist I told Uncle Charlie about. She's come to see the painting done by my ancestor."

I shook Elaine's hand, noting that she barely acknowledged Camilla, which made my feathers feel oddly ruffled on my former coworker's behalf.

"A genealogist?" Elaine repeated as she held the front door open for us. "That's such an interesting job to have. Do you do it part-time? Surely you can't make a good living out of researching family trees."

I heard this question quite a bit, so I pretended I didn't notice her slightly condescending tone and gave her my usual answer.

"I have to keep up a steady stream of work, yes, but if I do a good job for my clients, that usually gets me the referrals I need to work consistently." It was easy to change the subject after that, considering what greeted me in Charlie's living room. "Wow, Camilla, you didn't tell me your great-uncle also collects photographs."

Except for two modern sofas facing each other over a glass coffee table, the rest of the room was devoid of any furniture in order to showcase the walls, which were lined from baseboard to crown molding with black-and-white photos in simple black frames. Written in pencil on the white frame mats was each photo's description and date. There were family photos, landscapes, ones with a stark modernist feel, and others that were city or street scenes capturing a moment in time. They ranged in size from three by five to eight by ten, forming an eye-catching and slightly dizzying mosaic covering every available inch of all four walls.

"They're all incredible," I said, moving to the nearest wall to get a better look.

Out of the corner of my eye, I saw Camilla open her mouth to say something, but it wasn't her voice I heard.

"He doesn't collect them," Elaine said with a touch of asperity.

"No, Charlie took all these photos himself. He's a very talented, though amateur, photographer."

"I'm very pleased you like them, all the same," came a deeper, more formal voice.

I turned to see the same man who'd taught my wine class last year. Tall and barrel-chested, with a full head of snow-white hair, Charlie Braithwaite limped in, leaning heavily on his cane. He was clad in a tartan robe over dark blue pajamas, but somehow he retained a sophisticated air. I noted he had a cleft chin like Camilla and his gray eyes held humor, even though his overall appearance was one of exhaustion.

The past year had been hard on Charlie. His limp seemed more pronounced than I remembered, his cheeks were slightly sunken, and he now had so many age spots on his face and hands that he looked like he'd been splattered with drops of brownish paint. I was glad Camilla went over to him and kissed his cheek, because I was a bit speechless at the change in him.

"Uncle Charlie, this is Lucy, the genealogist I told you about. She says she took a wine class from you about a year ago. She remembers you fondly from that night."

Charlie assessed me for a moment, then held out his hand. "I remember you as well. If I'm correct, a young man had broken your heart that night, seemingly just before our class began."

I shook his hand, grinning. "You're correct, and you helped me get through that night by being kind to me—and not so much to my ex."

Charlie's smile lit up his tired face. "I hope he noticed as much as you did, and I hope you are well and truly rid of him."

I had to laugh. "He did notice, and I haven't looked back, I assure you."

Elaine cleared her throat, moving to his side. "Now, Charlie, you shouldn't be up and about. Let's get you back to bed where you can rest."

"Oh, Elaine, I wanted to dust all the photos," he replied. "You know it's my weekly chore. It helps me relax." He cast Camilla a fond smile. "And my lovely grandniece switched out some photos last night and added in several from just after my time in Vietnam. I want the joy of finding them as I make my way around the room."

"Yes, you told me as much, but you're not well, so I'm dusting for you this one time," she said, her tone suggesting he was being a stubborn child. "You can do it next week, when you're feeling better. Now, come on. You can show Camilla's friend—" She looked back at me.

"Lucy," I reminded her, even as Camilla shot Elaine a baleful look that she didn't see.

"Yes, thank you." Elaine took Charlie's elbow to guide him forward. "You can show Lucy that painting you love so much and then I want you back in bed." She turned to Camilla and me. "He has it hung in his office. If you'll just follow us."

Camilla was definitely irritated now, especially at being shown around her own relative's house by someone who was nothing more than a neighbor. She shook her hair back behind her shoulders with one heck of a twitch, but gestured for me to walk ahead of her down the narrow hallway.

NINE

"Well, Lucy, what do you think of it?"

Charlie had been helped into a comfortable-looking chaise longue by Elaine, who'd left the room after giving the framed panel of Charles Braithwaite's triptych a look that suggested she would never give such a work pride of place in her own home. Camilla, her jaw set and her arms crossed over her chest, had openly glared at Elaine's back. I had a feeling Elaine knew, and was deliberately playing up the fact that she held some sway with Charlie just to rankle Camilla.

For his part, Charlie had settled onto the chaise with a grunt of discomfort. His office was as neat as the rest of the house, yet with its calming slate-blue walls, well-loved armchairs, and dark wood shelves lined with books and more photos, it had a more relaxed feeling than the living room. The desk helped; there were papers scattered across the top, along with a box of letterhead, a leather blotter with a calendar insert, another couple of photos, and a handful of knickknacks. Two were small jade figurines—dragons, facing each other snout to snout. I couldn't tell if they were meant to look like they were kissing or about to breathe fire at each other.

Speaking of breathing fire, I noted that Charlie either didn't notice the animosity between his grandniece and Elaine, or wasn't feeling up to playing referee between the two women and was thus ignoring the situation. Either way, I couldn't blame him.

And part of me couldn't blame Elaine for her reaction to the painting in front of us. Camilla had described the battle scene as resembling folk art in the simplicity of the people, animals, and landscape it depicted, as opposed to truly realistic detail. I quite liked that style of painting, so I'd been looking forward to seeing this piece of the triptych.

This painting, however, was . . . not well done. It looked just short of cartoonish, in fact, with the Confederate and Union soldiers so crudely painted, they looked like a bunch of blue and gray rectangles with blobs for heads and various black markings representing belts, buttons, and gun holsters. More black lines represented rifles, and the one horse in the painting looked like a cross between an elephant and a giraffe; it was also a sickly shade of orange never found on any living equine. The background consisted of one big swath of green for the grass, a darker shade of greenish brown for the mountains behind it, and a wavy strip of blue for the river. As for the clouds, Camilla hadn't overstepped the mark by saying they were white blobs. Honestly, I could have attached a paintbrush to NPH's left front paw and he would have done a better job.

What made it worse was that the painting—already the size of a poster—was ensconced in a wide wooden frame that looked like it was made out of barnwood. The bottom-right corner of the canvas had also sustained some level of damage. The whole ensemble dominated a large portion of the short wall between the door and the room's south-facing window. I was now no longer remotely surprised the Alden museum had deemed it to have more sentimental value than anything else.

"It's . . . well . . . it's quite unique, isn't it?" I said. "And really colorful."

"You don't like it?" Camilla's voice registered another emotion I'd never heard from her: hurt. I realized she'd really wanted me to see the charm of it.

"Well . . . I . . . um, I mean . . ."

I slid my leather tote off my shoulder and onto a small side table, where it promptly tipped over and fell to the floor. I hastened to apologize as I bent and stuffed two file folders and my keys back inside. "I'm so sorry, really." Straightening again and feeling even more flustered, I said, "I saw the drawing your ancestor did of the 1865 Texas Emancipation Day celebration and those he did in his journal that's in the Alden museum. They were so wonderful, so detailed . . ."

Charlie held up a veined hand as my voice petered out and my face went hot with embarrassment. "No need, Lucy. You're right, it's horrible." Seeing Camilla's jaw drop as she rounded on him with a stunned, "Uncle Charlie! How can you say that?" he reached out for her hand and squeezed it with an affectionate smile. "It's true, and you know it, sweetheart." His eyes came back to mine. "Though I'll admit I still have a deep affinity for the darn thing, just like Camilla here does. It's part of our family history, and therefore precious to us."

I just nodded, not trusting myself to open my mouth again, lest I have to insert another foot. Camilla was still looking a smidge disgruntled, but when Charlie shifted uncomfortably in his chair, stretching out his bad leg, worry came into her face.

"I'll go get a pillow to prop your leg up," she told him, laying a hand on his shoulder. "Go on, tell Lucy the news, and I'll be right back."

Charlie smiled fondly after her as she disappeared down the hallway, then looked up at me. "Camilla has told me all about you, Lucy, and what a good genealogist you are. She read me that infernal article about our ancestor, and we're both hoping you can prove that reporter wrong. But I'm also hoping you can help us in another way."

"I—well, I'm very happy to try," I said.

Charlie still looked as unwell as he had moments earlier, but his voice now sharpened with excitement as he used his cane to point to the bottom-right corner of the painting.

"No doubt you noticed my piece of the triptych is damaged. It happened a few weeks ago, when one of my employees came over with his two-year-old daughter. She was toddling around, holding a stuffed elephant, being no problem at all." Charlie reached over to the side table next to his chair and laid his hand on another elephant. It was made of brass, about the size of a softball, and its trunk curled upward, emphasizing two long, pointed tusks. "Well, as always seems to happen, we looked away for two seconds and things went south. The little girl dropped her stuffed elephant, picked up this brass one, and began banging it against my painting, tusks first."

From the pocket of his robe, Charlie pulled out a plastic chopstick and a small flashlight. He handed me the chopstick. Nonplussed, I opened my mouth to jokingly ask if he was expecting me to follow the toddler's lead and take a jab at the painting, then thought better of it. He pointed his cane toward the damaged canvas and said, "Take a good look at the result and tell me what you see, Lucy. And here's a hint—use the chopstick to lift the canvas."

Curious now, I moved to take a closer look at the damaged corner. The painted scene in that area consisted of a dark blue rectangle that I guessed was a Union soldier standing beside a shapeless brownish-gray blob I could only take for a large rock. There, a small section of the canvas, about two inches high and an inch wide, had been ripped before being partially smoothed down. Using the chopstick as directed, I gently lifted the canvas to see underneath, helped by the beam of light from Charlie's flashlight.

I saw not a hole, but a neck. An actual neck, drawn to proportion, flowing down into a gray uniform collar and rising up under a few tendrils of dark, curling hair. There was also a long scratch that was likely caused by the brass elephant's tusks, but it didn't seem deep. The other fine lines I saw seemed to be the crackling of paint, and—if what I was looking at was real and not fake—they could be an indication of age. The detail, even in that little bit of neck and collar, was outstanding.

I turned around, whispering the words. "That's a person—the neck of a soldier. There's another painting, a whole other canvas, underneath this top one, isn't there?"

For a moment, Charlie's eyes brightened. "I think so, yes, but I'd like to know for sure. We tried to look at the back, in case there was evidence I'd never noticed before of another painting, but there's some sort of thick cardboard backing that's concealing it from view. I'm not confident enough in my art knowledge to try and take off the backing, either, and I'm afraid I haven't had the energy to research it further." He gave me a tired smile. "And despite my work and my love of photography, I don't really have any contacts in the art world. Not any living ones, at least."

He switched off the flashlight, then looked up at me again. "Lucy, would you happen to have any art-expert friends who might be able to look at this painting and see what's underneath? I'd really love to know if my ancestor Charles painted a real battle scene and then covered it up with this outer canvas for some unknown reason." Charlie's mouth twisted with a touch of dismay. "Or if maybe Charles took someone else's painting and covered it with this travesty, charming as I do find it."

"Travesty" was certainly the right word, I thought. Charming?

Well, maybe it had a little bit of charm, too—but only after you got used to the garishness of it.

Using his cane again, Charlie made an encompassing gesture at the painting. "I'd like to get it certified, so I can insure it if need be. Eventually, Camilla will inherit my piece of the triptych, since no one else on my side of the family seems to want it, and in case it might actually be worth something, I want her to be able to plan for it."

"Actually, I do know someone in the art world," I said. "Her name is Helen Kim, and she works doing art restoration but has some appraisal knowledge as well. How about I call her and ask her to come once you're feeling better?"

"That would make me very happy, Lucy. Thank you." He handed me one of his business cards. As I began taking photos to show my friend Helen, we heard arguing from out in the hall.

"He's fine, Elaine," came Camilla's voice. "He just needs his leg propped up."

"He needs to be back in bed," Elaine protested.

"I'm taking him to the doctor in an hour," Camilla shot back. "I think it would be better for him just to nap in his favorite chair in his office instead. Or dust his photos for a while, *like he wanted to before you took over.*"

"I know what's best for him, and that's rest," Elaine retorted.

Camilla strode back into the office, Elaine hot on her heels, both with blazing eyes and looking like forces to be reckoned with—yet Charlie staved off further arguing with great equanimity.

"Elaine, how about I nap while Camilla drives Lucy home? And then, Camilla, I'll spend a few minutes enjoying myself with some dusting before we leave for the doctor's. Sound good?"

Both of the women in his life nodded curtly, though refusing to look at each other, and Charlie shot me a surreptitious wink as he held out his hand and shook mine warmly.

I couldn't help but grin back. "I'll be sure to let y'all know as soon as Helen gives me a day and time when she can come over." Charlie thanked me again, and I stood with a fuming Camilla as Elaine bustled him off to his bedroom.

Once Camilla and I were back in her car, driving down Charlie's street, I decided she needed a good venting session about his pushy neighbor.

"So, Elaine . . . wow," was all it took to set her off.

"I know I'm not the most warm-and-fuzzy person sometimes," Camilla groused, then shot me a sideways look. I congratulated myself on keeping a straight face. "But I really couldn't even tell you what her problem is with me. She's been Uncle Charlie's neighbor for about a year, and she took an instant dislike to me when we met. This weekend, though? She's been nothing but a bossy, pushy witch, and I'm sick of it."

"Do you think you accidentally said or did something to offend her?" I asked.

"I didn't do either," Camilla insisted. "All I was doing was rearranging Uncle Charlie's photos like I always do. I mix them up and add new ones so the view changes. He's got thousands of photos stored in boxes, you know, and changes the photos regularly as well. He always tells me he enjoys the search and the memories it brings up when he finds one he hasn't seen in a while."

She scowled as she pulled into a visitor parking space, not yet ready to change the subject. "I also don't like it that she acts like my uncle Charlie is her boyfriend when they're not even dating. It's gotten worse since he's allowed her to spend time at his house, too. Until recently, he always finagled it so he would go to her place."

"He didn't like her to be in his house before now?" I said this with a frown as I unbuckled my seat belt. I hadn't gotten that impression.

Camilla canted her head. "It's more that he's never been a fan

of anyone being at his house for longer than a short social visit."
Her lips briefly curved up. "If you didn't notice, Uncle Charlie
is a bit of a neat freak, and very protective of his photos, so
he's always preferred to go to other people's houses for dinners
and such. Somehow, though, Elaine wore him down, and she's
started to spend time over there."

I pulled in my lips to keep from smiling. "Camilla," I said gently, "are you sure they're not dating, and Charlie just doesn't
want to upset you by telling you?"

She stared at me for a moment, then swore. "God, I've been
so dense. They *are* dating, and that's why she's acting like she
owns him."

"Well, at least she's looking out for him," I said, trying to be
positive but anticipating an eye roll from Camilla.

She surprised me again, however. "You know, you're right,"
she said on a sigh. "It's not as if Uncle Charlie is willing to move
back to Houston to be nearer to me, so it's important for him
to have someone he trusts and who will take care of him. For
whatever it's worth, he does seem to like her."

"I think that's a good way to view things," I said. Then the
weird silence of two people who'd established a fragile connection stole over the car, and I hastened to get out before it grew.

"I'll call you after I talk to Helen," I told her again.

Camilla gave me a stiff nod that was all too familiar, though
it seemed less abrupt now. I took that as a win.

TEN

Only two hours later, I was using my elbow to knock on the glass doors of *Helen Kim, Art Restoration*. I had no other choice, since my hands were full with two coffees and a box containing four sinful goodies from a little shop not far from my office.

"Cupcakes!" Helen exclaimed after unlocking the door and pulling it wide for me. "Oh, you are *terrible,* Lucy Lancaster." She took the box from me, then pulled me into a hug. "And I'm so glad you are."

"I brought all our favorites," I said, nodding toward the white box with blue lettering, "plus cappuccinos, just like every Friday afternoon of our junior year before History 303."

"And what an excellent tradition that was," Helen said, taking her coffee, her warm brown eyes dancing with good memories. Gesturing me over to a large worktable in the center of the room, she pulled back her long, black hair into a low ponytail like she always did when she was about to eat something with a high potential for messiness. We each chose a cupcake—red velvet for me and double chocolate for her—and began unwrapping them and cutting them in half with a knife, knowing we would share them just as we had back in college.

"You look wonderful," I told her. "I haven't seen you since your grand-opening party when you christened this place." I used a forkful of cupcake to make a sweeping gesture around the bright space Helen had moved into last October.

Her shop was located a few minutes from the Alden museum, in a short strip mall that was all modern white brick with black accents. Helen had snagged the corner spot, which also featured a loading bay for clients who needed to bring in larger items for restoration. Otherwise, it consisted of a long main workroom with one large countertop-height worktable in the middle and three smaller ones against the wall. At the far end of the room was a series of rollers holding different types of linen canvas, as well as another table Helen called her lining table. Among the paintings in various stages of restoration around the room, I saw a beautiful old mirror with a chipped frame, some pretty ceramics, a large blue-and-white Chinese vase, and a beautifully glazed majolica greyhound with some cracks and a leg waiting to be reattached. Through a wide, open doorway, just beyond a highboy chest of drawers that was awaiting some care, was a smaller room that held Helen's office, the garagelike door to the loading bay, and a steel door that led to a temperature-controlled walk-in vault.

Helen glanced around with pride. "It's a great location, and I've enjoyed it here, I have to say." She bit into her cupcake with a happy sigh. "Oh, so yummy . . ."

As we sipped our coffee, Helen and I fell into our old routine, segueing naturally from topic to topic. She and her longtime boyfriend were still going strong and thinking of marriage. When I told her about Ben and pulled up a photo, Helen grabbed my phone and let out a long, appreciative whistle. Swiping to a photo I'd snapped yesterday, when Ben had been walking toward me in nothing but a pair of faded jeans, she began to fan herself. "He's downright hot—*and* he looks like a young Harrison Ford. Do you realize this, Luce?"

"Little bit, yeah," I said, holding my thumb and index finger about a centimeter apart as a giddy smile spread across my face.

Laughing and joking, we kept talking for another quarter of an hour, until she checked the time. Knowing she had a customer coming in soon, I got down to business.

Opening my iPad to the photos I'd taken of Charlie's panel from the triptych, I asked if she'd heard of the Braithwaite family.

"Sure," she said with a shrug. "Mostly by reputation as being wealthy and philanthropic. I've never met any of them, though, and I didn't know they had any artists in the family."

I grinned. "I didn't think I'd met any of the Braithwaites, either, but it turns out I worked with one for sixteen months." Then I explained that I was doing some genealogy work for Camilla, and how the panels of the Civil War triptych done by her ancestor had been passed down through the three branches of the family. I told Helen about seeing Charlie's piece of the triptych and about the toddler incident that had led to him noticing another painting underneath the top canvas. "He then asked if I had any friends in the art world who could tell him how to proceed, and of course I thought of you."

"I'm honored," Helen said, beaming. "Now let's see this baby. You said they called it folk art in style?"

"For lack of a better term, I think," I said, then showed her a photo of Charlie's panel.

Helen glanced at it, then gave me a hilarious wide-eyed look.

"I had pretty much the same reaction," I said with a laugh.

Helen was a professional, though, and got to work studying the images, using two fingers to enlarge and better inspect certain parts.

"Hmm, well, I can tell you with some confidence that this

painting wasn't done by a trained artist," she said. "The brush-strokes lack refinement. The painting has a naive quality to it, to say the least, and just from these photos I'd guess the canvas wasn't prepped properly." She enlarged the photo again. "In fact, I'd bet it was hardly prepped at all, but I'd have to see it to be sure."

"Of course," I agreed. "Now, let me show you what Charlie found after the toddler accidentally ripped the canvas." I swiped to the last set of photos.

A hint of excitement colored Helen's voice as she examined them. "Now *this* was done by a true artist. If there's this much detail in such a little piece of a man's head and neck, I can only imagine what the rest of it looks like. You never know, there could be something really special under there. I'd guess at the very least it's a figural painting—meaning human figures are the primary subjects. Did you see the verso?"

My inner art geek had heard this term before. "That's the back of the painting, right?"

Helen nodded, but I shook my head. "Charlie said there's some sort of heavy cardboard backing that's concealing whatever is underneath. He said he wasn't confident enough to try and remove it."

Helen looked mildly horrified that Charlie had even contemplated this. "I'm glad he didn't," she said with feeling. "He could have damaged both the paintings, and if there *is* something special under the top one and he didn't use proper handling techniques, he could have reduced the value. No, I'll be happy to go over there to look at it. He definitely needs to have the painting seen by an art restorer like me who's also a conservator. After that, I'd recommend a good art appraiser."

"What's the difference between an art restorer and a conservator?" I asked.

"A lot more specialized training," Helen answered with a

smile. "Most well-trained art restorers are also conservators, but it's not always the other way around. I happen to love conservation, but being self-employed, it's the restoration part that's my bread and butter. Good thing I love that part, too."

"I understand that," I said. "I love all parts of my job, too, but I do wish I got to make more videos of my clients relating their family's stories. With the technology out there today, I can make them much more sophisticated and interesting than they were even a couple of years ago. I'm starting to do outdoor, documentary-like videos where my clients walk around their favorite spots and talk about their family memories and such. They're really fun to create."

"That sounds amazing," Helen said. She tapped my iPad screen again. "But talking about outdoor videos reminds me—is this a panoramic triptych? Do the three pieces form a panoramic scene when put together?"

"I'm afraid I don't know, but I think it's likely. Camilla did say the triptych was a battle scene, but she was talking about the outer painting, not what's underneath."

Helen said, "Well, it won't help the value of this painting, but if what's under it is better *and* a panoramic Civil War triptych? Now *that* would be very interesting indeed."

"Is there a big market for Civil War art?" I asked.

She nodded in an exaggerated way. "*Yes*. It's one of the biggest art markets there is in America."

"Even by an unknown artist?" I asked.

"Are you completely sure Charles Braithwaite is unknown?" replied Helen. Before I could answer, she reached across the table for her laptop, saying, "Let's check, shall we?"

She pulled up a website, explaining that it was a subscription-based site with listings of known artists and what their art had sold for at auction, as well as examples of their verified signatures.

"Yep, he's listed," she said. "Though there's not much on him except for his signature." She pointed to the image, where I saw Charles signed his works merely "C. Braithwaite" in bold, forward-slanting strokes, plus a longer than average cross-stroke on the second "t" in his surname.

Helen continued, "It was taken from an illustration he did titled *Life in the Lumber Mill* in 1887 that was sold at auction five years ago to a collector. He's not even known for Civil War art. He apparently mainly sold illustrations to newspapers as a side job and is best known for—"

"The Texas Emancipation Day announcement drawing," I said, reading the words on the screen out loud. Reaching for my tote, I pulled out the *Chronology* article. The sight of the magazine reminded me I'd wanted to call the reporter, Savannah Lundstrom. Problem was, I hadn't yet thought of a way to tactfully ask her why she'd felt the need to levy an attack on the Braithwaite family via their ancestor. Making a mental note to think about that later, I found the page I wanted and showed Helen the photo of Charles Braithwaite's drawing of the 1865 Texas Emancipation Day announcement in Galveston, Texas, adding, "His journal, which has some of his other sketches, is in the Alden museum." I pulled up one of the photos I'd taken that morning to show her.

Helen looked appreciatively at it, then found a magnifying glass and looked at the drawing in the magazine. "Both are highly detailed," she murmured. "He certainly had a knack for capturing people and their emotions."

She gave me the magnifying glass and I got a close-up look at Charles Braithwaite's painting for the first time. "Wow," I said. "He really was talented, there's no doubt about it."

"See, ninety percent of a painting's worth is who painted it, not just what was painted," Helen explained. "The fact that we have proof of Charles Braithwaite as an artist could potentially be helpful to the value of the painting that's underneath, if what is found is of an interesting enough subject, of course. And if there's a historical figure in the scene—such as Robert E. Lee—that could make it even more valuable."

That sense of excitement I'd felt in Charlie's office when I saw the neck of the soldier underneath the top canvas was coming back. Could Charlie have found something of real importance? I was looking forward to finding out.

"You said Camilla has another piece of the triptych," Helen said, interrupting my thoughts. "Has she found anything under hers?"

I groaned. "I didn't even ask her. Can you believe it?" I explained how I'd let Camilla grouse about Elaine Trudeau the whole way back to my condo. "And asking about her part of the painting just slipped my mind."

Helen was unperturbed, though. "What about the third panel?"

I tilted my head from side to side. "Now, that's where it gets a bit trickier. It's owned by someone in the third branch of the Braithwaite family, of course. Camilla descends from the younger son, and Charlie descends from the older son. Those branches have stayed in touch somewhat. The third branch, however—"

"Branched out?" Helen offered, grinning.

"Oh, that was a *really* bad genealogy pun," I said, and Helen affected a bow from her seat. "So, yes, that side of the family went off in their own direction. Presumably, they still have the painting, but we don't know."

Helen picked up her cappuccino. "Let's hope they haven't already found the painting underneath it and sold it sometime in the past."

I blinked at her. "I didn't think about that. Would we know if that actually happened?"

Helen went back on the website she'd showed me earlier, explaining that the database kept track of what paintings were sold and the prices they fetched. She tried several key words, but there weren't any matches for a painting that could possibly match what she believed was under Charlie's piece of the triptych. She tried other databases as well, with the same result.

"So does that mean it's never been sold?" I asked hopefully.

"Possibly," Helen said. "But it could have been sold to a private collector, or there's the faint possibility it could have been stolen ages ago and sold to a collector who lives in Japan." When I asked what she meant by that, she explained, "Most countries have reciprocal treaties to return stolen art. Japan, however, does not. If the third piece happened to end up there, then it's unlikely it will ever come back stateside—but I think it's less probable because there's not a demand for American Civil War art in Japan."

Angling my coffee cup to my lips, I said, "Then let's hope the third piece is still around and no distant Braithwaite cousin has decided it's so ugly, they're willing to sell it at a garage sale for ten bucks like Camilla's brother nearly did."

Helen laughed, then looked at the photo of Charlie's painting once more. "You know, I've always loved triptychs, so I can't wait to see this hot mess of a painting up close and personal. Plus, if it looks like any amount of restoration or conservation is warranted once I see it, I'll hint to Charlie Braithwaite with the subtlety of, oh, say, a freight train that he should use me for the job."

"High-five to that," I said, and she slapped her palm to mine.

ELEVEN

❧

Ben took my hand as we strolled across Pfluger Pedestrian Bridge. Charming carriage lamps illuminated the wide walkway that spanned Lady Bird Lake and spring flowers were bursting out of large planters set at intervals along the railings. A few other couples were doing the same thing we were, along with the inevitable joggers and bicyclists who used the bridge to cross to the other side of the reservoir.

Leaning against one handrail was a guy strumming a guitar. He had a full beard and gold hoops in each ear, and wore surfer shorts, hiking boots, a fisherman's sweater, and a silver-belly felt cowboy hat with a hatband made of old bottle caps. He was doing his best to keep Austin weird as he entertained us with an acoustic version of the Heart classic "Crazy on You."

The night air was cool, so I was glad I'd chosen to wear a cropped jean jacket over my sleeveless A-line little black dress. Ben and I had just come from a romantic dinner at a nearby French Vietnamese restaurant. Seeing as our meal had ended with coffees and—despite my cupcake with Helen earlier—two macarons each, we'd decided a constitutional was in order.

"I'm so full," I said with a laugh, my hand over my stomach. "But that was amazing. Thank you for taking me there."

"I'm glad you liked it. I'm not nearly as addicted to that place as you are to Big Flaco's Tacos, but I'm happy to go there any time you like."

"Which will be often, I think," I said. "Only, if Flaco finds out, I'm blaming you *hard*."

"Oh? Willing to throw me under the bus, are you, Ms. Lancaster?" Ben said.

"When it comes to keeping my standing as Flaco's favorite customer and honorary fourth child? Heck yeah, I'll hand you to him hog-tied and on a silver platter."

Ben's eyes crinkled as he laughed. "Somehow, I don't doubt it."

I walked sideways just long enough to rake my eyes up and down his lean frame like I was picking out choice cuts at my local butcher's. "You don't have enough meat on you to make more than a few *tacos al carbon*, I'm afraid," I said, and gave his firm backside a little pat, "but he could make some good carnitas off of this rump roast." Tapping my lips with one finger, I gave him a final, salacious once-over. "Oh yes, you'd do quite nicely."

Ben's face had smoothed into a blank mask. He pulled out his cell phone, clicked on the voice memo app, and said, "Note to coworkers: If I go missing, check walk-in freezer at Big Flaco's Tacos, and immediately slap handcuffs on my girlfriend."

This was heard by a passing couple, who looked at us in such shock, Ben and I burst out laughing. "All taco-themed cannibalism jokes aside," he said, pulling me in close, "I've no doubt Flaco would do anything for you."

"He does take his duties as my second father seriously," I agreed.

"No kidding," Ben said, grinning, as we started walking again. "This morning at breakfast, when you went outside to take that call from one of your other clients, he grilled me about my intentions. He's a damn good interrogator, let me tell you, and he made it very clear you're special to him and that I'd better ask for a transfer to another city if I screw this up."

I giggled, then stopped in my tracks, gaping up at Ben. "Wait. Are you serious?"

He nodded. "Yeah, but I didn't mind." He turned me to face him again, rubbing the back of my hand with his thumb, which I was fast learning was his sweet little quirk. "Look, Lucy, you've proven you can take care of yourself, but I have to admit it felt good to know that when I'm, ah, out of town for work, there's someone else here in Austin who cares about you and would go to every length possible for you."

I blinked, digesting what he'd said and all the sweet things it implied, before I used the lapels of his tweed sport coat to pull him down to my level for a passionate kiss.

The surfer-cowboy switched to another song as Ben and I stood there, wrapped in each other for a long moment.

Though he and I had spent some quality time together back in January, his next assignment had called him away just as we'd begun getting into that groove of how two people are around each other when you take out the romantic bits—and, in our cases, the fraught-with-danger bits. I think we'd both been happy and relieved to find our personalities still fit nicely together when we were just being the regular, everyday versions of ourselves.

Eventually, my mind pulled back to the here and now, and I glanced over to where the guy in the cowboy hat was crooning. "Huh. You wouldn't think Def Leppard's 'Rock of Ages' would make for a good acoustic ballad, but it kinda does. Surfer-cowboy dude isn't a bad singer."

"Actually, that reminds me," Ben said. "Mrs. Singer made me promise I'd tell you she wants to talk to you about doing her family tree."

For a second, I drew a blank, then the name rang a bell.

"Mrs. Singer, your neighbor who stocks your freezer with desserts?" I asked.

"Yep. She's been wanting her genealogy done for years, and now that her eldest son is married and expecting his first child, she's decided the time is perfect."

"I'd be happy to, then," I said. "Do you want to just give her my number?"

We turned and started walking again. "I offered," Ben said, "but Mrs. Singer is old-school. She likes business cards so she can put them in her alphabetized business card binder. She told me she hasn't decided whether to put you under 'G' for genealogist, 'A' for Ancestry Investigations, or 'L' for Lucy. She's going to wait to meet you to decide."

I grinned, pulling up the crossbody purse that rested on my hip to rummage for my leather business card case. "I have every respect for that. I was already predisposed to like Mrs. Singer after trying her turtle brownies, but now I'm really looking forward to meeting her."

"Oh, no doubt you'll love her. She's got a great sense of humor and keeps an eye on my condo when I'm gone."

I laughed. "Not to mention making you all your favorite desserts." I stopped my rummaging just long enough to tap his stomach. "Admit it, she has you pegged." Before he could retort, I stopped under one of the carriage lights to get a better look into my little purse.

"Missing something?" Ben asked.

"I can't find my case with my business cards," I said. I rummaged around once more, even though I knew the green leather case wasn't there.

"Okay," Ben said. "When's the last time you saw it?"

"This morning," I answered immediately, "after I realized you'd have lipstick on your face from our make-out session in the car." I flashed him a sassy wink, thinking back to the moment at the Alden museum when I'd dropped my phone in my tote after sending him my warning text. I'd seen the card case then. I snapped my fingers. "Wait. My tote bag tumped over at Charlie's house and a few things fell out. It happened right by a side table, and I was looking at Charlie most of the time, so maybe the case ended up under the table where I didn't see it."

Ben looked at his watch. "It's only seven twenty-five. I'm sure it's not too late to call Camilla and ask if she'll look for it."

I thought about this for a second, worrying I might wake up Charlie, then reasoned Camilla would probably have her phone on silent if her great-uncle was asleep. Sliding my phone from my purse, I found her contact and hit call. She answered on the second ring and I could tell instantly that she was in her car and distracted.

"Hi, Camilla," I said. "Did I catch you at a bad time?"

"What? Oh no," she replied. "I've just done a pharmacy run for Uncle Charlie's meds and now I'm trying to find his favorite deli to get him some soup. Are you calling about your green business card case? I found it just before I left."

I opened my mouth to suggest I could pick it up tomorrow, but at the same time, the surfer-cowboy launched into an energetic version of Willie Nelson's "Whiskey River."

"From the music I can hear in the background, it sounds like you're out, too," she said in my ear. "If you have time, you can swing by Uncle Charlie's and I can give it to you. He's feeling better after visiting the doctor and is napping right now."

"I'm so glad to hear that about Charlie," I said. "But I don't have to disturb y'all tonight. I can come tomorrow, if that's easier."

"Tonight's better," she said firmly. As if knowing she'd sounded abrupt, she added in a more normal tone, "Plus, I'll be waking him up anyway to make sure he eats a little dinner and walks around a bit to keep his circulation going." She paused, then said, "I found out that Uncle Charlie has had some heart problems for the past year or so that he never told me about, but the doctor doesn't think his current issues are related to it. In fact, she thinks he may be feeling stronger soon, but she wants him to rest tomorrow anyway, undisturbed."

"I'm glad the doctor is optimistic," I said, then I relayed Camilla's suggestion that we pick up my card case tonight to Ben. Unfazed, he offered me his hand. I took it and we turned back as I told Camilla that we would head in her direction.

"This is the guy who's got you glowing?" she said, but didn't give me a chance to answer. "Anyway, I'm at the deli now, so I'll be back at Uncle Charlie's in about twenty minutes or so. Come to the side door. It's off the driveway, kind of hidden by a trellis, and faces Elaine's house. The door has a touchpad combination lock. The code is the year Texas won its independence, plus the pound sign. I don't need to be more specific, do I?"

I grinned at the slight note of challenge in her voice. "Of course not," I said. "Thanks, Camilla. We're on our way."

TWELVE

Even without rushing, the light traffic heading away from the heart of the city meant I was pointing out Charlie's little blue house with the white trim in less than a half hour. The porch lights glowed as Ben and I walked up the driveway and to the side door, which was blocked from view by a tall trellis covered in yellow Carolina jessamine vines. Passing the kitchen window on the way, I saw Camilla had just arrived, too, and was unloading her purse and the take-out bags onto the counter.

After I entered the digits 1-8-3-6 on the backlit electronic touchpad, the dead bolt retracted and Ben and I walked through Charlie's mudroom and into the kitchen. It was galley-style and, unsurprisingly, as spotless as the rest of the house, except for a take-out bag from Barry's Deli and several cartons of food. I called out a soft hello to Camilla just as she was concentrating on placing a bowl of soup—matzoh ball, as it turned out—carefully in the microwave to heat up.

"They gave you cold soup? That's not nice," I said with a smile as the microwave began whirring.

Wiping her hands on a dish towel, Camilla shrugged with a

mildly disgruntled expression. Then her eyes fell on Ben. "Is this your boyfriend, then?"

"Yes, this is Ben Turner," I said, feeling my cheeks heat with pleasure—it was the first time I had admitted out loud to anyone other than my best friends that he was, indeed, my boyfriend. "Ben, this is Camilla Braithwaite. We worked together in Houston at the university library before I set up my own business. She's an accomplished researcher."

I didn't know if it was my compliment or Ben's full-wattage smile, but I could have sworn my former coworker melted a few degrees as the two exchanged pleasantries.

The microwave dinged. Camilla pulled out the bowl of soup and said, "Well, I'd better get this to Uncle Charlie before it cools down again. Your card case is just over there by the fruit bowl, Lucy."

She used her elbow to point to the far end of the kitchen counter, by the open doorway that led to the living room full of Charlie's photos. Earlier, at dinner, I'd told Ben about Charlie's art gallery of sorts, and had learned that my new boyfriend harbored a secret passion for photography and black-and-white photos were his favorite.

Picking up my card case, I said, "Camilla, do you think Charlie would mind if I let Ben have a quick look at his room of photos before we go? He loves black-and-white photography, too, and I told him how amazing Charlie's are."

"She did rave about them," Ben agreed.

Camilla hesitated, then said, "Go right ahead. Only, don't stay long, please. If Charlie knows you're here, he'll feel like he should play the host. I know he'd love to see you again, but he really doesn't need to overexert himself tonight."

"Of course," I said, and decided I would never tell her how much she sounded like Elaine Trudeau in that moment. I thought about pushing my luck and asking if I could let Ben see Charlie's piece of the triptych as well, but she was already walking down the hallway to Charlie's bedroom, tray in hand.

Ben followed me into the living room, and I found the light switch, then grinned at his instant expression of awe. From down the hall, I could just hear Camilla speaking to her great-uncle over the sounds of a movie playing on low volume. Her voice was cheerful and warm. "Knock, knock. Are you awake, Uncle Charlie? Your matzoh ball soup is here."

I didn't hear Charlie give a reply, since, true to our word, Ben and I weren't lingering. I pointed out a few cool photos I'd seen yesterday as we moved around the room. "Camilla told me that Charlie has thousands of photos and he likes to switch them up often, adding new ones, rearranging existing ones," I said. "It's almost never the same view twice."

It seemed that Charlie or Camilla had already been at it again, in fact. I gestured toward an area of wall with a photo of a stone house standing in a field of wildflowers in rural Virginia from 1993, one of a smiling, dark-haired woman walking in Paris on a windy day in 1971, and one from 1965 of two little boys hugging a huge Saint Bernard. "Case in point: I'm pretty sure yesterday this space had a photo of a cricket match in India from the mid-nineties, a moody view of the London Eye, and a neat one of two women and a man at the Kentucky Derby in 1982."

I looked around for that one. I'd remembered it not because of the fabulous hats, but instead for its emotion. The man, shouting with excitement in a straw fedora and seersucker suit, had his arm slung around one of the women's shoulders. Big sunglasses shaded her eyes and her long, dark hair shone in the sunlight under her feathered fascinator as she tilted her head back in exultation. The other woman, who was taller and had lighter hair under an enormous, wide-brimmed hat trimmed in ribbons, was grinning delightedly Charlie's way, yet his lens seemed to be irresistibly focused on the passionate woman in the sunglasses.

Several feet away and close to the floor, I finally spotted the photo of the London Eye. The other two, though, had either been switched out entirely or were lost within the myriad of photos covering the walls.

"You weren't kidding. These are incredible," Ben was saying as he took in a fish-eye shot of the Donegal coastline in northern Ireland and I admired a photo of a neighborhood soccer match in Kenya.

"Hey, look at this." Ben pointed to a photo near the ceiling. "It says 'Braithwaite Family Reunion, 1988.'" He then pointed at something in the background. "Is that the triptych?"

I glanced up, then put my hand on my hip, reminding him dryly, "Even in my heels, you've got more than half a foot on me, so I really couldn't tell you."

Grinning, he glanced toward the hallway, then pulled out his cell phone and snapped a photo of it, saying in an undertone, "I'll delete it straight away."

"You could have just taken the picture down," I teased.

"And run the possibility of it dropping and cracking and having Camilla chew me out for it?" Ben said in my ear, using his fingers to enlarge the photo on his phone screen. "No thank you."

I grinned and looked at his phone. Beside a handsome Charlie Braithwaite in his early fifties were three framed paintings hanging together.

"Holy frijoles, you're right, it's the triptych," I said. "Wow, and I thought Charlie's third was terrible."

Ben was staring incredulously at the photo. "So you're telling me that Camilla's ancestor—the guy who captured the first-ever Juneteenth celebration in 1865 with such precision and talent— painted *these*?" He pointed to the screen, and just as I was about to say "I told you they weren't pretty," I picked up on an odd sound.

We were near the other open doorway that connected to the hallway. I could hear Camilla's voice again, but it was no longer cheerful. Something was off. There was a keening noise between her words, for one thing, and she sounded choked up. I set one foot in the hall, craning my neck to better hear.

"Please, Uncle Charlie. Wake up. Please wake up. Don't be dead."

With a worried glance back at Ben, I started down the hallway.

"Camilla?" I called out. "Is everything okay?"

The keening noise I'd heard turned into full-scale wailing, and I ran the last few steps to the bedroom door, which had been left cracked open. I pushed through the door, Ben right behind me, and stopped to get my bearings.

The only light was coming from a television sitting atop a large chest of drawers. It was showing *Butch Cassidy and the Sundance Kid* on the classic movie channel, the volume now muted. Camilla, it seemed, had used the light from the television to put the tray with the matzoh ball soup on an upholstered bench, and now she was bent over the side of her uncle's bed. One hand was grasping a king-size pillow. Her other hand held Charlie's forearm, but there was no movement from her great-uncle.

"Camilla?" I said, inching closer. "What happened? Did Charlie go downhill all of a sudden?"

I reached out to put my hand on her shoulder, but stopped when I caught sight of Ben's face from the corner of my eye. He was staring at the bed, with its rumpled sheets and blankets. Charlie's legs were twisted in them and at odd angles, even his bad leg. It looked as if Charlie had thrashed around in his bed before dying.

"A seizure?" I said, as much to myself as to Ben.

"Doubt it," he muttered, so low I could barely hear it. His eyes were now narrowed at the pillow Camilla was holding.

"Ms. Braithwaite," Ben said. His voice was gentle, but underneath was the steely professionalism I'd heard last year when I'd first dealt with him on a case. "That pillow you're holding—where did it come from?"

Camilla turned to us, tears coursing down her cheeks, blinking as if she didn't understand Ben's question. Then she looked down and almost seemed surprised that she was grasping the pillow by the middle of its sham, which was navy with a white border and a crisp flange.

"It was on his face," she said in a whisper. "It was sort of half covering his face when I walked in. I was talking to him, but he never responded. Then I noticed he wasn't moving. I pulled it off him, and . . ."

She couldn't finish the sentence and I turned to look at Ben. I read in his face what he wasn't saying. Camilla must have understood what had happened at the same time, because she dropped the pillow and covered her mouth with her hands.

Someone had used that pillow to suffocate Charlie Braithwaite.

THIRTEEN

B en stepped forward and placed two fingers on Charlie's neck to feel for a pulse. He looked back at me and gave a small shake of his head. Camilla uttered a heart-wrenching sob and hid her face in her hands.

I glanced uneasily at my former coworker, then back at Ben. The ugly thoughts that were flowing through my brain made me feel terrible, but I couldn't help it. Could Camilla have just killed her great-uncle? Again, I noted the tangled sheets and the angles of Charlie's legs. Yes, he'd obviously thrashed around. But if Camilla had just killed him, surely the struggle would have made noises that Ben and I would have heard, right? However, it had been maybe two minutes between the time Camilla had taken Charlie his soup and the moment I'd rushed down the hall. Would that have been enough time to suffocate him? I didn't know.

I recalled how the back door had been securely locked, how the kitchen had been clean and orderly, and the fact that Charlie's photo-filled walls were as neat as I'd seen them earlier today. We hadn't noticed the front door ajar or any broken windows, so what did that mean? Had Camilla really been out driving around when I'd called her earlier? Or was my call just well timed and her suggestion—no, almost insistence—that Ben and I drive to Charlie's house tonight to pick up my business card case a convenient part of her plan to establish an alibi for herself?

From the way Ben's jaw had tightened, I guessed his FBI agent's mind was thinking along the same lines as mine. Though when I noticed his eyes darting toward the bathroom, then out toward the hall, I knew he'd realized something I hadn't: if Camilla hadn't killed her great-uncle, then someone else had, and that person could still be in the house.

Reaching under his tweed sport coat, he pulled his Glock from a pocket-like holster in his undershirt. I recalled him telling me that even off duty, he was required to carry his service weapon, but I was still surprised. It rested along his rib cage and I hadn't even noticed it was there.

He moved past Camilla, using the motion to steer me a few feet away from her without making it seem deliberate. "Stay here," he said to both of us, then moved swiftly to Charlie's bathroom and checked that it was free of unwanted visitors, stopping first to peer at the lock on the sliding patio door. I noticed his walk change from his normal, almost loping gait to smooth, small steps that no doubt reduced the possibility of stumbling.

"Bathroom is clear," he said. "Lucy, please call nine-one-one."

I pulled out my phone and we both looked at Camilla again. She hadn't moved, and appeared to be in shock as she stared at her great-uncle.

"I need to check the rest of the house," Ben told me. I looked up into his blue eyes, which were telegraphing a question to me: Did I feel safe being alone with Camilla?

I answered by projecting confidence in my voice as I said, "We'll stay here, and if something happens, I'll be ready with my self-defense moves." I added the merest glance in Camilla's direction for emphasis.

He nodded once and moved to the door. He'd been proud of me for signing up for self-defense classes last fall and taking my safety into my own hands. Just yesterday afternoon, in fact, he'd helped me practice my jabs and kicks. It had been fun then, with lots of laughing and joking around as he nevertheless corrected my stance and showed me a tip or two. Even though I only knew basic moves, they were still good ones, and Ben knew I wasn't afraid to use them.

"Be careful," I whispered to him, just as the 9-1-1 operator answered the call. Ben gave the merest of nods before I shut the door and locked it. He had lots of training, I reasoned, and I had to trust that he knew what he was doing. I needed to focus on what he'd told me to do.

Camilla hadn't shown a note of shock at my boyfriend pulling a gun from under his jacket. Her hands were still over her mouth and tears were causing her mascara to run. Keeping my senses tuned for any weird moves from her that would signal danger, I kept one ear trained toward the rest of the house for noises that might mean Ben was in trouble while I spoke with the emergency services operator.

All the while, I never let Camilla fully out of my sight as I glanced around the bedroom. Like the rest of Charlie's house, it was very clean and simply decorated. The bedside table by which Camilla was standing held a lamp, a couple of travel books, a bottle of water, a box of tissues, and a jade figurine of a horse sitting up with its legs tucked under its body. The other bedside table had a lamp atop a few more books, but nothing else. There weren't any medications by the bed, but I wondered if there had been at some point. After all, Charlie hadn't been well for some time.

I thought about possibilities. Could a desperate someone with a drug problem have broken in? Maybe he or she found Charlie sleeping, with some prescription pills by his bed, and when

Charlie woke up and found them stealing his meds, that person panicked and suffocated him.

I decided this was both as far-fetched and as equally possible as the idea that Camilla had killed her beloved great-uncle and was using Ben and me as her alibi. Then Camilla and I both started as a knock sounded on the bedroom door, banishing all other thoughts.

"Lucy?" It was Ben's voice. "You can open up."

I opened the door in relief and Ben held his hand out for my phone. I passed it to him and he gave his credentials to the operator, saying, "I've spoken with Detective Maurice Dupart of the APD, and he's on his way."

"Dupart?" I repeated when Ben hung up. "He's coming?"

He nodded, sliding his Glock back into the hidden pocket of his shirt. "We've been texting about grabbing a beer since I got back. He texted again just as I cleared the house. I called him, and he's on duty tonight, so he said he'd come. He's also calling a judge for a warrant to search the house."

Camilla hadn't spoken since explaining how she'd found Charlie, but my question about Dupart seemed to awaken her. She looked at us, her light brown eyes brightened another full shade with emotion, tear streaks down her cheeks.

"What's wrong with this Detective Dupart?" she asked, her brows knitting.

"Nothing whatsoever," I replied quickly. "He's very capable and honest. I've, ah, just dealt with him more in the past six months than I would like, that's all."

Camilla seemed to accept this explanation. Either that, or her mind was already elsewhere, and as if in a daze, she turned and picked up the jade horse from Charlie's bedside table.

"Please don't touch anything, Ms. Braithwaite," Ben said sharply, making Camilla convulsively pull the figurine closer to herself as she turned around in surprise.

"Why?" she said. Ben and I stayed silent a heartbeat too long, though, and Camilla read our silence. "Wait. You two don't honestly think I killed Uncle Charlie, do you?" Anger was replacing her sadness on the quick.

"We have to preserve the crime scene, that's all," I said, in what I hoped was a soothing tone. Though if I'd succeeded at all, I figured I wouldn't be seeing the rosy spots on her cheeks becoming blotchy.

Camilla was now palming the jade horse. "Are you kidding me, Lucy? I know you don't like me, but to accuse me of actually murdering my great-uncle? The man who was one of the most special people to me on earth? That's just despicable. I should have known you'd think ill of me the first chance you got."

"Put the figurine down, please, Ms. Braithwaite," Ben said. He hadn't moved from where he stood, an inch or so behind me, and I could see out of the corner of my eye that his right arm was at his side instead of near the hidden pocket where his gun sat, but his voice had lost all its gentleness.

Camilla stared at the green horse in her hand and gasped in shock. Then her voice went icy cold, the tone I was more familiar with, as she lowered the figurine.

"You can relax, Ben," she spat. "Or should I call you Agent Turner, now that I'm a suspect? Regardless, I wasn't going to hurt your girlfriend."

She turned away from us, put the figurine back on top of the books, and wrapped her arms around herself. Ben cast me a glance that six months ago, I wouldn't have been able to read. Now, though, I could see the slight flicker of something in his eyes. He had some more bad news to impart.

"Ms. Braithwaite," he began again, "when I cleared the house, I didn't see signs that any door was forced, and there weren't any broken windows, either."

Camilla turned slowly back around, her eyes narrowed at his careful tone. "But?"

I saw Ben's expression become what I referred to as his Fed Face. It was devoid of emotion, not giving away his feelings toward anything.

"The office was targeted, it appears. Did your great-uncle have anything of value in there?" he asked.

Camilla blinked. "Of course. His business papers, a few items from his travels that are worth a lot of money . . ." Her voice trailed off as her eyes met mine.

"The painting," we said, almost at the same time. "Oh no," I moaned when Ben confirmed it was gone.

"I have to see," Camilla said, and made to rush past us to the bedroom door.

"Camilla, you can't," I said, holding out a hand to stop her.

Ben nodded. "I'm sorry. I understand it's frustrating, but we need to stay here until the police and the crime scene techs arrive. There could be evidence in the office that you might disturb if you went in there."

Camilla looked at us, incredulity written all over her face. Then, uttering a noise that was half frustrated and half anguished, she turned away again. She was still standing with her back to us, shoulders hunched and occasionally sniffling as she cast forlorn glances toward her great-uncle, when Detective Dupart arrived at the front door a few minutes later.

FOURTEEN

B en and I were interviewed separately in the kitchen, while Detective Dupart spoke with Camilla in the photo-filled living room. Shifting my weight onto my back foot allowed me to look through the open doorway across the hall and see the back of Camilla's head as she stoically answered Dupart's questions.

As if he sensed my attempt to eavesdrop, Dupart's dark eyes lifted briefly and bored into mine for a half second before looking back at Camilla.

If he thought I would be cowed by this, he was wrong. As intimidating as Dupart could be, with his tall frame, broad shoulders, thin goatee that offset the strong planes of his face, and deep voice with a hint of Louisiana Creole that would be easy on the ears if he hadn't used it to bawl me out a couple of times, his attempts at a quelling look had nothing on Ben's Fed Face. I kept right on listening.

"Why did you tell Ms. Lancaster that you were at the deli picking up food when you had already been there twenty minutes earlier?" Dupart asked Camilla.

So that *was why she was microwaving Charlie's soup!* It had struck me as a bit odd that she had been heating the soup when she'd supposedly just returned home from picking it up.

"I don't know," Camilla replied stiffly, one hand clutching a fresh tissue. "Maybe I just didn't want to explain myself to her."

"Where were you when you said you were at Barry's Deli, then?"

Camilla gave an irritated sigh, then gestured out toward the street. "One of Uncle Charlie's neighbors is this divorced guy named Marcus Brewer. He lives a few houses down, and every time I'm in town, he tells me I'm welcome to meet up with him and his friends for drinks at the wine bar a few streets over. He's a nice enough guy, but . . ." Camilla hitched an indifferent shoulder. "I've never taken him up on it."

"And what was different about this time?" Dupart asked.

Crossing her arms over her chest, she said, "Well, he's implied more than once that he has some knowledge of Uncle Charlie's neighbor, Elaine Trudeau, who has been dating Uncle Charlie recently . . . or so I have come to figure out." This last part she said through gritted teeth, then added, "Look, Detective, you should know Elaine's not my favorite person, and vice versa, okay? I'll admit that. She's bossy more often than not, and possessive of Uncle Charlie, and it makes me angry—but she's been worse than usual this weekend. I've been wondering if she's hiding something, and I hoped Marcus would have something meaningful to tell me."

"All right," Dupart said, then prompted, "So you met him at the wine bar?"

Camilla nodded. "I know he usually goes there around seven and stays for a couple of hours. It was seven thirty when I drove by the bar, so I stopped in for a drink. Uncle Charlie was napping, it wasn't hot out, and everything I got from the deli could be served cold or reheated, so I took the chance." She looked sadly down the hall to Charlie's bedroom, and said in a quietly anguished voice, "If I hadn't, maybe I could have saved him."

"Or you could have been killed as well, Ms. Braithwaite," Dupart reminded her. When Camilla nodded like a robot, bringing the tissue to her nose, he asked, "And did Mr. Brewer say anything of note about Ms. Trudeau?"

"No," she said flatly. "He only said that Elaine never talks about her ex-husband, and he thought it was weird. I told him it wasn't so weird. I never talk about my ex, either."

I just stopped myself from saying, "Believe me, I know," out loud.

"Where is Elaine, by the way?" Camilla asked Dupart. "Why isn't she being interviewed? Her house faces the back door, and she's always watching Charlie's house. Yesterday I accidentally left the door ajar for two minutes, and she stormed out of her house and told me off for being careless. She could have seen the person who came in and murdered Uncle Charlie." Her voice became thick with emotion. "Or maybe *she's* the one who murdered him!"

"Ms. Trudeau was not at her house," Dupart replied, though I got the impression that he said this not just to give Camilla information, but also to see her reaction. "Her neighbor across the street said she saw Ms. Trudeau driving away sometime just after seven o'clock. We have not been able to contact her thus far."

"Well, that sounds suspicious enough for me," Camilla snapped. "Elaine had more than enough time to come over and kill my great-uncle. You should be interrogating *her*."

I watched as Dupart's face took on its now familiar inscrutable mask. "We are looking for Ms. Trudeau and we will be checking out every angle thoroughly, I assure you."

Camilla looked like she was going to protest, but Dupart

smoothly moved to another question. "Besides items in your great-uncle's office, of course, is anything else missing from the house so far as you can tell?"

"Well, Detective," Camilla replied icily, "since I came home, fixed my uncle's dinner, spoke to Lucy and her FBI boyfriend, walked down the hall to find Uncle Charlie dead with a pillow over his face, and then was kept cornered by Lucy and said FBI boyfriend until you arrived, I haven't exactly had a lot of time to go through the house room by room. You barely let me see Uncle Charlie's office, if you recall."

Dupart remained unruffled. "Speaking of the office, is anything else coming to mind as being missing from the room? Besides the items you listed already, including Mr. Braithwaite's computer, a purple-quartz chess set, two small jade figurines of dragons, and the painting—" He looked down to check his notes. "The folk art–style painting of a battle scene, one of three panels painted by your ancestor circa the mid- to late 1860s."

Camilla had absolutely insisted on seeing Charlie's office for herself when Dupart arrived. Thus, as Ben and I followed them out of Charlie's bedroom, on our way to the porch where we would wait, separated, until Dupart's request for a consent-to-search was approved by a judge, I was able to get a brief look inside the office before Ben took my hand and pulled me after him down the hall.

Charlie's office had been wrecked. Books were all over the place. Some of the photos had been smashed, others knocked to the floor. His laptop was gone, papers were strewn everywhere, and his desk had been cleared of everything except a few scattered pens and the box of letterhead, which was resting halfway off the desk. The last thing I saw was the leather chaise longue he'd rested on yesterday, which had been pushed so roughly aside that it had rocked up onto its side legs and was caught in that position, leaning against the French doors. I didn't get to confirm for myself that Charlie's piece of the triptych had been stolen, but I'd caught the look on Camilla's face as she stared up at the wall. She'd looked as if she simply couldn't believe it was gone.

Camilla was rubbing her forehead, but she finally answered wearily, "I'd have to look again, but I didn't notice anything else right off."

Dupart moved on. "Does your uncle's house have any security cameras?"

Camilla shook her head, then reconsidered. "Well, he has one of those doorbell cameras."

"Can you access it to see if the camera picked up anyone coming to the house?"

Dupart called out to one of his techs to bring him Charlie's phone, and saw me at the same time. Without thinking, I'd stepped into the living room. "What are you still doing here, Ms. Lancaster?"

"I just wanted to check on Camilla," I said lamely. Ben walked up behind me, but stayed silent. Unlike me, he knew when not to interfere.

Camilla had not seemed to notice either of us as she stared forlornly at Charlie's wall of photos. For a moment, Dupart watched her before turning back to me. "Since you're already here, why don't you stay until we've finished our interview?"

This seemed to bring Camilla around and she surprised me by saying, "Yes, please stay, Lucy."

"Of course I will," I said. Dupart gave me a discreet nod of thanks as a crime scene tech handed him a plastic evidence bag containing a cell phone.

Dupart worked the phone with Camilla telling him the password. He accessed the doorbell camera and called up the events it had recorded, with the most recent on top. The camera appeared to have a far reach and picked up things like a neighbor walking by with their dog at 8:22 p.m., Ben and me parking on the street and walking up the driveway at 7:48 p.m., Camilla returning home at 7:44 p.m., and a car pulling out of the driveway, nose first, and turning onto the street at 7:12 p.m.

"That's Elaine's car," Camilla said, jabbing a finger at the sedan accelerating past on the screen. She was frowning. "Elaine's driveway is right next to Uncle Charlie's, but I don't recall the camera ever picking up on her pulling out of her own driveway." She looked up at Dupart, her eyes alight and intense. "She must have been in *Uncle Charlie's* driveway."

"Meaning?" Dupart asked noncommittally.

Camilla pointed to herself. "I left the house at six forty-five to pick up his meds and food and got home more or less an hour later," Camilla said. "So, it means that Elaine had enough time to come over, suffocate Uncle Charlie, trash his office, steal the painting and other valuables, pack everything into her car, and drive off." She looked first at Dupart, then at Ben and me, before half turning to point toward the driveway. "Look, the back door is hidden by a vine-covered trellis. Elaine could have backed into the driveway and the trellis would have helped hide her while she loaded things into her trunk. The neighbors wouldn't have thought it strange if she was coming in and out of Uncle Charlie's house, either." Her voice rose with her vehemence. "I just know she had something to do with this!"

Dupart dutifully made notes, then called another officer to have the crime scene techs pay close attention to the area around the back door. Then, looking down at Charlie's phone, he said to Camilla, "There's some more events logged here. Do you recognize any of these people?"

The next event was from 7:08 p.m., a young couple out for a stroll, the woman with a hand over her belly. "That's the Kapoors. Vidya is pregnant and likes to walk after dinner," Camilla said, and Dupart clicked on the next event, from 6:56 p.m. Camilla frowned when she watched what had triggered the camera. She also shifted toward Dupart, blocking my view of the screen.

"Do you know this woman?" Dupart asked Camilla, indicating the video.

She shook her head. "I've never seen her before."

Ben, who could see better than I, said, "There's another event that says 'Doorbell Notice.' See if it's the woman arriving. Maybe you can get a cleaner shot of her face."

Since I still couldn't see the screen, I was glad that Dupart felt the need to narrate it.

"Okay, it's six fifty-five p.m. She pushes the doorbell; she's smiling as someone answers the door. Now she's saying something. Introducing herself, from what it looks like."

Camilla was squinting at the screen. "I can't lip-read, but she's acting like she has an appointment or something." Camilla looked up at Dupart, then her eyes slid to me. "But Uncle Charlie didn't say he had any appointments. In fact, I can pretty much guarantee he didn't. He writes everything on his big desk calendar." She pointed into the office. "It's in there. The calendar was torn, but I saw it on the floor. After our doctor's appointment this afternoon, he spent some time dusting and rearranging his photos, and then sat at his desk for a half hour and made phone calls. I heard him the whole time because I was changing his sheets and folding his laundry. I never heard him talk to anyone about a meeting tonight."

Dupart called out to the crime scene techs working the office. "Hey, Raza. Do you see any appointments scheduled for tonight on Mr. Braithwaite's calendar?"

We heard the tech moving around. After a pause, Raza called back, "No, sir. Nothing for yesterday or today. There's 'Expect call from Lucy Lancaster re: art appraiser' scheduled for Tuesday, then nothing else until Thursday."

"Art appraiser?" Dupart asked me. "Is this referring to the painting?"

I nodded, then glanced at Camilla, who said, "Tell him."

"Charlie saw that there might have been another painting underneath the top layer of canvas," I explained. "He asked if I had any friends in the art business who could help him determine what was underneath. I said I did, and that I would contact her."

"And have you?" Camilla asked.

"I have, yes," I said. "I should have updated you earlier. I went and saw her this afternoon, not long after you dropped me off at my condo. She said she'd be happy to come look at the painting. I gave her Charlie's card and she said she would call him."

Ben was still looking at the phone screen. "From the time stamps, it looks like this woman left exactly one minute later."

"And she looks angry," Camilla said. "Do y'all see her expression? She looks like she could spit nails."

Dupart asked, "Is it possible Mr. Braithwaite got out of bed and answered the door?"

Camilla considered this. "It's possible, I guess. He was feeling better after seeing the doctor, who told him that while she didn't know what was causing his current issues, they didn't seem connected with the heart problems he has. But then, like I said, he worked the rest of the afternoon with his photos and making phone calls, and he was exhausted after that." Finally, she shook her head. "Honestly, I don't know. If he did answer the door, what could he have possibly said to this woman to make her so upset? Uncle Charlie was unfailingly polite."

"I can attest to that," I said.

"And if he didn't answer the door," Ben said, "that meant someone was already inside."

Dupart checked the camera log again. "The camera doesn't show anyone coming in through the front door prior to this, so if someone else was already in the house, they would have come in through the side door or the garage door, correct?"

Camilla nodded.

"Does Ms. Trudeau or anyone else have the key code to that door?" Dupart asked.

"Elaine does, yes. I told Uncle Charlie that wasn't a good idea, but he said he trusted her." Frowning again, she looked back the phone screen. "I want to know who this woman is, though."

Dupart played the video again, and this time, I moved to Camilla's side to watch it.

"Yes, Ms. Lancaster?" Dupart said, his eyes trained on me. "Do you know the woman in the video?"

I hadn't realized that I'd sucked in a sharp breath. She'd let her hair down, and was wearing glasses, but I recognized her easily.

"She's my art restorer friend. That's Helen Kim."

FIFTEEN

❧

I got up from my desk and leaned against the windowsill, staring out of the tall, paned windows of my office into the bright morning. A mockingbird fluttered down onto the railing of the balcony while across the room Josephine was listening to a conference call on a headset, every so often breaking in to clarify something in French to one client or in English to another. On my computer screen were the scans of Charles Braithwaite's Civil War journal, but I hadn't been able to concentrate on them. Instead, I was thinking about Camilla and her uncle Charlie.

Last night, as Ben and I had walked out of Charlie's house and headed to the car, we could still see the rear lights of Dupart's sedan with Camilla inside, taking her to the station to make her formal statement. Before they'd left, I'd told her to call me if she needed anything, even if it were at some ungodly hour of the night. I'd taken the chance and reached out to squeeze her fingers, whispering with emotion, "I'm so very sorry about Charlie, Camilla." Her eyes had shimmered with tears, but she'd only nodded before turning away.

"You're worried about her, aren't you?" Ben had asked me as he started his Explorer.

"You overheard what the tech said to Dupart," I replied. "While they have to run the prints, it looked like there were only two sets in the bedroom, which are likely hers and Charlie's. She could really be a suspect."

"Dupart's a good cop," Ben said, taking my hand. "He'll flush out every lead before doing anything."

"I know," I said, thankful for the warmth of his hand in mine because I'd begun to feel cold all over as we drove into the night. "But there's also the question of Helen. What on earth was she doing there? And if Charlie answered the door, what could he possibly have said to her to make her give him such an angry look when she left?"

"And if Charlie didn't answer the door, then who did?" Ben said.

"True." I shook my head in consternation. "I wish Dupart hadn't told me I couldn't contact Helen."

"He said he would prefer you didn't until he spoke with her," Ben reminded me. "Not the same thing. He'll have interviewed her by noon tomorrow. You can call her after that."

At a stoplight, I'd loosened my seat belt to lean over the console and kiss him. If there was one thing I'd learned in encountering death so much recently, it was to not forget to enjoy the lovely things in life, like being with someone you care about. I'd only known Charlie Braithwaite a short time, but I felt like he would want me to smile and kiss the man who treated me well.

Something featherlight hit my back and I jerked back to the present and the sunny morning outside my window. I swiveled around; Josephine had just shot a rubber band at me. Headset still on over her curls, she said something in French to her clients and then laughed at their response. Then, to me, she mouthed the word *Tea?* and theatrically mimed sipping from a teacup before mouthing, *And toast?* and acting out the buttering of toast and then biting into it with such relish that I had to grin. Giving her a thumbs-up, I was turning toward our break room when our office door opened and Serena breezed in.

"Why are you here?" she demanded, though she was careful to whisper so as not to interrupt Jo's conference call. "Why aren't you at home doing all sorts of heavenly things with Ben?"

"Ben and I are definitely not slacking on the heavenly things," I replied as we moved behind the upholstered screens that separated our break room from the rest of our open-floor-plan office. Then I gave her the shortest possible explanation of last night's events while filling the tea kettle and cutting two pieces of scratch-made sourdough bread and popping them in the toaster oven.

"That's awful," Serena said. "I truly feel sorry for Camilla, but even still, it's you I care about. You doing okay?"

"I am, but you're wonderful for asking," I assured her as I added a pat of butter to each piece of bread as it toasted.

Serena eyed me, then nodded, convinced I wasn't pulling the wool over her eyes. "All right, then. I'm only here for another minute. Hasana Pritzger asked me to be her personal stylist for an episode of *Making a House a Home*. I have one hour to get everything I need before I drive to the Hill Country with a car full of outfits and shoes."

"Where exactly is the house in question that will be made into a home?" I asked, pulling down the teapot and filling the strainer with English breakfast tea leaves.

Serena had pulled a short, lightweight wool wrap coat in petal pink off the mannequin she used to test outfits for her blog. "It's in the town of Junction," she said, slipping on the coat and tying the belt in an expert way that I'd never mastered. "Somewhere on a gorgeous stretch of the Llano River. I'm at the Whitehurst B-and-B for two nights, and I'll be back on Thursday."

"You look smashing. Have a safe trip," I said before she hustled to the door again, looking chic with the soft pink coat over her smart-looking all-black travel ensemble that flattered her curves and made her blond hair seem brighter.

Josephine covered her headset's microphone with her hand and whispered, "And have a lovely time!"

"I always do," Serena replied with a wink, and then she was out the door, blowing us an air kiss as she left.

I arranged teacups, saucers, a little pitcher of milk, apricot jam, and extra butter on the antique cherrywood rolling cart we'd found during our last trip to the Round Top Antiques Fair. Then I rolled it out so it sat between Jo's desk and my own. Pouring her a cup, I added a splash of milk like she preferred it, and then handed it to her with her toast, which I'd also prepped to her liking—slathered edge to edge with apricot jam.

Thanks, love, she mouthed, then spoke into her headset in a torrent of fluent French.

Taking my own toast and tea, sans milk, to my desk, I tried to focus on Charles Braithwaite's journal entries. It's not that they weren't interesting—they definitely were—it's just that my mind was simply elsewhere. A moment later, my computer flashed a notification of a couple of new emails, and I saw that one was the latest digest from *Chronology* of their ten most popular recent articles. Clicking on the email, I read with some dismay that the article on Charles Braithwaite was coming in as their fourth most-read.

Rats. For Camilla's sake, especially after the tragedy of last night, I was kind of hoping the article would be a dud for the magazine and no one would care. I felt a renewed surge of determination to research Charles Braithwaite's military service with an open mind. I didn't know if contacting Savannah Lundstrom to understand why she had chosen the direction she did in her article would help me or not, but I figured it would be worth a try. Plus, I needed to ask her for her source citations as well, so I had double the reasons to call her.

I looked over toward Josephine; she was still on her call, concentrating on what her clients were saying as she chewed on a piece of toast. Snagging my own piece, I went out on the balcony, looking up the number for the *Chronology* office in Washington, DC, as I bit into one buttery, jam-covered corner.

I was surprised to find Savannah Lundstrom's direct office line listed on the magazine's website. I was less surprised to have my call go straight to voice mail. I listened to her message, noting a hint of a Texas accent in her confident voice.

"This is Savannah Lundstrom, senior journalist for *Chronology* magazine. Please note that for the first three weeks in March, I will be traveling in Texas and Louisiana for articles I'm researching, along with two speaking engagements. However, I check my messages regularly and will return your call at my first opportunity. If you are calling to suggest a story to our magazine, please email our offices at—"

I was gearing up to leave her a polite message explaining who I was and requesting a callback regarding her most recent article on Charles Braithwaite when my call-waiting beeped in my ear.

It was Camilla. Hurriedly, I ended the call just as the tone sounded for me to leave a message on Savannah's voice mail.

"I was hoping you'd call," I told Camilla. "How are you doing?"

Camilla's voice dripped with sarcasm. "Well, let's see. My great-uncle was murdered last night, I'm still a person of interest, and, as I understand it, the person who I think killed him simply waltzed down to the airport and left on a plane. How do you think I am, Lucy?"

Suppressing a sigh, I took another bite of toast and said through my mouthful, "I take it you're talking about Elaine Trudeau?" I certainly understood Camilla's stress, and I had immense sympathy, but I didn't need the attitude. If I was going to be snapped at, I deserved carbs.

"Of course I am. I overheard Detective Dupart telling one of his minions," Camilla replied tightly, before adding, "What *are* you eating? Oh, never mind." I heard a door open. From the whirring sound of a lock retracting, I guessed she was at Charlie's house.

"Did Dupart say where Elaine went?"

"No," Camilla said in an acid tone. "I asked, but it appears they don't tell murder suspects information like that."

"Right," I said, taking another bite of toast.

My suspicion that Camilla was in her great-uncle's house was confirmed when I heard her curse and say, "Stupid, disgusting fingerprint powder. It's *everywhere*."

I told Camilla I had some experience with the stuff and had the name and number of a service that could clean the house for her. After forwarding her the contact, I said, "Did Dupart tell you anything of note?"

"Yeah, he implied that because of how Elaine's timeline played out, the chances she could have killed Uncle Charlie are slim, but I call bull crap on that." Camilla's voice was becoming heated. "You watched the doorbell camera footage, Lucy. We saw Elaine speeding off in her car. Before that, she could have come in the house, smothered Uncle Charlie, and been gone with the painting in under ten minutes. I called a friend of mine who's a doctor and she confirmed that with Uncle Charlie's health issues and weakened condition, three minutes is all it would have taken to suffocate him."

I had to admit, Camilla probably had a point, and cool, efficient Elaine Trudeau seemed like she could smother someone, artfully trash an office to make it look like someone else had done it, and walk out with a large painting without appearing remotely ruffled. Not to mention having a discerning eye that would lead her to pick out the Vietnamese jade dragons and a few other expensive items to steal.

But there had also been the jade horse in Charlie's bedroom, so why wasn't that taken, too?

My phone tucked between my ear and my shoulder, I leaned on the iron railing of our balcony, looking out over Congress Avenue, chewing my toast, and thinking about timelines and what items could have been carted off in a hurry. The jade dragons were small enough to fit in a pocket, unlike the horse. If I had only a few minutes and I knew I had to risk walking outside holding a big painting, I wouldn't go for a heavy figurine that couldn't easily be concealed, either. Nope, I'd take smaller ones that I could stash in my pockets as I traipsed out, brazenly holding a potentially valuable piece of art.

"Lucy, are you listening?" demanded Camilla. "I said, can I ask you to do me a favor?"

"Of course," I said automatically.

"Detective Dupart requested I not leave the city until they verify my alibi, and I need to make sure my third of the triptych is safe," she said. "Since I can't go, will you go get it for me?"

SIXTEEN

I t took me a moment to realize what she meant, and once I did, I nearly choked on my toast. "You want me to drive to Houston and take the painting from your house?"

"Yes," Camilla said, an edge to her voice. "I know Detective Dupart will be able to confirm everything I told him soon, but I'm worried that Elaine"—the reasonable side of Camilla seemed to be coming back because she sighed and amended it with— "okay, *fine,* that *whoever* killed Uncle Charlie will go after my painting next. My ex has been staying at the house with my boys. But, it's their school's spring break and they're leaving this afternoon for a camping trip, so the painting will be unprotected. And I don't have an alarm system."

Turning so the railing was at my back, I saw the deep frown on my face reflected in the big windows of my office. Working my expression into a more relaxed one, I strove to do the same with my reply.

"Camilla, we don't yet know whether what happened to Charlie was a deliberate act by someone wanting to get to the painting or a robbery gone terribly wrong. It's possible someone had noticed Charlie was in a weakened state and therefore targeted his house for a robbery, then resorted to murder when—and I'm only guessing on this—Charlie woke up and threatened to call the police. That would make it an extra-heinous act, yes, but still a random one."

I heard the sound of our balcony door opening and looked up, then smiled as Ben stepped over the threshold. Another guy, this one with smiling brown eyes and thick dark hair, stuck his head out the door as well and waved at me. It was Ahmad, Josephine's boyfriend. I grinned and waved back, all the while keeping track of my point to Camilla.

"So, with a random act being a possibility, why do you think your part of the painting is at risk?"

"I just do, okay?" Camilla said.

"I'm afraid that's not enough for me, Camilla," I said, as Ben leaned up against the railing and wrapped his arms around my waist. I turned my phone out a little so he could hear, too, and added, "Especially if you want me to drive all the way to Houston for you."

I heard Camilla make a frustrated noise. "Okay, look," she said finally, "a couple of weeks back, when Uncle Charlie told me he thought there might be another painting underneath his piece of the triptych, I remembered that my panel had a small bit of damage along the left side of the frame. It happened ages ago, when I was a kid, courtesy of my cat trying to use the barnwood frame as a scratching post and catching part of the painting in the process. It was so minor you couldn't really see under the canvas at the time, but since the damage to the canvas was already there, I just made it a bit bigger—and I found the same thing Uncle Charlie did."

"Oh, wow, that's cool," I said, the little part of me that was art obsessed perking up again.

"Yes, it is," Camilla said, "but as I didn't quite realize what we might have on our hands, I went and told everyone I know about it. About both Charlie's find and mine."

I glanced up at Ben, who was listening intently.

"Everyone?" I echoed.

"Yeah, pretty much everyone," she replied. "My ex-husband, my coworkers, my brother, my hairstylist, two other cousins . . ." She paused. "And Neil Gaynor."

So much had happened, it took me a second to recall the name. "You mean the PhD candidate who is trying to sue your family for monies his family lost back in the 1920s?"

"That's the one," Camilla said, a bleak note in her voice. "I told him about a week before I was notified of his lawsuit. After that, I quit talking about our paintings and didn't mention them to another soul until I told you."

But it was possible the damage had already been done, I thought, and one of the people she told could have set their sights on obtaining all three triptych pieces, even if it meant killing to get them.

"Did Neil Gaynor seem unduly interested in this news?" I asked, and felt Ben nod his approval at my question.

"Yeah, he did," Camilla said. "Who doesn't like the idea of stumbling upon a bit of history and then possibly making money off it?" She let out a dry laugh. "You see stories about that all the time on *Antiques Roadshow* and in publications like *Chronology,* and I don't know anyone who doesn't find them fascinating."

She was right. I followed the magazine on all its social media platforms, and every so often there was a post about an exciting find. I couldn't resist reading them each and every time.

"That's true," I said. "Did your brother and two cousins have the same reaction as the others when you told them about the hidden paintings?"

"My cousins did," Camilla said, "but I highly doubt they

thought much about it after I told them. Both have more money than they know what to do with. One shows horses and is currently on the show-jumping circuit. The other cousin is pregnant with twins and has been on bed rest for the past six weeks. Unless I'd told her there was secretly a how-to guide on parenting twin boys underneath our ancestor's paintings, I'll bet she forgot about it ten minutes after I left her house."

"And your brother?" I said, bracing myself for a snappish reply. If anyone insinuated to me that my sister, Maeve, might do something as terrible as intentionally hurt someone, I'd jump down their throat faster than double-struck lightning. Still, Camilla brought it up, so why not ask?

Camilla, however, just scoffed. "Tor? Yeah, he joked about how it was a good thing I pulled the painting out from his garage sale a few years ago, and then spent the next twenty minutes telling me about the new fishing boat he just bought. I think he was about as interested in the painting now as he was back when he tried to sell it."

Ben had moved to my side and was looking skeptical at Camilla's statement in a way that said he doubted Tor Braithwaite wasn't interested in the painting anymore. To be honest, I did too.

I thought about going to Houston. It was my home, I loved it, and I hadn't been back there in months. This was mostly because my parents, now proud retirees, were avid travelers and were gone so much of the time that it was pointless to go back to Houston except for holidays or the occasional trip to see friends Serena and I had known since childhood.

I thought about it. It wouldn't be so bad. I could drive the two and a half hours to Houston, go over to Camilla's to snag her painting, then hang out with my parents and sleep in my old bedroom overnight. I always loved seeing my parents, so it would be fun, even if it meant missing out on twenty-four hours with Ben.

Plus, if I had enough time, I could go to the Clayton Library Center for Genealogical Research and get some work done on Charles Braithwaite's war records. It wasn't that I couldn't research them from my laptop; it was more that it would be hard to get any work done at my parents' house from the moment I drove into their driveway.

I glanced up at Ben, noting how the particular shade of blue of his casual button-down gave the color of his eyes a lovely intensity. We'd only been dating in person a couple of weeks, even if, technically, it had been just over two months since we'd gotten together on New Year's. I then thought back to Nick, my previous boyfriend. When I'd initially begun dating him, I was still living in Houston, and the first few times I tried to get him to drive in from Austin to meet my parents, he had come up with ten different reasons why he was too busy. However, when he finally met them, during our sixth month of being a couple, he'd loved them, as everyone does.

Later, Nick told me I'd just moved a bit too fast with the parents thing and it had made him nervous. As much as I wanted to harangue him for being weak and commitment-phobic, I'd actually understood. So, I could hardly expect Ben to want to go to Houston with me when we'd spent so little in-person time together, couldn't I? In fact, I decided I wasn't even going to ask.

Covering my phone's speaker with my hand, I whispered, "Camilla's asked me to do her a favor and go to Houston to get her third of the triptych. I'll stay with my parents and be back tomorrow. Sound good?"

Before he even had a chance to reply, I'd thought of another question.

"Camilla," I said into my phone, "just curious—why can't one of your other friends go get your painting? Or maybe your ex-husband? Or even Roxie or Patrice? I've never even been to your house—I don't even know what part of town you live in—but I know Roxie and Patrice do. They were always talking about how y'all would do brunch every so often. So why not ask them?"

Camilla was silent for a second, then sighed. I moved closer to Ben so he could hear.

"All right, I'll just say it," she began. "You're the only person I trust for this, Lucy."

She seemed to know I would be suspicious of this comment, because she continued. "My nonwork friends in Houston are great and thoroughly trustworthy, yes, but there's various reasons I don't want to bother them with this. For instance, one is about to get married and is in major bridezilla mode. Another one's car is in the shop. Two more are in the process of moving—"

"I get the idea," I said, rubbing my forehead with my free hand.

"As for Roxie and Patrice . . ." Camilla paused, then rushed out, "Even though we're friends, I just don't want them involved in my personal life any more than they already are. If that makes any sense."

Well, wasn't *that* an interesting statement? I looked at Ben and he tilted his head in a way that said he was going to refrain from commenting on the way women chose to conduct their relationships with other women.

Probably a smart move on his part. We're an interesting, but complicated, bunch.

Camilla was still talking. "I mean, they know about the lawsuit because I got the call when I was at work. And they know about what happened"—I heard her take in an emotion-filled breath and blow it out—"to Uncle Charlie. I did a conference call this morning to tell them so they'd know I won't be in this week, and so they wouldn't hear about it from the news or anyone else." She paused. "Um, you should know that in the stress of it all, I mentioned being on the phone with you while I was out picking up dinner."

"Oh? Okay," I said, for lack of anything better coming to mind.

"But they don't know you were with me when . . . I found Uncle Charlie." She had to clear her throat before she continued. "Anyway, when Roxie asked why you and I were talking, I told them you had an appointment with Uncle Charlie to get the maternal side of his genealogy done and I was setting up a meeting with you and Uncle Charlie for when . . . he felt better." She said these last three words quietly, which made me feel a real pang for her that mingled oddly with the exasperation I felt at hearing that Camilla felt she had to lie to her coworkers about why she was in touch with me. I kept the latter feeling out of my voice, though, and replied with kindness instead.

"I understand that there are certain aspects you might not want others to know," I said. "What about Gareth? Could he possibly take the painting from your house and store it somewhere safe before he and the boys go camping?"

I heard sounds like she was pacing, and several moments ticked by without her answering me.

"Camilla?" I said finally, after indulging myself in an exaggerated heavenward glance. "What gives? Is there something weird going on with your ex?"

Camilla paused another second, then said, "Gareth has been having money problems, okay?"

"All right," I said. Then it hit me what she wasn't saying. "Are you concerned he might try and sell the painting or something?" I looked into Ben's eyes and asked her, "Or do you think Gareth came into town and stole Charlie's third of the painting and—?"

"No, there's no way he would have hurt Uncle Charlie," Camilla said firmly, but there was anguish in her reply. "I can't imagine it. He loved Charlie, and he actually cried when I called him to tell him what happened."

"But . . . ?" I prompted.

"But he's struggling to pay his bills. He lost his job a few months ago and he was never good at planning for the future in terms of finances." Camilla sounded like she was hating saying every word, but she added, "And he was one of the people who was most interested in both Uncle Charlie's find and mine. He thinks there might be a Civil War battle scene underneath the top painting, and he spent hours researching prices of battle scene paintings."

"What did he find out?" I asked.

"That, under the right circumstances, the paintings could be worth quite a bit," Camilla said. "Even if we never found the third piece, there's what's called 'crossover markets' or something like that, which could still bring in good money for the two pieces, depending on the subject."

"I think a crossover market is when, say, you have a group of interested buyers who will pay more for a painting because it has a certain theme or subtheme," I said. "Like if the painting or photo or whatever has, say, Irish wolfhounds, or a poker-playing theme."

"Yes, *I know*," Camilla said, through gritted teeth. "That's what I was about to say, Lucy. Christ, and you wonder why we didn't want to be around you all the time at work."

I felt myself flush and was thankful that Ben had received a text and was currently concentrating on typing a reply. Blinking, I felt the threat of tears pricking at my eyes. Hurt, embarrassment, and the desire to hide all those emotions from Ben didn't make it any better. I turned away, trying to center myself again.

Not that Ben didn't already know I could be a know-it-all sometimes. Heck, I'd said the same thing about him, preceding it with the word *insufferable* as an extra descriptive adjective, and I'd repeated my assertion many times. Still, I'll admit I wasn't quite ready to have someone else take me to task for, well, anything in front of Ben quite yet. I mean, logically, I knew it was just a matter of time—especially with *my* mouth—but a few more days of the particular ignorance-filled bliss that is new-coupledom would be great, thank you very much.

I hadn't said a word in response, and it seemed Camilla understood she'd gone too far. "I'm sorry, Lucy, I shouldn't have said that," she said. "I'm stressed out and worried and I let my temper get away from me. Please forgive me."

"It's fine," I said, trying not to sound curt, and failing. Out of the corner of my eye, I saw Ben's head come up at my tone as I continued. "Look, I'll go to Houston for you, Camilla. I'd like to see my parents anyway. You'll need to send me your address. Would you either be able to bring me a key or meet me halfway? I'd like to get out of town and into Houston before the going-home traffic hits."

"You won't need a key," she said. "I have the same automatic door lock that Uncle Charlie has. We actually have the same code, so you already know it. That's another reason I'm worried. It really looks like someone gained access to the house without force, so they either had a key or they knew the passcode for the door."

Now it was my turn for gritted teeth. If she had started with this information, I might not have spent the last five minutes questioning her. I could be halfway to my condo by now, with maybe enough time to do some heavenly things with Ben before I left. Turning back to him, and knowing my color was back to normal, I looked him up and down, my mind going to a more pleasurable place. A slow smile spread across my face as my eyes lingered on his mouth.

This time, when his eyebrows went up, it was with a smile that clearly said he was fully okay with my objectification of him, and would be willing for me to act on it in any way I chose. He beckoned me forward. When I complied, he bent and let his breath tickle my ear in delicious ways.

"Mind if I come with you to Houston?" he said.

I don't know what made me weaker in the knees: his words or his lips. Putting my hand on his stomach, I managed to lean back, cover my phone's speaker with one hand, and goggle at him.

"You want to come to Houston with me? Really?" Then I gave him a slanting look. "You know this will mean meeting my parents—for real this time, not just the quick handshake and hug you got when they came in after New Year's."

With the FBI claiming his time for wrap-up meetings on the separate case he'd concluded at the same time I'd unmasked a killer who'd targeted my grandfather and me, my parents had met Ben for literally one full minute. Enough for an introduction from me, a warm handshake from my father, a teary hug and several thank-you kisses on the cheek from my mother, and another grateful handshake from Grandpa before Ben's phone had rung and he'd had to leave again.

"I know," Ben said.

My eyes narrowed some more. "This also means staying at their house . . . actually conversing with them—potentially for hours—and you should know my mom's a talker."

Ben tried to work his face into not smiling, and failed completely. "I've been in a few dangerous situations in my career, and I survived working with you last fall. I *think* I can handle the people who created you." Then he pointed at my phone. "I think Camilla is trying to get your attention."

I'd been hearing a distant squawking, and now it came again. *"Lucy!"*

"Apologies, Camilla," I said hastily, putting my phone back up to my ear. "I'm back, and Ben's coming with me. We'll leave for Houston as soon as possible."

"You will?" she said. Relief was flooding her voice. "Oh, that makes me feel better."

Ben was already indicating that we should get going. Camilla, too, had moved on to explaining some of her house's quirks that we should watch out for, including a squeaky floorboard that, if stepped on in the right spot, made a moaning noise that sounded almost human, and a light switch in the hallway that was wired incorrectly and would set off the garbage disposal.

Back inside the office, Josephine was still on her conference call and Ahmad was pouring himself some tea. Ben picked up my tote bag for me and made small talk with Ahmad as I shut down my computer and scrawled a note to Jo about going to Houston, all with my phone still to my ear. Camilla was still talking as Ben and I started down the three flights of stairs, hand in hand.

"And watch out for the rug when you get to the living room. One edge is curling up, and if you're not careful, you'll trip over it and go sprawling into the coffee table . . ."

SEVENTEEN

After one quick stop at Ben's place to let him pack, and a longer stop at my condo, where packing was the last thing on our minds as soon as we stepped into my bedroom, we dropped by Big Flaco's Tacos long enough to grab a to-go order and then cruised an hour and a half down highway 71 before heading east on I-10 toward Houston.

On the way, I called Helen, hoping to talk to her about why she'd been at Charlie Braithwaite's house last night before he was murdered. I also hoped she might help me with another of Camilla's requests—to get an appointment with a reputable art conservator in Houston to have her piece of the triptych inspected.

Helen didn't answer, so I left a voice mail. Around the time Ben and I made a brief pit stop for gas and kolaches at Hruška's Bakery in Ellinger, Texas, I received a text from her. It was lacking Helen's usual effusive use of exclamation points and the occasional emoji, making it read rather curtly.

"I think she might be angry with me for ID'ing her to Dupart," I said, feeling down as I read the text again, which merely gave me a time—3:45 p.m.—the name Cisco Ramos, an address for Morris Art Conservation, and instructions to meet Cisco at the side-entrance loading dock. "Helen's one of the coolest women I know, and we've been friends for a long time. But I've seen her upset a couple of times, and she doesn't cool off quickly." I sighed, adding, "Damn."

"You only did what was right," Ben said as we walked into the bakery. "She'll come around to that, especially if she has nothing to hide."

"I'm sure she doesn't," I said with a fierce glare.

At this, Ben smiled. "I agree with you, and so does Dupart."

I turned and walked sideways so I could face him. "Wait, what? How do you know this? What exactly did Dupart say?"

Ben, however, merely put his Fed Face back into action as we stood in line for a dozen of Hruška's famous kolaches to take as a gift to my parents, including Mom's favorite, peach, and Dad's favorite, cherry and cream cheese. No matter how many ways I tried phrasing my question to get him to tell me what Dupart had said, it was to no avail. Once in the car, though, he pulled me into a long kiss that did a pretty good job of making my mind go blank, so that was some consolation.

Just over an hour later, as we were in the heart of Houston and fighting the traffic while crossing town, I attempted to regale Ben with stories of how all our freeways went by multiple names.

"It even confuses the hell out of longtime residents, but it doesn't stop us from calling US 59 the Eastex Freeway when it heads—get this—*north*east, then change to calling it the Southwest Freeway when it heads, logically speaking, southwest." I held up a finger. "Oh, but there's more. With the new interstate from Mexico to Canada, US 59 is also I-69. And don't even get me started on how I-45 is both the Gulf Freeway and the North Freeway, and I-10 is both the Katy Freeway and the East Freeway."

Ben thought about this. "So, basically, each freeway is nicknamed in different places for whatever direction it takes you when you're heading out of town."

I stuck my tongue out at him. "Insufferable know-it-all."

Ben laughed all the way to our exit ramp, which put us out onto Kirby Drive, heading south.

More ridiculous stop-and-go traffic later, we both muttered, "Finally," as Ben took a right turn into the quiet beauty of the West University subdivision, so named because it was situated west of Rice University, one of Houston's multiple institutions of higher learning. Others included the University of Houston, Texas Southern University, the University of St. Thomas, and my former workplace, Howland University.

A couple more turns as directed by GPS, and we were on Camilla's street, which was tucked away into an even quieter part of the subdivision. Here were mostly older one- and two-story houses, and unlike on the other streets, there were no residents on the sidewalks, walking with their kids or their dogs as they enjoyed the warm spring weather without the intense humidity that is the usual tropical norm for Houston. Ben parked on the street in front of Camilla's two-story, redbrick colonial with ivy trailing over the garage. We were both ready to get out and stretch our legs.

Unbuckling my seat belt, I checked the time. "We've got an hour until our appointment at Morris Art Conservation at three forty-five. Let's get this painting and then drive a few streets over. There's a little restaurant with a walk-up window that serves nothing but warm chocolate chip cookies and coffee."

"What? Why didn't you say so sooner?" Ben asked, getting out of the car with renewed vigor as I grabbed the blanket in which we would wrap Camilla's painting.

As directed by Camilla, we walked up the driveway, then let ourselves through a wrought-iron gate just before the garage. It led into a back courtyard that had been marked up to resemble a small basketball court, with a hoop at the far edge. Through another gate was the backyard and a trampoline.

I went to the door and punched in the 1-8-3-6 code, then the pound sign, and the dead bolt retracted. We walked into a mudroom, which held a long picnic bench, painted white, with several pair of shoes underneath, most of them athletic shoes. From the size of them, and from the men's-size coats hanging on two of the pegs, Camilla's boys were no longer little.

We moved into the kitchen, which had been left clean and fairly tidy by her boys and ex-husband before they left on their camping trip. It had been remodeled sometime in recent years with granite countertops, a large island with upholstered bar-stools, and walls in that gray-beige color that had been dubbed "griege" when it was the chicest neutral and being touted on every design show and website. A basketball sat on the middle barstool, a wicker basket held mail and a few odds and ends, and two six-packs of Dr Pepper were on the counter, waiting to be put in the fridge. The floors were wood and looked original to the house.

"Watch for the floorboard," I told Ben, a moment too late. An eerie moaning sound filled the quiet of the house as Ben's weight found just the right spot, but stopped just as quickly when he removed his foot.

"Yep, that was just as creepy as advertised," he said after we stared at each other for a second with equally wide eyes and then started laughing.

Next up was the living room, where big, comfy sofas in an L shape dominated and a television was mounted on the wall above the fireplace. Much like her great-uncle, Camilla had photos everywhere, though on a more reasonable scale. I finally got a look at her two boys courtesy of a series of professional photos, similar to the ones my parents made Maeve and me take every couple of years. Taken in a pretty green parklike setting, the photos showed the boys posed by themselves, together, and with Camilla.

They were tall and lanky, with tousled dark hair and blue eyes. The taller likely took after his father, but the younger one—I determined that by the bit of youthful plumpness still in his cheeks that made me guess he was thirteen or fourteen years old—took decidedly after Camilla, getting the Braithwaite high forehead, cleft chin, and reddish tint to his dark, curly hair.

We glanced around, but didn't linger. Even though we were here at Camilla's request, Ben and I both felt awkward looking around her house without her express permission.

"Come on, this way," I said, just managing to steer him away from the edge of the area rug, which was indeed curling up at just the right spot for someone to trip over it.

"This house has its own security system," he joked as we went through and found the staircase in the front part of the house. He put his hand on the banister. "Second-floor study, right?"

We climbed the carpeted stairs and found the study next to Camilla's bedroom, as promised. I glanced into Camilla's room as we passed it, but all I really saw was a queen-size sleigh bed with a flowered duvet, lots of pillows, and a painting above the headboard.

"More frilly than I would have imagined," I said to Ben as I followed him to the study. Turning in, he barely managed to duck as a nine iron came swinging at his head.

EIGHTEEN

❧

I wasn't as quick as Ben and stood, oddly frozen in place, as the nine iron went whooshing just over my head before lodging in the drywall with a deep *thunk*.

Occasionally, there are advantages to being short, and this turned out to be one of them.

Ben charged like a linebacker going in for a sack. With a guttural cry, he tackled our assailant, his shoulder going into the solar plexus of a tall, dark-haired man, who emitted a loud *"Oof."*

They landed in a heap on the floor, both struggling for the upper hand. Dropping the blanket, I lunged to where the golf club was embedded in the darker-griege-toned wall, and yanked it out. Wielding the nine iron over my head, I took two swift steps and stood over the stranger, bellowing, "Cut it out, or I'll conk you right on the head!"

He looked up at me, fright and anger mingled in his features, and continued to struggle against Ben, who had managed to pin him. Then I saw it.

"Ben—stop!" I said. "I know who he is!"

Both men turned to stare at me in shock, breathing heavily.

"Y-you do?" said the dark-haired man.

I kept the nine iron ready. "Do you have ID on you?" I asked. He nodded.

I looked at Ben. "This is Camilla's ex-husband. I don't know his last name, but his first name is Gareth."

The man's eyes, almost navy blue in color, went wider. "How do you know Camilla? And what are you doing here, sneaking around the house? How did you even get in?"

Something on Ben's face changed, from a suspicious, well-trained FBI agent to a person resigned to having likely given himself sore muscles for nothing.

"I'm going to let you go," he told Gareth. "My name is Special Agent Ben Turner and I'm with the FBI. But if you make any sudden movements, *she'll* conk you with the nine iron." Ben jerked his head at me, and I tightened my grip on the golf club, just in case.

Ben continued, "I want you to sit up and pull out your ID. Slowly, please. Understood?"

Gareth nodded. Ben released him and swiftly got to his feet. As directed, Gareth slowly reached into his back pocket and pulled out a wallet. He handed it up to Ben, who found the driver's license. "Gareth Louis Fishwick," he read.

I had a feeling I now knew why Camilla had gone back to using Braithwaite for her surname.

"It's pronounced the French way," Gareth said from his position on the floor. When Ben and I both looked blankly at him, wondering how "Fishwick" could possibly be made French, he said, "*Lou-ee*, not *Lou-iss*."

"Right," Ben said, managing to stay perfectly straight-faced. "My apologies, Mr. Fishwick."

Gareth looked up at me, suspicion all over his lean features. "How do you know who I am? And how do you know Camilla?"

"I used to work with her at the Howland library, over four years back," I said, lowering the nine iron. "I'm a genealogist, and Camilla hired me to research her ancestor's Civil War service." I leaned on the golf club, realizing I was breathing almost as heavily as they were. "As for how I recognized you, we just passed through the living room, with the portraits of Camilla and your two sons. The eldest is practically your spitting image."

Gareth's face, which had retained a hard look, softened somewhat as he went to get up.

"Before you do that," Ben said without heat, but holding up a hand to stop him. "If you would, please explain why you're here, and what you were doing taking down the painting done by Camilla's ancestor."

I looked to where Ben was gesturing. Sure enough, Camilla's piece of the triptych was on the floor, propped up against the wall and partially covered by a patchwork quilt.

"Since I heard what y'all were saying in the hallway, I could ask the same thing," Gareth said, though his tone was calm as well and he didn't try to rise again.

"We're here at Camilla's request," I said. "We've come to take the painting for safekeeping."

Pulling out my phone, I found the texts Camilla had sent me with her address and a request that if we saw any mail in the front foyer, could we please pick it up and put it on the kitchen counter? I turned my phone around so he could read them.

Gareth's eyebrows came together. "Funny," he said, "because she asked me to do the same thing."

We stared warily at each other.

"When?" I asked. When Gareth looked confused, I said, "When did she ask you to do this? Did she call you? And where is your car? Because we didn't see anyone parked in the drive."

He shrugged. "It was about two hours ago, I guess. I'd have to check my phone. The boys and I were just about to head out of town for our annual camping trip with my brother and his kids when I heard from her. I left the boys with their cousins and came back here and parked in the garage. But Cam didn't call me, she just texted." His mouth twisted a little in what was either sadness, annoyance, or both. "Cam and I are in a much better place than we used to be, but she still doesn't call me unless she has to."

I'd never heard Camilla called "Cam" before, not even by Roxie or Patrice. It sounded odd to my ears. It must have to Ben's as well.

"Would you show us the text, please?" he asked Gareth, his tone still one of easy politeness.

Gareth jerked his head toward my right. "It's on the desk."

Camilla's desk turned out to be a glass table with a straight-backed upholstered chair covered in a chintz fabric adorned with red and pink cabbage roses. Looking around the room as I picked up the phone, I noticed the plethora of feminine touches that seemed incongruous with the Camilla I knew. Maybe my vision of her needed to be revised? I decided the jury was still out on that.

At a nod from Ben, I handed Gareth his phone. He opened it, tapped the screen a couple of times, then turned it around and handed it back to me. With Ben looking over my shoulder, I read the text.

> I'm worried about my ancestor's painting being stolen. Please do me a favor and go get it. Will send a friend to pick it up from you. Thx

Camilla's last text to me had been in much the same tone—to the point and without much emotion—and had ended with her typing "Thx" instead of spelling out "Thanks" as well. Still, I hovered my thumb over the top of the text. Where Camilla's name should have been, there was only a phone number. "Didn't you think it odd that the text came up with Camilla's phone number instead of her name?"

When Gareth shook his head, Ben said, "No? I'm not sure I'm buying that."

"Look at my other texts," Gareth said. "You'll only see a few names. I use it as a privacy measure because—well, I recently lost my job, but at the last place I worked, there was this one guy who would watch other people's phones for clients calling, get their names, and then try to steal those clients." He lifted one hand, turning his palm up in almost embarrassed supplication. "I've got a talent for remembering phone numbers, so I started removing my clients' names from my contacts list. I did the same with Cam's so that on the occasions she would call, I could act like she was a client. It drove the guy crazy."

Gareth glared into the middle distance with satisfaction for a moment, then back at us. I'd shown Ben his other text messages in that moment. Sure enough, there were only three or four that actually had names.

"I think the best way to check this is to call Camilla," Ben said.

"I agree," Gareth said, clearly confident that his story would be corroborated. Using my phone, I tapped on Camilla's contact, then put it on speaker.

"Hey, Lucy," Camilla answered, her voice sounding strained and rushed. I could hear elevator music in the background. "I'm on hold with the funeral home," she explained, and I guessed she was using the landline I'd seen in Charlie Braithwaite's office. "Is everything okay?"

"Yes," I said automatically, then amended the statement. "Except when we got to the house, Gareth was here. He said he got a text from you to get your third of the triptych."

"What?" Camilla said, and I could hear the confusion in her

voice. "I never texted Gareth to go to my house for the painting. I told you why I wasn't going to do that."

"Cam?" Gareth called from the floor. "What the hell do you mean by that?"

"Is he there? He's listening?" Camilla hissed through the phone. Then she groaned and uttered a couple of frustrated oaths. "Why the hell did you call on speakerphone, Lucy?"

Gareth was looking angry now, and went to get up again, but Ben said firmly, "Sit down, Mr. Fishwick."

"What's going on?" Camilla said. "Did your boyfriend arrest him?" She called out, "Gareth? Are you all right?"

Now I was irritated. "Of course he wasn't arrested," I snapped. "Though he probably could have been, since he tried to take Ben's head off with a nine iron."

"Only because I thought you two were robbers," Gareth shot back loudly.

"Um, hello?" A timid, unfamiliar voice could just be heard on Camilla's end. "This is Dot from Shady Hills Funeral Home. May I, ah, assist you with something?"

I heard Camilla politely ask Dot From Shady Hills to please hold on a moment. Then her voice came through my phone clearly again. "I hope all three of you are listening," she said to us. "Look, I don't know what happened there this afternoon, but I didn't send Gareth to get my painting." She addressed her ex with a growl. "Gareth, if this was some ploy of yours to take my ancestor's painting and hock it like you did my grandmother's opal necklace this past Christmas, I won't be so forgiving this time."

On the floor, Gareth was sputtering, a flush creeping up his neck. "I got the necklace back, Cam, and you know it! I explained the situation to you. Are you really going to keep throwing that in my face?"

Still holding my phone out like a conduit between the feuding exes, I glanced at Ben. He looked like he was forcing himself not to roll his eyes.

Camilla ignored her ex-husband and continued. "Lucy, I have to go. Please do as I've asked you, and please show Gareth the door. If your boyfriend wants to frisk him for other objects before he leaves, I wouldn't tell you it was unwarranted. Now, I have to plan a funeral for Uncle Charlie. Goodbye."

My phone screen went black. Gareth had gone red in the face and was looking mutinous. Ben looked like he could do with some of those warm cookies I'd told him about, only with a double scotch instead of a coffee to wash them down.

"You can get up now," he said to Gareth. "Only, the Austin PD will want to be in touch with you about investigating the origin of this text message. If you'll allow me to take a photo of the text and give me your information, I would appreciate it."

Gareth got to his feet. It was only then that I realized how tall he was. Possibly six foot four or more. Though lanky, he was muscular, like a basketball player. It was lucky Ben hadn't waited to use his center of gravity and a football tackle because, had they started a fight now, Gareth looked like he wouldn't be so easy to take down.

Luckily, though, Gareth didn't seem to want to do anything but get out of the house. Mutely, he turned his phone around and let Ben snap a photo of the text, then he handed Ben a business card.

However, it appeared he was still smarting from Camilla's remarks, because he made a show of turning out his pockets, saying, "See? Look, completely empty." He even lifted up his shirt to show he wasn't storing anything in the waistband of his jeans.

Ben nodded his thanks and gestured for Gareth to walk in front of him. "I'll see you out, as Ms. Braithwaite requested."

Gareth shot him an angry look, but Ben stayed calm and courteous. It occurred to me then that Ben had his service weapon hidden in that clever pocket of the T-shirt under his button-down, but his hand had never gone near it.

"Fine," Gareth said in an aggrieved tone. "If that's how Camilla sees me, as a thief, then at least I know not to try to do her any favors in the future."

He went to exit with dignity, but I stopped him with a light touch to the arm.

"Gareth, I think Camilla is just stressed out after what happened to her uncle Charlie," I told him. "I've no doubt she'll feel terrible for saying those things when she's calmed down."

He'd been scowling down at me but, at my mention of Charlie Braithwaite, his expression faltered.

"I'd ask you to tell Camilla that I loved Charlie like an uncle myself, and if she needed any help with his funeral arrangements, that I would do it in a heartbeat. But now I know she'll think I'd show up just to steal something, so I won't bother asking you to pass along the message."

He was out the door, with Ben a pace behind, before I could reply.

NINETEEN

Feeling better now?" I asked Ben as he polished off his second chocolate chip cookie. We were sitting side by side at one of the small picnic tables by the walk-up cookie window. My lips twitched with amusement when he grunted through a sip of his black coffee and eyed the last half of my second cookie.

I broke it in two, giving him one piece as I stuffed the other in my mouth. That got a small grin out of him, though I could tell his mind was elsewhere.

"I hate having to do that," he muttered.

"Which part?" I asked dryly. "Having to do a quick dodge of a flying nine iron? Or the subsequent tackling of my ex-coworker's ex-husband? Or was it the lovely speakerphone spat we had to witness?"

He rolled the shoulder he'd used to plow into Gareth Fishwick. "If I have to use my training to defend myself or someone else," he said on a weary sigh, "I always prefer that it be the absolute last resort and for a very good reason."

"Like last fall, when you tackled the guy who tried to hurt me and was looking to throw a knife into Senator Applewhite's chest," I said.

Ben nodded, a frown on his face. "If Gareth hadn't swung the club, especially with the force that he did, I wouldn't have rushed him. I would have tried reasoning with him first."

I put my hand on his shoulder and used the heel of my palm to gently rub circles into the deltoid muscle. "I never doubted it for a second," I said, smiling a little when he made a sound of relief at my massage techniques. I smiled more with the knowledge that Ben loved using his brain, but that being forced to use his brawn, of which he had a considerable amount, was not to his liking.

The cookies, however, proved to be the right move, as the easygoing personality I now knew to be more Ben's regular temperament began to resurface. But then, cookies are pretty fail-safe for improving anyone's mood.

Ben's phone buzzed with a work call he'd been expecting. Kissing his cheek, I said, "I'm going to go check out Camilla's painting." He handed me his keys with a wink, though his voice was all business as he answered the call.

I got up and strolled back to Ben's car, slowing further as the two vehicles on either side of Ben's Explorer tried to back out of their respective spaces at the same time and nearly collided. A guy in a black Suburban made a rude hand gesture at the person in the other car, a gray BMW. Then the BMW tore out of the parking lot, music blaring. The Suburban gunned it to the edge of the lot, too, but then turned the opposite direction, nearly cutting off another driver at the same time.

"Jeez. That's all we would have needed today, a road rage incident," I muttered. I was glad to see them go, however, as it left only Ben's Explorer and two other cars on the opposite side of the small parking lot, giving me space to inspect Camilla's piece of the triptych without having to worry about anyone bothering me.

A rush of cool wind hit me as I neared the car. Rain was forecast for the overnight hours, and the sky had gone from gloriously sunny to moody and cloudy in the last half hour. As a safety precaution, Ben had backed the Explorer into the parking space. The back window was just touching a tall stand of holly shrubs lining the edge of the parking lot, keeping anyone from being able to easily access the trunk. I unlocked the car and was about to hop in the driver's side and pull the car forward enough to pop the trunk when I noticed the rubber weather strip that helped keep air and water out of the driver's-side window was damaged. It looked like something had been wedged between it and the window, taking a tiny nick out of the hard rubber.

Had someone tried to break into Ben's car? I grimaced as I ran my finger over the damaged strip, then looked around as if the culprit might be standing a few feet away, holding up a confessing hand. I considered the two vehicles I'd just seen reversing out of their spots at the same time, but I hadn't seen anything untoward before they drove away, so I thought about other culprits.

Could it have been Gareth Fishwick? I asked myself. After all, Ben had walked him outside, but had then come back up to Camilla's office to help me wrap the painting and take it downstairs. It had been, oh, about another ten minutes before we made it to the Explorer with the painting. If Gareth had been attempting to use a slim jim to open Ben's car for whatever reason—to get back at Ben for tackling him?—only to be interrupted when he heard us coming outside, he could have been in his own vehicle and gone before Ben and I could have witnessed his attempts.

Starting the Explorer and driving it forward a few feet, I also reasoned the damage could have been there for ages. Maybe Ben had lost his keys at some point and used a slim jim to spring the lock. Deciding Gareth was guilty before I'd even shown the issue to Ben was not fair.

Popping the trunk and getting out, I turned back toward the picnic tables and caught sight of Ben. He was still on his phone call, running his thumb thoughtfully along the healed cut over his eye, from which I'd removed the stitches just before we'd left on our road trip. I made a mental note to show him the damage to the car. Then, pulling from my purse a small flashlight and pair of tweezers I'd brought with me, I went to inspect the painting.

Carefully, I loosened the blanket until I could lift it up over the front of the canvas. It was framed in the same wide barnwood as the piece I'd seen at Charlie Braithwaite's house. It didn't matter that I'd seen the photo of all three panels in Charlie's house and knew they were all similarly painted, it was different seeing it up close. The rectangular soldiers looked almost like LEGO figures and the horses like Play-Doh creations, but all in one-dimensional paint. Then there were several white cloud-blobs, something looking like it might be a mountain, and the blue, snakelike thing that I'd already guessed was supposed to be a river.

I bit my lip to keep from laughing as I took it all in. It really was truly horrible.

Yet then my eye caught a two-inch piece on the leftmost side where Camilla had carefully made a hole in the canvas. Using my tweezers to lift up the edge, I angled the flashlight into the crevice, and all my laughter disappeared.

The detail of the soldier's face was astounding. He was looking back over his shoulder and upward. It seemed his eyes were looking straight into mine. Every plane of his unwashed, unshaven face—down to the dirt and the scraggly beard—was depicted in stark detail. What made me unable to look away, however, was the fear etched across his face. It widened his blue eyes and flared the nostrils of his nose. His brow was sweaty, and the kerchief he wore around his neck was darkened and limp with perspiration as well. He wasn't a boy like the young man named Powers whose tragic death Charles Braithwaite had supposedly witnessed and then written about in his journal. No, this soldier was very much a man, and he was plainly terrified.

"Everything all right, Lucy?"

I turned to see Ben approaching, looking concerned.

"Come look at this," I said, moving aside so he could bend over to see where I was shining the flashlight. He took it in for several long moments, then met my eyes.

"I mean, wow," he breathed. "That soldier has incredibly realistic detail, like the people depicted in Norman Rockwell's paintings." He peered once more at the soldier's face. "He almost looks alive."

I ran my finger along the edge of the frame, wanting to touch the face, but not daring to. "And it's as if he's, I don't know, beseeching you to understand the horrors he's witnessing."

Ben nodded, still in awe. "No kidding. I'm really glad Helen made an appointment for us with a conservator. I can't wait to see what else is under here."

I glanced at the time. "Speaking of, our appointment is in twenty minutes, so we'd better hustle."

Soon, Ben and I were driving east down Bissonnet Street toward the museum district, passing two of Houston's independent bookstores within seconds of each other. Morris Art Conservation was just a few blocks farther on, within walking distance of the Museum of Fine Arts.

"If we have time on the way back, I want to stop in at Murder by the Book," I told him. "It's pure heaven for anyone who likes mystery and crime fiction."

Ben smiled, keeping his eyes on the road. "First stop is to find out what secrets this painting has been hiding. Next stop is pure heaven."

TWENTY

A stocky man in his thirties wearing a white lab coat met us at the side entrance to Morris Art Conservation. He had a cart for transporting the painting and a wide, friendly smile.

"I'm Francisco Ramos—but please, call me Cisco," he said.

After quick introductions, Ben hopped back in his car to move it to the parking lot at the back of the building while I followed Cisco, who pushed the cart holding Camilla's piece of the triptych into the loading dock. In no time, Ben was rounding the corner and striding our way as a gust of wind blew back part of the blanket protecting the painting. I gave Cisco a peek at the soldier's terrified face and Cisco's eyebrows rose in a way that told me he might be impressed despite himself.

"I think I'll be as interested as y'all are to see what's under there," he said. "Though I don't know if Helen told you, but I can't start on this until later today or tomorrow morning."

Ben and I exchanged glances. Helen hadn't mentioned this in her text, and it made me more concerned than ever that she was still angry with me. Or, worse, that Dupart had actually found a reason to keep Helen on his suspect list.

"I'm sorry," Cisco said, misreading my expression, "but

Helen's request was last-minute and I've got another painting I absolutely have to finish up today."

Without going into details, I told him that we were grateful for his willingness to look at the painting on such short notice, but we were hoping to keep it in our possession.

Cisco smiled. "No need to worry. I'll be able to keep the painting safe. Do it all the time, and with paintings far more valuable than what's under here, even if it's a Civil War masterpiece."

It wasn't hard to believe, but I still hesitated. After what had happened to Charlie Braithwaite, and then the possibility that someone had found a way to fake-text Gareth Fishwick and make him believe his ex-wife had asked him to take the painting, I truly believed someone was after it because they knew something special was underneath. I really didn't want it to leave my sight. Ben looked like he was thinking along the same lines.

Cisco, sensing our hesitation, launched into the security measures at Morris Art Conservation, which were considerable and made me feel a bit better. "I'll be giving you documentation for your painting as well."

"Thanks, Cisco, we'd appreciate that," I said, and we followed him though the loading dock, where he touched a key card on a retractable lanyard to a scanner. It beeped and he opened the door. Ben held it open as I walked in, followed by Cisco with the cart.

From the direction Ben and I had come, Morris Art Conservation appeared to be a small, two-story office building. However, it felt much bigger on the inside, with large workrooms on either side of a long center hallway that made a right turn near the far end of the building.

As we walked down the hall, Cisco told us there were a total of ten workrooms, all specializing in different types of conservation, from paper artifacts to paintings to sculptures, earthenware, and other artistic mediums. Each workroom had a security door that could only be opened by a key card and every door had a small window set in the upper third. Craning my neck as we walked past, I caught a glimpse of two conservationists in white lab coats lifting a modern-art sculpture from a protective crate. Through another window, I saw what looked to be equipment for digital photography. The whole time, Cisco was telling us about everything Morris Art Conservation offered.

"Besides treatments, retouching, and all kinds of restoration, we can do various reports on your art's condition for insurance purposes and the like, help get rid of pest infestations, and even make mounts and displays for collectors to best display their art." As Cisco rolled the cart around a corner, he pointed to a staircase at the end of the hallway. "Then the second floor is part art gallery and part museum. We have a couple of docents and everything, and we often host small, but really well-curated exhibitions." His enthusiasm for his job was infectious as he led us to the first workroom on the right after the corner.

Inside the bright, clean room were three huge tables. Two had paintings on them in various states of conservation. Working on one was a smiling young woman sporting lavender-tinted hair tipped with pink at the ends and very short bangs going straight across her forehead. Cisco introduced her as Abbie, his assistant. She smiled at us and then went back to what she was doing, gently applying what looked like a long-handled cotton swab dipped in a clear liquid to the surface of a painting of three racehorses galloping toward the finish line. When she saw me looking interested, she explained.

"I'm doing a cleaning of what we call accumulated surface grime on this eighteenth-century painting. Different paintings require different types of cleaning, so I performed a couple of patch tests until I found the right solution to best remove the smoke, dust, and whatnot. Then I wrap cotton around a wooden stick and use small, circular strokes, letting the solution and the swab do the job instead of pressure." She waved the swab over the haunches of a dark bay horse that was in the lead. "See? He's two shades lighter under all the years of grime. You can now see the flashes of coppery red in his coat that have been hidden for so long."

"That's amazing," I said, and Abbie beamed.

Cisco then rubbed his hands together with a cheerful expression. "All right. Let me get some paperwork going for y'all."

I caught Ben watching me as Cisco moved off to another desk. "Are you sure you're okay leaving the painting here?" he asked.

"Yes," I said, nodding. "But should we have some extra safety measures, just in case?"

Ben grinned. "I like the way you think, Ms. Lancaster. Why don't we set up some security questions? You know, a question that Cisco is required to ask of anyone calling about the painting or attempting to come get it?"

I nodded. "Good idea."

Again without going into too much detail, I explained to Cisco that some weird things were happening around the pieces of this triptych, and that no one except for Ben or me was allowed to come collect the painting once it had been uncovered and assessed.

"If you get a phone call or a text message—even if you think it comes from Helen, or Ben, or me—you need to be suspicious," I said.

"Can do," Cisco said. "We won't let it out of our sight, will we, Abbie?"

"We'll take good care of it," Abbie agreed.

After spending a few minutes setting up some security protocols, Ben and I left the painting with Cisco and Abbie showed us the door to the parking lot. Ben received a work call as he and I got in the car, leaving me a few minutes to stew in my thoughts.

Earlier, while we were enjoying our cookies and coffee, Ben had forwarded Dupart information about Gareth's bogus text. Ben said that it was best to let Dupart handle looking into it, as it was his case, and I agreed, but there was nothing against thinking over other details, right?

I was now sure someone knew there was another potentially valuable painting underneath the unsophisticated artwork both Charlie and Camilla Braithwaite had been proudly displaying for so many years. But who could it be?

Camilla had admitted she'd told many people of her and her great-uncle's finds, including Roxie and Patrice, PhD candidate Neil Gaynor, her brother, Tor, and others. All of them, presumably even Neil Gaynor, could have known Camilla was going to Austin to see her great-uncle. Yet Camilla hadn't left her house empty and vulnerable. Instead, her ex, Gareth, and her two teenage sons—three tall, healthy males—had been there, making targeting Camilla's house to steal her piece of the triptych a less-attractive idea than having to contend with her eighty-four-year-old great-uncle who was known to have a bad leg. Did they also know Charlie was weakened from other health issues? It was possible, of course. Whoever this person was, they clearly knew some level of detail about both Camilla and Charlie Braithwaite.

So, could one of the people Camilla told be looking to steal the paintings and profit off the potential Civil War art underneath? Could they have driven into Austin Monday night, murdered Charlie Braithwaite, stolen his computer and various other items, and then driven back to Houston in time for work the next day?

Even though it sounded ludicrous, timing-wise it was possible. The drive was only two and a half hours. And with Camilla in Austin for a few more days, the murderer-slash-art-thief would have had the opportunity to dupe Gareth into stealing the second painting. All the other suspects on my list, save for Neil Gaynor, had closer relationships with Camilla than I had and could have known about her ex-husband's money problems.

Heck, they probably even knew about Gareth's habit of not putting names with the phone numbers in his contacts.

As for who was the least likely to be in Camilla's confidence, and therefore the least likely to know her plans, whereabouts, and details about her ex-husband, that was Neil Gaynor. However, Camilla said he was constantly in the Howland library, right? That meant he was no doubt friendly enough with the staff to ask a few questions.

A rustling noise made me come back to the here and now. As Ben pulled out of the parking lot, he'd dug into his cup holder and was handing something to me. I looked down and saw it was a penny. "I understand it's still the preferred currency for thoughts," he said. I hadn't even noticed he'd gotten off the phone.

With a smile, I took it. "I've been thinking. Before we go back to Austin tomorrow, it might be worth it to try and talk to some people."

"We could do that. Who do you have in mind? Though, remember, we only have until tomorrow afternoon, so not a whole lot of time. Also, Dupart will be interviewing people associated with Camilla, especially the ones she talked to about the painting. We need to be careful not to interfere."

"Of course," I said. "I've no desire to incur Dupart's wrath, believe me—and I'll just ignore that snort, Agent Turner. Anyway, I was thinking the city council member might be worth talking to."

Ben, however, shook his head. "We can cross her off. Dupart hasn't mentioned any other potential suspects here in Houston, but he did say the city council member had checked out."

This was actually a relief, as talking to her would have meant tracking her down first, and with only a few hours to play with tomorrow before heading back to Austin, finding her would cut into our limited time.

"All right, then. My next thought was Neil Gaynor, because Camilla mentioned he's at the Howland library all the time. And possibly even Camilla's brother, Tor Braithwaite."

Ben mused on this, then said, "Because Tor's a family member, Dupart will be checking him out fully, so I think we should worry about him only if we have time."

"Then Neil Gaynor it is," I said. Rubbing my thumb over the penny, I added, "And hopefully this baby will bring me luck, because while I'm at my former workplace, there's no reason not to have a chat with my two other least-favorite former coworkers as well."

TWENTY-ONE

I'd been so caught up with everything concerning the triptych that I hadn't had time to stress out about the crucial first true meeting between my parents and Ben. It wasn't until after we'd left Murder by the Book—Ben and I having bought two mysteries each—and were headed in the direction of my childhood home that I felt butterflies erupt in my stomach. My parents were wonderful, caring people, but not easily impressed when it came to my boyfriends. Not even the fact that Ben had literally saved my and Grandpa's lives would be enough to make them like him in the long run if they didn't feel he was worthy. I cast a sidelong glance at Ben. While Grandpa had pegged him as "a keeper" almost instantly, I could only hope my parents would feel the same.

As Ben navigated the Houston roads, I found myself studying him. He seemed a little nervous as well, which somehow made my butterflies chill out. It took Ben waving his hand in front of my eyes for me to blink and realize he'd asked me a question.

"Sorry, what was that?"

"Your dad's initials?" he asked with a grin. "When I met him on New Year's Day, he asked me to call him G.W. What do they stand for?"

"Oh, right," I said with a laugh. "It stands for George Watson."

"He's named after your grandfather, then?"

"Only the George part," I said. "Watson was my gran's maiden name."

"And your mother's name? It's Nita, of course, but is that short for Anita?"

"Right you are. High-five," I said, holding out my hand, and he indulged me.

"Okay, then. G. W. and Nita Lancaster," Ben said, as if he was approaching them as suspects in a case and committing their details to memory, all while absentmindedly using his left hand to rub the shoulder he'd used to do his linebacker impression on Gareth Fishwick. "Your dad is an architect, right?

"Yes, he's a retired structural architect," I said, reaching out and taking over for him, getting another little kick of satisfaction at the grunt of relief he let out as I massaged his arm muscle. "He specialized in designing things like bridges and skywalks, stuff like that."

"That'd be a neat job," Ben said, leaning into my massage after successfully navigating onto the freeway. "And what about your mom? You never told me what she does."

I chuckled. "Well, let's just say you have her to thank for my massage techniques."

He blinked, then it sunk in. "Your mom's a masseuse?"

"Massage therapist," I corrected. "Specifically, a sports massage therapist. She's basically retired, too, but still owns a small company that specializes in massage for athletes."

Ben grunted again as I continued working his shoulder and upper arm.

"Remind me to bow and kiss her feet, then," he said.

As I thought they might be, Mom and Dad were outside in the front yard when Ben and I drove up.

"Were they waiting for us?" he asked out of the side of his mouth.

"Yep," I said, grinning, "but they'll think we don't know that, so act cool."

My mom was on the porch with a glass of iced tea and a book, and my dad was pulling bags of potting soil out of the back of his pickup truck and stacking them to one side of the garage. There looked to be about fifteen bags of soil still left in the truck, plus a couple of flats of what were likely young vegetable plants. It seemed everyone was going crazy for spring planting.

"I'd forgotten just how much you look like your dad," Ben said, glancing at my very blond mother with her pale Irish skin, then at my dad, with his dark hair and naturally tan skin from his mother's Spanish and Mexican side. "Has anyone ever mentioned that to you?"

"Not one soul," I quipped. He laughed and we both got out of the car. I grinned widely at my parents and called out, "Hi, Mom. Hi, Dad."

"Hi, pumpkin," Dad said, his arms wide to show that his light blue T-shirt was dusted in soil. "I'll let your mother hug you for the both of us, as I got bombed by a torn sack of compost. Good to see you, Ben. How do you feel about helping me with some of these bags?"

"Daaaad," I drawled in mock exasperation, but Ben was already heading to Dad's tailgate, saying, "Happy to—and good to see you again, sir."

My dad reminded Ben to call him G.W. Ben inclined his head respectfully and was reaching for a bag of soil when my mom called out, "Wait! Don't you dare move a muscle!"

Ben stopped in his tracks, looking unsure. A second later, my mom was whipping around the tailgate and grabbing Ben in a big hug.

"Hello, Ben. I wanted to get in my hug before you got all dirty."

Ben returned the embrace with a laugh. "It's so good to see you again, Nita."

That earned him a kiss on the cheek and then Mom released him and came for me, arms outstretched.

Dinner was my mom's famous roast beef—or "Roast Beast," as she always called it—with mashed potatoes, salad, steamed asparagus, and balsamic-and-red-wine-glazed mushrooms. The conversation, however, mainly centered around the Braithwaites, from Charles to his descendants Charlie and Camilla to the family members we'd never met, and the triptych that seemed to connect them all. My parents, being art lovers themselves, were riveted by what we'd found on Camilla's piece of the triptych today, and couldn't wait to hear what Cisco at Morris Art Conservation discovered when he removed the top canvas.

"I just wish I knew where the third piece of the triptych is," I said, taking a sip of the excellent pinot noir Dad had selected for us to share.

"Why, you should talk to Jensen Hocknell," Mom said, her face lighting up.

"Who's Jensen Hocknell?" I asked, perplexed. "Are they related to old Mrs. Hocknell down the street?"

Mom, who was sitting to my left, reached out to push a lock of hair out of my face. "Jensen *is* old Mrs. Hocknell, dear." Then she lightly slapped my knee. "And don't call her old. She's younger than your grandfather, for goodness' sakes."

"Yeah, but Grandpa is young at heart," I said with a grin. "Mrs. Hocknell has never exactly been known for her light and carefree ways." I turned to Ben. "She used to come out on her porch and yell at Maeve and me for riding our bikes past her house too loud. I'm still wondering how anyone could ride a bicycle loudly."

Ben smiled, rubbing his hand over his chin in what looked like an effort to not laugh. Since pretty much the moment we'd arrived this afternoon, I could tell he'd been highly amused at the way my parents and I teased and joked with each other. My parents had noticed as well, which had served to increase the level at which we ribbed each other, almost as if the three of us were in an unspoken competition to see who could make Ben laugh out loud first. Would it be my sweet mother, who could surprise you with her devilishly cheeky comments? Or my dry-witted father, who was a true ham underneath it all? Or would it be me, the one who had bits of both their traits?

"But why would I need to talk to Mrs. Hocknell about the Braithwaites?" I asked Mom.

"Don't you remember? She told us she was a Braithwaite. It's her maiden name."

I racked my brain while staring at my mother, then finally said, "When did she say this? I can't even remember the last time I talked to her."

Mom took Ben's wineglass for a refill. "Oh, it was a while ago. You were twelve or thirteen, I'd say."

"So, just seventeen or eighteen years ago," I deadpanned, waving my hand around airily. "Like yesterday."

Mom giggled at my sarcasm and Dad grinned broadly. He angled himself toward Ben, whose eyes had lightened two whole shades with suppressed mirth, and stage-whispered, "I commend you on your ability to keep your mouth shut. It comes in handy in this household."

Ben just rubbed his face even harder and I pretended to give my father a withering look that he returned with an innocent smile very reminiscent of Grandpa's. I turned back to my mother.

"Are you sure Mrs. Hocknell is a Braithwaite?" I said.

"Of course I'm sure. She's mentioned it to me several times since then. She even has some family photos on the wall in her living room."

I goggled at my mom. "You've been in her house?"

Mom smiled at me with infuriating calm. "Many times. I partner with her for bridge every couple of months, too, when her usual partner, Ruthanne, is out of town."

Naturally, Mom mentioned Ruthanne like I should know who she was, but I asked the more pertinent question. "I know you love gin rummy and poker, but when did you start playing bridge?"

Mom smiled at me fondly. "Oh, I always played. Tried teaching you and Maeve when you were young, but neither of you were interested. I just haven't played much until the last few years."

I looked at my dad. "Is she having me on? I don't remember anything about her trying to teach Maeve and me bridge, or having Mrs. Hocknell as a friend, much less as a bridge partner."

My father leaned back in his chair, crossing one ankle over his knee. "Oh, she's serious, all right. It's been another one of her secret talents all these years, and she and Jensen are quite the sharks. I've begun to suspect Jensen is lying about Ruthanne being out of town as often as she claims. Jensen wins much more often when she teams up with your mother." He pointed to the pretty new wine decanter that was helping to aerate our pinot noir. "She won that decanter a couple of weeks ago. A few weeks before that, she brought home a very nice gift card to one of our favorite restaurants. We took Dan and Suzy out to dinner and had a great time."

I stared at my father, then at my mother, who cheerfully poured Ben another glass of wine.

I turned to Ben, whose grin was wide as he raised the glass to his lips, and pointed to myself. "Am I in the Twilight Zone here?"

At this, he choked on his wine then started laughing, sending my mother into delighted giggles as well. My father handed Ben an extra napkin while sending me a wink.

"You think this is funny, do you?" I said to Ben, trying to give him a beady stare even as my own lips were twitching—not just because it was funny, but because I'd been the one to make him break. "You just wait until I meet *your* mother."

This had no sobering effect on either him or my parents. Or me, when it came down to it. Honestly, it was right then that I knew Ben was in, as far as G. W. and Nita Lancaster were concerned.

TWENTY-TWO

Mom suggested that she and I walk to Mrs. Hocknell's house after an early breakfast at my favorite diner the next morning.

"Another secret you're keeping from Flaco?" Ben teased in my ear when the staff at Buffalo Grille greeted me like an old friend. I turned, batting my eyelashes up at him with my sweetest smile.

"Snitch on me, bucko, and I'll let it slip that you raved about the corn tortillas at that new taqueria by your house. That's right, you heard me." I made bring-it-on movements with my hands before sidling up to the counter to order my favorite pancakes, eggs, and thick-cut bacon, Ben chuckling as he followed me.

It was just after eight a.m. when Mom and I set off, leaving my dad outside working in the yard and Ben in their library to take some work calls, yet not before Mom gave Ben's sore shoulder a professional once-over. She declared him well on the mend, but nevertheless microwaved a heating pad for him to use during his calls.

Mrs. Hocknell lived on the opposite side of our street and seven houses down. Mom and I decided it wasn't long enough of a walk to work off our breakfast calories, so we took an alternate route that first wended us around a couple of other streets in the subdivision.

When we approached Mrs. Hocknell's house, she was standing out on her porch in knit pants, a white shirt, and a long gray cardigan with wide sleeves. Her hands were on her hips, staring grumpily in the direction we would have come had we taken the direct route.

"Jensen, yoo-hoo!" Mom called gaily, waving even though Mrs. Hocknell was still stubbornly looking the wrong way. "Over here, Jensen! We came from the other direction."

Slowly, Mrs. Hocknell turned, glaring at me like she was determined to find something in my appearance or my approach for which to call me out.

"She's all bark, no bite," Mom said out of the side of her mouth, her smile still in place.

"Yeah, she's looking like she remembers my 'loud' bike riding about now," I muttered back, making Mom giggle.

"Anita, you didn't tell me you would be coming from the opposite end of the street," Mrs. Hocknell snapped as we made our way up her walkway.

I willed my face to not show surprise. The only person who had ever called my mom Anita was her late father, my maternal grandfather, and I'd never heard him say it in the brusque way Mrs. Hocknell had.

Yet my mom just grinned. "Oh, we just wanted a bit more of a jaunt. My, your hydrangeas are already looking like they're producing flowers. They'll be absolutely gorgeous in no time. And your azaleas!" Mom clapped her hands together, holding them to her chest. "I never cease to be jealous of how beautiful yours look. Mine always seem to look so thin and wimpy in comparison."

"Acid!" Mrs. Hocknell fairly barked. "They need acidic soil to thrive. I keep telling you that, Anita. You're not acidic enough."

Mom swiftly grabbed my fingers to stop us both from giggling after I gave her a look that implied Mrs. Hocknell had enough acid for the whole street's azaleas.

Luckily, Mrs. Hocknell didn't seem to notice, as she was craning her neck over her porch to inspect her full and thriving purple azaleas. Clearly Mrs. Hocknell, or someone else, had been sprucing up the garden, as a recently added layer of fresh, dark soil was visible under her shrubs. A wheelbarrow stood just around the corner of the house; in it, I could see a couple of small boxwood shrubs in pots, ready to be planted, along with some empty brown bags of soil and gardening tools.

As we ascended the stairs and onto Mrs. Hocknell's porch, Mom's charm went up another notch. "Jensen, I'm sure you remember my daughter Lucy?"

I smiled. "Good morning, Mrs. Hocknell. It's very nice to see you again."

Mrs. Hocknell, who my mother had told me was now in her early eighties, frowned imperiously at me through rimless glasses. Her hair was arranged in the same one-length bob it had been for years, parted to one side and ending about an inch below her earlobes, only it had finally gone from a storm-cloud gray to a frosty white. Though her cheeks had a few broken blood vessels, her face wasn't heavily lined until you got to her neck, which sagged with loose skin from a lifetime of a slightly hunched posture. With her thin, patrician nose, lines around her lips that gave her a look of perpetually sucking lemons, and eyes that had faded to the blue-gray color of sagebrush, she looked like the person I'd cast in a play as the modern version of the Dowager Countess of Grantham.

"So, you want to talk to me about my family, do you?" she asked me in lieu of pleasantries.

"I would, yes, Mrs. Hocknell. If you wouldn't mind."

Out of the corner of my eye, I could see my mother suppressing an indulgent smile that encompassed both her friend's stubbornness and her daughter's attempt to keep her inclination to be sassy at bay.

With a nod, Mrs. Hocknell gestured for us to follow her into the house. "Come on, then. I know your mother likes tea. I assumed you do as well? I've brewed some Irish breakfast for us to enjoy."

"Thank you," I said. "That sounds wonderful."

Mrs. Hocknell's house was a two-story colonial painted butter yellow, and had black shutters, white trim, and three dormer windows. I'd always loved the look of her house, and I told her so as we walked over the threshold.

"Have you?" Mrs. Hocknell said, a measure of doubt in her voice as we followed her through her entryway. "By the way you and your sister always tore past my house, either on your bicycles or on foot, I assumed you thought the Wicked Witch of the West lived here and my house was to be avoided at all costs."

A minute shake of the head from my mother told me any reply I gave wouldn't be good enough. Thus, I let Mom make small talk with our veritable crosspatch of a neighbor as I looked around the house. I took in the abundance of artwork around the room and how the morning sun highlighted comfortable furnishings in pretty fabrics, beams of light streaking across a large leather ottoman covered in coffee table books on various subjects. A tray with tea things straddled two of the book stacks, while a tortoiseshell cat was perched atop another stack, surveying us with interest as we filed in.

Mrs. Hocknell went around the ottoman, stroked the cat, who began purring loudly, and sat down in the armchair closest to the windows.

"Anita, you sit there," she said, indicating the other armchair, "and Lucy, you may sit on the sofa."

I did as directed, and the cat immediately came to me, begging for attention.

"You're a pretty thing," I told the cat, scratching her behind the ears.

"That's Turtle," Mrs. Hocknell said before I could ask, and began to pour the tea. She glanced around the room. "There's another one hiding around here somewhere named Dove. I adopted them on the same day two years ago, though they're not related." She passed Mom the first cup of fragrant tea. "Turtle never wants to be away from people, and Dove is more than happy to be in my presence only when it's breakfast or dinnertime." Handing the second cup to me, she added, "She's not mean, you understand, just a loner."

I smiled at Mrs. Hocknell, but she merely observed me for a moment before pouring her own cup. Mom and I briefly met each other's eyes and she gave me a little wink.

"As I understand it from your mother, you know my grandniece?" Mrs. Hocknell said, getting down to business. "And you were with her when she found my cousin Charlie?"

I hesitated. Mrs. Hocknell was watching me, waiting for my answer, her expression giving me the idea she wanted facts, not sympathy. This morning, I'd texted Camilla about my discovery that her great-aunt had been my neighbor when I was growing up, and that Mom and I would be going to visit with her this morning. Camilla's reply had been frustratingly brief—she was still dealing with the funeral home but encouraged me to talk to her aunt Jensen. I had no idea what details Camilla had given her great-aunt, if any at all. Thus, I decided that information regarding Charlie's death should come from Camilla, and I would steer the conversation in other directions.

"I was with her, yes," I said, nodding. "Camilla actually came to me a few days ago regarding the article in *Chronology* magazine—" I stopped, then switched gears. "Have you read the article about your ancestor, Mrs. Hocknell?"

"I read a great deal, Lucy, and *Chronology* is a magazine I pick up from time to time, but I have not yet read the article."

I went to explain it, but Mrs. Hocknell made a sweeping-away motion with one veined hand, causing her cardigan to draw back to the elbow and expose three large age spots I hoped she was getting checked by a dermatologist. "You do not need to explain it to me. Camilla has already done so. She called me the night before she went to Austin to see you and—" Her voice didn't so much falter as go quieter. "And Charlie."

"May I say how very sorry I am about Charlie?" I said when the tiny crack in her armor gave me my chance. "I met him once at a wine tasting, and then, as you may know, I spoke to him a bit the afternoon before he was . . . well, before he died. He was a lovely man."

Mrs. Hocknell's jaw shifted side to side for a moment and then she nodded. "Charlie and I were always close, even though we didn't see much of each other. I knew he was unwell, but it's still a shock. And that someone killed him and then robbed his house, stealing our ancestor's painting?" She shook her head. "I'm still trying to wrap my head around it." Her voice was quiet when she added, "I shall miss him terribly."

My mother reached out and squeezed Mrs. Hocknell's hand, releasing it when the older woman's chin lifted once more. Mrs. Hocknell took a sip of her tea, then looked at me.

"If you're wondering if I have any knowledge of the truth—or lies—of my ancestor Charles Braithwaite's claims of continuing to fight in the Civil War and being promoted to corporal," she said, "I'm afraid I don't. All the artifacts from his life were handed down through the male heirs in my time and before."

She sniffed again, but this time it was out of derisiveness, not sadness. "Many of them cared, some of them didn't, and no doubt some interesting things got lost along the way when they passed to a descendant who didn't give two hoots about our forefather. All I can say is that I'm glad Camilla stepped in before her fool of a brother gave away all our ancestor's things, including their piece of the triptych."

I wanted to ask about the triptych panel, but curiosity prompted me to ask a different question.

"Did Camilla happen to tell you about the man looking to sue for monies his family lost back in the 1920s? And about the woman who's looking to strip the Braithwaite name from the elementary school and the park?"

Mrs. Hocknell's eyes flashed, but she merely sighed. "Yes, I know about it. It makes me furious, of course. They're just doing it for the publicity."

Luckily, I was already taking a sip of my tea, so I was saved from having to agree or disagree with her before she went on.

"Don't get me wrong, Lucy," Mrs. Hocknell said, giving me a shrewd look. "For the past several years, I've been telling my family we should quietly ask the city and the school district to give up the Braithwaite name. I'm happy to say my relations finally agreed."

"Camilla mentioned as much to me," I said, nodding.

"Yes, it was time. Even though Charles's true legacy was not that he lived to be the last surviving Civil War soldier, but that he was a man who worked his whole life against racial oppression—not to mention advocating for good things like education, proper medical care, and women's right to vote—I can nevertheless understand the opinions of those who think his name might be more linked with the Confederacy than with the upstanding man he was after the war." She leaned forward to put her teacup down on the tray. "I would love for his name not to be an issue for the park and the elementary school, but it is, and my mind was and is open to comprehending that. In fact, I strongly believe that my ancestor would be open to the change, too—and, luckily, my extended family felt the same."

I realized I'd been smiling at her without thinking, and I saw one side of her pinched mouth twitch a bit like she might actually be pleased about it.

I couldn't think of any other questions to ask about her ancestor, so I turned the subject to the triptych. "Do you remember seeing all three pieces together?" I asked.

"Oh yes, but only once, at our last family reunion, in 1988," Mrs. Hocknell replied with the first true hint of a smile. "Horrid, all three parts. I never liked it, but it was passed down, so it became like—" She pointed to a small table in one corner. It held a couple of fading photographs in silver frames, a candlestick lamp with a pleated shade, and a squat, misshapen flowerpot colored in varying shades of blue and holding a small dieffenbachia plant. "Like that flowerpot," she continued. "It's hardly a showpiece, but Camilla made it for me when she was about seven years old. She looks for it every time she comes over, so I keep it, and I cherish it. Our family cherishes those paintings for the same inexplicable reasons."

"It makes perfect sense to me," I said, "and I hope Charlie's panel will be recovered quickly so that it can be returned to your family."

Mrs. Hocknell considered me for a moment, then nodded, looking pleased.

Across the ottoman, Mom gave me a smile. I'd done well. Then she gave a surreptitious movement of her left wrist and, hence, her watch. It was time to get back on track. Mom had things to do today, and Ben and I would be going back to Morris Art Conservation to pick up Camilla's painting.

Mrs. Hocknell was sharp, though. I was beginning to see how much she and Camilla were alike, even though they didn't physically resemble one another. "Go on, Lucy. We all have busy days today and I know you have more questions for me. Ask away."

She sounded a little tired now. I cast my mom another glance as Mrs. Hocknell was adjusting the sleeve of her cardigan. Mom, whom I was using as a barometer of her friend's energy levels, gave me an encouraging nod, but one that also told me not to go too far.

I settled on the one question I really wanted the answer to: "Camilla explained how the triptych panels were handed down through the three main branches of the family. She said she doesn't know any of her cousins from the branch descending from Charles's daughter—which isn't unusual at all after so much generational distance in the family tree. However, do *you* happen to know who in your family has the third piece?"

"No, I don't. I know who used to own it, though," she replied with a touch of disapproval. "Back in the eighties, when we had the reunion, it was owned by one of my older distant relatives, though I only met him a couple of times. I don't even recall his first name because he went by his surname, which was Smith. What I do remember was that he had more than one older sister, but he inherited the painting because he was the eldest male." Mrs. Hocknell shrugged and glared at me, but this time I guessed she wasn't seeing me, but her distant cousin who received the triptych panel because of patrilineal inheritance and nothing more.

"Anyway, Smith died from some sort of cancer less than a year after the reunion. He had four or five children, if I remember correctly, though they didn't attend the reunion so I've never clapped eyes on any of them." She gave me a sidelong look and asked, "Incidentally, what would their relationship be to me?"

"Well, you have to go back to your nearest common ancestors," I told her, "which would be Charles Braithwaite and his wife.

Camilla determined Charles was her fourth great-grandfather, which makes him your second. It depends on Smith's generational relationship to Charles, but if he's Smith's second great-grandfather as well, then you two are third cousins. And therefore, his children are your third cousins, once removed."

"And if Smith was a generation older than me?" Mrs. Hocknell asked, one white eyebrow arching with curiosity.

"Then he's your second cousin, once removed, and his children are your third cousins."

Mrs. Hocknell turned to my mother. "Isn't that interesting, Anita? And she can do it in her head. I'm astounded, and impressed."

My mother practically glowed with pride, and Mrs. Hocknell turned back to me with a look that told me I could continue, if I wished.

"So, Smith's children . . . do you think one of them inherited the painting?" I asked.

"It's likely," Mrs. Hocknell replied tartly, her mouth going back into a thin line. "But I don't know any of their names or where they are now. You would be better at finding them than I would, I think."

I nodded, mentally filing the information away. I felt like Mrs. Hocknell was beginning to look tired, too, but when she raised her eyebrows once more, I said, "Did Charlie tell you about the incident with his employee's young daughter accidentally gouging a hole in his piece of the triptych, and that he believed there to be another, more detailed painting underneath?"

This time, as Mrs. Hocknell nodded, she blinked and I saw a wave of exhaustion come over her. My mother saw it as well.

"Jensen, is everything all right?" Mom asked, reaching over to put her hand on Mrs. Hocknell's arm, right over her wrist. I guessed she was checking her friend's pulse and felt thankful my mother, as a massage therapist, had some medical knowledge.

Mrs. Hocknell pushed Mom's hand away and said in a tone that was reminiscent of the days when she'd groused at Maeve and me, "I'm fine, Anita. Don't fuss. I've been up since five and I've been cleaning the house and working in some new soil into in my vegetable garden out back. I'm just a bit tired, that's all."

"All right," Mom said. "If you're sure."

Mrs. Hocknell took a deep breath, then focused on me again. "Yes, Charlie mentioned that he saw another painting underneath. Camilla said she found the same thing under her painting as well."

"Did you happen to mention what they'd found to anyone?" I asked.

"I haven't, no," she said. "Why do you ask?" Before I could answer, though, her doorbell rang. Turtle, who'd been purring next to me, hopped off the sofa and trotted to the window to look outside.

"Now who could that be?" Mrs. Hocknell said, pushing herself out of her chair and walking to the front entry. My mom watched her with a trace of worry, but Mrs. Hocknell seemed to have regained her strength.

A moment later, we heard the door open, then Mrs. Hocknell say wryly, "Tor. I should have known you'd show up here."

TWENTY-THREE

"Aunt Jensen," a deep voice said with warmth. "I was in the area, so I thought I'd drop by to see you. May I come in?"

Now Mrs. Hocknell's voice sounded amused. "Oh, of course. I know that your sister sent you to check on me, but you're always welcome here, you rascal. I do have guests at the moment, though. Let me introduce you." We heard the front door close, and Mom and I stood up, exchanging a look. Not two minutes ago, Mrs. Hocknell had called her grandnephew a fool, but now she seemed charmed to see him.

I gave my mom a shrug. Families and family dynamics were strange and complicated things, and it wasn't for me to decide how Jensen Hocknell should feel about her grandnephew.

Though when Tor Braithwaite walked in the room, striding over to clasp my mother's hand, I saw how Mrs. Hocknell could have been charmed just by his smile alone. Then there was also his tousled reddish-brown hair, lean build with broad shoulders, and eyes an even clearer shade of brown than his sister's.

As Tor moved to take the opposite end of the sofa and we both sat, I looked back up at the sound of my mother's voice. "If you two will excuse us for just a few minutes, Jensen is going to give me her recipe for a double-chocolate Bundt cake I had at our last bridge game. We won't be long." She had her arm through Mrs. Hocknell's, whose face was obscured by my mother's angle.

I nodded distractedly at her. I'd given up on the thought of trying to talk to Camilla's brother after Ben said Dupart's team would be checking him out thoroughly. But here was my chance—I felt like fate had smiled upon me, and I wasn't going to waste time.

"I used to work with your sister, actually," I said as he languidly crossed one leg over the other. "And she's hired me to look into your ancestor's Civil War records. I'm a genealogist."

Tor grinned, but it wasn't at my last statement. "You worked with Camilla?" He leaned back into the corner of the sofa to look at me head-on. "Good God. Don't tell me my sister was a fun coworker, because I won't believe you."

When I opened my mouth, then closed it, he chuckled. "Don't worry, I'm just teasing you—and my big sister. She's been a bossy, no-fun managerial type since the day I was born, and I love her for it."

I decided changing the subject away from my relationship with Camilla would be the way to go here. Folding my hands in my lap, I said, "Tor, may I say how sorry I am about your great-uncle Charlie? I didn't know him well, but I liked him very much. It's such a tragedy what happened."

Tor's hand went through his hair and his smile disappeared, making him look older, and also showing me he had a cleft in his chin like his sister and his uncle Charlie. "Thank you. Yes, it was a great tragedy. Uncle Charlie was always in our lives. He was irreplaceable, and it will be really different without him." There was a heartbeat of silence, then his face twitched with realization. "Wait a minute. If you're the genealogist, then you're the friend who was with my sister when she found him. The one who's helping to get our ancestor's painting checked out."

I nodded. I didn't clarify that I was in the living room when

Camilla found their great-uncle dead, so not exactly with her. Nor did I correct him that Camilla and I weren't exactly friends. At least, not in the traditional sense. Instead, I latched onto the topic of the triptych painting.

"I understand your sister told you a while back that she found the same thing Charlie did—that there's another canvas under the top one." When he nodded, I asked, "Did you happen to mention it to anyone? About what she or Charlie found, I mean?"

"Why would you ask that?" Tor said. His eyes slid in the direction my mother and Mrs. Hocknell had disappeared to, then back to me. Part of me wondered if he was hoping his great-aunt would interrupt us, and the other part wondered if he was afraid she would and hear his answer. It made my suspicion levels jump up a notch.

"Well," I said, "there's the possibility that whoever killed your great-uncle knew there might be a valuable painting underneath, you know what I mean? It just makes me wonder if anyone you or Camilla told might have been unduly interested in the story."

Tor turned one of his palms up. "I mean, sure, I told a few people a couple of weeks ago, and they all thought it was pretty cool, but they were my buddies—guys I go out drinking with and such. We talked about it, I joked about bringing the painting on *Antiques Roadshow* and having some antiques dude tell me it was worth millions, and how I'd be all, 'Sold! To the first bidder who will take this piece of crap off my hands!'" Tor threw up his hand with a flourish, index finger up, and then chuckled at the memory. "Then my buddy's girlfriend showed up and brought a couple of her friends with her. I hit it off with one of them, and let's just say, the conversation didn't come up again," he added, flashing me a bad-boy grin.

Fighting not to roll my eyes, I persisted. "Not with anyone else? It didn't come up again later?"

Tor watched me for a long moment, and I saw his flirty

jocularity disappearing, though he kept his tone even. "You know, Lucy, you're sounding like you might be working with the police, who have already questioned me. They showed up on my doorstep early this morning." His eyes briefly flashed with irritation, though I couldn't tell if it was directed toward me or the police. Probably both. Nevertheless, he remained polite.

"Look, I don't think I owe you any explanations, but since you're helping my sister, I'll tell you the two things you need to know. First, I would never hurt anyone, much less my uncle Charlie, who was like another grandfather to Camilla and me. Second of all, I've had the same alibi for the past week—all day, every day, and definitely all night." Dipping his chin, he gave me a significant look.

"Yep, I'm tracking your meaning," I said dryly.

"Her name is Mellie," he added nonetheless, "and she's the woman I hit it off with at the bar with my buddies. Since meeting her, I haven't left Houston, and she's been staying with me this past week. She sold her town house and can't move into her new one for another couple of days. So my whereabouts are known and solidly confirmed."

Well, rats. I felt like I'd just failed my first test at questioning a potential suspect, and my frustration made me blurt out the first thing that came to mind.

"Okay, then. Camilla told me you nearly sold your family's piece of the triptych to someone for ten bucks at a garage sale. You knew this painting was created by your Civil War–veteran ancestor, right? Why on earth were you willing to practically give it away?"

"Because it hung outside my bedroom my whole life," he shot back. "I looked at it every day, ten times a day, and I couldn't stand it." He rubbed the back of his neck, seeming to deflate a little. "Plus, this was six years ago, and just a couple of months after my dad died and my mom moved to California to open a yoga studio with her best friend. I'd just graduated from college, Camilla was going through her divorce, so she was distracted, and it was up to me to clear out the house. I wasn't thinking straight, okay?"

I felt like a serious heel now, and it reminded me that there are often difficult moments hidden behind a person's bright smile. "I'm sorry," I said, my tone softened.

"It's okay," he replied. "But for what it's worth, I'm glad my sister saved the painting. It may be ugly as hell—at least the one on the outside is—but I get that it's part of our family history."

I could see now why Mrs. Hocknell seemed to fluctuate between being exasperated and charmed by her grandnephew. The minute he seemed to be nothing but an overgrown frat boy, he said something that made you feel like he had a much deeper side. "I'm glad Camilla saved it, too," I said.

From the other room, I heard my mother's laugh. I turned in my seat to find Mom walking back in with Mrs. Hocknell, who looked a bit pale, but was smiling at whatever my mother had just said.

I stood up, reading an almost imperceptible glance from my mother that said it was time for us to head out. Tor Braithwaite stood as well, and after one assessing look, offered me his hand.

"Thank you for speaking with me," I said as we shook. "I apologize if—"

"Water under the bridge," he said with a rueful smile and a wave of his free hand. "I promise."

"Lucy?"

I turned around. Mrs. Hocknell was coming toward me, both her hands held out. Surprised, I took them.

"I just want to say that I appreciate the fact that you were with Camilla when she found Charlie, and that you were willing to help Charlie when you owed him nothing." She squeezed my hands a bit tighter and lowered her voice. "That goes for my grandniece, too. Oh, I know she's paying you and all, but you didn't have to take the job. Thank you."

Mom waited until we were halfway down the street, headed toward home, to laugh at my expression. "You look like I could knock you over with a feather."

I laughed, too. "I'm not sure it would even take that much. Mrs. Hocknell, being nice to me, and *thanking* me? Who would have imagined it?"

"Wonders will never cease," Mom said, and I smiled at her. I always loved how she said it as a statement she was stubbornly sure of rather than posing it as the traditional sarcastically surprised question.

Glancing at her hands, I asked, "So, where's the recipe for the chocolate Bundt cake? Is it on your phone?"

Mom gave me a confused look, then nodded in recollection, saying, "Oh, right. I'm afraid that was just a ruse."

"Why?" I asked. "Did Mrs. Hocknell need to have a good cry about her cousin Charlie?"

"Yes, and no," Mom replied. "We both saw Jensen looking a bit weak earlier, and I noticed it again after her nephew—but he's her grandnephew, correct? And why isn't it 'grandaunt,' when Jensen is the sister of Tor and Camilla's grandfather? We say 'grandfather' and 'grandmother,' so why not 'grandaunt' and 'granduncle'?"

"Technically, it should be 'grandaunt,' and all the other 'grands,'" I said. "With the next relationship being 'great-grandaunt' and so on. Only somewhere along the way, it got corrupted, and 'great-aunt' and 'great-uncle' stuck around, confusing everyone forevermore." I held my hands up in mock surrender when Mom looked exasperated. "Don't ask me how. I don't know."

Mom grinned. "All right, then, to get back on the subject. I figured Jensen wouldn't want me to make a fuss, so I covered with the Bundt cake story." I saw Mom's brows knit. "I'm worried that she's not feeling well. She has a bit of a strange rash on her arm and stomach. But I got her to at least promise me she would make an appointment with her doctor."

"I noticed that she was doing some spring planting like most everyone else." I pointed to another neighbor's yard, which looked much the same, with freshly planted flowers, crepe myrtle trees just beginning to leaf out, and a mound of fresh soil ready to be spread. Then I recalled seeing the shrubs and empty bags of soil in Mrs. Hocknell's wheelbarrow. I frowned. Something flitted through my brain, but I couldn't hold the memory. Shaking it off with a shrug, I said, "Maybe she's allergic to one of her plants."

Mom nodded. "Yes, that's definitely possible. Anyway, we argued a bit about her taking care of herself, and after that, yes, she did have a brief cry about her cousin. I think it made her feel better, though."

"I'm glad," I said, and I meant it.

Mom hooked her arm though mine as we turned in to my parents' driveway. "I'll be checking in on her later—but speaking of things to make you feel better . . ."

We'd arrived to find Ben and my dad putting together two raised vegetable planters that Maeve and I had bought my mom for Christmas. They seemed to be engrossed in their work, and Ben was laughing at something my dad was saying. Even nicer, Ben's muscles were rippling under his shirt and he looked like he was happy—always an attractive combination.

"Amen to that," I said.

TWENTY-FOUR

It was my phone dinging with a text that made me look away from Ben—just before my father noticed, luckily. I may be an adult, but practically salivating over my boyfriend was not something my father likely wanted to see, or something I wanted him to see, thank you very much.

"Is it from Cisco?" Ben asked, jutting his chin in the direction of my phone.

I nodded. "He said the painting is ready for pickup. We can come by any time after ten a.m., except for between noon and one p.m."

Dad, who had been tightening a bolt on the planter, asked, "Did he say what was under the painting?"

"No, darn it," I replied.

Mom looked at Ben and me like we were nuts and flung up her hands. "Why are you two just standing there? It's already after nine and it takes almost half an hour to get to the museum district with our Houston traffic. Go, get dressed and see what he found!"

A little while later, we were at Ben's car, both of us having taken quick showers and dressed in jeans. I'd just thrown another blanket borrowed from my mother in the back seat for extra protection for Camilla's painting when I realized Ben was standing at the driver's-side door, looking down and frowning. He ran his finger along the edge of the window, his blue eyes irritated.

"What's wrong?" I asked as he finally opened the door and slid in.

"It looks as if someone tried to break into my car last night," he growled. He looked up at the motion-activated floodlights my father had installed near their front porch, where Ben had parked his Explorer. "I guess the lights came on and scared them away."

I put my hand on his arm just as he jabbed the button to start the car. "You mean it wasn't there before? The damage to your weather stripping?"

His head turned my way. "You saw it? When?"

"Yesterday, at the cookie place. You took a work call and I went to look at Camilla's painting. I noticed it then, but I guessed it had happened at some other point because you didn't mention it when we got in the car." I grimaced. "I'm sorry, Ben. I figured you already knew, and I guess I forgot all about it with the excitement of meeting Cisco and finally getting to know what's underneath the painting."

"You noticed it yesterday afternoon?" Ben asked. "Are you sure? And did you see anything suspicious at the time?"

I said I was sure and told him about the black Suburban and gray BMW trying to leave the lot at the same time. "I didn't see anyone standing outside your car or anything that indicated they'd been doing anything underhanded, though."

"Any chance you caught any license plates?"

I shook my head. Now I was feeling irritated on Ben's behalf. "You know, I kind of wondered if Camilla's ex, Gareth Fishwick, might have done it. He seemed angry enough at being walked out of Camilla's house like a criminal. And you and I spent, what, almost ten minutes getting the painting out of the house after that. He would have had time."

"I'm thinking not," Ben said, shaking his head as he reversed onto my parents' street. "I don't think Fishwick did it, I mean. I watched him drive away, and I stood there until I was sure he was gone."

"That doesn't mean he didn't come back," I said.

Ben tapped his driver's-side window with his knuckle. "Agreed, but why would he try and break in?" He made a gesture around the inside of his car. "I don't keep anything of value in here."

It was true. The only things visible were two half-drunk bottles of water in the cup holders from our drive into town yesterday and a roll of mints. Even in his glove compartment, which he'd popped open yesterday to store his Glock while we drove, there had only been the requisite car manuals, plus a pack of latex gloves for, as he put it, "the occasional crime scene."

"I thought Gareth might have done it for some sort of unspecified revenge," I said with a shrug. "Just because he was ticked off."

Ben seemed to consider this, then shook his head again. "I don't think so. He was angry, yes, but he also seemed glad to get away from the whole situation." He switched lanes as we merged onto Loop 610. "Plus, I ran a check on him, and he was clean other than some debt that's a hair's width away from being serious."

I laughed. "You know, you could have led with that part."

He flashed me a quick grin. "Hey, it's never a bad thing to talk out the ideas that are swimming around in your head, especially when they're negative. It can help you make sense of things faster."

I had to agree with that, but then remembered something else.

"Speaking of Gareth and checking on things, did you find out who sent him that text that was supposedly from Camilla?"

Ben's mouth thinned into a grim line. "Burner phone," he replied. "I checked in with Dupart while you and your mom were at Mrs. Hocknell's. It was sold at a Walmart in Quincy, Massachusetts, three weeks ago, and then an app was used so that the text looked like it came from Camilla's phone number." He glanced my way, anticipating my next thought. "And Dupart checked both Camilla's and Gareth's recent whereabouts using what's called 'historical pings' from each of their phones. It's location data taken from nearby towers and can give us a good idea as to where they've been lately. Neither Gareth nor Camilla has been anywhere near Massachusetts in the past month."

We'd just navigated an interchange when my phone beeped with a text.

"Is it from Helen?" Ben asked.

"No, unfortunately," I said. "I texted her again this morning to check in, but she hasn't answered back." My face must have looked as gloomy as I felt on the inside, because Ben replied in a voice that was both soothing and confident.

"Hey," Ben said. "Don't worry. I don't have any further updates on her from Dupart, but, like I told you, I didn't get the impression he thought her a viable suspect. And if she's upset with you about having to ID her, she's smart and she'll eventually understand."

"Yeah, I know," I said. "I just wish she'd call me, even if it's to chew me out, you know what I mean?"

"Maybe she's really busy and she can't call right now," Ben suggested. Giving me a wink, he added, "I know how frustrating that feels."

"Let's hope that's the case," I said, then explained that the message was actually from Camilla. "I texted her this morning, saying I was thinking of talking to Neil Gaynor. She thinks it's a good idea. She's been recalling that he showed a lot of interest in what she had to say about finding another painting under her piece of the triptych."

I typed a reply and my phone soon dinged again with another text. "I asked where he usually hangs out in the Howland library and she said he goes to the Duchess Reading Room nearly every day. It's reserved for PhD students only." I looked over at Ben. "What if we show up and just so happen to engage him in conversation?"

At first, I thought Ben might decide this came too near interfering or maybe suggest a different approach, but instead he nodded approvingly, glancing at me as he exited the freeway. "You're liking all this investigative stuff, aren't you?"

I thought about it. "You know, I am, actually. Though it's with mixed emotions. I wouldn't be doing this if someone hadn't been killed, and, I'm not going to lie, that part tears me up inside." At this, Ben reached out and took my hand. I squeezed it gratefully, adding, "That being said, being able to help right those wrongs in some way, shape, or form feels good, especially when it involves using my talents as a genealogist. I think the helping suits me."

"It *does* suit you," Ben said, casting an assessing look my way.

"But don't worry," I said with a toothy grin. "I've no desire to go into law enforcement. I'm happy to stay a genealogist who just swoops in with awesomely helpful information from time to time. Your and Detective Dupart's jobs are quite safe."

Ben let out a bark of laughter. "I'm going to be sure and video his reaction when I tell him you said that."

"Oooh, tell him right when he's taking a drink. Ten bucks says it makes him do a spit take."

"I think you'll win that bet," Ben said. "Anyway, your suggestion about showing up and engaging Neil Gaynor in conversation isn't a bad one. Ask Camilla if she knows what time he's likely to be at the library. If it coincides with what time we have before we need to head back to Austin, we can find Neil and play off each other and see what we can get out of him."

"Like good cop, bad cop?" I asked, frowning a little. I was hoping for something more subtle than that.

"Actually, I was thinking more like a Tommy and Tuppence Beresford act. Play the affable couple and pull him into conversation and then steer him in the direction we need. Sound good?"

I felt a thrill of excitement, both at the idea of actually teaming up with Ben to interview a suspect and at doing so in an improvisational style that was reminiscent of two of my favorite Agatha Christie characters. Oh, yes, it definitely sounded good.

"I'm in," I said, and got to work texting Camilla for more details on Neil Gaynor's schedule.

TWENTY-FIVE

I didn't have much time to think about ways in which Ben and I could engage Neil Gaynor in some breezy conversation that would naturally segue toward Camilla's painting because Ben was soon dropping me off at the side entrance to Morris Art Conservation. Abbie, Cisco's assistant, was waiting for us with a smile.

"I'll go park and meet you in a few minutes," Ben said, raising a friendly hand to Abbie, who said she would come back to let him in after escorting me inside.

"Cisco has some great stuff to show you," Abbie told me, pulling her key card out of her white lab coat and touching it to the scanner. "He's been jumping out of his skin for y'all to get here."

"Oh, now you have to give me a hint," I said, giving her a pleading look as we made our way through the security door and into the hallway that would take us to the workroom.

She laughed. "No way. Cisco would demote me if I did."

"Hey, Abbie!" called a voice from an open doorway we were passing. "Can you come help me for a mo'?"

"Sure, Fazil, just a sec," she called back. With another smile, she pointed me down the hallway. "You remember where to go, yes? Down this hallway and then hook a right. First door after that. If Cisco doesn't answer when you knock, he'll be back momentarily. He knows you're here, but he had to run upstairs for a minute."

I smiled. "No problem. Thanks, Abbie—and thanks for letting Ben in, too. He shouldn't be too long."

She nodded, the pink tips of her hair swinging forward. "I'll be back to get him in a jiffy."

Abbie disappeared into the doorway we'd just passed and I continued on down the hallway. Rounding the corner, I saw another woman in a lab coat was holding her key card up to the scanner at Cisco's workroom. Her graying fair hair was pulled into a sleek bun and one hand was holding a cart like we'd used yesterday to transport the triptych piece. The scanner beeped obligingly, and she turned the handle, pulling the door open.

Another beep sounded, but this was from the phone in my hand. It was a distinctive two-tone I'd set up to alert me to emails from my various genealogical societies. Glancing at the notification, I noted the email as being from the North American Genealogy Conference, with the subject line *Conference Panel Invitation*. A zing of excitement coursed through me as I flipped the little side switch to silence my phone. I'd never been asked to be on a panel before.

Grinning, I looked up as I was steps away from the workroom, already intending to help hold the door open for the employee, only to see her pushing the cart away again, toward a service elevator at the far end of the hall. She twisted her right wrist up to read a message on her smartwatch, shaking her head in an irritated way at the same time. Though she moved swiftly, the workroom door was closing at a more sedate pace. Seeing my chance, I dashed the last couple of steps and caught the door just before it shut.

"Cisco?" I called into the cavernous room, but it was quiet

except for some unidentified humming that sounded like the air-conditioning system.

I was all alone, it seemed, so I wandered over to a worktable where a painting lay under a drop cloth. Beside it was a folder labeled *Untitled Triptych Piece, 1866, Charles Braithwaite, artist*. I was about to open the folder when I heard the door beep again and Cisco walked in, stopping to hold it open for someone else as he called out, "Ah, Abbie found you, then."

I jumped guiltily, accidentally making the folder slide halfway under the drop cloth.

"Now, no peeking, Lucy," Cisco admonished me. "I at least get to do the big reveal."

"I'm backing away from the table," I said, holding my hands up in mock surrender and stepping back two paces. Following Cisco into the workroom was a woman with intelligent green eyes, high cheekbones, and brown curly hair streaked liberally with blond. She wore slim trousers, a pair of feminine penny loafers, and a dusky pink blouse with the effortlessness of a runway model, and she looked at me with interest until a noise made her turn around. It was Ben, and her mouth dropped open in surprise.

"Well, Ben Turner, as I live and breathe," she said, her voice infused with Southern charm.

Ben, whose eyes had gone straight to me, turned toward the woman. "Savannah? Er . . . hi. It's been a long time. How are you? And what are you doing here?"

Cisco shot me a look to see my reaction, but if he expected me to be jealous, he was in for a disappointment. I'd recognized Savannah Lundstrom the moment I saw her. Even better, while yesterday's attempt at leaving a message on the *Chronology* reporter's voice mail had been truncated, I'd been considering trying again as I really needed to talk to her regarding her article. Now—hot damn—I could talk to her in person.

I moved to stand beside Cisco as Savannah Lundstrom held out her arms to Ben, saying, "I'm here to interview Mr. Ramos. Now, come here, you, and give me a hug."

She was only a couple of inches shorter than Ben's five-eleven and didn't have to stand on tiptoes as she wrapped her arms around his neck and pulled him into an affectionate embrace. When she released him and turned my way again, Cisco was already hastening them into the room, explaining, "I'm being interviewed about my conservation work by Ms. Lundstrom for *Chronology* magazine. She showed up a bit early to take a peek at the museum upstairs and asked to see some of the workrooms. I thought I'd give her the ten-cent tour before y'all showed up, but I misjudged my timing. Looks like it all worked out, though." He looked back and forth between Ben and Savannah. "You two know each other?"

Savannah's eyes sparkled. "Yes, Ben and I took some classes together one summer at UT." She turned to Ben, a reporter-like gleam in her eye. "I understand you're with the FBI now. Is that true?"

Ben's smile was all friendly politeness. "It is. White-collar division, though. I mostly handle fraud cases, so fairly uninteresting."

Before she could reply—or I could snort at hearing pretty much the same brush-off he'd used with me last year, which had been true at the time but had since become a lie—Ben turned, gesturing to me.

"Savannah, this is my girlfriend, Lucy Lancaster," he said. "Lucy, this is Savannah Lundstrom, my former classmate, and currently a reporter for *Chronology*."

Savannah's voice was warm as she walked to me, holding her out her hand. "It's really lovely to meet you, Lucy."

"It's a pleasure to meet you, too, Savannah," I said, smiling. "I'm a longtime subscriber to *Chronology*—it's one of my favorite magazines. I've read some of your work recently, and Ben recognized your name in the byline. You're an excellent writer."

"Oh, thank you," Savannah replied with a big smile. "Which piece did you read?"

"It was actually the one on Charles Braithwaite," I said. "I found it very thought-provoking, and I've been hoping to get in touch with you to see if I could talk to you more about it." When Savannah raised her eyebrows in question, I explained, "I'm a genealogist, and I was just curious as to what made you take the angle you did with the story."

Though her smile was holding, I sensed a reserve coming over her at the idea that I might be criticizing her article.

"Well, after extensive research, it was simply how the story presented itself," Savannah began as we moved closer to the table where Camilla's piece of the triptych lay, still covered. "If you're a longtime reader of *Chronology*, then you know it's our job to unmask the parts of history that have presented a facade to our nation and our world for so long. Sometimes it makes for pieces that are thought-provoking in a good way, and sometimes in a way that ruffles a few feathers. Yet when the true history is uncovered, it always ends up being better for us all going forward, don't you agree?"

"Of course," I said, taking the tactful approach. While I agreed with much of the sentiment, if Savannah and I had been alone, I might have challenged her on the part where she used the "unmasking of history" to belittle a family that, while no doubt imperfect, had remained an upstanding part of the Houston community for decades. However, while Ben's eyes were registering admiration for my gumption, I'd caught Cisco looking slightly uncomfortable out of the corner of my eye. Now was not the time to continue this conversation.

Savannah seemed to sense it as well and changed the subject.

"You know, I've actually been wanting my genealogy done," she told me. "Do you happen to have a card, Lucy?"

"Of course," I said, reaching into the crossbody purse for my green card case. "I'd love to work on your family tree. Which side are you considering focusing on first?"

"Hmm?" Savannah said, her attention already distracted by the covered-up painting and the folder that was peeking out. "Oh, my mother's side, I think." She plucked the card from my fingers and gave it a quick read. "My dad's side is mostly Scandinavian and the family's kept pretty good records, but my mom's family didn't, so I don't have as much information on that side." She'd seen the folder, including the words *Charles Braithwaite, artist,* on its label. She gestured toward the covered painting, looking a little stunned.

"This was painted by Charles Braithwaite? I mean, I know from my piece on him that he did some artwork, including that marvelous drawing of the Texas Emancipation Day announcement, but I didn't know he did any actual paintings. Is this why you wanted to discuss my article?" She looked at me, her fingers already taking hold of the covering. "May I see it?"

Cisco was there in a flash, his hand preventing any further lifting of the drop cloth. His tone became polite, but professional. "I'm so sorry, Ms. Lundstrom. It's for Lucy's and Ben's eyes only at the moment, as they are the agents for the owner. If, after I give them my report, they wish to contact the owner and obtain permission to tell you about it and let you see the results, that's their prerogative." He smiled almost apologetically, and held out an arm to gesture her back toward the workroom door. "If you wouldn't mind waiting upstairs until I'm finished here and they take possession of the painting? I'll be, oh, thirty or so minutes, I think. Then I'll be ready for any questions you might want to throw at me about conservation work."

For a second, I thought Savannah was going to argue, but she merely gave him a beatific smile, gracing Ben and me with it as well, and said, "Of course. I shouldn't have been so presumptuous—and it was my fault for showing up early in the first place. Where would be the best place for me to wait for you in the meantime?"

"Oh, you should enjoy more of the museum, of course," Cisco replied genially. "Let me get my assistant, Abbie, to take you up through the staff doorway." He pulled out his phone, which was ringing.

"Talk of the devil. Hey, Abbie . . ." As she spoke, he began rubbing his brow wearily. "She can't find it anywhere? And she's sure she had it on her when she arrived?" He listened to Abbie's response, then sighed. "All right. Have security revoke the access for that card and issue her a new one—and tell her no one's going to chew her out for it. It's happened to all of us." He let out a wry chuckle. "Including me, a couple of weeks ago. She just needs to be more careful. Nope, don't worry about what I was going to ask. I'll do it. Thanks, Abbie."

"Someone lose their key card?" Ben asked, moving to my side, subtly blocking Savannah's access to the painting at the same time.

Cisco gave a rueful grin, nodding. "New intern. Hardworking, but hasn't quite got the hang of things yet. She will, though." He looked expectantly at Savannah, who smiled, inclining her head in acquiescence.

"And this is my moment to exit stage left—until our interview, at least," she said.

I piped up in an attempt to subtly remind Savannah that I would be calling her. "If you like, I'm happy to contact the painting's owner to see if we can share the information we find with you when you and I talk."

Savannah's reporter's intuition sharpened her gaze, and one

eyebrow lifted. "Do you think it might change the conclusions I drew in the story I wrote on Charles Braithwaite's life in some way?"

Though I felt a subtle tension emanating from Ben at the question, I was about to answer that it could. Yet it was Cisco, out of Savannah's eyeshot, who stopped me with an emphatic shake of his head.

"Honestly, I have no clue," I replied, turning my palms over for emphasis. "I'm only acting on the owner's behalf."

Savannah persisted. "Is this owner a Braithwaite?"

I raised my upturned palms and shoulders at the same time, but didn't answer. Though since her eyes warmed with success, I figured my nonanswer was as good as a yes in her book.

Her smile was as innocent as mine. "Will you at least give me a hint as to why the panel is here? Is it to be evaluated for sale?" She whirled to look at Ben, excitement coloring her voice as she asked, "Wait. Is the FBI involved? Is this a painting that somebody stole?"

At this, Ben laughed, tucking his thumbs in the belt loops of his jeans. "You haven't changed a bit, Lundstrom." He shook his head in amusement. "I commend your persistence as a journalist, but no, the FBI is not involved in any way, shape, or form. You're welcome to call and check up on that, if you like."

The truth was ringing through his words, and I could tell Savannah heard it, too.

"All right, all right," she said with a laugh. "I give." Smiling at Ben, she tilted her head to the side, saying, "It was really good to see you again, Ben Turner. You look happy, and I'm glad."

Ben smiled back at her. "It was good seeing you, too, Savannah."

She turned to me. "You're a lucky woman, Lucy. I hope to work with you on my genealogy in the future and I'm happy to talk to you about my article whenever you like." Then she added in a humorously dramatic stage-whisper, "And maybe you'll tell me about the Braithwaite painting at the same time."

I grinned, but she followed Cisco out the lab door without waiting for a reply.

TWENTY-SIX

H oly frijoles," I said in a half whisper.
  "You said it," Ben agreed.

We were both turned around in our seats, looking at the inconspicuous dark blanket spread across the laid-down back seat of Ben's Explorer. Underneath it was Camilla's painting, lying there silently as if it hadn't just given up some rather mindblowing secrets.

"It's like finding a dusty black rock, washing it off, and realizing you're holding a seriously big diamond," I said.

"And knowing that it's one of three," Ben said. "It's just incredible."

"The whole scene," I breathed, one hand going to my heart. "Oh my stars, it's so detailed, so *beautiful,* and so heartbreaking all at the same time. The look of fear and desperation on some of the soldiers' faces—from both sides of the battle—as they did their best to simply survive the chaos of the fighting around them. It was *palpable.*"

"I think Charles Braithwaite was trying to show the absolute pointlessness of the war," Ben said. "He did one hell of a good job, too."

I nodded, looking into Ben's blue eyes with the green around the pupils, remembering another set of blue eyes, those of the terrified soldier we'd been able to see in the painting yesterday in the spot Camilla had uncovered. When I'd finally seen all of that soldier, witnessed his the tautness in his neck, the strain of his muscles, and almost felt the lurch of his body as another soldier bore down on him, I was so moved that tears had briefly welled in my own eyes. Thankfully, Ben's blue eyes were smiling as he added, "And the piece has Braithwaite's signature and the date he painted it, too."

Cisco had been like a kid in a candy store when he'd shown us Charles Braithwaite's signature—the same bold, forward-slanting "C. Braithwaite" with the long horizontal stroke over the second "t" that I'd seen when Helen had found the example in her art database. Just underneath the distinctive "t," almost as if it were directing the eye, was the year 1866. Charles had painted his triptych likely not long after returning home, when the war and its horrors were still very fresh in his mind.

"I was floored to see that—the whole thing is just amazing." I put my hand on Ben's arm. "Oh, I'm *so* hoping I can find proof that Charles didn't desert his regiment. You heard what Cisco said—an appraiser has to confirm it, but if Charles Braithwaite really remained a soldier and painted the triptych from his memories of battle, that could make it significantly more valuable."

"And maybe even more so because Robert E. Lee is in the painting," Ben added, the excitement in his voice increasing. "I'm no art expert, of course, but I think that was one of the best likenesses of Lee I've ever seen."

"Charles had such a talent for painting faces and expressions," I said. "And he was a dab hand at horses, too. Lee's horse was magnificently done."

We turned to face forward, staring out to the street, in awe of all we'd just learned.

"What I really can't believe," Ben said, "is that the artwork on top was simply another piece of canvas that wasn't prepped well and was laid over the first painting. It was literally just sitting on top. To know there's likely to be little or no damage to the painting underneath—except for where it was gouged by that brass elephant—it's simply unreal."

I smiled. "I'm so glad Camilla has agreed to let Helen do the restoration—if Helen still wants to, of course. It would be a huge boost for her business. And thank goodness Dupart cleared her of any wrongdoing so she could be offered the job." I smiled at Ben. "Thank you for texting Dupart and asking, by the way." Then I frowned. "Though I wish he'd given you more details in his reply."

Ben had received the text as Cisco was escorting Savannah to the staff stairwell that would take her upstairs to wait in the museum. Showing me the text chain, I saw that Ben had messaged Dupart about Helen earlier in the morning, when Mom and I were at Mrs. Hocknell's house. Dupart had replied with only one word, but it was a good one: *Cleared.*

Then, when Ben and I realized the importance of what Cisco was telling us about the painting, we'd called Camilla on Face-Time so she could hear all the details herself. Though she still looked like Uncle Charlie's death was weighing heavily on her, Camilla had been breathless with excitement. Afterward, when I'd suggested Helen do the restoration and Cisco had assured Camilla that Helen would do a bang-up job, Camilla had agreed that supporting a small, woman-owned business would make her happy.

"Ben," I said, turning to him, worry now entering my voice, "what if we can't find the other two pieces? One's stolen, and the other is who knows where. What if they're gone forever?"

He held out his hand and I took it, relaxing somewhat as he rubbed the back of my hand with his thumb. "I've already called

Dupart, when I went to get the car. He'll make finding Charlie Braithwaite's piece of the triptych a high priority. He'll also alert the FBI and put it on the NSAF—the National Stolen Art File."

"Good," I said forcefully. Using my finger, I made air circles at his expression, which had taken on a look of forced seriousness. "What's with this look, though?"

Ben worked his jaw, but a twinkle was coming into his eyes. "As far as finding the third piece, Dupart requested that I ask you to research the Braithwaite family to locate who might have inherited it."

My own jaw dropped as if on a hinge. "You're joking. Dupart's actually asking me to get involved?"

Ben tilted his head to one side. "Well-l-l-l, I don't know if 'involved' is the right—"

I put my finger over his lips. "Shhh . . . I want to savor this moment." Closing my eyes in satisfaction, a grin spread across my face. I heard the rumble of laughter in his chest, and felt his breath tickle my finger. Then my eyes flew open, another thought having occurred to me. "So what are we going to do with the painting now?"

"How do you mean?"

"Well, we're going to go interview Neil Gaynor, remember? You even had me ask Camilla if she knew his schedule, and she said he's usually at the library from about twelve thirty to two thirty." Jerking my thumb over my shoulder toward our concealed treasure, I said, "We're toting around what's likely an extremely valuable piece of art. One of the pieces has been stolen, resulting in a murder, and yesterday someone tried to break into your car and steal this piece. I don't think we can leave it in the car."

"You're right," he said with a grimace. "One of us needs to stay with it while Gaynor is being interviewed."

"It might need to be you who goes in," I told him. "Roxie and Patrice aren't my favorite people, as you know, but both of them are extremely intelligent, and they notice everything. If I manage to slip by them when I'm walking in, they'll no doubt find me talking to Neil Gaynor, and they'll know something is up."

Ben fished in his pocket, pulling out the key to his Explorer. "Happy to do it, then. Show me the photo you found of him again?"

I opened my phone and found Neil's Instagram account, having checked with Camilla via text to make sure I had the right guy. He was short and wiry in his photos, with dark brown hair, eyes that could have been hazel or brown, and a long nose. I'd read several of his posts, most of which were reviews of the latest craft beer he'd found. However, scattered throughout his photos of ales, lagers, and hefeweizens, were photos with various friends, the occasional anecdote about his PhD studies—usually accompanied by a photo taken at the Howland library—and a handful of humorous posts about searching for the best pizza in Houston with his younger sister, Dina. The most recent one, posted ten days earlier, showed Dina, who was a blonde but resembled her brother in stature and nose, enthusiastically gesturing toward a pizza topped with ground beef, olives, jalapeños, and pineapple. In the caption, Neil had both teased his sister about her pizza-topping choices and praised her for her hard work getting into law school, writing that he and his sister were the first two people in his immediate family to even go to college in the first place.

In general, Neil Gaynor seemed, well, like a decent guy. But I'd had to remind myself that people often showed only their best side on social media. Neil could have posted this tidbit about his family history in an attempt to add credence or sympathy—or both—to the lawsuit alleging that his family had experienced decades of hard times as a result of Charles Braithwaite's so-called greed back in 1925. Heck, Neil could have possibly been the person to try to steal the magnificent painting lying quietly behind me, too. I had to remember anything was possible.

"Luce?" Ben was still holding out the key to his car, but I didn't take it. I shifted in my seat to look at him straight on.

"I need to change my mind," I said. "Um, the last thing I want to do is put either of us in any kind of danger, but if someone should try to break into the car again or whatever, you *are* a trained law-enforcement officer and I'm just your basic, everyday citizen." I splayed my hand and made air circles over my frame, then did the same toward Ben's. "You are quite a bit bigger than I am, too."

"You're right, I should have thought of that. Of course I should be the one to stay with the painting." He gave me a sidelong look. "But are you okay going into the proverbial lion's den of former coworkers? We could take the painting to your parents' house and then I could come back to the library and try to find Gaynor, if you don't want to mess with having to talk with him, or see Roxie and Patrice."

I smiled at him. "Thanks, but Howland University is not far from here, and my parents are all the way across town—and you saw what Houston traffic is like. Plus, I'm not concerned about talking to Neil Gaynor if I'm in the safety of the library. And I'm certainly not afraid of Roxie and Patrice—not that they ever did anything that was intended to make me fear them. They just gave into their own petty jealousies, which made for a very unhappy workplace environment for me." I straightened my shoulders. "I'm willing to let bygones be bygones, though. Maybe they'll turn out to be like Camilla—never going to be my best bud, but better than I remembered."

I expected Ben to laugh, so I was surprised when he gave me another appreciative look. "If you handle them the way you handled Savannah Lundstrom, then I think you'll be all right. Same goes for Gaynor."

I felt like he'd just given me a gold star to put on my shirt. "I do think I need to learn some interview techniques, though," I said.

"The fact that you're not an expert is probably better, in your case. You don't come off as slick, and it makes people trust you more," Ben said.

"Not in Savannah's case," I returned with a laugh. "But then again, I was questioning her work, even if nicely." Determined not to worry either about Savannah or the fact that I was about to face Roxie and Patrice again, I changed the subject, adding briskly, "All right, then, Agent Turner. Our next mission is to get me some food so I don't eat my former coworkers alive. There's a really good Greek place not far from here. What do you say?"

Instead, he pulled me into a long kiss that was only interrupted when we noticed a car had drawn up beside us. Feeling eyes on us, we looked over to see an elderly lady in the passenger seat sending us a big wink. Chuckling, Ben started the car, and we were soon on our way to lunch, then my former workplace.

An hour later, I was walking along a pretty, tree-lined walkway, admiring the classical buildings of Howland University just like I always used to. The university's buildings and layout had been modeled after Yale University in Connecticut, and the campus continued to be one of the prettiest areas in Houston. As such, I saw more than one person taking selfies in front of the ivy-covered buildings and another couple of people taking photographs of the equally beautiful university library.

Officially named the Barbara A. Kazen Library, with its grand columns and Beaux Arts architectural style, it was often likened to a much smaller version of the New York Public Library when viewed from the Fifth Avenue entrance. Built in 1913, when Howland University opened to its first batch of students, there were even two statues flanking the stone steps—one a lion and the other a lioness, both wearing wreaths around their necks. The lion's wreath was of elm leaves, representing inner strength, and the lioness's was of birch, signifying new beginnings. Supposedly, the two statues didn't have names, but everyone called them Nick and Nora, as they were both put on their plinths on May 25, 1934, the day the Myrna Loy–William Powell hit comedy *The Thin Man* came out, bringing to life Nick and Nora Charles from the Dashiell Hammett novel of the same name.

I stopped at the base of the stone steps, taking in a deep breath, just as a tousle-headed student trotted down them, after stopping to put a penny at the base of Nora's left front paw. He saw me watching him and gave an embarrassed smile before hurrying on.

I smiled, too. There were traditions surrounding the two statues. If someone left a penny at Nick's feet, it was for good luck for one or more of Howland's sports teams to win their upcoming match. Nora was the one who got all the pennies, though. Leaving one by her right front foot was for good luck on exams. A penny next to her tail was for inspiration, and one at either of her back feet was for safe travels on a journey. But as for leaving a penny at Nora's left front paw? That was to wish for good fortune in matters of the heart.

Digging into the side pocket of my crossbody purse, I came up with the penny Ben had given me yesterday afternoon. Placing it alongside the others at Nora's left front paw, I smiled, inhaled another deep breath, and marched up the steps and through the ornately carved double doors into the library.

As soon as I did, a voice hissed from the direction of the welcome desk to my left. "Lucy? What the hell are you doing here?"

TWENTY-SEVEN

I froze in mid-step after crossing the short, empty foyer onto the carpet of the library. No matter what I'd told Ben earlier, I turned with a slight feeling of doom, only to get another surprise at who I saw.

"Helen?"

Before I could say anything else, Helen got up from the desk and jerked her head for me to follow her back outside, slinging a large tote over her shoulder as she did so. I hesitated for a moment, glancing around at the area we'd always called the bull-pen, where the reference desk stood. A few students were milling around, but I couldn't see any of the library staff, or anyone resembling Neil Gaynor. Turning, I hurried to follow Helen as she sailed down the steps, past a couple of students walking by the library's entrance, and aimed toward an empty stone bench underneath a sprawling oak tree. Reaching it, she whirled around. I braced for a dressing-down, but instead, she pulled me into a hug.

"Please forgive me for not calling you earlier. I was upset at the police showing up and questioning me," she said in my ear as she gave me an extra squeeze, "but only for a little while." Pulling back, she tilted her head back and forth, and her brown eyes had humor in them. "And most of it was because Detective Dupart showed up when I was talking to a very important new client about their artwork. It was *super* awkward, let me tell you. And then having to verify my whereabouts and all that stuff wasn't a ton of fun, either." She cast me a mock glare. "And everything was on the up-and-up, of course."

"I never doubted it," I said. "Oh, Helen, I'm so sorry."

"Don't be, Luce. I would have done the same thing in your position. It was just weird for a while, that's all." Extracting her phone, she brought up a half-started text to me. "I was replying to you when you walked in, actually. Now *that's* what I call serendipity." Then she grabbed my arm in excited anticipation. "But never mind all that. What did Cisco say about the painting?"

"Oh my gosh," I breathed. "I've got so much to tell you." Pulling out my own phone, I showed her photos I'd taken of Charles Braithwaite's long-hidden painting, and related our meeting with Cisco as she went through the photos with fascination. When I got to the part where Camilla had said she wanted to hire Helen to do the restoration, she blinked at me for a moment, then threw her arms around my neck again in delight.

Pulling back, she said, "Wait, did you come here to the Howland library to tell me this?"

I gave her a sideways look. "How would I have known you were here?"

"Detective Dupart didn't tell you?"

"Are you kidding? He doesn't tell me squat," I said in exasperation. "He'll give Ben the occasional bit of information—like the fact that you were cleared in the investigation—but only out of professional courtesy." Pulling her down to sit on the bench, I said, "Now, spill, please. And don't forget to explain the part about why you were at Charlie Braithwaite's house in the first place."

Helen turned in her seat to face me, her dark hair swinging forward in front of her shoulders. "I'm here to pick up some rare maps of Texas that a Howland University student brought here a couple of days ago, thinking the library would like them. They're from Spanish colonial times, and one is particularly interesting. Anyway, one of the librarians, Patrice Alvarez—did you work with her?—regardless, she convinced the kid to gift them to the Harry Alden museum instead, but they need some conservation work first. I was hired to do the job and offered to drive down here and pick them up. I called Detective Dupart to make sure I was free to do so, and that's when he told me I was cleared."

"That's really interesting about the maps," I said, "but why were you sitting at the reception desk?"

Helen rolled her eyes. "Even though I confirmed with Patrice that I would be here by eleven forty-five and she said she goes to lunch at noon, apparently she decided that was not the right journey for her today and went to lunch early." Glancing at her watch, she added, "Another staffer, whose name was Trent, if I remember correctly, told me Patrice would be back by twelve thirty, so I said I'd wait and welcome people to the library. He looked at me like I was bonkers—clearly he doesn't get my sense of humor—but told me to knock myself out."

I grinned, but my impatience was getting the better of me. "But Helen, I have to know—what happened the night Charlie Braithwaite died?"

My words seemed to remind her that something much worse had occurred than her being interrupted by the police at work or being inconvenienced by one of my former coworkers. "I'm so sorry about Charlie. I didn't know him, but it's still such a terrible thing." When I agreed that it was, she said, "Remember me telling you I would call him to make an appointment to see the triptych piece?"

I nodded.

"Well, I did, and left him a message. He called me back a while later, apparently after being taken to the doctor by Camilla. As it turned out, Charlie felt so much better after seeing his doctor that he asked if I wanted to stop by to chat while Camilla was out running some errands and picking up food." Helen shrugged. "It worked perfectly with my schedule, so I drove over to his house at about ten till seven. I expected Charlie to open the door. Instead it was a woman who introduced herself as his next-door neighbor. Excellent posture. Looks to be in her late seventies or so, but she's very well preserved." Helen tapped her chin with her finger. "I would bet there's a picture of her somewhere that's aging, because she's clearly not, except for the gray hair."

Though I was interested to hear Elaine Trudeau had indeed been in Charlie's house the night of his murder, the thought of Elaine having a Dorian Gray–like painting somewhere almost made me laugh. Nevertheless, I wanted Helen to get on with it, so I only nodded.

"Anyway, she let me inside for about five seconds put together. Basically just long enough to tell me I should be ashamed of myself for forcing my way onto Charlie's schedule when he was so frail and ill. When I told her he had *invited* me, she said that he always updates his calendar and she'd just been dusting in his office and my name wasn't on there. I tried to protest, but she told me I had two choices. I could leave right there and then, or I could try to get past her and see where that got me."

I opened my mouth in shock. "She threatened to fight you?"

Helen shrugged, her eyes fiery with indignation. "I'm not saying we were destined for a cage match or anything, but there was a framed photo in her hand that had four very sharp corners, and she was holding it in a defensive position. She may have been thinking she could bean me on the side of the head with one of those corners and it would take me down. Regardless, I decided it was best to just leave."

"Well, you certainly told her how you felt with that look," I said with an amused grin. "If looks could be an equally sharp-cornered picture frame to throw at her, yours did the job."

Helen snorted. "Until I turned around and tripped on one of those bags of soil lying on the walkway and nearly ate dirt—literally. One of the bags was opened and I landed inches from it."

Now I laughed. "We didn't see that part. Dupart stopped the playback at your dirty look and missed the eating-dirt bit."

"Yeah," Helen muttered. "'Soils from Heaven,' my left foot. Should have been 'Soils from Hell.'"

Even as I snickered, another piece of knowledge was playing hide-and-seek in my brain, like it had when Mom and I had been talking about Mrs. Hocknell having been gardening. What was the connection? I recalled Grandpa's and Ben's advice to try not to think about it and let my subconscious work it out, but it turned out I didn't need to. Images were already flashing in my brain.

Uncle Charlie, soil, spots on his arms, weakness. Mrs. Hocknell—Charlie's cousin—with the same issues, only on a lesser scale. Both had been gardening.

The image of the brown paper bag with the name Soils from Heaven in its swirly font swam before me. I hadn't seen Mrs. Hocknell's bags close up, but I recalled that they'd looked like the same type of industrial brown paper as the bags at Charlie's. I gripped my phone. I needed to check with Mom.

"Helen," I said. "Can you hang on a minute?"

"Sure thing," she said, crossing her legs and taking out her phone. "I'm just waiting for Patrice to decide to come back to work. Might as well do it here as in the library." She looked up at the gorgeous blue sky. "Houston hasn't let loose the dogs of heat and humidity yet, so it's quite pleasant out here."

Being the weirdo I was, I thought the current sixty-five degrees was cold, but I stood up and walked around the other side of the immense oak tree, typing "Soils from Heaven" and "Houston" in the search bar of my phone. A simple but well-designed website came up. The site explained how their land's long-fallow ground had been found to contain optimal organic potting soil, and that packing and distributing the soil gave young men and women a great job that allowed them to work outside and learn about gardening. Packaging was kept as simple as possible to keep plastic waste to a minimum. And the land was located in a nearly uninhabited part of a tiny, nearly deserted town just outside Houston by the name of Potter's Hill, Texas.

My mind was really clanging with another memory now. Another internet search led me to just the information I needed. I called up the favorites on my phone and tapped the one for my mother's cell phone.

"How's it going, hon?" Mom asked upon answering.

"Great," I said. "Ben and I have lots of fun things to tell y'all, but that's not what I'm calling about." Looking around to make sure no one could hear me, I said, "Mom . . . about Mrs. Hocknell and her weakness, rash, and spots on her arms. Her cousin Charlie had similar issues."

"Did he?" Mom asked, concerned. "You didn't mention it."

"I sort of forgot about that aspect in the moment," I explained. "But the point is, do you remember seeing the brand of potting soil Mrs. Hocknell had at her house? There were bags of it in the wheelbarrow at the corner of her porch."

Mom's voice was musing as she said, "No, I don't recall seeing the name, but I know they weren't the same brand your dad and I bought from the garden center because the packaging was different." Then excitement came into her tone. "Want me to sneak over there and see?"

"I'm not sure you have to 'sneak,' necessarily, but if you could go over there and take a photo of the bags, that would be great. If they happen to say 'Soils from Heaven,' then ask Mrs. Hocknell if you can take one—and tell her not to touch any of the soil or any of her plants until she hears from us."

"Ten-four," Mom said smartly, making me grin.

"And take some gloves with you, okay? Be sure and use them when handling the bag or the soil."

Now Mom sounded concerned. "Do you think there's something wrong with the soil?"

"Yes," I said. "I think the company got at least some of the soil from an old, abandoned cemetery on the outskirts of Houston. A cemetery that's virtually unknown now and is privately owned, but it's where a number of Civil War soldiers from poor families or without families were buried after the war. It's possible the company doesn't even know they're getting soil from an old cemetery, especially if they're not digging deep enough to unearth bones."

I could practically see my mother's baffled expression in my head. "Why would the soil from this cemetery be an issue—other than the fact that they are digging up graves, of course?"

"Because when Civil War soldiers died on the battlefields, their organs were removed from their bodies," I explained. "Then, before being sent back home to their families via train, the body cavities were stuffed with sweet-smelling herbs and arsenic."

"Arsenic?" Mom said. "Really?"

"Really," I confirmed. "The arsenic acted as a preservative, while the herbs helped fend off the smell. And as the bodies decayed over the intervening years, the arsenic leached out into the soil. It naturally occurs in soil, of course, usually to a low degree that doesn't cause issues to the casual gardener. However, this company is unwittingly selling potting soil that has it in a higher concentration—and Mrs. Hocknell spends a lot of time in her garden. Mom, I think Mrs. Hocknell might have low-level arsenic poisoning."

TWENTY-EIGHT

❧

I felt a sense of relief when Mom assured me that, after confirming the name of the potting soil Mrs. Hocknell had purchased, she would make sure her friend saw a doctor immediately. Hanging up, I turned and walked back to where Helen was still sitting on the bench.

"So, I know why I'm here, but why are you?" she asked, looking up at me. "If not to tell me the fabulous news that I'll get to restore a very cool piece of art, that is."

I explained my thinking that it might be worth interviewing my former coworkers and the PhD candidate who was suing Camilla's family. I grinned. "And Ben didn't think I'd be interfering too much, so here I am."

Helen rose and we strolled back toward the steps of the library together, my friend listening intently to my tale of working with Roxie, Patrice, and Camilla, though I watered down my experiences significantly. I didn't want anyone's pity, even from a friend who was definitely on my side. But she'd picked up on my pained expression as we aimed for the library doors and I had to give her the gist.

Specifically, she said, "Luce, you look like you're about to face a firing squad, not just talk to a couple of people you used to work with. What gives?"

Now, after hearing my reasons, she said, "How about I do my best to keep Patrice engaged while you go hunt down Neil Gaynor? That way, you'll only have to deal with Roxie at most."

"You'd do that for me?" I said. "I mean, I plan to talk to both Roxie and Patrice, but I think it would be best to find Neil first. I don't want to give him time to find out I'm asking questions and hightail it out of the library."

"Of course," Helen said. Then she added with a wicked grin, "It would be my pleasure to waste some of Patrice's time after she left for lunch when she knew I was going to be here. What does she look like, so I can spot her without having to go through that Trent guy again?"

I whispered, "I don't have to describe her. There she is." I nodded my head to the walkway in front of us. A good twenty feet away, Patrice was walking and typing on her phone at the same time. She wore a black pencil skirt and cranberry-hued sweater that flattered the warm tones of her skin, and her thick dark hair was pulled up into a high ponytail. She seemed oblivious to everything but what was on her phone's screen.

"I wish I could text and walk that well in heels," Helen said as we watched Patrice expertly ascend the stairs and disappear through the main doors, all without looking up once.

"Tell me about it," I agreed. "I'd be stumbling into people and tripping over everything in sight if I tried."

"No kidding. So, what about the other librarian you worked with? What does she look like?" Helen asked.

"Roxie? She's just a bit taller than me, fairly curvy, with an upturned nose," I said as we walked the last few yards to the library at a leisurely pace. "I can't tell you what color her hair will be since she's always changing it." I explained that Roxie's longtime girlfriend, Layla, was a hairstylist. "Layla likes to experiment with bolder looks, too," I said. "In the six months before I quit, Roxie's hair was a chocolate brown with chunky purple highlights. Before that, it was a dark red with blond streaks around her face. And when I first started working here, her hair was ombré—you know, darker on top and gradually lightening so the last few inches are a couple of shades lighter—only her girlfriend gave her two shades of gray."

"Was that attractive or hideous?" Helen asked.

"Believe it or not, that one looked really nice. You might not think so, but it did."

"All right, then," Helen said, lifting her chin as she took hold of the brass bar that served as a door pull. "Give me one minute to engage Patrice before you come in."

"Ten-four," I said with a grin.

I spent my sixty seconds checking to see if Neil Gaynor had a Twitter account. I found him easily but didn't read through his tweets. When I finally walked into the library, Patrice was near the reference desk, talking to Helen, who had indeed positioned herself so that Patrice's back was to me. Her ponytail bobbed in acknowledgment of something Helen had said, and she gestured toward a nearby hallway, where the staff offices were. I knew they would go to Camilla's office first, however, as it also housed the vault where anything important was secured.

A few feet away was a wide set of stairs leading up to the second floor, and I locked onto Roxie walking downstairs. She was dressed in a black wrap dress, and her hair was now cinnamon brown with subtle blond highlights, and cut to just below her shoulders. I had to admit, it flattered her coloring, though the effect was lessened by the bossy, supercilious look on her face.

She was holding a couple of books and talking to a harried-looking student who was following in her wake. From having witnessed this scenario many times, I could tell Roxie was lecturing him, likely about his research techniques. Or, perhaps, simply for asking what she considered to be a silly question. Both gave Roxie that distinctly smug glow.

As they were nearing the bottom step, Roxie looked my way. Luckily, at the same time, two tall students passed between us, conveniently shielding me from my former coworker's view.

Ducking my head, I made a fast ninety-degree turn, passing a set of kiosks holding pamphlets ranging from campus maps to tips on stress relief before pushing open another set of doors. I entered the reading room, and reveled in the weighty yet calming hush you found only in a room where the loudest sound was the occasional turn of a page, creak of a book spine, or shuffling as a student sat down, stood up, or arranged their belongings on one of the twenty long wooden tables. I felt myself relax and, after passing the fifth table, made a left to another door and up another set of stairs to the second floor. Bypassing several seating areas occupied with students, I made my way purposefully toward the southwest corner, where another, much smaller, reading room was situated. This was where Camilla told me Neil Gaynor would likely be working.

Just before the door was a sign on a brass stand reading *The Duchess Reading Room is reserved for PhD candidates only.* Usually called simply the Duchess Room, the funds to create it had come from the mother of the library's namesake, who, though not actual royalty herself, was known as "Duchess" by her family. The room—with eight smaller tables, ornate crown molding, dark wood shelves, huge picture windows, and walls painted a classic library green—was my favorite room in the library, and apparently Neil Gaynor's usual haunt.

At the door, I looked through the glass panes of the reading room. It was empty.

"Rats," I murmured. I'd been hoping Neil would already be there so I wouldn't have to spend more time tracking him down.

I texted Ben to tell him my plan had fallen through. Shortly, his reply came in, reminding me that it was worth a try, and that Dupart would soon be questioning Neil anyway.

I texted back that I'd wait ten more minutes, then I'd go downstairs to tackle Roxie and Patrice. *Metaphorically speaking, of course,* I joked.

Ben's reply was a funny tackling-themed gif featuring characters from *The Office*. Then he wished me luck and asked if he could pick me up in an hour, adding cryptically that there was something he wanted to check on.

By this time, I'd already leaned up against a shelf of reference books and opened Neil Gaynor's Twitter feed. He hadn't posted for weeks, but I clicked on "Likes" and found he was still very active on the platform, just mainly in liking others' tweets. Many were about beer, which was unsurprising. A few were posts about poverty or growing up in poverty. He'd also liked posts on everything from movies to politics to one feed featuring nothing but cute puppies. I kept scrolling, and then my eyebrows rose. A week earlier, Neil had liked two tweets from a series posted by an art museum in England. Both contained links to articles about art and recognizing potential value in a painting.

"Huh," I murmured. "Maybe he's not such a decent guy after all."

Checking the time to find it had been ten minutes already, I walked toward the glass doors of the stairwell, looked through them, then immediately whipped around and rushed back behind another row of bookshelves. Moments later, the wiry form of Neil Gaynor came through the doors and strode past me, a black messenger bag slung around his shoulders, aiming for the Duchess Room. Much like Patrice earlier, he'd been concentrating on his phone as he ascended the stairs and hadn't seen me. Quickly, I replied to Ben's text.

An hour is fine. Gaynor is here. I'm going in.

Ben's reply was swift, and made me smile.

Go get 'em, Tuppence.

But I didn't go in right away. I began to pace the row, realizing I hadn't thought properly about how I would handle the issue of surreptitiously questioning Neil Gaynor now that Ben wasn't here to play off. And now that I knew Neil had been reading art-related articles, I was even less sure of how to approach him.

Should I go in and try to charm the information I want out of him? Or confront him head-on, hoping that a surprise attack might shock him into speech? Or maybe just use the honest approach, and appeal to his sense of decency?

Still pacing, I decided to go with straight-up honesty. Being an honest person myself, I felt like I would be able to carry that off best. Taking a deep breath, I walked with purpose into the Duchess Room, the heavy door opening with silent smoothness. Neil's name was already on my lips, but I stopped myself before uttering it.

The room was still empty save for Neil, who was standing at one of the windows with his back to me. He was on a phone call, though using wireless earbuds. Strictly speaking, calls were frowned upon in the Duchess Room, but, as a former staffer, I knew the PhD students often took phone calls in here if they were alone, and promptly got off if another person walked in. It was clear, however, that Neil hadn't heard me come in. Staring out the window, he had one hand on his forehead as if he was hearing bad news.

"What? God, no, I didn't know that." His voice then went sharp. "This detective is going to interview me? Why?" A pause, then, "I mean, yeah, one of the library staff told me about the painting a while back."

At this, I stilled, standing just inside the room.

His voice went thoughtful for a moment. "I mean, it's cool and all, but—Wait, *what*?" I glanced at his reflection to see his mouth agape as he said, "No, it didn't even cross my mind that it could be really valuable. I mean, I read a couple of articles and figured maybe ten grand or so. *Incredibly* valuable, though? Not for a second—but I don't know much about art, Dina, you know that."

He's talking to his sister, I thought, remembering the photo of the young woman with blond hair from Neil's Instagram account. He was still so utterly focused on a point outside the window that he had yet to notice me. I debated whether to take a seat like someone showing they deliberately meant to be there, or to continue standing at the door like some odd, snooping statue. Regardless, I decided I could use overhearing his conversation as a reason to introduce myself. It would be easy, natural. And yet I didn't move.

Dina had evidently asked him another question, because Neil flung up a hand and replied, "I don't remember telling anyone about the painting. I think it may have come up again later with one of the other library staff. I was asked if I'd heard the story—I said I had—we both said it was a pretty cool find, and that was about it."

There was silence for a few seconds and I surreptitiously watched as Neil once more put his hand on his forehead. He sounded weary now.

"Look, Dina. I've been having second thoughts about this for a while now, but what you told me about Camilla Braithwaite's great-uncle being murdered kind of seems like a sign. I know we decided to go through with this lawsuit. I mean, yeah, if we win, the fifteen grand or so will be helpful in paying Aunt Frieda's caregiver bills. In reality, though, it really won't help for much more than a month or two."

Dina must have argued, but Neil stood his ground. "I don't feel right taking money from the Braithwaite family to help ours when they've just had one of their own murdered. Not even if her painting turns out to be worth a fortune."

Dina had apparently begun arguing again, but Neil cut her off.

"Yes, our family has financial issues because of Camilla's ancestor. But, Dina, our family has had a lot of years—almost a hundred total—to rectify that, and they haven't. You and I are the first ones to even give a damn about our education. I just don't think the right way to start on a better path is through a stupid lawsuit that we might not even win. It won't look good for either of us going forward. I think we'll feel better about ourselves if we go about this the right way—yes, I mean earning our own money." He sighed, and I heard a tightness in his voice when he continued. "On that note, I've made up my mind. I was offered a job recently. It's a good one, and I'm going to take it."

Now, for the first time, I could hear Dina's voice issuing from his phone, and her tone wasn't happy.

"Yes, *I know* that means leaving my PhD unfinished, Dina," Neil replied, "but it also means I'll have a good salary with enough left over to take care of the woman who helped raise us so she doesn't have to go into a home. It also means you can stay in law school." His voice strengthened and there was a finality to it. "Tell your professor friend thank you for being willing to represent us pro bono, but that we're backing out."

Turning, I slipped out of the reading room as he continued to argue with Dina, who didn't seem to want to back down. After the door closed, I turned and peeked through the glass panes, half expecting to see Neil Gaynor looking back at me, shocked and angry to discover someone had been listening to his private phone call. But the only thing I saw was Neil rubbing his fore-head, looking strained as he continued to stare out the window.

It was I who experienced the shock, as a whispered voice came from directly behind me.

"Lucy Lancaster, I presume?"

TWENTY-NINE

I whirled around, my heart pounding. In doing so, my shoulder bumped the sign reminding everyone the Duchess Room was reserved for PhD students. I reached out and grabbed the brass stand just before it toppled over. Glancing back through the door's windowpanes to the reading room, I saw that Neil Gaynor was still on the phone, looking resolved, and completely oblivious to anything else.

"You okay there?" asked the man who'd said my name, a hint of amusement in his voice nonetheless as he watched me struggle to steady the sign. He'd continued to keep his voice at library levels but was no longer whispering.

He was tall, thirty-five or so, and had wide-set gray eyes, thinning wheat-colored hair, and a narrow face that was somehow balanced by a close-cropped beard. "I'm Trent Marins," he said. "It's nice to meet you."

It took me a second, but then his name clicked in my brain. "The new genealogist."

"Well, not so new anymore. I've been here over six months now," he said, and there was a slight note of something mocking in his voice. "But I guess I'm new to you."

"Yes, that's what I meant," I said, tamping down a prick of irritation. "It's a pleasure to meet you, Trent. Camilla tells me you're a very good genealogist and the students like you."

Trent tried to look modest, but then his face split into a wide grin. "I've heard much about the famous Lucy Lancaster as well." I looked up at him questioningly, but he was peering over my shoulder. "Were you in a rush to get away from Mr. Gaynor?"

I craned my neck and saw that Neil was now pacing the length of the small reading room, gesticulating, wireless earbuds still in his ears. I turned back around, thinking fast.

"Not a rush, no," I said. "I know I'm no longer a staffer here, but I've always loved the Duchess Room. I thought I'd go in there to make a few notes on some things I wanted to look up for a client while I'm here, but that man was on what sounded like a private phone call, so I left."

Trent smiled in an understanding way that felt a little patronizing. "I came up here to rescue you from him, actually." He leaned in slightly and put his hand up to the side of his mouth, then whispered, "We've had more than one woman complain that Mr. Gaynor's a bit of a creeper."

I didn't truly know Neil Gaynor from the man in the moon, but I had a feeling Camilla would have mentioned it if he were the creepy type. And after what I'd just overheard Neil telling his sister, somehow Trent's assessment didn't seem to fit. I decided the students here at Howland University might like Trent Marins, but I wasn't so impressed with him thus far.

"How did you even know I was here, Trent?" I asked, keeping my tone light as he and I began moving toward the stairwell.

"Roxie," he said. "She saw you walk in and watched you on the monitors as you came upstairs. Then she saw you seemingly hide from Mr. Gaynor. She said it looked like you may have been texting someone for help, so she sent me to find you."

Well, hell's bells, Roxie *had* seen me earlier. I'd forgotten the librarians had access to security feeds and could see just about everywhere on the monitors. It irritated me that she'd sat there and watched me, even if she did think I might have felt unsafe. Oh well, time for another fib, I thought.

As Trent held the door open for me, I gave a tinkling laugh, and it echoed in the stairwell. "Oh my goodness, I can't believe she saw that. I'm so embarrassed." I grinned up at Trent as we took the first steps down. "I saw Mr. Gaynor, and he looked like a guy who used to ask me out all the time. I did indeed hide from him—or from the guy I thought he was—and I texted my boyfriend. But when Mr. Gaynor actually came upstairs, I realized I'd mistaken him for someone else. That's why I felt safe going in the Duchess Room."

We reached the landing and I gave another laugh, letting my eyes crease with feigned mirth so I could assess Trent's face without letting on that I was staring at him. Good, he seemed to be buying it. I topped it off with a philosophical shrug. "But then, like I told you, Mr. Gaynor was on what sounded like a personal call. I thought about reminding him that he shouldn't be on the phone, but I'm not on staff anymore, so I kept my mouth shut and waited for a minute or so to see if he would hang up." I gave another unconcerned hitch of my shoulder. "When he didn't, I left. Plus, he seemed upset and I felt like I was interfering, you know?"

Trent looked around the stairwell for listeners, then said in a conspiratorial way as we started down the last set of stairs to the first floor, "Was he talking to his lawyer about the lawsuit?"

Only the fact that my phone vibrated with a text at the same moment and I performed the Pavlovian response of looking down at the screen kept the twitch I gave from being an obvious tell. The text was from my mother, and I just made out the words *You were right! SOILS FROM HEAVEN!* before my head came back up to look at Trent. My shock, both at his question and at Mom's text, must have given my expression a suspicious edge, and Trent rushed to explain himself.

"Gaynor was talking to another student, just before he came upstairs. They were making plans to meet for a paper they're working on jointly, and Gaynor said he had a call with his lawyer first." Trent shrugged, looking pleased with himself. "I simply overheard, that's all."

I felt a bit pleased with myself, too, because I'd realized something: Trent Marins was a gossip, and a gossip was someone I could mine for information.

"He *was* talking to his lawyer, as a matter of fact," I said in a low voice. Then I pretended to give him a hesitant expression. "You do know what it's about, then? Because I wouldn't want to talk out of turn . . ."

"Oh, honey, *everyone* here knows," he said with a roll of his eyes. "Gaynor's suing Camilla's family because Gaynor's ancestor had Camilla's ancestor, some rich old Civil War vet, over to dinner." Trent gave me an incredulous look, then shrugged. "I mean, as genealogists, you and I both know that happened a lot in earlier centuries. Hell, half of England's landed gentry became gentry after having a member of royalty stay at their house."

"True," I said. "And the money they shelled out to impress their royal guest was astronomical. It was a very common thing."

"It certainly was," Trent said, "but it still stuns me. One dinner with Braithwaite—that's it, one measly dinner—and it set Gaynor's ancestor back so much money that it affected his family for ages. You may have read about it in the latest issue of *Chronology*." Trent's eyes lit up. "The whole article was about Camilla's ancestor, you know. The reporter really ripped the Braithwaite family a new one with her claims, don't you think?" He gave me a sidelong look. "I mean, you *have* read the article, haven't you?"

"I have—and *wow*," I said, letting my eyes go round as we reached the bottom step. We stopped just before the doors to the main reading room. "I've subscribed to *Chronology* for years and I've never read an article quite like it."

A student came breezing through the doors and dashed up the steps, barely taking notice of Trent and me. I took the opportunity to steer the conversation.

"So, tell me," I said, moving a bit closer to him. "Camilla said her ancestor was a painter and she's got part of a triptych done by him." Pointing upstairs to the Duchess Room, I said, "I overheard Mr. Gaynor saying something about the painting being worth a lot of money. Something about another painting being underneath the top one. I mean, how freaking cool! Did she ever say anything to you about it?"

Trent's eyes narrowed. "We knew she found what looked to be another painting underneath, but I don't know anything about it being worth that much." His voice took on the purr of someone who's just heard something particularly juicy. "Well done, Camilla."

I nodded emphatically. "Mr. Gaynor said something about someone from the library staff telling him about it. Do you think it was Roxie or Patrice?"

Trent tapped his lips with one long finger, assessing me with amusement as he did so. "Lucy, are you helping our Camilla with an 'investigation'?" he asked, using air quotes.

"How do you mean?" I hoped my face was an innocent mask, but I could feel the heat in my cheeks. It only got worse when he swiped his finger along the side of his nose as if to assure me that I didn't need to worry, he would keep my secret.

"Come on," he said, tilting his head toward the bullpen. "Let's go find Roxie and Patrice so you can see what they have to say for themselves." And he yanked open the door to the main reading room.

It was all I could do not to slump as I walked through. In seconds, Trent Marins had seen right through my attempts to extract information from him. And the sinking sensation I felt when I met Roxie's cold stare as I neared the reference desk told me things weren't likely to get one bit better.

THIRTY

I was wondering if you were going to come say hello or if you were going to keep running scared from us," Roxie said in her slightly raspy voice from her perch at the reference desk. As it sat higher than the other two desks in the bullpen, I felt like a peasant being led to an imperious-looking queen.

"Now, Rox, don't be prickly," Trent said. "Lucy here was going to come say hello. She just had some work to do first. Isn't that right, Lucy?"

I nodded like a robot. Roxie, whose hazel eyes seemed to laser in on any level of bull, didn't look convinced. For his part, Trent left me and headed upstairs again, but not before turning around and giving me two thumbs up in encouragement behind Roxie's back. He also mouthed, *Patrice is in her office,* and pointed to the hallway just beyond Roxie's desk, where the librarians and the in-house genealogist each had a small private office. I wondered if Patrice and Helen were still there talking rare Texas maps.

Roxie continued to look at me, unsmiling, but a student stepped up to the desk and asked her for the Wi-Fi password, giving me a temporary reprieve. I sent a quick reply to my mother's text, telling her where I was and that I'd call her back soon.

Then, almost as if Helen knew I'd been wondering if she were still here at the library, my phone buzzed in my hand with a text. She wrote that she had waited for me as long as she could after accepting the maps from Patrice, but had to get back on the road to Austin. She told me to keep her updated, wished me luck, and finished with a good reminder.

And if either of those catty women hisses at you, remember, you've got fangs, too. Use them.

I looked up from my phone, my lips twitching. Roxie was giving me a look like there was a bad smell in the room.

"Your hair looks really nice, Roxie," I said by way of breaking the ice. "Layla's outdone herself this time."

Even the mention of Roxie's girlfriend and a compliment on her hair didn't thaw her. "Why are you here, Lucy?"

Suddenly, I realized how tense I was—just like I had been every day I worked here—and I didn't want to feel that way ever again. I lifted my chin and stared back at her. I didn't raise my voice, nor did I sound defensive. I merely spoke with resolve.

"Roxie, I have every right to be here, for whatever reason I like, and I'll thank you to drop the attitude with me."

For a moment, Roxie didn't do anything but glare at me. Then she sat back in her chair, almost looking impressed.

"Grown a spine since you were last here, have you?"

"No, I already had a spine," I said. "You just chose to see my niceness as a weakness instead of that of a strong woman who chooses to embrace the positive and lift up other people along with her. What's changed is that now I know you're the one with the problem, not me."

When the silence between us stretched into its third long

second and I gave no sign of unlocking my eyes from hers, Roxie glanced at her computer screen, then back at me. Her gaze was as cold as ever, but I thought I saw a flush creeping up her neck. "Fine," she said. "What can I do for you, then?"

From the moment I knew I was going to come here and try to get information out of Roxie, I'd been dreaming about finessing and finagling details out of her so she wouldn't know how sneaky I'd been until she thought about it later. I wanted her to think, *Damn, Lucy Lancaster got the better of me!* and give me some respect for it, even if it was begrudgingly.

However, I'd forgotten what a force Roxie was, even when someone had just knocked her down a peg. I might have been able to at least somewhat use Trent's love of gossip against him, but with Roxie? I couldn't play games.

So, I made a decision. Camilla may not have wanted her co-workers to know how closely she was working with me, but a murder had occurred—of her own close relative, no less—and if I wanted information from Roxie, Camilla and her desire to keep secrets were just going to have to lump it. I moved closer to the reference desk and spoke in a low voice.

"Look, what Camilla didn't tell y'all was that I was with her when she found her great-uncle Charlie. The Saturday before, she'd hired me to look into the accusations made in the *Chronology* article about her ancestor." I'd pointedly left Ben out of the picture, and on an inspired whim, I corroborated Camilla's lie by adding, "And Charlie wanted his maternal line researched, too, so it was a double deal. Anyway, I'd gone over to Charlie's house to have a quick meeting with him, and I was in the living room when Camilla found him." I saw Roxie's mouth open just slightly as I continued. I had her attention, which was rare, so I wasn't going to let it go just yet. "Then there's another side to this. If Camilla didn't tell y'all, her uncle Charlie had another piece of the triptych painted by her ancestor, and that piece was stolen the night of the murder. I know Camilla told you about *her* piece of the triptych, that it had another painting underneath it. I'm here to ask you if you mentioned that to anyone."

Roxie was quiet for a moment, and I wondered if she was going to refuse to answer me just to be contrary. Instead, she picked up a pencil and started rolling it between her fingers. I recognized it as her habit when she was thinking. After a few more moments, she sighed and said, "I told Layla, of course, and my mother, and a handful of other friends. Layla and I had a dinner party one night and it segued nicely into the conversation." She shrugged. "That was it."

Somehow, I wasn't buying this. It was the way my former co-worker looked almost too blasé. At the same time, over Roxie's shoulder, I'd noticed someone with a cranberry-colored sweater and dark hair lurking just beyond the reference desk, at the edge of the hallway leading to the back offices. When I chanced a look, however, Patrice had disappeared. Had I caught her frowning at what Roxie said as well? I was pretty sure I had.

I was just about to push away from the desk and go in search of Patrice when Roxie moved her computer mouse and an invoice came up on her screen, catching my eye.

"You bought Soils from Heaven potting soil, too?" When her eyes flicked irritably my way, I said with a shrug, "I noticed some bags at Camilla's great-uncle's house."

I was about to add my suspicions that the soil was tainted with arsenic from the bodies of dead Civil War soldiers, but I stopped when I saw Roxie's face become somewhat animated. I'd forgotten she enjoyed gardening.

"I've been hearing great things about it from Trent," she said. "I'm sure Camilla told you that he sells it, and we've all bought a bunch. I just got twenty bags the other day, and Layla and I are going to plant tomatoes and other veggies this weekend."

"*Trent* sells it?" I repeated. "I didn't know that."

Roxie nodded as she closed the window on her screen. "It comes from land his family bought that used to be a farm many decades ago. It's all organic and supposedly really great soil." She looked up at me, and—seemingly remembering to whom she was talking—her expression shut down again. I made my reply light and breezy.

"Well, my parents just bought some standing vegetable planters, so I may get some bags for them. They love anything organic." Roxie didn't respond. She wasn't going to offer up any more tidbits to me, about gardening or anything else.

All right, then, so be it.

Not that I was going to let her harm herself by using the soil or anything. Roxie wasn't my favorite person—and obviously I wasn't hers, either—but I'd never put her in danger. Thankfully, though, I had a couple days to figure out what was going on with Soils from Heaven—especially now that I knew Trent Marins was involved—before she planted her vegetables. Once I did, I'd do what was right and warn her about the potential for high levels of arsenic.

"Well, thanks for the information, Roxie," I said. Inclining my head in the direction of the back offices, I said, "I'm just going to go say hi to Patrice, and then I may use the computers upstairs for some genealogy research until my boyfriend comes to pick me up."

"Still dating that rich pretty boy?" Roxie asked in a snide voice. She was, of course, talking about my ex, Nick, who, unlike the stone lion with the same name outside, had never brought me luck.

"Nope. My new one's a whole lot hotter," I said with a broad smile, and left her scowling after me.

I found Patrice in her office, staring at her computer screen, seeming to be in another world. My encounter with Roxie having left a bad taste in my mouth, I resolved to go into my conversation with this former coworker in a more positive mindset.

"Knock, knock," I said with a smile, rapping lightly on her doorframe. "May I come in?"

"Lucy!" she said, sitting up straight and smoothing back a stray lock of dark hair from her face. A bit of pink came into her cheeks and her words came out in a rush, like they always did when she was embarrassed or uncomfortable. "How are you doing? I was just speaking to your friend Helen Kim. She, ah, overheard Roxie saying you were here—she said she ran into you outside."

I took the seat across from her desk, acting like it was no big deal that Roxie had alerted Patrice as she watched me on the security monitors. "Helen and I went to college together. She's fantastic. I didn't know she would be here, but she told me about the maps. That was pretty cool of you to convince that student to donate them to the Alden museum in Austin instead of keeping them here."

Patrice shrugged modestly, but I could tell she was pleased, and it served to return her voice to its normal speed. "They were really special maps, and as much as I love it here at Howland, so few people would see them. They belong in a true museum. I'm just glad the student and his family agreed."

I glanced at the framed photo on her desk, trying to keep a positive vibe going. "Wow, Anamaria and Esteban have really shot up," I said, leaning forward for a better look at the young boy and girl mugging for the camera. Though the sun was high in the sky, they wore sweatshirts under their hiking vests. A distinctive rock formation loomed in the background, with what looked like a huge egg-shaped boulder balancing precariously on its side between two other upright rocks, the taller almost in the shape of a crude obelisk.

"They have," Patrice said, casting a warm glance toward the photo. "They're seven and six now, if you can believe it."

"No kidding?" I said. She nodded, and despite my efforts, we lapsed into an uncomfortable silence.

I thought about how Patrice had always taken all her cues from Roxie, from how to handle any project to how to deal with students to how to treat her coworkers. In some ways, imitating Roxie had been good for her. Roxie was an excellent researcher and librarian; therefore, Patrice was now, too. But in other ways, Patrice hadn't helped herself at all. Of the three librarians, it was Patrice whom the students went to the least. I had always suspected that Patrice's problem was that she tried too hard to mimic Roxie's prickly manner, and the students could sense it was inauthentic. Roxie may have been intimidating to them, but somehow they seemed to appreciate that her personality wasn't a shadow of someone else's.

Now, however, I sensed something was different with Patrice's demeanor, but I couldn't quite put my finger it. Shaking off the feeling, I got to my point.

"Patrice," I said. "I'm here to help Camilla in finding out some information." I went on to tell her the same details I'd told Roxie, and she replied with much the same gaping silence. "I'm trying to figure out just how many people knew about the triptych, and if anyone was unduly interested in it. Did you happen to tell anyone what Camilla found under her painting?"

Patrice's complexion seemed to turn sallow for a moment. She acted like she wanted to look out her office door to see if anyone was there. I got up and did it for her.

"All clear," I said, sitting back down, and she nodded, putting her elbows on her desk and leaning forward.

"The answer for me is no, I never mentioned to anyone."

I was skeptical, and it clearly showed on my face.

"Honestly, Lucy, no one." She looked earnest, then frowned with a memory. "That day Camilla told us, my mother called maybe twenty minutes later. My dad had fallen downstairs and broke his leg in two places. He's all right now, thank goodness, but I took several days off to help my family, and then a holiday came around. By the time we came back to work, Camilla's find had been forgotten." Patrice paused, lowering her voice. "By most of us, at least."

"How do you mean?" I asked.

"I heard Roxie telling you that she only told Layla and some friends she'd had over for a dinner party, and that was probably true. They're all her longtime friends." Then her voice became laced with sarcasm as she said, "But they're not her most recent best buddy, Trent, who she seems to talk to about everything now. And that includes Camilla's painting."

Ah, I thought, hearing the jealousy in Patrice's voice. I recalled how Trent had referred to Roxie as "Rox"—something no one but Patrice had ever done when I worked here. And also how he'd told Roxie to chill out, another thing no one ever said to her. Now, not only was Patrice actually talking to me like we'd always been friendly, she was also giving up dirt about Roxie.

Yes, I thought I had it figured out now. Trent had displaced Patrice as Roxie's favorite, and the green-eyed monster was making Patrice loose-lipped.

Well, if spite and jealousy got me good information, then so be it.

"Are you saying that Roxie and Trent showed an undue interest in the painting?" I asked, and she nodded, before hesitating and looking nervously out in the direction of the hallway again. We could both hear someone heading our way.

Quickly, I said in a bright voice, "So y'all enjoyed hiking in Big Bend National Park over the winter? How cold did it get?"

For a second, Patrice looked confused. I gave her a slightly exasperated look and jutted my forefinger toward the photo of her kids. "That's Balanced Rock, isn't it?" I asked, indicating the rock formation in the background. "My parents took my sister and me to Big Bend a couple of times as kids, but I need to go back again as an adult."

Patrice cottoned on just in time. As Trent walked by, talking on his cell phone, she said, "Yes, it was lovely in the winter at Big Bend. It was about sixty degrees as the high and the kids *adored* it." I could see Trent's reflection in the eight-by-ten wedding photo on the credenza behind Patrice's desk. He turned his head, looking at us with interest while holding the phone to his ear, but kept going. We heard a door open, then close, and the hallway was quiet again. I jumped right back in with my questions.

"Patrice," I said, "I know it's a long shot, but any chance you know where Roxie and Trent were two nights ago?"

"Why?" she asked, suddenly suspicious, and I realized I'd overstepped my boundaries. When it came down to it, Patrice was still more likely to side with Roxie than me. I'd been foolish to even ask.

"Um, it's just information worth knowing," I said.

Wow, that sounded *really* weak. My gold star for interrogation was fading real fast.

Patrice's eyes had narrowed as she correctly read into my question. "Are you seriously thinking one of them did something to Camilla's great-uncle?"

"Not at all," I said, my voice a shade too high to sound believable. "I'm thinking that one or both of them may have . . . you know . . . opened their mouths to the wrong person about the painting, and *that* person targeted Camilla's great-uncle."

Patrice stared at me, but didn't reply either way. Her computer had dinged a couple of times thus far with the sound I recognized from my time on staff as incoming emails, and I'd seen her eyes straying back to her computer more and more. Now she'd clicked on one and started a reply.

I understood what she wasn't saying—she'd griped enough about Roxie to make herself feel better, but she wasn't going to be a full-on sneak.

Inwardly sighing, I gave up. Though when I stood, I remembered the other question I wanted to ask. "Patrice, did you buy some potting soil from Soils from Heaven as well?"

She looked up at me, frowning. "Why?"

Not wanting to alarm her until I knew more, I responded with valiant lightness. "Oh, I saw it at Camilla's great-uncle's house. It looks like good soil and I wanted to know if anyone had used it yet. Roxie said she just got her bags, so she couldn't give a firsthand report. I'm thinking of buying some for my parents."

Patrice had already turned her attention back to her computer, but said, "I bought some for both my parents and for my house—but the company does things in such small batches, we won't receive our shipment until next weekend, I think." Her computer dinged again and sarcasm came back into her voice. "But who knows? It's Trent's brainchild, and he doesn't feel the need to keep me updated."

She stood up as well. For a moment, she watched me uncertainly, a range of emotions skittering across her face, landing on a tentative smile. I felt like she was half regretting sounding snappish with me just now and she also half preferred the dismissive way she always used to treat me.

"It was nice seeing you again, Lucy," she said finally, sounding like the part of her that was regretful might have prevailed. "I hate to rush out, but I have to go relieve Roxie at the reception desk. She's got a budget meeting in a few minutes. If you want some soil, you'll need to ask Trent."

Before I could say anything else, she slipped out past me, her ponytail swishing behind her as she headed to the bullpen.

THIRTY-ONE

✺

I rapped lightly on Trent's door and called his name.

"Trent? May I come in?"

There was no answer. Turning the handle, I pushed the door open a smidge to find the room empty and dark, except for a bluish light emanating from Trent's computer screen.

Standing in the hallway, I wondered where he might have gone, since he hadn't passed back by Patrice's office. Then my eyes landed on the door just beyond his, which I'd nearly forgotten existed. It was a blank door the same color as the wall and served as a private stairway to the second and third floors, requiring a staff key card to get in. He must have gone upstairs.

I heard a ding from his computer, and once more noticed the blue glow of his screen. He hadn't locked the computer before he left, I thought, and sent him a mental *tut-tut*. That was a faux pas at any company, including a university library.

Then my mind repeated the thought. *His computer is unlocked.*

Quickly, I ducked into the office, forgetting the lights were motion-activated. They came on immediately, which would alert Trent as soon as he came downstairs, but I was already around his desk and at his computer before I could even really think twice about it. I'd been hoping to ask Trent if he knew about the arsenic in the potting soil he was peddling as a side job. But what if I could find the answer on his computer or in his office without having to deal with him again?

I was just a moment too late. No sooner had I lunged for his mouse, hoping to reengage the computer's internal sleep timer, than Trent's computer recognized the allotted minutes of inactivity and the screen automatically locked, going black.

Feeling unsettled by my unethical—and unfruitful—attempt at snooping, I turned to his paper-strewn desk.

I spotted a notepad above his mouse. There were a bunch of doodles and scribbles, including a notation reading *Katherine Sabom—10 bags* and *Heather Horwitz—15 bags* and the words *bill to credit cards*. Underneath he had written *Testing? Call A&M?*

Pulling out my cell phone, I snapped a photo of the notations. My alma mater, Texas A&M University, had a world-renowned agricultural extension service that did, among many other things, soil testing. That had to be what Trent's last note was about.

Just above the notepad was one of those refillable calendars with two U-shaped silver prongs holding the pages in place. On today's date I saw he'd written *Mary Paredes* in blue ink, but that was it.

I lifted my head, listening for footsteps in the hall. All I could hear were the murmurs of students talking and the soft *burr-burr* of the telephone out in the bullpen.

Scanning the papers on Trent's desk again, I noticed a familiar-looking logo with a swirly font sticking out from under a book bound in green leather. It was a printed invoice from Soils from Heaven. Lifting the book up carefully so as not to disturb the placement of the invoice, I saw that it was made out to Jensen Hocknell—Camilla's great-aunt. She had bought thirty bags of soil, which had been delivered six weeks earlier. A code of some sort—*P7*—next to the quantity had been circled. Quickly, I snapped a photo of the invoice. I was just taking a second, close-up photo when I heard a sound.

It took me a second to place it, then I realized it was someone coming down the stairs next to Trent's office. With a little squeak of fear, I went to put the book back on top of the invoice. *Wait . . . had one inch of the logo been showing, or two?*

The muted ringing of a cell phone—weirdly reverberating since Trent was in the stairwell—made me jump. Hastily, I tried the book a couple of different ways, but all that served to do was to shift the papers underneath more with each try. Dang it, now it was really obvious someone had been in his office.

I heard the handle of the stairwell door slowly turn and the muffled sounds of Trent speaking to someone on the phone. There was nothing else I could do. I rushed out of his office, pulling the door closed quietly behind me, and streaked into the next office down—Camilla's, as it happened—just as the door to the stairwell opened.

I clapped my hand to my forehead. What in the ever-loving name of all that was stupid was I doing?

I heard footsteps, Trent's door opening, and then a pause. He'd no doubt noticed his light was on, if not that his desk looked slightly rearranged. I gritted my teeth and leaned up against Camilla's desk, fanning myself to try to calm down and not look so guilty. I heard Trent's door closing, but no footsteps. He must have gone in.

My phone buzzed with a call, making me start again, but this time my heart soared at the name and photo I saw on my screen. Hurriedly, I closed Camilla's office door as I answered the call.

"Grandpa!" I said excitedly, though as quietly as I could.

"Lucy, my darlin'!" Grandpa's voice was so reassuring, I nearly wilted with the sound of it. Then his tone sharpened. "You sound upset, love. What's wrong?"

Growing up, I'd always thought my beloved, now ninety-two-year-old grandfather was simply more perceptive than most grandfathers. Heck, more perceptive than most men of any age. It wasn't until just before New Year's that I discovered Grandpa's extra-good perceptiveness came from the fact he'd been an honest-to-goodness spy. He'd begun his career with the Office of Strategic Services during World War II and then continued on as a handler with the CIA, as the OSS became, until just around the time my father was born.

With a slightly hysterical giggle, I moved to the back of Camilla's office, by the big standing vault, and said, "Oh, nothing at all, Grandpa. I just nearly got caught snooping in the office of a guy who I think is selling the public potting soil laced with arsenic from the bodies of Civil War soldiers—including some to my client's great-uncle, who may have been dying because of it before he was murdered."

"Now, *that's* one I haven't heard," Grandpa said without missing a beat. "Where are you?"

"Hiding in my client's office," I said. I gave him the briefest of rundowns on what I'd been doing and why. The good thing about Grandpa being a former spy was that he didn't require a lot of information to make a decision.

"Well, love, that's your first mistake. Don't hide. It makes you look guilty. Open the door and act like you just closed it to take a private call."

This sounded good. "Okay, thanks, Grandpa." I paused, biting my lip. "Then what?"

Much like the other G-man in my life, Grandpa's first thought was for my personal safety.

"Are you in any danger from this man?" he asked.

"No, I think I'm more embarrassed about being caught," I replied with a wry laugh.

"What about when you leave the library?" Grandpa asked.

No doubt his levelheadedness had made him a good handler for his operatives out in the field. For a split second, I almost felt like I was a real spy making contact with my trusted handler, who was assessing the situation and giving me instructions that would take me to the nearest safe house.

"Ben should be texting at any moment," I said, checking the time on my phone. We were coming up on the end of the extra hour he'd said he needed. "He'll be picking me up about five hundred yards from the library."

"Good," Grandpa said. "Though I have no doubt you could handle yourself no matter what the situation. Here's what you need to do."

I listened, then said, "Really?" At the same time, I heard what sounded like Trent's office door opening.

"Yes," he said, "and do it with confidence."

"Grandpa, I think he's coming," I whispered, moving closer to the door.

"Confidence, my love," Grandpa repeated. I leaned up against Camilla's desk again, hoping I looked casual, just as Trent pushed open the door, his expression no longer friendly.

THIRTY-TWO

◈

My phone still to my ear, I held up a finger for Trent to be patient as I said, "Yes, of course, Mr. Halloran. I'm honored you asked me to research your wife's side of the family. How about I call you when I'm back in Austin and we can set up a meeting? Yes, I'll be back in the office tomorrow."

I paused, hearing Grandpa's low voice in my ear. "Excellent, my love. Report back as soon as you can."

"Of course, Mr. Halloran," I said. "It was great to talk to you again as well. I'll call you tomorrow." Keeping my phone turned toward me, I touched the screen to end the call and make Grandpa's name disappear. Then I looked up at Trent with a smile.

"What are you doing in here?" he asked. His eyes scanned the office for signs of snooping, including Camilla's desk, which was free of anything except a stack of papers and a few other office odds and ends. I'd noticed there were still no photos of her family. I'd read once that the absence of personal details in a person's workspace was an indication that they didn't enjoy their job. It kind of made me wonder if Camilla truly liked working here.

I held up my phone. "Just taking a call from one of my old clients who wants his wife's side of the family traced."

Trent's nostrils flared. "And were you in *my* office, poking around in my papers, before you took this call?"

Thanks to Grandpa, I didn't stutter. "I was," I said.

His eyebrows lifted. "You were? You don't deny it? Want to tell me why?"

I pushed away from the desk so I was standing up straight. Grandpa had told me to go on the attack, and that's exactly what I did.

"I think it's *you* who needs to tell *me* why, Trent," I said. My heart was hammering in my chest, but I pretended it wasn't.

His eyes went shifty. "What do you mean?"

I said, "I know you're selling soil that's laced with arsenic, Trent. I know it's because you're taking the soil from an abandoned pauper's cemetery where soldiers from the Civil War are buried. And from a notation I saw on your desk, it sounds like you're aware of the affected soil. What I don't know is how long you've known about it and whether or not you were going to tell Camilla that her great-uncle had possibly become ill from handling your soil."

Trent had gone still, his eyes watching me like a snake's, and, suddenly, I was regretting telling Grandpa that I felt safe confronting this man. After all, I was backed into Camilla's office. Much like Camilla's ex-husband, Trent Marins was also tall and looked very fit. If he decided to become violent, I now realized, he might be able to overpower me quickly, render me unconscious—or even dead—and lock me in Camilla's office. He could be long gone before anyone found me.

Casually, I slipped my phone into the pocket of my crossbody purse, widened my stance, and gently curled my fingers toward my palms, ready to perform some of my new self-defense moves. So, it took me a couple of heartbeats to realize what I was seeing.

Trent had brought his hands to his face. With a groan, he sunk down into one of the hard chairs opposite Camilla's desk.

"Oh my God," he said, looking up at me with pleading eyes. "How did you know? We—my partners and I—just found out a couple of weeks ago about the higher levels of arsenic in our soil."

"Simple," I said. "I noticed Charlie Braithwaite's symptoms, read your advertising on your bags of soil and on your website, and did my research." I squinted at him. "But what do you mean, 'partners'? I thought the land was family owned."

"It *is* family owned," he said with a hint of snappishness. "My partners are my family. My aunt and uncle bought the land nearly a year ago and had been giving the soil away to friends when they realized they could make a business out of it. When I changed jobs and moved here to Houston last August, they asked me to help with sales and billing." With this, he momentarily closed his eyes and tipped his head back so it was resting against the office wall, then looked back at me. "You're wrong on one count, though. The cemetery isn't on our company's land, it's adjacent to it."

When I looked a bit disbelieving, Trent stood up slowly, as if exhausted, and motioned for me to follow him. "Come to my office. I'll show you an email. One that you *clearly* missed when you were looking through my things."

I bristled at this. What cheek to try to turn this around on me. I returned his gaze steadily. With a slight twitch that could have been an irritated shrug or another flash of guilt, he turned without further comment and led the way back to his office.

At that moment, my phone buzzed with a text. *Oh, thank heavens*—it was Ben.

Ready for an extraction? I'll be at the drop-off point in 10.

I texted back, in all caps, *AFFIRMATIVE,* as I followed in Trent's wake. Once in his office, he lifted the leather-bound book and underneath the invoice I'd seen earlier were printouts of two emails. The first was from a woman named Perrie Wigglesworth.

In the email, Mrs. Wigglesworth described taking possession of her shipment of forty bags from Soils from Heaven nearly five months earlier. An avid gardener, she began using it immediately in her greenhouse and had worked with the soil, without gloves, on a daily basis. It was her husband, a dermatologist, who noticed the first spot on her stomach about three weeks ago. She had thought it might be an age spot, as she was in her sixties and had had a few of them crop up on her face in the past. Mrs. Wigglesworth wrote that her husband then tested her for many things, with arsenic poisoning being the last, but it was the arsenic test that came up as positive. She went on to state that she knew trace levels of arsenic were naturally occurring in soil. However, she felt compelled to alert Soils from Heaven, because it was clear that there was a higher concentration in their soil, and did they know?

Below Mrs. Wigglesworth's email was Trent's response. He had apologized profusely, explaining that they'd done soil testing on the land, but would be performing those tests again to a more extensive degree to determine how much land was affected. He offered her a full refund on her soil and said he would send two employees, at her convenience, to remove any unused bags and replace them with organic soil from a local landscape nursery.

The second email was a report from an environmental laboratory. A total of thirty samples of dirt, each representing a plot from five acres of land, had been sent in by Soils from Heaven for specialized arsenic testing.

"As you'll see," Trent said, "only two plots have higher-than-normal concentrations of arsenic. They believe the ones marked 'P1' and 'P7,' for plots one and seven, respectively, are the only ones affected. This is likely due to erosion and runoff over the decades, since they're located directly downhill from the grave sites in question."

"Plot seven has the higher concentration of the two," I said, checking all the numbers again. "Why is that?"

"It's because there's a dip in the land at plot seven," Trent replied. "If you look at a topographic map of our acreage, the areas that form plot seven look like they may have been the site of a man-made watering hole or something similar back in the day. Regardless, it seems the runoff accumulated most in that area, increasing the arsenic levels."

I wished I had a good reason to take photographs of the email and the report, but since I couldn't come up with one, I handed him back the sheets of paper.

"Do you know from which plots of land you got the soil that went to Camilla's great-uncle Charlie Braithwaite?" I asked.

Trent blinked rapidly at me, and then his expression smoothed into blankness. Somehow, I knew what he was going to do. He might know the answer to my question, but he wasn't going to give me any more specifics that could incriminate him or his company. And I wasn't disappointed.

"Was Camilla's great-uncle having symptoms of arsenic poisoning?" he asked instead. "She never said as much, if so. All Camilla told us before she went to Austin was that he hadn't been feeling well. And all she told us when she called yesterday was that, before the tragedy, she'd taken him to the doctor for some tests and he felt better when she brought him home."

I blanched as Trent began picking up papers from his desk, straightening them, and putting them into piles. Dang it, he had me there. Camilla didn't even know that Charlie had been feeling unwell until a few days ago. It was possible his doctor hadn't received any test results back yet as to what had been causing Charlie's symptoms. I was the one who recognized that

Charlie could have had arsenic poisoning. Hell, I hadn't even told Camilla.

My phone vibrated with a message from Ben—he was parked on campus, waiting for me—just as Patrice buzzed Trent's intercom.

"Trent," I heard her say in a bored voice, "there's a student here for your office hours."

I'd completely forgotten Trent had professor duties and, hence, would have office hours for genealogy students to visit him. For a second, it seemed he'd forgotten as well, as he muttered a curse word before hitting the intercom button and saying, "Thank you, Patrice. Please tell Ms. Paredes I'll be there in just a minute."

Patrice didn't reply. Trent and I looked at each other, neither of us smiling. He seemed as frustrated at the situation as I was.

"Look," I said, keeping my tone even, "I know Roxie and Patrice have bought bags of your soil—"

"Theirs isn't from the affected areas," he interrupted tersely. "We've stopped working the soil in those two plots. Also, you have to remember, most soil has some level of arsenic in it. It occurs naturally. Our soil just has a higher concentration in those two areas." Gesturing at me with a handful of papers he added, "But, if the customers wear proper gardening gloves like our employees do, there's not an issue. None of the teens and college kids we employ have had any health problems."

"Thank goodness for that," I said. "And, yes, that's true, arsenic *is* naturally occurring. But even so, you need to tell Roxie and Patrice, as well as your other customers. You'll need to put out a press release or something to alert them all. I don't know, of course, but I expect you've shipped out a lot of soil from those two plots. If others aren't using gardening gloves when they work with the soil, then they may be experiencing issues as well."

Trent looked unhappy about this, but didn't refute it. Finally, he rubbed his brow again and said, "This will be the end of the company. We're too small to recover. And we've given a lot of underprivileged kids some good work."

"Truly, I'm sorry about that," I said, feeling like a heel at the thought of some kids losing a good place to work, out in the fresh air and sunshine. "I mean it. However, if I don't see a press release on your website telling your customers about the issue and giving them options for how to handle it—whether that means y'all refund them or pay for soil tests or what have you—I'll have to report it."

Trent gaped at me, clearly shocked that I would go this far.

Clasping my hands together, I thought of Mrs. Hocknell, but chose my words to be deliberately vague. "Trent, I happen to have another friend who's been using your soil recently. Shall I tell my friend that Soils from Heaven will be emailing their customer list about this issue?"

He didn't look at me now. His face was turning red with frustration. Nevertheless, he nodded.

Just then a pretty brunette came walking up to the door holding a genealogy textbook I recognized as one I'd used myself in grad school.

"Professor Marins?" she said tentatively. "I was told to come back. Is this not a good time for office hours?"

I gave her a smile, mutely thanking Patrice for ignoring Trent and sending the student anyway. "No, no, I was just leaving." Turning to Trent, I said, "Thank you for your time, Professor Marins. I'll let my friend know to expect your email." Then I strode out of his office, through the bullpen, out the doors, and past Nick and Nora the lions into the crisp afternoon air, gulping it like I'd been suffocating in that library.

Then I realized it wasn't the library that was the issue. The toxicity had been coming from the people I'd been dealing with.

Down the tree-lined walkway, I could see Ben's Explorer parked with its hazards on. Feeling relieved, I texted Grandpa to tell him his advice had worked and I'd update him soon, and smiled when I immediately got a thumbs-up emoji from him in return.

"Lucy! Hey, Lucy!"

I whipped around. "Patrice?" I said, pushing my hair out of my eyes.

She rushed up to me, looking uncertain.

"What's wrong?" I asked. "Did I leave something in the library?"

She shook her head. "I wanted to tell you something, but I didn't want Trent or Roxie to overhear."

I just stopped myself from rolling my eyes at the mention of both their names.

Patrice glanced back at the library, then said, "I don't know where either of them were two nights ago." She wrung her hands for a moment, then seemed to decide to continue. "What I do know is that the two of them have been even more tight than normal recently. I think . . . I think they're planning something."

Frowning, I said, "Like what?"

"I don't know. A couple of weeks ago, I overheard Trent tell Roxie that she would definitely be getting a commission. Roxie seemed to think her split wasn't high enough, and they argued over it, but they were smiling afterward, so I guess they came to a good number."

"This was probably about Trent's soil business, don't you think?" I said.

"That's what I've been thinking, too," Patrice said. "But you know when you asked if anyone had talked about Camilla's painting?" When I nodded, she said, "Well, during that conversation, I overheard, very clearly, the words 'Camilla' and 'the painting,' At the time, I guessed it was a side conversation because I only heard parts of the whole thing, but now I'm not so sure."

I felt a chill come over me. Roxie and Trent had both known about Camilla's and Charlie's finds. Were they working together to somehow get ahold of one or both paintings? Had Trent lied to me about when, exactly, he had discovered his company's soil had higher levels of arsenic? Did he deliberately send bags of poison-laced soil to Charlie Braithwaite's house in an attempt to sicken Charlie, or even to kill him? And had Roxie encouraged him to do so, then demanded a higher cut from the sale of the Braithwaite paintings for her part in thinking up the plot?

Despite the fact Trent and Roxie were definitely not people I enjoyed being around, something about the scenario I was floating in my mind wasn't ringing true. I didn't want to fuel any more fires in Patrice, though, so I just said, "Thanks for letting me know." When she nodded, seeming relieved to have said her piece, I looked at her questioningly. "But why did you decide to tell me this?"

Patrice's mouth twisted in thought for a moment, then she said, "I'm not sure, really. I heard about the case you were involved in last fall—how you helped save a senator. Back in my office, you told me you were trying to help Camilla, and, well, if something underhanded *is* going on, I guess I felt you were the best person to tell."

She nodded to me, this time with a genuine smile, then turned and went back into the library, leaving me staring after her in complete surprise.

THIRTY-THREE

Ben and I were soon on the road back to Austin, but not before first filling my parents in on the day's events. After Mom and Dad listened intently to the exciting news of what was under Camilla's painting, then about my adventures at my former workplace, Dad hugged me fiercely, gave Ben a hearty handshake, and then left to buy some more potting soil. "Only not from Soils from Heaven," he joked. Mom, on the other hand, declared that we needed something sweet after all our running around and made sure Ben and I were loaded up with baked goods for the trip home.

"I made y'all some of Lucy's favorite cinnamon-pecan coffee cake cupcakes," she'd told us, handing me a bakery box that made Ben's eyes light up. "I've also put travel mugs in the car for you. Lucy, yours is Darjeeling tea, and Ben, yours is dark-roast coffee with a dollop of cream."

This earned my mom a second hug from both Ben and me, especially once he got a whiff of the heavenly scented mini coffee cakes, each topped with a swath of glaze and a single pecan half.

Once we were on the road, I took one out and peeled back the pleated cupcake liner halfway. "Oh, you're going to love this, Ben.

Mom makes the best sour cream coffee cake. It's got a cinnamon-butter swirl in the middle and just enough pecans, and they're absolutely scrumptious. She started making small ones in a muffin tin a few years ago, and I actually think they're better this way."

Ben was only too happy to taste test. He bit in and, casting me a stunned look, held up the rest of it like he'd discovered the pinnacle of coffee cakes and it deserved to be on a pedestal.

"*Oh my god,*" he said through his mouthful.

As I was about to select one for myself, I stopped, staring at him, as he brought his right arm down to bring the coffee cake back to his mouth. Why was that move familiar? I began thinking of everyone I'd spoken with yesterday.

Trent Marins? No.

Roxie or Patrice? Hmm, not them, either.

Had it been when I'd been listening in on Neil Gaynor's phone call? Nope.

I thought for a second that it might have been Tor Braithwaite, but that didn't seem right, either. I found myself mimicking Ben as if doing so would make the little snippet of film in my memory bank flow out into the short film I knew it was.

"What are you doing?" Ben asked with a grin, before taking another bite.

Rats; it simply wasn't coming. I shook my head.

"I saw someone doing that same move you just did, but I can't remember who."

"Do you think it's important?" Ben asked.

"I don't know. Possibly?"

"All right, then," he said. "Let's talk about other stuff while we let your subconscious try to spit it out." He finished the last bite, licked a bit of glaze off his thumb, and said, "We spent most of the drive back to your parents' house updating your grandfather on what was going on, so we haven't been able to go through everything we've both learned."

I nodded. This was true. After Ben had picked me up on the Howland University campus, I called Grandpa using FaceTime. I loved it that I could see my grandfather's smiling face as he sat in the little sunroom of his house in Wimberley, his blue eyes crinkling with impish excitement that he'd caught me in the throes of another adventure. After recounting my semi-disastrous attempts at interrogating my former coworkers and then my completely terrible attempt at searching Trent's office, I'd felt buoyed when Grandpa commended me on how I'd sold my confrontation with Trent. Seeing the proud and delighted look on my grandfather's face had made every second I'd spent at my former workplace worth it, let me tell you.

Grandpa had signed off just before Ben and I arrived at my parents' house, saying, "I'm off to the senior center, my darlin'. Some of the ladies are teaching me how to play mah-jongg." He sent me an exaggerated wink, adding, "And if I tell them the latest on my beautiful granddaughter, they usually forget to collect the money they've won from me . . ."

Now, as Ben and I cruised west on I-10, I peeled off the wrapper of a coffee cake muffin for myself and said, "Okay, you go first. While I was at the library, you went back to the cookie place to check out those two cars I saw. What did you find out?"

Flicking on his turn signal, Ben moved into the other lane to pass a slower vehicle. "After you told me how those two cars left in a hurry when you walked out to look at Camilla's painting, I realized it was strange they chose to flank my car when almost no one else was in the parking lot at all. Why did those two cars feel the need to park on either side of mine when there were at least fifteen other open spaces?"

I hadn't even thought about that. "And what did you find out?"

"Well, since I had the painting in the car and wasn't willing to leave it, even just to go into the restaurant and ask to see their security camera footage, I had to call in a favor from a local buddy. I doubt you'll ever meet him, though. He does hush-hush stuff." When he saw me perk up at this information, he laughed. "Your grandfather has been a bad influence on you."

"Heck yeah, he has," I said proudly.

"Anyway," Ben said, "my buddy went into the restaurant and asked to see the security footage. The two cars arrived within minutes of each other, but the guy in the gray BMW was just there to pick up a to-go order. He's a regular and the staff know him."

"And did you see the driver of the Suburban?"

Ben nodded. "Somewhat, at least. Looked to be an older white male. He was mostly hidden by the Suburban, but the camera caught him raising a slim jim with his back to his car, which meant he was facing my driver's side window. Then a passenger in the Suburban alerted him to your approach. In the footage, my buddy could just see the person's shadow, and he could tell the passenger warned the driver because of the driver's body language. The driver then hopped in and drove away, as you know. We think the passenger would have been the one to drive off in my car had the driver been able to open my door."

"Were you able to run a license plate?" I asked.

Ben shook his head. "The vehicle had paper plates. We're giving the footage to Dupart, but it looks like a dead end."

"Only partially," I corrected, licking glaze off my finger. "We already guessed that someone was after the pieces of the Braithwaite triptych, especially after a burner phone was used to send a fake text to Gareth Fishwick so that he would inadvertently steal Camilla's piece. Now we've all but proved that someone tried to break into your car to get to the painting. To me, that says there's a person who knows the value of the triptych and they're going to great lengths to find all three pieces." I paused, then said, "And even scarier, they were watching us as we took it from the house and followed us to the cookie place. I wonder if it was the same person who sent Gareth the fake text. Or maybe that person hired professional car thieves."

As I'd said this, Ben had been encouraging my thoughts, making a keep-going hand gesture that had his watch glinting when it hit the afternoon sunlight. I went to take a sip of my tea and stopped.

Ben had just set me up, hadn't he? By giving me information and then claiming it was a dead end, he'd encouraged me to think about what other facts we'd learned from it, and to put those facts into play within my mind.

It made me want to kiss him. You know, even more.

"And?" Ben prompted, making another encouraging wave with his hand. "What next?"

"And so now we have to think about who would be the most likely to know about the painting's importance."

"Which would be whom, in your estimation?"

"Someone in Camilla's family, or someone she worked with," I said automatically, but my eyes were on his watch as it glinted.

"Let's keep talking it out, then," Ben said. "Who would be your first guess?"

But instead of answering him, I reached out and grabbed his wrist. "Hot damn, my subconscious spit it out," I said. "I remember what I saw, and I have a wild hunch. I have to call Cisco."

Cisco picked up on the third ring, his friendly voice coming though my phone speaker so Ben could hear.

"Lucy, hi. Are you and Ben back in Austin yet?"

"We're on our way," I replied, "but I have another question for you."

"Hit me with it, then," Cisco said.

"Remember how your intern lost her key card? Do you know if your security people looked up the last time it was used before it was reported lost?"

Cisco's voice was curious as he said, "It's standard procedure, but they never mentioned it to me as being suspicious. Why?"

And I told him about how I got into the workroom at Morris Art Conservation without a key card. How there had been a woman with a cart opening the door, but when I looked up from my phone, she was rushing off. "I only saw her briefly and from a distance, but she was taller than me, in a lab coat, with graying blond hair pulled back into a bun. I'd say she was in her fifties at least."

"Huh," Cisco said. "That description doesn't fit anyone in conservation, but I kind of think it fits one of the docents in the second-floor museum. They only work part-time and I rarely deal with them, so I don't know any of them well. I don't know why this woman would be down in the workrooms, or wearing a lab coat, though."

I glanced at Ben. As smart as Cisco was, I didn't think he was putting the pieces together.

"Cisco, I think this woman might have stolen the intern's key card in order to try to steal the Braithwaite painting," I said.

Sure enough, this elicited a loud exclamation from him. "I'll need to talk to security. This is terrible."

Ben, though, had been looking thoughtful. "I wonder if Savannah Lundstrom noticed anything."

"Why? Did she mention something like that?" Cisco asked, his voice now sounding anxious through my phone's speaker.

"No," Ben replied, "but you said she'd arrived early for your interview and had been looking around the upstairs museum for a bit while she waited for you to give her a tour, right? She may have seen this docent doing something suspicious."

Cisco's voice was wry now. "Well, you're going to have to be the ones to ask her, because after I finished telling y'all what we'd found under the painting, I went upstairs for our interview and she'd left me a note telling me something had come up. I'm now supposed to contact the *Chronology* offices to reschedule our in-person interview as a phone call. I have a feeling that when she saw we had the triptych panel and there was something special about it, she decided there would be a bigger interest in a follow-up story on Charles Braithwaite than one on art conservation." Sounding glum, he said he'd get back to us on the name of the docent, and hung up.

Ben and I exchanged a glance. I said, "I mean, let's face it, Savannah could tell there was something up with the triptych painting. Do you think she really is on the hunt for another Braithwaite story?"

"That'd be my guess," Ben said, glowering as he watched the road. "Why don't you call the *Chronology* offices, ask for Savannah's editor, and see what you can find out?"

Deciding this was a good idea, I looked up the magazine's number online and made the call. The main receptionist listened to my request to speak with Savannah's editor, and said, "That would be Sal Ferrara. He's on vacation, but I'll put you through to his assistant, Danica."

She forwarded my call before I could even thank her, and a voice picked up almost instantly. "Sal Ferrara's office, Danica speaking, how may I help you?"

I introduced myself, keeping my tone easygoing and respectful. Unlike a lot of people, I knew never to be rude or dismissive to the boss's assistant, and my polite inquiries on what Savannah Lundstrom might be working on next earned me the reward of two tidbits of information.

"I don't know if she's planning a follow-up to the Braithwaite article," Danica said, "but since she pushed hard to have the first article published in March instead of May, when it was supposed to run, I kind of doubt Sal will be willing to shift things around again to accommodate her if she is writing a second story."

Why March? I thought, and I asked the question. "Do you know why she wanted the article to run in March, specifically?"

"Couldn't tell you, especially because she didn't tell me," Danica replied with disapproval in her voice. "But you can ask her yourself. You said you're in Austin, right? Well, she has a speaking engagement there tomorrow, before she comes back here to DC. I'm looking at her calendar. It's at the Hamilton American History Center, do you know where that is?"

"I do," I said with a smile.

"Great," Danica said. "It's for a lecture series titled 'History Then Happy Hour.' From three to five p.m. She goes on at three thirty. It's in the Brownsville Room."

I thanked her profusely, then hung up, though I barely had time to tell Ben what she'd said before I got a text from Cisco.

"Cisco says that security is backed up because they're expecting some high-profile dignitaries for the opening of a new exhibit tomorrow," I said. "He'll get back to us as soon as he can."

To me, this was frustrating. It would be so simple to check into the whereabouts of their docents earlier today and why one of them had stolen—presumably stolen, at least—a key card. To Ben, however, the delay was nothing new or unusual. Perhaps sensing my annoyance, he took my hand and we drove on, talking of other things. Then a work call came in, which he'd warned me to expect. I pulled my noise-canceling headphones and iPad from my tote bag, put the headphones on, and used the time to resume my look into Charles Braithwaite's war records.

Since I didn't yet know which Braithwaite descendant owned the third piece of the triptych and I couldn't figure out who was after the pieces themselves, I was determined to find something—anything—that would prove definitive regarding Charles's Civil War service. Good or bad, I didn't care. I just wanted to feel that something about this project was going right.

THIRTY-FOUR

T hink you've put on enough layers?" Ben teased as I pulled the zipper of my fleece-lined yellow jacket up to my neck. It covered a sweatshirt that was itself over a long-sleeved T-shirt.

"I don't understand you people who like the cold," I grumbled, shivering, as I fit the key into the gate that would take us from the back of my condo complex to Little Stacy Park.

On a whim, we'd decided some fresh morning air would be good after so many hours, utterly enjoyable as they were, holed up in my condo. We'd been so ensconced in our own little romantic world last night that we hadn't even noticed it had rained and a minor cold front had come through. Our glimpses of warm spring weather now seemed like a memory, as the temperature dropped to fifty degrees and the wind chill made it feel even colder. As the stiff breeze blew my ponytail into my face and made my eyes water, I somewhat regretted agreeing to this venture—even more so because it was only seven o'clock in the morning.

For Ben's part, his only concession to the weather was a half-zipped running vest over his T-shirt and shorts, and I was pretty sure he wore the vest to hide his service weapon rather than to keep out the cold.

"I think I'm with the majority in saying the temperature's perfect for a run," he said, gesturing toward the number of joggers already out and seemingly enjoying the cold, most of them wearing nothing heavier than a fleece jacket.

It's hard to pull off lifting your chin defiantly and holding your gloved hands over your ears to warm them at the same time, but I managed it. "I should have brought my beanie," I added for a touch of extra dramatics.

Ben tugged on my ponytail with a grin. "Let's get going, then. Work could call at any minute, and I'm hoping we can get in our run and a trip to Flaco's for breakfast before I have to go in."

The idea of breakfast got me going, and a few strides later, we were settled into a nice pace. The rising sun was already brilliant, sending beams through the trees and then making me squint and wish I'd brought my sunglasses when we ran through an open stretch, the grass glistening with last night's rain. We talked about meeting up with Camilla yesterday afternoon at Helen Kim Art Restoration. There, Camilla had gotten her first true look at the gorgeous battle scene her ancestor had painted in 1866, which had been covered up for an untold number of decades. As we all gazed at it, Helen had explained what restoration processes would need to be undertaken, all of them minimal.

"I don't know that I've ever seen Camilla smile like that in all the time I've known her," I told Ben as we jogged. I recalled Camilla even looking somewhat misty by the time it was all over, and I heard her tell Helen that she wished her uncle Charlie could have seen it, which made me a bit misty, too.

"I think anyone would be moved by that painting, but Camilla's reaction was a great one, no doubt," he agreed. "I have to admit, I'm still amazed by the fact that so little restoration needs to be done, and also really relieved that Helen has the ability to store the painting safely and properly while she works on it."

Helen had showed us the temperature-controlled walk-in vault where Camilla's piece of the triptych would be stored at night. She also explained her shop's extensive security system and introduced us to the security guard who would be watching the place overnight. The guard—polite, well-muscled, and a former member of the special forces—promised to be extra vigilant until the painting's restoration was completed.

"Helen is so excited about working on the painting," I told Ben earnestly as we jogged. "And being hired by Camilla will also help dispel any issues with any clients as to her being questioned about Charlie Braithwaite's murder. Speaking of, I'm sure you and Dupart talked over more details about the case last night . . ."

After waiting several long seconds, I began casting blatantly expectant looks at Ben every few strides. When he remained silent, I finally huffed, "Okay, now this is not fair. You got an update on Charlie Braithwaite's murder from Dupart last night, and you haven't spilled the details. And I was being super obvious that I wanted the latest, too. What gives?"

Ben turned around, jogging backward for a few steps and giving me a wink. "As for last night, I got distracted—and I think you remember why, Ms. Lancaster." Turning back around, he said, "Plus, you never told me what you uncovered in your research yesterday, either."

"Fine, we distracted each other," I said, trying and failing to keep a straight face as he laughed. "But tell me what Dupart said. You know it's not cool that you have access to this information and Dupart would laugh and hang up on me if I tried to get it."

Ben looked highly amused at this, and I had a feeling it was a pretty funny scenario in his mind. When I reached out and playfully smacked his arm, he laughed. "Okay, okay," he said. However, a second later, he was slowing to a walk, pulling his lit-up phone from the pocket of his vest. He answered, "Turner," listened for a second, then put his hand over the speaker. "Give me five minutes?"

I nodded, indicating that I'd run down the path, then back to him.

After checking my phone for the time, I zipped it into my jacket pocket and moved off, finding my stride again and finally enjoying the cold air on my face since I'd warmed up a bit, even though I continually had to squint from both the brisk wind and the bright, rising sun.

A woman with a stroller ran past me the opposite way, followed by a guy running with a pretty German shorthaired pointer. As I rounded a bend, I thought about how Gran and Grandpa had owned German shorthairs when I was growing up. Seeing one always brought up lovely memories of my sister and me visiting our grandparents.

As I came upon a huge oak tree, I was still happily musing on how that dog had looked like Grandpa's favorite named Belle Starr when, out of nowhere, two hands reached out and shoved my shoulder, hard, sending me twisting and flying sideways. The world was a transitory blur, and then I was facedown in a sprawling heap on the soft, wet ground.

For a second, I was too stunned and out of breath to move. Then, gingerly, I turned onto my side, doing a mental check of my body.

The rain-soaked earth, thankfully, had made my fall a softer one, though I could feel a burning on my cheek. I'd scraped it on the fist-sized rock protruding from the ground. Touching the scrape with the back of my hand, there wasn't any blood, so I hadn't hurt myself in any significant way. When I looked up, I shivered, but not from the cold. I'd missed the tree trunk by mere inches. Had it not been for chance or physics or a combination of both, I might be unconscious—or with a broken nose, at the very least—from a forced face-plant into the tree.

With a grunt, I rose to my feet, looking around for my assailant. There wasn't a single person anywhere near me. In the distance, I could see two college-age girls walking toward me from the direction I'd just come, talking animatedly to one another, but that was it. Soon they were passing me, too absorbed in themselves to give me a second look.

The ground being more wet than actually muddy, and my jacket being water- and dirt-repelling, I mostly had to brush off damp leaves. Equally fuming and frightened, I pulled my phone from one pocket and, from the other, my set of keys, which also held a whistle and a tiny canister of pepper spray. Threading the keys through my fingers, I began walking stiffly back toward Ben, eyes darting everywhere, looking for who might have pushed me.

Think, Lucy, I told myself. *What did you see or hear?*

I racked my brain to recall any snippet. My eyes had been half closed against the sun and wind, and my mind had been on memories of Grandpa's favorite hunting dog. The pounding of my feet on the ground, the sound of the wind, and the rustle of my jacket had dampened any approaching footsteps. Really, I'd glimpsed nothing but a flash of running shoes and black running tights. I had a vague recollection of arms clad in black running gear as well.

A runner sped by me on the path and I jumped, then stared after him, my senses heightened as I looked around for more danger. The runner had been dressed in all black, including black running tights. Turning around, I looked back to the girls who'd passed by without noticing me—they were both wearing all-black gear as well. It was a pretty common look, and one that would allow my assailant to simply blend in with half the other runners out here.

"*Dang it,*" I whispered with heat, then I started again as my phone rang. It was Ben.

"That was work," he said. "I have to go in, and, ah, they need me there in thirty. Have you already turned around?"

"I have," I said, making my voice sound calm and unconcerned. I really wanted to run to him and have him wrap his arms around me, but I couldn't keep him from his work when I was just fine. "I'm not far, and I've got my pepper spray, just in case. I'll be all right. You go ahead."

"Good thing you gave me your extra set of keys," he said. "But while I'm heading back, want to hear what Dupart said?"

A wash of relief came over me that he would stay on the phone with me as I walked back home. "Yes, spill it," I said. Hearing someone coming up behind me, I whipped around, but it was just two elderly ladies walking together, hand weights in each hand. They met my eyes and smiled. I returned their smiles weakly.

"Whoever did this was really careful," Ben began. "They wore gloves and protective booties on their shoes, like crime scene techs do. However, there's evidence that there were two people in the house at the time of Charlie's murder, not just one."

I was coming up on a stretch where there were multiple people around, which made me feel a little safer. "Well, one must have been Elaine Trudeau, right?"

"Nope. She admitted to being in Charlie's house to check on him, just after she got a call from a friend who works for one of the airlines. She was able to get a last-minute seat on a flight to go see her grandkids in California. She said she nearly just called Charlie on her way to the airport, but decided instead to stop in for a proper goodbye at the last second."

"That must have been why the doorbell camera caught her driving out of Charlie's driveway," I mused.

"That's what she told Dupart. She evidently pulled out of her driveway, then backed into Charlie's when she changed her mind. She said she spent a few minutes with Charlie, answered the door to find Helen, turned Helen away immediately, and then took off for the airport. Security footage at the airport's long-term parking lot shows her arriving right within the most likely time frame that Charlie was killed."

"Okay, then how do they know there were two people in Charlie's house?" I asked.

"Evidently, in his struggle, Charlie scratched one of them. Not enough to draw blood, but enough that there were skin cells under his fingernails."

For a brief second, I closed my eyes, feeling heartsick for Charlie. "And the other evidence?" I asked.

I could hear Ben jogging up my steps to my condo. "One of them bumped into the corner of the doorframe in Charlie's office. Likely whenever they were taking the painting out. Again, it wasn't enough to do much, but there was a tiny speck of blood and some skin cells, and they didn't match the first set of cells. However . . ."

He stopped, and in the background I heard a voice say, "Mornin', Ben. How's our Lucy today?"

"Good morning, Jackson," Ben called out to my condo manager. "I have to go into work, but Lucy is on her way back from the park. I'm on the phone with her now." Then, to me, he said, "What's your ETA?"

The adrenaline was draining away now, leaving me colder than ever, but I kept my voice strong. "Less than five minutes, I think."

Ben relayed this to Jackson, who said, "I'll keep an eye out for her."

Through the phone, I heard Ben unlocking my door. I stepped up my pace, looking around me while I listened to Ben explain that one of Charlie's neighbors said they noticed a car pulling into Elaine's driveway sometime after seven p.m. But the neighbor couldn't remember a thing about the car and noticed Elaine's driveway was empty not long later, so they didn't think it was suspicious at all. "And Elaine doesn't have any cameras at her house and no other neighbor saw a car pull in or out of her driveway."

"Damn," I said. "Was there something else you meant to tell me about the skin cells?"

"Oh, nearly forgot," Ben said. He'd put me on speaker phone to change his clothes and I heard him unzip his running vest. "Dupart's people used a forensic method called FDS. Have you heard of it?"

I had heard of it, actually. "It stands for familial DNA searching, right? I read an article a few months ago about how it's used to help with cold cases, among other things."

"Correct," Ben said. "Not all states use FDS, but Texas is one that does. Anyway, a match on some level was found in the DNA from the two sets of skin cells. There's a high probability the two people who were in Charlie's house are related."

Jackson and NPH were both waiting for me at the gate, and as I walked up, NPH trotted to me, then pounced on my feet, batting at my ankles for a split second before racing off with his tail held high and springing up onto the nearest tree. In a trice, he was sitting on one of the lower branches, tail swishing, eyes already on a bird fluttering away.

"Lucy, my God, what happened to you, darlin'?"

Jackson's Mississippi drawl, always a charming sound, nevertheless deepened when he was stressed, making it sound like "mah *gawd*." In his usual cashmere sweater, jeans, and driving moccasins, he ran a hand agitatedly through his thick auburn hair as he covered the distance to me.

"Someone shoved me, nearly into a tree," I replied, explaining what happened. Jackson fussed over me all the way back up to my condo, insisting on coming in with me to make sure it was safe.

"Ben was just here two minutes ago," I said, unlocking my door and pushing it open with more force than was necessary. I was angry now at what had happened. Angry that someone had had the nerve to do that to me, and even angrier that I hadn't been observant enough to get any tiny shred of a hint as to who they were. I recalled Ben telling me last year that details would come back to me, but in this case, I wasn't so sure.

"Be that as it may, sugar, I'm coming in and making sure all your locks are working." Jackson breezed past me, and after a quick thunderous sound that heralded NPH following us up the stairs, he streaked in after Jackson. I, however, was frozen on the spot.

"Jackson," I said, shutting my front door. "Are you wearing a new cologne?" He'd always favored a sandalwood-based men's fragrance, and it smelled heavenly on him. Today, however, it was lighter, more flowery.

He was checking the French doors that opened onto my balcony, and replied with amused exasperation. "Oh, that. My niece and I went shopping yesterday and she made me help her find a new scent." He gave the neck of his aqua-hued cashmere sweater a tug. "I wore this sweater, not realizing until I got home how much I smelled like I'd been bathing in perfume. I decided I'd better wear it again today to let it air out some."

"What perfume is it?" I asked.

He told me the brand, which was a very famous and popular one. "It's their hot new scent, called Magnolia and Red Plum, or something like that. Why? Do you like it?"

"Not really," I answered. "But the person who pushed me does."

Jackson stared at me for a full two seconds before clearing his throat loudly.

"Lucy, darlin', you know being kept in suspense isn't a good look for me. For the love of God, who was it?"

"My client and former coworker," I told him. "Camilla Braithwaite."

THIRTY-FIVE

"Camilla, good morning," I said, gesturing to the booth seat across from me in the far back corner of Big Flaco's Tacos. "Thank you for coming so quickly. I ordered you some coffee, but Ana should be back around any second to take your order."

Camilla sat down, her jaw set in irritation, no doubt at my insistence that she stop what she was doing and come meet me, pronto—and especially because I'd refused to tell her why. Over her shoulder, in the next booth, Josephine grinned at me from under the baseball cap covering her dark curls. She gave me a thumbs-up. Serena, whom Camilla had never seen before, didn't need to be incognito, and sat calmly sipping her coffee. I could see only the back of her blond head, but noted that she'd shifted so as to better listen in on our conversation.

Yeah, I wasn't going to confront Camilla alone, even in a place as safe for me as Flaco's. I wanted witnesses. Jackson had offered to come with me to the taqueria after I'd explained that Camilla had worn that flowery scent with a hint of something fruity underneath when she'd appeared at Flaco's last Saturday and then hired me. She'd also been wearing it when we went to the Harry Alden Texas History Museum, though it had been much more subtle then. In the end, though, we'd decided that Jackson should stay alert for anything strange happening at my condo complex and I would call upon my best friends to meet me at Flaco's to witness my takedown of my former coworker.

Flaco and Ana were in on what was happening, and would be on the alert for Camilla attempting to run out or, worse, do something silly. Flaco's dark eyes had flashed when he heard someone had tried to hurt me, and he'd muttered something menacing-sounding in Spanish.

After Josephine, Ana, and I nodded our heads in stern agreement, Serena had put one hand on her hip and said, "Um, hello? We've been through this before. Y'all know I don't speak Spanish. Is someone going to translate for me?"

"In essentials?" Jo said. "Woe betide anyone who tries to hurt his Lucia, or tries any shenanigans in his taqueria."

Then Flaco had to ask what the term "shenanigans" meant, and our whole tough-sounding vibe went to hell in a handbag as we all defined it a little differently. Finally, Flaco shooed us away with a flick of his kitchen towel, though his mustache was twitching as he encompassed all of us in an indulgent *"Ay, chiflada,"* before going back into his kitchen.

Camilla had walked in ten minutes later, however, and any lightheartedness disappeared. Especially when I saw what she was wearing.

"I don't care for it that you summoned me here, Lucy," she said, pulling her steaming mug of coffee toward her and adding a packet of sugar. "Nor do I care for your tone when you did so." She picked up the plastic spoon that was on a paper napkin by her coffee, along with a plastic fork. "Why do I have plastic silverware and you don't?"

Ana arrived at that moment, giving Camilla a falsely warm smile. "Our dishwasher broke. My apologies, miss. May I take your order?"

Camilla began stirring her coffee with an unimpressed expression. "Two bacon-and-egg tacos. I'd like the bacon extra crispy."

Ana waited for a "please." When it didn't come, she wrote the order, her expression turning frosty. "And you, Lucia?"

I smiled. "I'll do the same, please. *Muchas gracias*, Ana."

I was graced with one of her sassy winks as she tucked her pen behind her ear. *"De nada, chiquita."* Unbeknownst to Camilla, Ana gave her a brief, hard stare before walking by Josephine, who held out her hand for a quiet high-five as Ana breezed past.

"So?" Camilla said. "Why did you call me? And what happened to your face?"

Though it hadn't bled, per se, the nearly two-inch-long area where my cheek had grazed the rock was now red, smarting, and streaked with small scrapes. Nothing I did made it look better, either. Even the outfit I'd chosen in anticipation of Savannah Lundstrom's event this afternoon—a pair of crisp navy trousers, heels, and a pretty blouse the color of a robin's egg that made my eyes bluer—hadn't taken away from the slightly swollen look of my cheek.

I stirred cream into my own coffee, feeling my anger rising like the steam, but my voice was ice cold. "That's what happens when you shove someone down, Camilla. Only, I'm sorry I didn't hit the tree like you intended. Instead, I went down in the dirt." I pointed to my cheek, "But there was this one rock that still caught me, so bully for you."

Camilla had taken a sip from her mug, and I saw her clear brown eyes widen with confusion as I spoke. Now she was choking on her coffee, covering her mouth with her napkins.

"What are you talking about?" she sputtered.

I leaned across the table, my voice bristling with anger. "I know it was you who pushed me this morning at Little Stacy Park, Camilla. I could smell your perfume. Before I report you to the police, I just want to know why you did it, and if you planned it in advance. Or was it just happenstance, and you took your chance when you saw me running alone?"

My former coworker stared at me, napkins clutched tightly in one hand. I kept going.

"I also found out, as I'm sure you know, that there were two people in Charlie's house the night he died. Two people who were related, as evidenced by a DNA match. Were you one of them? Did you kill your great-uncle, Camilla?"

Now the color was draining from her face. I'd never seen her so pale, and it almost frightened me.

"How can you say such things?" she whispered. "I loved Uncle Charlie. Why are you being so horrible? Is this some sort of payback for the fact that you never got along with Roxie, Patrice, and me? God, Lucy, do you really hate me that much?"

Now I was stunned. "Excuse me? *I* didn't get along with *y'all*?" Then I stopped abruptly, shaking my head. She was trying to direct the conversation away from what mattered. "No, that's not what this is about, Camilla."

"Then what is it about?" she asked, her color beginning to rise again. "Because I don't know what the hell you mean, Lucy."

Her voice had risen, too, and I looked around to see a few patrons watching us. This issue was quickly quelled by Ana and two of the other waitresses, who bustled around, checking on the diners and drawing their attention away from us. I noticed Flaco had also turned up the music that was coming through the loudspeakers, which was apparently Julio Iglesias's greatest hits. Suddenly, "To All the Girls I've Loved Before," Julio's duet with Willie Nelson, was in my ears. Flaco had actually started singing in his kitchen, though with one eye firmly on Camilla and me in the back booth.

Camilla, though, was too angry to notice any of it.

"Are you going to answer me? Why the hell are you accusing

me of pushing you? For heaven's sake, I don't even know where Little Stacy Park is." She plunged her spoon in her coffee again, then cursed as some of it splattered out onto her hand. Her eyes were fiery as she snatched more napkins from the dispenser. Then she thrust out her wrist. "And I'm not even wearing perfume today, either."

This stopped me for a moment. I hadn't been able to smell the perfume on Camilla like I had this morning—but I reasoned this was because it had worn off as she'd run.

"Yeah?" I said anyway, still angry enough that backing down wasn't a clear option yet. "Then explain your outfit to me, because the person who tried shoving me into a tree was wearing both the perfume you wear and an all-black outfit. You have clearly been exercising. Explain *that*, Camilla." I gestured toward her face, which, having regained some of its color again, had a healthy glow and was free of makeup, making the smattering of freckles across the bridge of her nose stand out. Her reddish-brown hair was up in a ponytail, the finer hairs around her face having come loose in the windy morning.

Now Camilla was looking at me like I was certifiable. "Of course I've been exercising. I've just come from running at the park by Uncle Charlie's house with my friend Sarah. Then you called me, got all"—she made her voice sound prissy and demanding—"'Camilla, you need to meet me *now*,' and I got in my car and came."

Over Camilla's shoulder, I could just see Josephine's look of scandalized shock at the way Camilla had imitated me.

"Can you verify that?" I said.

"Are you kidding me?" she returned.

"No, I'm not kidding," I snapped. I leaned forward again. "Camilla, I talked to you yesterday and confirmed that there were three—*three*—separate times where someone attempted to steal your piece of the triptych. The first time through spoofing your phone number and texting your ex-husband to take it from your house. The second, by trying to break into Ben's car." I swung my arm up in irritation. "And the third, by audaciously attempting to take the painting from the freaking Morris Art Conservation building in broad daylight."

A lock of hair had dropped onto my face, touching the scrape on my cheek and making it smart. Hastily brushing the hair away, I added, "And then this morning, with my FBI boyfriend only a couple of minutes down the path from me, someone shoves me down so hard that I was nearly slammed into a tree. So you'd better believe I'm not kidding when I say I want you to verify where you were."

Once more I made an emphatic gesture with my hand, though I lowered my voice. "And this doesn't even include the fact that your poor, sweet uncle Charlie—someone who was so kind to me during a not-great night in my life—was murdered three nights ago. He's dead, Camilla, and it's because of something to do with that triptych. And now *my* life has been put in danger, too. So if you weren't responsible for what happened today, I want proof."

Camilla, who'd been looking outraged, had paled again when I spoke of her uncle Charlie, tears filling her eyes. Without speaking, she found her phone and pulled up some text messages, then handed it to me.

They were between Camilla and her friend named Sarah from this morning. Camilla wrote of just needing to get out, because planning her uncle's funeral, and living in his house while doing so, had been emotionally horrible. Sarah immediately offered to meet her at the park by Charlie's house. Camilla took the phone back from me and pulled up an Instagram account for her friend, who had posted a photo less than an hour ago. The two were standing on a little footbridge I knew to be in that park. Sarah's arms were around Camilla's shoulders in a comforting hug, and

Camilla was in the exact same outfit she wore now, with no makeup and tendrils of her hair already escaping her ponytail. In the caption, Sarah wrote of seeing her friend and how strong Camilla was staying with what she was going through. She'd tagged Camilla's account.

"Satisfied?" Camilla said, her voice tight. She'd been dabbing at her eyes the whole time, and they were still welling up. Hers were no crocodile tears.

I nodded, handing back her phone. "I apologize for accusing you," I said, "though I hope you can see how I came to the conclusion I did."

I felt like Camilla was going to snap back at me and tell me what an awful person I'd been, but instead, she nodded, albeit a bit stiffly. Glancing toward the scrape on my face, she said, "I'm sorry someone did that to you because of me." I saw her swallow. "I never should have hired you for this, Lucy. Ever since Uncle Charlie announced he was willing his piece of the triptych to me, I've had a bad feeling, like I knew something was going to happen. I just expected it to be some relative who would come out of the woodwork and challenge me for rights to the panel, though." She gestured toward my face, then made a sweeping motion as if to encompass the last few days. "I never dreamed of anything like what's been happening."

But I was staring at her. "I'm sorry—what did you say? Charlie *announced* that he was willing it to you?"

Camilla frowned. "He told you, that day in his office. You knew he'd willed it to me."

"Yes," I said, "but neither of you said anything about announcing it. Did he put out a press release or something?"

For the first time since she walked in, her expression lightened. "No, nothing like that. He just sent out emails to various members of our family, informing them of his decision so it would be official. The emails were sent to those in his line and mine, but he requested that the email be forwarded if anyone had connections with the third branch descending from Charles's daughter, Henrietta. No one in his line has wanted the painting, including his actual nieces and nephews."

I leaned forward on the table, the smarting irritation on my cheek nearly forgotten.

"Camilla, do you know if he received any responses to those emails? And was this before or after he discovered the painting underneath?"

"Uncle Charlie told me that nearly every cousin replied," she said. "As for the timing, this all happened last June, so nearly, what, nine months before the incident with the toddler that caused the hole in the canvas."

Briefly, I wondered if one of the descendants in Charlie's line would contest his will once they realized what was under the top painting. Then I course-corrected my thoughts, deciding that wasn't something I needed to be worrying about.

"Dang it, Charlie's laptop was stolen, though, wasn't it?" I said. "So we can't get a look at the emails." I tapped my fingers on my coffee cup, thinking out loud. "I wonder if Ben could convince Dupart to hack Charlie's email account."

"There's no need," Camilla said. "Uncle Charlie printed the emails out."

I goggled at her. "Are you serious? Do you know where they are? Will you show them to me?"

Camilla nodded. "I found them yesterday. They were in that box of letterhead, underneath a few blank sheets. I only found them when I went to print some letters on Uncle Charlie's official stationery to send to his wine distributor contacts."

"That's probably why the police didn't notice," I mused. "And why the box wasn't rifled through by the killers, because they thought it was merely blank letterhead." Picking up my coffee, I said, "Can we go get them after breakfast?"

Next to me on my seat, my phone pinged and I looked down at it. Serena, who'd been listening, had sent me a text.

You're not going anywhere with her without one of us.
Just in case.

I felt a warming knowledge that my friends had my back and sent back a heart emoji, even as Camilla asked, "Why? Do you think they might be important?"

"Yes, I do," I said. "This morning when Ben told me there were two possibly related people in Charlie's house the night he was murdered, it confirmed something that's been going around in my brain."

"Which is?"

"Which is, whoever murdered Charlie, they're also related to you."

THIRTY-SIX

※

Once Ana had brought our breakfast tacos with a smile and extra-crispy bacon for both of us—easing up on Camilla once she'd seen that I was no longer acting like my client was the enemy—Camilla and I had eaten, and began to both feel and act like normal humans again. Later, when Serena and Josephine popped up from the booth next to us, Camilla had taken it with relatively good grace that I'd brought friends along for backup.

"I guess I would have done the same thing," she said, and wisely didn't question it when Serena said she was coming with me to Charlie's house.

As promised, once we arrived Camilla gave me the letterhead box, which contained a sheaf of printed-out emails totaling about sixty-five pages in all, each with the subject line *Charles Braithwaite Triptych*.

"Were there any names you recognized as being from the Braithwaite line that descended from Charles's daughter?"

"No, unfortunately not," she said. "Plus, some of them only signed their emails with their first names, and their email addresses are vague." She lifted the box top, rifled through a few sheets, and pulled one out. "Like this one. It's from a cousin

I've never met who signed his name as Arthur, but his email is 'ironmanrunner9191'—there's nothing else that gives away his last name."

"Darn it," I said. "I'll take a look anyway, though."

We walked back through the living room, where Serena was waiting for us. Seeing me, she pointed to the photo of the smiling, windswept woman on a Paris sidewalk that I'd seen the first time I visited. "With her long, dark hair, she kind of reminds me of you, Luce."

"I like that one, too," I said, running my finger along the edge of the frame. I looked around the room, marveling once more at the beautiful collage made by Charlie's black-and-white photos. "They're amazing, aren't they?"

Serena's reply was to gasp, "Oh, I *love* this one." The writing said *Spanish Steps, Rome, 1980*. Charlie had taken a photo of a model in a ball gown ascending the famous steps as she was being photographed by a professional photographer.

"What will you do with them all?" I asked Camilla.

"I haven't decided," she said. "I found Charlie's will, and assuming he didn't change it recently, he left a few of them to family members, including Tor, my aunt Jensen, and me." She pulled a face. "And four go to Elaine. As for the rest, I'm thinking of doing a showing, and maybe auctioning some off for charity." She smiled at Serena. "I might be open to selling others, too."

"I think Charlie would approve of your ideas," I said. "And since you mentioned Elaine, have you spoken with her?"

Camilla shook her head vehemently. "She's called me twice and left me messages to call her, but I'm not interested."

After seeing how Elaine had treated Camilla, I couldn't very well blame her.

A few minutes later, Serena and I were walking out the front door. Seeing a patch of Charlie's garden, I asked, "Camilla, have you received an email from Soils from Heaven?"

"Not an official one, no, but Trent called and told me about the elevated arsenic in Charlie's bags of soil," Camilla replied with a sour look. "I told him he got lucky. I won't be suing his company."

"Not that I would have encouraged you to sue, but why aren't you?" I asked.

Camilla looked back into the living room, at Charlie's beloved photos. Her eyes were emotion-filled again, but she held herself together. "Honestly, beyond the fact that Uncle Charlie's doctor couldn't say for sure that the arsenic issues would have killed him, I just don't think Uncle Charlie would have wanted me to." Her expression hardened. "Still, I'm spitting mad at Trent for not telling me as soon as he found out. He felt so bad, he's coming up here himself tomorrow to pick up the rest of the bags of soil and dispose of them. I told him he'd better send someone to do the same for Aunt Jensen, too."

"Good for you," I said.

"Speaking of," Camilla said, "I spoke to Aunt Jensen a little while ago, too. She said your mother took her to the doctor and a course of treatment has been mapped out for her. She's going to be fine, and I'm grateful to your mom for being such a good friend to her."

I explained about her great-aunt and my mom being the team to beat in their bridge games, which made Camilla laugh. As Serena and I were about to walk down the porch steps, I said I would let her know what I found from the emails, and then reminded her I was going to the Hamilton Center later today to talk to Savannah Lundstrom. I'd mentioned it to her yesterday at Helen's studio, but the excitement of looking at the beautiful painting again had quickly overshadowed everything else. Now, however, Camilla's eyes sparked with irritation.

"If she's planning on writing about my ancestor's paintings

in order to make more false accusations about my family . . . oooh, I just don't know what I'll do!"

"Let me find out what her plans are before you let it stress you out any further," I said as I started down the steps. Then I turned back. "Camilla? Are you doing all right after everything that happened with your uncle Charlie?" With my free hand, I gestured inside the house and the general feel of loss that was permeating it. "Are you okay staying here and everything?"

She nodded, the fire in her eyes petering out. "It's tough, but yeah, I'm doing okay. My friend Sarah is going to come over tonight for some wine and to help me do some more cleaning, so that will help."

I nodded. "You can call me, too, if you're ever not okay," I said.

She hesitated, then said, "Thanks, Lucy. I appreciate that," before closing the front door.

Back at my office, I made copies of all the email responses Charlie received from his relatives, then returned the originals to the box. Technically, I knew I should give the emails to Detective Dupart, but first I was going to give myself a few hours to see what I could get out of them. I wanted to construct a more detailed family tree descending from Charles Braithwaite and his wife, Violet, on down to as far as I could go. After that, the emails would be all Dupart's, if he wanted them.

First, I pulled out the family group sheets I'd begun creating for the three main branches of the Braithwaite clan, which allowed me to keep track of the members inside each specific family within a branch, along with such information as birth dates, marriages, death dates, and other notes. As I learned from the *Chronology* article and confirmed through my own research, Charles's three children had been, in order, Nathaniel, Edward, and Henrietta. Because even I could get confused sometimes in such an extended family tree, I also found my notepad on which I'd scribbled some quick-reference notes on who descended from which child of Charles and Violet Braithwaite:

Charlie Braithwaite descended from eldest son, Nathaniel.

Camilla, Tor, and Jensen Hocknell descend from second son, Edward.

TBD: descendants of third child and only daughter, Henrietta.

During my research thus far—mostly done during Ben's and my drive back to Austin yesterday—I'd quickly had a stroke of luck when I went on one of my favorite genealogy sites. I'd found that another descendant of Nathaniel Braithwaite, who posted her family tree under the screen name MargaretB213, had done a lot of the work for me on her branch, including source citations and other proof documents. MargaretB213 had also done enough research on the branch descending from Edward to give me a lovely head start.

When it came to Henrietta's branch, though, information had been thin. MargaretB213's family tree had shown that Henrietta had married one Ezra Jepsen in 1889 at the age of twenty and had one daughter with him before he died of typhoid fever. In 1892, a widowed Henrietta met and married a man named Olney Smith. There was a notation that Henrietta had five more children with Olney Smith, but no names or other dates were listed.

The one thing I did know, courtesy of Mrs. Hocknell, was that one of her distant cousins who went by his surname, Smith, had been the last known owner of the third piece of the triptych. This meant that I needed to focus on finding the descendants of Henrietta Braithwaite and Olney Smith.

However, given that "Smith" is the most common last name in the United States, I had to be extra careful in confirming that I had the *right* descendants. Needless to say, researching them had eaten up the bulk of yesterday's drive home. By the time Ben and I pulled into the loading dock at Helen Kim Art Restoration to unload Camilla's piece of the triptych, I'd made a bit of headway into Charles Braithwaite's war records. However, I hadn't come much further in tracing his daughter Henrietta's line than finding the names of her five children with Olney Smith—three girls and two boys, all born between 1893 and 1903.

Now, as the morning sun rose higher in the sky, shining through our office windows, I had narrowed the field somewhat by finding the spouses of the five Smith children, but ran into issues after finding out the surname Smith had quickly died out. This was because Henrietta's two sons, Roger Smith and Frank Smith—one of whom was the descendant who inherited the third piece of the triptych—both had multiple children, but they were all girls. That meant the surnames in Henrietta's line all changed each time a daughter or granddaughter married.

I kept working, running search after search, hoping one or more of the names—or partial names, as the case often was—from the email replies Charlie had received would match up with a descendant of Henrietta Braithwaite Smith. Then, at exactly high noon, and as if announcing a showdown, my phone rang.

"Detective Dupart," I said, my voice the epitome of respectful politeness. "How are you today?"

"Ms. Lancaster," he said dryly. "I just got off the phone with Ms. Braithwaite, telling her she is free to return to Houston at any point. She told me that she has decided to stay a few more days to finalize plans with her great-uncle's estate. However, she then mentioned a few interesting tidbits to me."

"Oh?" I said.

"Yes. Something about arsenic in potting soil, and the fact

that you took some papers from Charlie Braithwaite's house."
His voice grew weary. "Now, I'm aware I asked you through
Agent Turner to help me in researching the third branch of the
Braithwaite family—"

"And thank you for that," I interjected. "I'm honored, and
I'm working on it right now."

Dupart merely paused, then continued. "Agent Turner has also
kept me apprised of your little jaunt down to Houston and how
Camilla's piece of the triptych is now here, in Austin, being restored. I've allowed this interference into my investigation because I trust Agent Turner and I know he'd handle things to the
letter if anything untoward took place. He did not, however,
mention any arsenic in any soil. Care to explain?" Now he modeled my polite tone. "And please do remember to add in the part
about the papers you took."

I did explain, all the way to the part where I gave Trent seventy-
two hours to contact his customers.

"As for the papers," I said, "I was going to turn them over to
you right after I spent some time looking into Camilla's family
tree. Specifically into the third branch of her family tree. And
I'm guessing it would be safe to say you agree with me that due
to the interest in the triptych painting—and 'interest' is putting
it lightly—there's a high likelihood the two people who killed
Charlie Braithwaite are from that third branch."

There was silence for several seconds, then Dupart said, "I'll
give you twenty-four hours to see what you can come up with,
Ms. Lancaster, but you are not allowed to contact any of the indi-
viduals Mr. Braithwaite emailed. Not in any way. Understood?
That would be our job, if needed."

"Understood," I said.

"In the meantime, make copies of those papers you took from
Ms. Braithwaite and have the originals ready for an officer to pick
up in a half hour."

I smiled. "You can send an officer now, Detective. I'm already one step ahead of you."

After we hung up, I began sorting my copies of the emails into four piles, one each for the descendants of Nathaniel, Edward, and Henrietta, plus a fourth pile of those who it wasn't immediately obvious to which branch they belonged.

Not surprisingly, the pile for Henrietta's descendants was the smallest. In fact, it was only one piece of paper. The emailer—whose name was Ephraim—had expressly identified himself as a descendant of Henrietta. Sadly, Ephraim did not know the location of the third piece of the triptych. Nor did he seem to care, either, as he'd written, *Ugliest thing I ever saw. Good riddance to it.*

Twenty minutes later, one of Dupart's officers arrived and I handed off the originals. By that time, I'd read through a good portion of the responses, as well as researched a few of the names from the "uncertain" pile and filed them under the right descendant. By the time one o'clock hit, Serena and Josephine insisted I go to lunch. Twirling a strand of hair around my finger, I tried to say I wasn't hungry because of our late breakfast at Flaco's, but that didn't work with my best friends.

"I always know when you're getting hungry because you start playing with your hair," Serena said, hauling me out of my office chair. "Come on. A new ramen place opened up across the street last week and we've heard it's really good."

"Yes, love, and they close at two p.m. for the afternoon, so chop-chop," Josephine added, motioning me to hurry up when I didn't move fast enough.

"I think it's you two who are hungry," I said, pointing at my friends. Nevertheless, they were right. I needed to eat before I gate-crashed an event to talk to Savannah Lundstrom. Grabbing up the last five of Charlie's emails, I said, "I'm taking these with me, though. Dupart is giving me only twenty-four hours, and I'd like to see if I can figure out which branch of Braithwaites they belong to before I head over to the Hamilton Center."

"We'll be happy to ignore you the entire time. Now, shake your tail feathers, honey," Serena said, picking up my purse as Jo linked my arm with hers and pulled me toward the door.

By the time we ordered, I was ravenous, and the three of us ended up taking our sweet time enjoying our steaming-hot bowls of ramen. Halfway in, I received a text from Ben saying he'd likely be busy the rest of the workday, but to continue texting him updates. He'd told me that he would read them, but warned me that I likely wouldn't get more than an "OK" in response.

And I had been keeping him abreast of things. Well, mostly. I still hadn't told him about being attacked this morning at the park. I knew it would affect his concentration at work, and since I was fine and sticking close to my friends, I didn't feel it necessary to add that bit. I felt better knowing that he'd seen my texts, though, and I hoped that in a couple of hours, he would be done for the day and could meet up with me. If not, he knew I was keeping myself safe and out of trouble, and that was what mattered.

It wasn't until Serena and Jo started discussing a new streaming series I hadn't yet seen that I remembered the emails I'd brought along. I used my chopsticks to maneuver the last of my noodles into the porcelain soup spoon filled with tonkotsu broth, and slurped it up as I read the top email.

Charlie,
　　Thank you for your reply. If you change your mind about letting other family members purchase it, my two kids (one a "step" from L's 2nd marriage) would be interested.
Hoping you're well,
Renee

Then I inhaled sharply, making my soup catch in my throat and sending me into a coughing fit. The original exchange had not been printed, but the email came from the username "reneethedocent."

After Josephine thumped me on the back a couple of times, I found my phone and texted Cisco, who'd never written me back to tell me the name of the docent who he'd thought resembled the woman I'd seen opening his workroom door. Not thirty seconds later, he sent a reply.

Sorry - forgot to send. Name is Renee Behrens.

This time, it was I who chivvied my two best friends back to the office. It was now almost two o'clock and Savannah's event began at three. I had about forty minutes before I had to leave for the Hamilton Center, and I was determined to find out who Renee Behrens was in the Braithwaite family tree before then.

THIRTY-SEVEN

Josephine insisted on following me to the Hamilton Center to, as she put it, "make bloody sure no attackers jump out at you." I was smart enough not to object.

After I parked, having been lucky to find a parallel-parking space not far from the entrance, I walked up to Jo's driver's-side window.

"You'll have a security guard escort you out, yes?" she said.

"Cross my heart," I said, drawing an *X* over my heart with my finger for emphasis. Slipping my phone in my purse, I didn't realize I'd huffed out a breath, but Josephine heard it.

"I know that look, love. I can tell you're frustrated that you didn't have enough time to find that woman in Camilla's family tree."

"I *am* frustrated," I grumbled. "I just really feel like Renee Behrens may be a key somehow, but I couldn't find her name connected to the Braithwaites at all."

"You couldn't find her *yet*," Jo reminded me. Using one hand to gesture toward the entrance of the Hamilton Center, she said, "Can't you blow off this meeting with the *Chronology* reporter? Do you really have to talk to her today? Surely you can call her or something, right? That way you can go back to the office and keep working."

I exhaled another breath. "True, I *could* call Savannah and try to get her to talk to me over the phone about her article and if she's writing a follow-up that might be even more damaging to the Braithwaite family. However, I doubt she would answer my call, or call me back if I left a message." Shaking my head, I said, "No, I think asking her face-to-face would be the best option, and today's my only chance, because she'd heading home to DC tomorrow." I jerked my thumb over my shoulder. "I'll just go talk to Savannah—it shouldn't take long, hopefully—and then I'll head back to the office and get on the hunt again." I blew her a kiss and turned to make my way into my other former workplace.

Walking into the Hamilton Center was a different feeling altogether than visiting the Howland library. I'd loved working here, and had made many good friends, and that thought made me smile even as I passed a display of somber photos taken during the Great Depression and headed to the elevators.

Once on the third floor, I walked confidently toward the north end of the building, where the Brownsville Room was located, keeping my eyes peeled for Savannah Lundstrom. As I reached the hallway leading to the room, however, I was stopped by a baby-faced student with a badge on his shirt that told me his name was Oscar.

"Can you show me your emailed invitation, ma'am?" Oscar asked politely. He held up an electronic device for scanning bar codes and QR codes.

"I'm afraid I don't have one," I said, affecting an embarrassed grin. "I just need to have a few words with Savannah Lundstrom, the speaker, but I won't take long. Would that be all right?"

Oscar shook his head, though I could tell by the way he was looking at me that he wasn't liking having to say no. "I'm really sorry, but I can't let you in. This particular 'History Then Happy

Hour' is a charity event, and only those who bought tickets are able to be admitted."

Briefly, I thought about calling one of my friends who still worked here at the Hamilton Center to see if they could get me in, but I decided against using my connections in that manner. I also mulled over trying to sweet-talk Oscar. I had a strong feeling that I could convince him if I played it just right.

I was just about to attempt some mild flirting when, from over Oscar's shoulder, I saw Savannah, walking with another woman who had the air of a professor. Savannah's head was turned away from me, but I heard the professor say, "The ladies' room is just down the hall if you'd like to freshen up before you go on."

Smiling at Oscar, I shrugged. "Well, I tried. Thank you so much." Then I turned on my heel and wove through a group of guests as they lined up to present their cell phones with the invitation's QR code showing.

Within seconds, I was in the lounge area, with a long mirror over a counter on one side and two armchairs on the other. A swinging door at the far end would take me into the bathrooms themselves.

Catching my reflection in the mirror over the countertop, I made a face. The lighting in the Hamilton Center bathrooms was notoriously bad, and with my scraped cheek starting to bruise, it didn't flatter me at all. Even the pretty blue blouse I was wearing looked a little sickly in this lighting. My hair was pulled back at the crown to keep it from touching my face, but I thought about letting it down to help distract from the scrape. I had other things to discuss with Savannah than how I came to be banged up.

I went to release my hair clip just as my phone dinged. Pulling the phone out to silence it, I read the text. It was from Cisco.

Dang. Siri misheard me. Just noticed. Not Behrens.
Marins.

My breathing felt stifled and I read his words again, just to be sure I hadn't imagined them. Hurriedly, I googled the name "Renee Marins," though of course I already knew where I'd heard the last name. And since Renee had referenced having two kids in her email to Charlie Braithwaite—one who was a step-son or -daughter—I'd bet my last dollar that Trent was her son.

I itched to call Dupart to alert him, and to call Patrice and Roxie to warn them they were working with someone danger-ous, but I knew I needed to verify my hunch first. As much as I didn't care for Trent Marins, I couldn't accuse him of being an art thief—and likely one-half of a murderous duo—without making sure of my facts. I hadn't yet come across the surname Marins in any of my checks into the Braithwaite family tree, so I aimed for the easiest route to researching her first: social media.

"Hot damn, there she is," I whispered and clicked on the link that would take me to Renee's account. I'd barely seen her that day in the Morris Art Conservation building, but in her pro-file, she listed herself as a docent at the Morris Art Museum in Houston, Texas, convincing me I had the right person. She posted regularly and it took me scrolling through a few posts before I murmured, "Bingo."

It was a throwback photo from a year earlier. Trent, tall and grinning in a cocky way, his fair hair a little less notice-ably receding, was clean-shaven, but clearly the same person I'd met at the Howland library. Something else caught my eye, though. Enlarging the photo, I focused in on what his beard had hidden.

"Well, would you look at that," I whispered. "He's got the Braithwaite cleft chin."

I took a screenshot of the photograph, then scrolled further. Several posts later, I was staring at the screen, my thumb hover-ing over another photo from ten months ago, of Renee Marins and two other people sitting in deck chairs on the edge of a lake, cocktails in hand. Her caption gushed about spending time with her two kids—and she'd tagged both of them.

"I can't believe it." I breathed as I read the words that were automatically generated when the account holder tags someone.

Renee Marins is at Canyon Lake with Trent Marins and—

I looked up at the sound of the door opening. The other person tagged in the post, Savannah Lundstrom, had just walked into the ladies' lounge.

She stopped when she spotted me. Looking utterly glamorous in a red sheath dress and heels, the bad lighting seemed not to affect her it all. Her curly hair was free and hanging to her shoulders, and the matte red lipstick she wore emphasized her lips even more as she pursed them, her expression confused for a moment, as if she couldn't quite place me. The action, I now noticed, emphasized her own cleft chin, though hers was much more subtle. Then realization appeared to come to her and she said, "Why, hello, Lucy. Are you here for my talk?"

"No, but I did come to see you, Savannah," I said, my tone mild. My thoughts were racing as I slid my phone into my purse. It suddenly hit me that Trent knew I was working for Camilla, and thus, he would have told Savannah. I needed to change my whole plan of action to be able to walk this particular line. And I needed to change it on the quick.

"Oh? And you felt the best place to wait for me was the ladies' room?" she said with a touch of sarcasm, turning toward the mirror and putting her purse on the counter so she could fluff her hair and check her lipstick. Then she glanced at me in the mirror with a put-upon expression. "Is this about Ben? Are you jealous that I hugged him or something? Look, he's gorgeous, yes, but there's nothing between us. We were just classmates, that's it." She shrugged and resumed checking her makeup, each movement of her arms sending a whiff of her perfume my way. It was floral, with a fruity undertone.

Almost in response, the scrape on my cheek started to smart again. Savannah hadn't even asked what had happened to my face, though her eyes had lingered on the contusion. I steeled myself against the anger threatening to rise up inside me. Instead, I kept my voice calm. A plan was forming in my mind.

"No, it's not about Ben," I said, waving off the notion. "It's about Charles Braithwaite, and his descendants, of course. Cisco told me that you ditched him and his interview after you noticed the painting in the workroom at Morris Art Conservation was done by Charles." I then gave her a decidedly worried look and blurted, "Savannah, are you going after another Braithwaite family story for *Chronology?*"

For a moment, Savannah had stilled, but when her eyes flicked back to me, my expression as earnest as they come, she seemed to relax.

"And if I am?" she replied, the reporter's gleam back in her eye.

Something about that look made me flash back to Cisco's workroom, and how Savannah, after attempting to peek at the covered-up piece of the triptych, had asked, *Will you at least give me a hint as to why the panel is here?*

She'd called it a "panel," not simply a "painting" or "piece of art" as any other regular person would who thought there was only one canvas, total. Until recently, while Charles Braithwaite had been somewhat known as an artist, only the Braithwaite family had known he'd painted a three-paneled piece of artwork. Plus, while Cisco's folder had been labeled *Untitled Triptych Piece, 1866, Charles Braithwaite, artist*, the word "triptych" hadn't been visible, because I'd accidentally pushed some of the folder under the drop cloth. Yet Savannah had already known the painting was one of three panels, hadn't she?

She wasn't at Morris Art Conservation to interview Cisco at all. No, she was there to help Renee—her stepmother—steal Camilla's piece of the triptych. Was it Savannah who stole the intern's key card and passed it off to Renee? Or did Renee steal it, and Savannah was there to pick up the painting when her stepmother rolled it outside? Though Savannah had no doubt made a real appointment to interview Cisco, just in case, mind you.

Now Savannah was eyeing me. I leaned forward in conspiratorial fashion. "Look, my client—"

"Your client *is* a Braithwaite. I'm right, aren't I?" Savannah said, a note of triumph in her voice.

"Okay, yes, you're right," I said, as if I were conceding the point to a worthy opponent. "My client is Camilla Braithwaite, and the painting at Morris Art Conservation was part of a triptych painted by her ancestor that's been covered for decades by another canvas that looked like a bad folk-art painting. The painting underneath—a battle scene—was discovered by accident." Now I inflected my voice with insistence. "Look, Camilla is adamant that you not write another follow-up on her ancestor and her family. She wants her family's name preserved, not further questioned, and she's hired me to look into Charles's Civil War records to prove your assertions wrong."

"Has she, now?" Savannah asked with a smirk.

I nodded and gave a sigh. "I'll admit, I haven't found anything thus far that verifies Charles Braithwaite wasn't a deserter, so I'm up against a wall there. But since you still seem interested in writing about the Braithwaites, what if you wrote about the triptych instead, and the mystery surrounding it?"

"Which is?" Savannah asked, turning back to check her reflection again as if she didn't care.

I glanced at my own reflection, pleased to see my wide-eyed, earnest look was pretty darn Oscar-worthy.

"Well, the other two pieces are missing—one's whereabouts have been unknown since the eighties and the other one was recently stolen and its owner *murdered . . .*" I made an isn't-that-shocking face in the mirror at Savannah, whose eyes had cut over to me. "Anyway, this kind of thing is right up *Chronology*'s alley, right? How a family has been thinking some hideous painting was done by their ancestor, only to have an accident uncover the true painting underneath that could be worth a fortune? And now there's a hunt for the other two pieces?" I affected a hesitant smile. "So, what do you say? If you're going to write about the Braithwaites again, why not make it about the triptych?" I leaned in toward her, my hand to my heart. "And the painting is *amazing*, Savannah. Oh. My. God."

My countenance was lit up now, but it wasn't that hard because I was recalling the painting and its astounding detail. "You should see the scene that's underneath. It's just *incredible*. We brought it back here to Austin. It's at my friend Helen Kim's restoration shop near the Harry Alden Texas History Museum. There's only minor work that needs to be done—can you believe it? Helen's doing it now, of course. She'll be finished by this afternoon and then the painting is going to a secure location after that." I bit my lip, then said in an excited whisper, "And Helen called me this morning. She had Camilla's piece appraised and it's likely worth—"

At that moment, the door to the ladies' room opened and the professor who'd been talking to Savannah earlier walked in, looking a little harassed.

"Oh, Ms. Lundstrom, there you are. Dean Trezzi of the history department would love to ask you a couple of questions about your presentation, so I told him I'd come find you. Do you need more time to freshen up?"

Savannah's eyes had been laser focused on me, hungry for my next words. I saw her jaw tighten, but when she faced the professor, her calm demeanor was intact. "No, not at all. I'm ready," she replied. Briefly turning back to me, she graced me with a smile. "It was good to see you again, Lucy. I'll think about what you said. It might just be the angle I'm looking for."

I gave her a hopeful smile in return, holding it until the door to the hallway beyond had closed once more before saying under my breath, "Yes, let what I've said really sink in, Savannah. I've no doubt you'll find the temptation irresistible."

I waited until I was in the elevator, riding down to the first floor, to call Detective Dupart.

"You're suggesting *what*, Ms. Lancaster?" he said after listening to my tale.

"An undercover op, detective. Mark my words. Savannah Lundstrom is going to try and steal that painting again. How fast can you get a team over to Helen Kim Art Restoration?"

THIRTY-EIGHT

I sat next to Helen, watching her do a gentle surface clean of Charles Braithwaite's painting.

"You know this will be pretty boring for you, right?"

"No way," I said, my eyes glued to her process, watching as the rich golden tones of one soldier's hair—a soldier with a cleft chin, I noted—took on even more dimension with the removal of the dust that Helen said had likely been on the painting before it was covered by the second canvas. "I'm utterly fascinated."

Helen laughed, but I noticed her eyes flicked back and forth to the front door, and I answered her unasked question.

"Officer Park should be here in about twenty minutes," I said. "And several undercover officers with her, including one to follow you home and stay with you until this is over."

Helen glanced up at me. "This is surreal, Lucy. You're so calm."

"I'm not really," I said, and it was the truth. I was nervous as hell, but this time was different. This time I wouldn't be in danger, nor would my friend. This time, the police were going to be handling the bad guys. I was just going to be watching the takedown.

"But you look like butter wouldn't melt in your mouth," Helen said on a laugh. With one hand, she gestured toward the door. "It's crazy to think someone is going to stand in for me, pretend to *be* me, while the police set a sting to catch Savannah Lundstrom attempting to steal this painting." She looked down at Camilla's triptych piece, then back up at me. "Speaking of, tell me what Savannah did to make you figure out she was doing something that was more than reporting."

I explained it to her as I'd figured it out. "First, there was the article. It was well-written, but as I began to research Charles Braithwaite's military records, there were a couple of places where her fact-checking was tenuous, especially when she claimed he deserted."

"Yeah, but didn't you say that there was an actual card in his CM-whatever—"

"CMSR—it stands for 'compiled military service record.'"

"Yeah, that. Wasn't there a notation that listed him as deserted?"

I nodded. "There was, but what you have to understand about Civil War records is that you'll see a lot of soldiers with notations like that in their files. And then the next record will say they're back on active service. The record keeping—for Union and Confederate forces alike—was fairly shoddy. They only took roll call—called a muster report—every two months. With the exception of the Bowie List, which is a list of soldiers who died during three battles in Maryland, including Antietam, and the exact locations where the soldiers were buried, there's nothing in any Confederate records that will definitively tell you whether a soldier actually fought in a particular battle or skirmish. So basically, there's not a ton you can rely on one hundred percent within the CMSR files."

"Sounds like some of the provenance records I see," Helen said wryly as she wrapped fresh cotton around a long stick and began to work her way onto the fair-haired soldier's face, which was distorted with pain from a bloody gash on his upper arm.

"I would expect the discovery process can be quite similar at times," I agreed. "In Civil War cases, I have to carefully work from the outside in. In general, that means finding other records that prove, say, that Charles was or wasn't in the hospital at the time—because, let me tell you, these soldiers were always in and out of hospitals. Or maybe Charles mentioned certain other soldiers in his journal and they were proven through other means to be at a particular battle. I basically work my way inward, fitting puzzle pieces together, until I can make the best case I can that Charles was in one place or another at a given time."

Helen nodded thoughtfully as she worked. "So, Savannah didn't make a good enough case?"

"Not in my mind," I said. "Though, I will admit it was done well enough that I might not have thought twice about it if it hadn't been for Camilla hiring me to prove the article wrong."

Helen continued to work on the painting, but asked me what else made me think something was up with Savannah. "Was it that she showed up at the Morris Art Conservation building in Houston?" she said.

"Actually, not really. At least, not until today," I replied. "She's from Dallas and other stories I've read of hers prove that she writes about the South and Southwest quite a bit. She claimed she was there to interview Cisco on what sounded like a legitimate article at the time—though when I called the *Chronology* offices as I drove over here, I confirmed that, while she *was* in Houston to research a story, she'd never cleared writing an article about art conservation."

Helen made an indignant sound on my and Cisco's behalf.

"Anyway, what seemed weird, thinking back, was that she really seemed more interested in looking around the workroom than she did in talking to Cisco. Also—and, again, I didn't recognize this until much too late—but when she saw the painting, she specifically used the term 'panel,' making me fairly certain she knew the painting was part of a triptych, even though we never told her as much." I explained how there was a folder label that had identified the painting as a triptych piece, but Savannah couldn't have seen those words.

I added, "Plus, the woman I saw trying to wheel a cart into the workroom, and then rushing off when she heard someone coming, made everything even more odd."

"And that woman was Renee Marins?"

I nodded. "She was the first wife of Savannah's father, and the mother of Savannah's half brother, Trent Marins. Trent and Savannah have the same father, and are therefore both Braithwaite descendants, but Trent goes by his stepfather's surname."

I was about to explain more, about how I'd sat in my car outside Helen's shop for a bit, doing some genealogy work that linked several things together. And how I'd called Camilla and tried to tell her the update. Helen's mind was elsewhere, though. She was frowning at the scrape on my cheek. "Do you think she followed you to Little Stacy Park? Savannah, I mean."

"I don't know," I said, "but my gut is actually saying she didn't. Savannah must have been staying in the area because of her talk at the Hamilton Center"—I checked the time—"which should be over in about thirty minutes, by the way. Anyway, I think she simply saw an opportunity and took it." I scowled. "If she'd planned it, I have a feeling I wouldn't be here right now."

Helen's tone was fierce. "Well, the police had better find out after they arrest her." Then her expression switched to uncertainty. "You're sure she'll come?"

I remembered the way Savannah had looked at me while I'd rambled on, giving her details she needed to find out where the painting was—if she didn't already know—and warning her, without acting like I intended to do so, that she had a finite amount of time before the painting went to a secure location. "I'm pretty darn sure," I said.

"So, then, do you think she killed Charlie Braithwaite, or do you think her half brother did?"

I was about to say I didn't know, but paused at a knock at the shop's front doors.

Helen checked the security cameras, then looked at me with a slightly panicky face. "It's Camilla. Did you not call her and tell her this was going down?"

My eyes shifted from Helen to the screen where I could see Camilla standing outside, having changed from her earlier exercise outfit into a pair of jeans, ankle boots, and a bright fuchsia sweater. Her dark red hair had been let down and was framing her face in a becoming way.

"I mean, I called her and said I had news for her about the painting and she should sit tight and lock her doors, but she was in a seriously bad mood. She cut me off, telling me she was safe, that she was finalizing plans for Charlie's funeral, and she would call me back. Before she hung up, I told her that Dupart was sending a cruiser to her house, just in case. She said fine and hung up. *Dang it.*" I huffed for good measure.

"Well, what should we do?" Helen asked as Camilla knocked again.

Sighing, I threw up my hands. "Seriously, this whole mess is driving me to drink, but water will have to do for now." I gestured to the screen. "If you let Camilla in, I'll go grab us some bottles of water and explain what's happening. Since she's here now, I'll get one of Dupart's officers to escort her home, though she might want to stay and watch with me from a safe distance. I'd say she deserves to."

Helen nodded and I walked to the back, passing the security vault, and into Helen's office, where she had a small refrigerator.

"Camilla," I heard Helen say brightly as I grabbed three waters. "Nice to see you again." There was a pause, then she said, "Oh, I didn't see your friend on the cameras. Hello, I'm Helen Kim."

On the tablet on Helen's desk, another security camera was rolling. I watched, shocked, as a familiar tall man with light brown hair and a close-cropped beard I knew hid a cleft chin sidled up to Camilla and threw an arm around her shoulders. His voice was amiable and charming.

"Hi, Helen, I'm Trent. Camilla's cousin."

Stunned at his casual pronouncement, anger flared in me. Had they pulled the wool over my eyes? Was Camilla actually colluding with Trent and Savannah and I hadn't yet figured that out? Then Camilla gave that familiar stiff jerk of her head to push her hair back, and I knew right then. Something was very wrong.

Luckily, Helen kept her composure. "It's nice to meet you, Trent. What can I do for y'all?"

I saw Camilla open her mouth, but it was Trent Marins's voice I heard out in the main part of the shop as they walked in. "We've come to collect our ancestor's painting. We've opted to have it restored in Houston instead."

I could no longer see them on the security camera, but I could hear how Helen's voice had become strained. "Camilla, is this true?"

"Yes, it is. I'm so sorry, Helen," she answered.

Helen paused. "I see. Would you at least tell me why?"

Trent began, "The three of us have been talking this over for some time, Helen."

"The three of you?" Helen echoed, as I noticed I could change the security view. I tapped on the screen that showed the main workroom as Trent nodded. They were standing just inside the door.

"Camilla, my sister, Savannah, and me," Trent said. "Well,

she's my half sister, but we've always been close." I saw him pause and smile, then say, "She and I, and Camilla here, are the only cousins who care about our ancestor's triptych, and we want to see it put together again. Savannah has had one piece for years, stored away at her place in DC. I was helping her move last summer, and"—I heard him emit a chuckle—"I said something that displeased my sister, and she threw a shoe at me. A four-inch stiletto heel, to be exact. Well, I hid behind the painting, and the stiletto heel slammed into that godforsaken top painting like a dart hitting the bull's-eye." He raised his hand and made a motion like he was throwing a dart. "When we pulled her heel out, it had made a pretty decent hole." I could see Trent gesturing toward the table holding Camilla's piece of the triptych as he said, "And I think you know what we found when we looked through that hole."

"What did you do with it after that?" Helen asked.

"We took it to an art restorer like you, of course," Trent said, beaming. "After that, we began searching in our family line for cousins who might own the other two pieces." I saw him bring a stressed-looking Camilla in for a side hug as he said, "Turns out, I was already applying for a job that would put me working with Camilla here, and in no time at all Cam and I then started talking and making plans. She helped us acquire the third painting, owned by our older cousin, who recently passed away, bless his heart."

Helen said, "Okaaay," and from the screen I saw her address Camilla. "So, why did you send Lucy to Houston to get your piece of the triptych? And why did you then agree to have it evaluated at Morris Art Conservation and brought back here for me to do the restoration work?" Helen pointed to herself for emphasis.

Camilla looked uncomfortable. "I'm really sorry, Helen," she said. "I'm happy to discuss this with you later, but for now, could we have my painting back? I'll pay you for whatever work you've done, plus extra for being so patient. Um, is Lucy here, too? I saw her car outside."

I was starting to see red now. I could tell Helen was angry as well and she didn't answer Camilla's question about me. Instead she said, "It's your painting, Camilla, so of course you can have it, but first I want to know why you used Lucy this way."

When Camilla didn't reply, Trent did, his tone one of embarrassment. "She doesn't want to say, but it was because of her ex-husband. Gareth had researched the painting, too, and wanted to try and make a claim for it since he's the father of her two sons. Cam here felt that Lucy going to get the painting would be the simpler solution." I saw him crane his neck. "Where *is* Lucy?"

I couldn't contain myself any longer. I was out the office door in an instant and striding into the main room.

"Oh, I'm here, and I heard what you said," I snapped, slamming the bottles of water down on Helen's worktable.

"Lucy," Camilla began in a somewhat strangled tone, but I just glared at her.

"I'm not the simpler solution, I'm just the more naive, trusting one, aren't I?" My fists were clenched in anger, but I pointed at Camilla as I came within steps of them. "How *could* you? How could you be in cahoots with those two and hurt your uncle Charlie like that?" Now I jabbed my thumb at myself as I got up almost in Camilla's face. She and Trent seemed to be mesmerized by my fury. "And how could you use *me* like that?" I heard my voice crack. "Good God, Camilla, do you really hate me that much?"

When she opened her mouth and began, "Lucy, I'm—" I didn't hesitate. I pivoted toward Trent and slammed the heel of my hand up into his nose.

We heard the crunch, then came the blood. Trent released Camilla as a reflex, howling with pain while he did so and drowning out Camilla's and Helen's gasps.

"My nothse!" he wailed thickly, and then I stomped my three-inch heel into the soft top of his shoe. He dropped to his knees, one hand over his nose and the other reaching down for his foot, and I called back to Helen, "Find something to tie him up with!"

Helen was around the corner in a flash and I turned back to where Camilla had been standing, frozen in place. I pointed at Trent, ready to tell her to knee him in the groin if he tried to get up, but what I saw made me go still, too.

Savannah Lundstrom had appeared in the doorway. She grabbed Camilla from behind, yanked one of her arms up and back, eliciting a gasp of pain from my former coworker. Then she encircled Camilla's neck with the crook of her other arm, so tightly that her left hand was hidden in Camilla's hair.

"Get the painting, Lucy," Savannah said in a cold voice, seemingly oblivious to the wailing of her brother on the floor. With a push at Camilla's back, she and her cousin stepped just out of his reach. Jerking her head toward the table, Savannah said, "Do it now. We're going to walk it out back, nice and easy. Once it's in my car, I'll let my sweet cousin here go."

"They're going to kill me, Lucy," gasped Camilla. "Trent told me."

To this Savannah tightened her hold around Camilla's neck, hissing, "Shut up." Then she glared at me. "I said, get the painting. *Now.*"

I held up my hands in surrender, taking a step backward. "What about him?" I said, indicating Trent.

"*Him.* He's lived off me for far too long," she said in a poisonous tone. "I did all the work on this—all the research, all the planning, not to mention the writing of the article that would question our ancestor's war record and integrity. I'm the only one who did anything to help devalue the paintings if Camilla here and Charlie decided to get their pieces appraised. I also worked to convince my editor to run the article early, and even found our buyer . . ." She glanced disdainfully down at Trent. "And *he* still wanted half of the massive payout we would get."

"You already had a buyer in place?" I asked, my mouth dropping open.

She sneered, not looking half so pretty now. "Do you honestly think I would have gone through this without one?" Giving Camilla's arm another jerk and seeming to enjoy the cry of pain from her cousin, she said, "The guy's a major collector of Civil War art, an American expat and rich as Croesus. He's been visiting family in Houston, but he's going back home the day after tomorrow. He's promised us an unbelievable amount for all three paintings."

Something Helen had said to me the other day came floating back. "He lives in Japan, doesn't he?"

Savannah's lips curled up in a smile. "Your friend Helen told you about countries with no extradition treaties, did she?" Then, from under Camilla's hair, Savannah's grip shifted, giving me a look at what she'd been pressing into her cousin's neck. It was a dark red cylinder, about four inches long and two inches in diameter, that had blended into Camilla's russet-colored hair. Savannah's middle finger also ran through a square protrusion in the middle with two small silver spikes. There were two more lethal-looking inch-long spikes on the end of the cylinder. Camilla, I could see, was trying hard to get a look at what weapon was being used against her, but she couldn't, since it was being held against the side of her neck.

"That's some stun gun," I said, hearing my voice go high with dread. I didn't know how much stunning would injure Camilla, but there was no doubt that jamming those spikes into her neck could do some serious, possibly fatal damage. I saw Camilla's eyes go wide as she looked at me, but I looked at Savannah, whose green eyes stared coldly back into mine.

Strangely, it was at that point, when the two women's faces

were next to one another and Trent just a few feet away, that their one common physical trait, their cleft chins, was the most obvious. It was almost nothing more than a slight dimple in Savannah's chin. Trent's, though covered by a scruff-length beard, was more visible as he held his hand over his bloody nose, whimpering, his lower jaw tight with pain. Camilla's I'd noticed the very first day I'd met her at the Howland University library. It linked all three of them, and had been passed down from their ancestor, Charles Braithwaite.

Savannah brought me back to reality, tilting the stun gun up and down so that the long red spikes on the end seemed to be waving at me. "Yes, it is a nice little number. I wish I'd been running with it this morning in Little Stacy Park." When my hand went involuntarily to my scraped cheek, she said with a satisfied snarl, "Now get the painting, Lucy."

I put both my hands up again, backing away toward the table where the painting lay. Savannah shoved Camilla forward again, glancing briefly at Trent, who was moaning loudly in the fetal position on the floor. Momentarily, I was at a loss as to what to do next.

Then Camilla did something shocking, something I never thought I'd see her do. She imitated me.

It happened in the blink of an eye. Camilla raised up one of her ankle boots and slammed it down on Savannah's toes. I saw Savannah's eyes close with the pain as she yelled, "You bitch!" But her grip on Camilla had loosened.

With renewed strength, Camilla grabbed the wrist that held the stun gun and pulled it away from her neck. I gasped as the two cousins began struggling. Before I knew it, they were stumbling toward me, toward the painting, grunting and growling, the flash of Savannah's red dress and Camilla's bright fuchsia sweater making for a colorful blur.

Yet now Savannah was flailing as the two spun. Camilla was

half a head shorter, but she was strong, and she wasn't in heels. Camilla was struggling hard to get away as they moved nearer and nearer to the table that held the triptych panel. Somehow, Savannah still held fast to the stun gun and the thought reached my brain that if she managed to jam the spikes into the painting, she could rip a hole in it several inches long.

I skirted away from them, grabbing the first thing that caught my eye, though not without a slight struggle because it was heavier than it looked. Stumbling a step or two myself, I managed to hoist myself onto my knees on top of the stool I'd been sitting on earlier. With a grunt, I lifted the heavy piece over my head, yelling, "This way, Camilla!"

Automatically, she responded to my voice and swung around, bringing Savannah with her like a two-headed spinning top. I roared with effort as I brought down the colorful majolica greyhound on Savannah's pretty, curly head.

The earthenware dog cracked into several large shards and Savannah dropped to the floor, unconscious, just inches from her ancestor's painting.

I quickly clambered down off the stool and whipped around, holding one of the greyhound's legs out like a weapon toward Trent, who'd uttered a long yell.

I needn't have worried, though. His shout was only because Helen had dashed back into the room, yanked his arms up, and begun tying his wrists together tightly with a length of baling twine and a satisfied look on her face.

Bending down, I checked that Savannah was still alive. She was, though a lump was forming on her head. Helen shoved a long piece of twine across the floor, and I picked it up and swiftly tied Savannah's hands together, then pulled the stun gun out of her limp hand and kicked the pottery shards out of her reach.

"Sorry about the dog, Helen," I said. "I hope it wasn't an antique."

"Oh, it was," Helen said cheerfully. "But I can fix it, don't worry."

I turned to Camilla. She was breathing hard, one hand to her cheek where one of the shards from the vase had scraped her face. Holding up a hand, I said, "Well *done*. High-five to you."

She looked at me like I was nuts for a second, then grinned and slapped her other palm to mine.

THIRTY-NINE

Officer Park showed up about thirty seconds after I finished tying up Savannah, and when she took in the scene, she immediately called in the other undercover officers. One of them was Detective Dupart himself, looking almost unrecognizable in a pair of jeans and a tie-dyed *Keep Austin Weird* T-shirt.

Later, I told him I was never going to take him seriously again after seeing him in his undercover getup, and for once, I got a laugh out of him.

While Helen stood with Dupart and gave him her statement, Camilla and I waited on two stools at the far end of Helen's workroom, both of us sporting scrapes on our cheeks and Camilla also holding an ice pack to her left knee, having twisted it in the scuffle.

Camilla herself had just finished telling Dupart how she'd been packing dishes in Charlie's kitchen when Trent had shown up and walked in the back door, bold as brass. She'd been so shocked, it had taken her a few moments to realize he'd known the door code.

Within seconds, Trent had pulled a knife, forced her into a chair, bound her wrists with duct tape, and was planning on holding her there until he could rendezvous with Savannah after her event at the Hamilton Center. The two siblings would first use Camilla to get Helen to release the painting, then Camilla would be deadweight—literally. But when I'd called, ignoring Camilla's snappishness and telling her that a police cruiser was heading her way, the timeline had been pushed forward. Trent had texted Savannah the news and forced Camilla into his car, and they'd driven off before Dupart's officer had arrived at Charlie's house.

"How did you know?" Camilla asked me. "That I wasn't in cahoots with Trent and Savannah, I mean. He'd cut the duct tape off my wrists, so I wasn't tied up. And I was worried that he'd hurt you or Helen, so I was cooperating with him. So what gave me away?"

"Well, for one, you did this." I imitated the way she jerked her head to swing her hair behind her shoulders. "You do it only when you're stressed." She looked surprised that I'd noticed this. "I also couldn't imagine you being in league with Trent all this time in the first place. You're too . . ." I tilted my head side to side, searching for the right phrase. "Too straightforward. There was also something about the way you spoke to Helen. If you really had been in with those two, I think you would have sounded more like your usual self."

Then, realizing what I'd just said, I clapped my hand over my mouth, mortified.

Camilla was shaking her head, though. "No, don't be sorry. I do tend to sound . . . unfriendly sometimes. It's something I need to work on."

"Well, I have things to work on about myself, too," I said, then I grinned. "Isn't it the worst that life is mostly about constantly having to improve yourself?"

"It sucks really big rocks," Camilla said with a laugh. "But I guess it's worth it." Then she added, "Though one thing you don't need to change, Lucy, is your willingness to give people second chances. Too few people are open like that these days. Don't give it up, okay?" Then she laughed again at the nonplussed look on my face.

I kept goggling at her until the sound of struggling made us look over. Savannah, who had woken up a few minutes ago and was being looked over by the EMT crew, had tried to get up and lunge toward us when she'd heard Camilla laugh. She'd been caught instantly by Officer Park and was being walked to the door, where an ambulance waited to take her and her half brother for medical evaluations before heading to jail.

"You won't find the other two pieces of the triptych, Camilla!" Savannah yelled to us with maniacal glee as she was being led away. "You might get a decent price for your painting, but it will be small potatoes compared to what all three would fetch!"

Camilla, who had been staring at her long-lost cousin with a mixture of horror, anger, and loss, called back, "You're too late, Savannah. While you were passed out, Trent was only too happy to talk, especially after hearing you say you would leave him in the wind. He already told us your piece and Uncle Charlie's piece are hidden in his storage unit, and Cisco and the Houston police are on their way there now. He also told us that your father, Lucas, is the rightful owner of the painting, so it was never yours to begin with." Then she added, "And it was never about the money for me in the first place!"

Savannah's eyes had gone furiously horrified with this knowledge, and she uttered a frustrated noise followed by a stamp of her foot. Camilla and I both had to bite our tongues to keep from laughing when Savannah howled with pain, having just stamped the foot Camilla had smashed with her boot, and was escorted, hobbling, out the door.

Camilla wasn't kidding, though, when she said Trent was happy to talk. Seeing his sister passed out, he'd immediately offered Dupart testimony in return for a lighter sentence. While Dupart didn't agree to anything, Trent spit out information anyway.

After Trent and Savannah had been taken away, Camilla and I explained the finer points to Helen.

"So, Savannah and Trent share the same father, whose name is Lucas Lundstrom," I said. "Lucas is the eldest grandson of Roger Smith, Henrietta Braithwaite's eldest son. He, Lucas, inherited the third piece of the triptych from his grandfather."

"Then why is Trent's last name Marins and not Lundstrom?" Helen asked.

I replied, "Because his parents—Lucas and Renee—divorced very quickly, and Renee married another man named Marins, who legally adopted Trent as a toddler. Renee made sure Trent had a relationship with Lucas, though. And if you're wondering, I found this out from Renee's social media posts."

Camilla said, "Then Lucas Lundstrom married Savannah's mother soon after that?"

"You're correct," I said, unscrewing the cap of my water. "Savannah and Trent are only two years apart. Renee Marins got to know Savannah, and they became a blended family of sorts—to the point that Renee referred to Savannah as her stepdaughter."

Helen said, "They sound like a decent family. What made Savannah and Trent feel like they needed to steal two paintings? Not to mention committing murder as they did so?"

Camilla said, "This is where I can help a bit, only because Trent talked while he had me tied up. Basically, Trent and Savannah became aware of their connection to my family as they grew up. Trent described his family as 'comfortably middle class' themselves, but he and Savannah were both very ambitious."

"I'd call it greedy," Helen said flatly.

"I can't disagree," Camilla said. "Anyway, Trent admitted it was their connection to my family and our shared history that made him become a genealogist—though he told me he never liked working with clients and preferred to teach the theory rather than do the work in practice."

"It's wonderful to teach, of course," I said, "but I think Trent taught so he didn't really have to do the constant legwork of an actual genealogist."

Camilla's lips thinned. "There always seemed to be something lazy about him, even if he was smart. That's one of the many reasons I came to you, Lucy, instead of going to him."

I blushed. It was nice to hear the true compliment in Camilla's voice.

"Anyway," Camilla continued, "Trent had done his family tree, of course, and knew he had lots of Braithwaite cousins in Houston, but at the time it was just interesting information to him. He then found out that one of his relatives—me—worked as a librarian at Howland University, when he coincidentally met our former genealogist, Ginger, at a conference last year and they got to talking. Ginger also mentioned that she was retiring soon, and Trent considered applying for her job—but, again, it was nothing more than a thought in his mind because he and Savannah hadn't found what was underneath their piece of the triptych yet."

"I take it things changed rapidly when that happened," Helen said.

"Oh, from what Trent told me, things moved really fast," Camilla replied dryly. "After he and Savannah saw what was under their painting and were told the potential value of it—and then the value of all three paintings together—Trent pursued Ginger's job as soon as it was posted. He figured if he got to know me, maybe he could buy my part of the painting. But when he and Savannah quickly realized how attached Uncle Charlie and I both were to our paintings, and how proud we were to be Braithwaites, they knew we wouldn't sell. That's when they hatched their plan, and Trent went about researching me, so to speak."

"Like asking questions about her ex-husband and finding out that he doesn't put names with phone numbers in his phone," I explained to Helen. "And things like the specific way Camilla would text someone." Opening up my text messages, I brought up Camilla's texts and pointed out a couple. "Such as the fact that she uses 'Thx' for the word 'thanks,' and tends to text in short sentences."

Helen smiled. "Unlike me, who texts like an emoji-happy fifteen-year-old."

"Hey, if you ever see a text from me without at least one ex-clamation point, you know something's wrong," I joked, before becoming serious again. "Anyway, Trent did this so that when he texted Camilla's ex-husband from the burner phone Savannah purchased on one of her work trips, he could sound like Camilla and Gareth wouldn't question it when he saw the request to go back to Camilla's house and get the painting."

Camilla nodded sadly. "Trent also found out that my door code is the same as Uncle Charlie's. Roxie knew what it was because she and Layla stayed at my house one weekend, and he finagled it out of her."

"Speaking of Roxie, was she involved?" I asked. I'd confessed what Patrice had told me about how it seemed Roxie might be in on the scheme somehow.

"No, I think Patrice simply misheard or misinterpreted the conversation," Camilla said. "Roxie was only involved with Trent in helping Soils from Heaven bring in more customers. She wanted a cut for her participation, and when Trent came back with a low number, she insisted on better terms."

"What about the soil company?" Helen asked. "How did that fit in?"

"It was ninety-nine percent exactly what it appeared to be," Camilla said. "Trent and his other Marins family members had no clue about the arsenic in the soil until they began to hear from customers. That's it—though it sounds like his behavior when Lucy confronted him made her more suspicious of him."

I made a kinda-sorta gesture with my hand. "I knew you'd told him about your painting, but I didn't know he was related to you at the time. My suspicions were that he might have been trying to poison Charlie in order to get to your painting."

"Well, you weren't entirely wrong," Camilla said, her jaw set with anger. "Trent says he truly didn't know that Uncle Charlie got soil with higher levels of arsenic in it, but when he realized it, he and Savannah hoped that it might make the painting easier to steal if Uncle Charlie were bedridden and weak. That's the reason why they made their move to steal it when they did. They knew he was ill enough that I was worried and taking him to a doctor."

Camilla went on to explain that Trent had confessed he'd driven into Austin to meet up with Savannah the night Charlie was killed. The siblings had staked out the house, waiting for Camilla to leave to pick up food, then used the key code to walk in the door. They'd planned on taking the painting and leaving without touching anything else. Charlie, however, had surprised them by waking up and getting out of bed when he heard them in his office.

Beyond that, the details became murky. Trent claimed Savannah pushed Charlie back into his bed and smothered him. However, one of the first things Savannah said upon coming to and seeing officers standing over her was, "Trent killed him, not me."

This issue seemed to be on Camilla's mind, too, as she and I sat on our stools while Helen went back to speak with Dupart. "Do you think I'll ever know who actually killed Uncle Charlie?"

"It's a toss-up," I said, "though I kind of wonder if it's best, the not-knowing. Neither of them are worth trusting, anyway."

"Very true," Camilla said. She was silent for a moment, then asked, "Oh, but do you want to know how Savannah knew you'd taken my panel to the conservator in Houston?"

"Um, *yes,*" I said with an exaggerated nod.

"So, Trent told me Savannah hired some guy with a shady background to follow you and steal my panel out of your car after you took it from my house." Camilla paused at the way my jaw dropped, but I waved off her concern.

"I'll tell you later how I know about that. Just keep going."

"Well, the shady guy reported you'd taken it to Morris Art Conservation and, even though her stepmother was a docent there, Savannah wanted the shady guy to break in and take my panel—or something to that effect." She rolled her eyes, adding, "Trent was chintzy on the details at this point. However, somehow the shady guy found out that Ben is with the FBI and got cold feet. He backed out, and then Savannah apparently ended up convincing her stepmother, Renee, to dress up as a conservator and attempt to steal my panel."

"So Renee wasn't part of the main scheme?"

Camilla shrugged. "It sounded like she wasn't, but I guess that will be for Dupart to figure out." She tilted her head thoughtfully. "I have to say, though, I got the impression Trent told me all this because he felt like Savannah might double-cross him."

"And he was right, wasn't he?" I said.

"He sure was," Camilla agreed, and we both sighed at the sadness of it all.

Then Camilla's phone rang and I saw the name Elaine Trudeau on her screen just as Ben walked through the door, making a beeline toward me with a relieved smile.

"You know, maybe you could try that second-chances thing now," I said, nodding toward her phone. "Whatever Elaine's faults, she truly loved Charlie."

Camilla nodded, and I heard her answer the phone with a very pleasant "Hi, Elaine" as I hopped off my stool and walked into Ben's arms.

FORTY

The days following our thwarting of Savannah and Trent's attempt to steal the triptych panel were filled with revelations and explanations, one of which was surprisingly assisted by my grandfather and brought a long-standing mystery to a close.

A huge clan of Braithwaites came into Austin for Charlie Braithwaite's funeral, including Camilla, Tor, and Mrs. Hocknell—or Jensen, as she'd asked me to call her.

After the morning service, which I attended along with Helen, I invited all sixty-eight Braithwaite family members to the Harry Alden Texas History Museum. There, the Civil War exhibit area had been temporarily roped off, and chairs added so the family could sit while I spoke. Movable curtains had been placed in front of what had been the exhibit on Charles Braithwaite.

Standing in front of the curtains, I introduced myself and Helen, who was manning my laptop to help run my presentation.

Having not told Camilla or any of the family what I'd found, I began in a serious tone.

"The opening sentence in Ms. Lundstrom's article about

your ancestor's life was this: *His name was Charles Edward Braithwaite, and he was a coward, a deserter, and a charlatan.*" I paused just long enough to feel the tension from the assembled Braithwaite clan and to see Camilla's face cloud over with dread.

Then I smiled, and added, "However, I've found definitive proof that the only true part of this sentence is that your ancestor was, in fact, named Charles Edward Braithwaite."

The relieved laughter was exactly the happy tone on which I wanted to start off my findings.

I explained that researching a Civil War soldier's military duty wasn't as simple as finding their name on the muster roll of a particular battle and then being able to say that without a doubt, that soldier was in precisely that town, at that battle, on that day.

"Roll calls were only taken every two months, and records of events were sometimes detailed, sometimes not. Also, records pertaining to the Confederacy can be especially spotty because many were lost or destroyed after the war."

I went on to explain that per the article, Charles had deserted his regiment, the Fifth Texas Infantry, after the Second Battle of Bull Run.

"Charles's compiled military service records—his CMSR— seemed to confirm this," I explained. "He is listed as having deserted on September first, 1862, and, upon first inspection of the files, this appears to be the end of it." I grinned. "Until you look closer."

Helen called up my first photo, which indeed showed one of Charles Braithwaite's CMSR abstract cards. I explained that when the files were re-created by the War Department to aid in authorizing pensions as well as veterans' benefits, cards were preprinted with lines to fill in details of the soldier's name and company designation—such as Company "A"—at the top, plus any other information relevant to his service. However, it wasn't the same War Department staffer filling out all the abstract cards.

Thus, some had lovely, easily readable handwriting; others did not.

Knowing what I wanted her to do, Helen flipped through a few of Charles's abstract cards. Some were company muster roll cards and others were regimental returns—which, I explained, helped show a regiment's strength through a listing of soldiers who were present, absent, sick, deserted, and the like. I pointed out how the handwriting could differ, and how sometimes it was nearly undecipherable.

Using a laser pointer, I sent a red stream of light onto a Regimental Return card that showed "Confederate" at the top, with a space for the company designation below. Next to that was printed a number five, and then the word "Texas."

Under the words "Enlisted men on Extra or Daily Duty" was a nearly illegible scrawl.

"I found I couldn't decipher these words," I said. "What I have that most people don't, though, is a fellow genealogist friend who is also an expert at untangling handwriting such as this. When I sent this link to my friend Ginger, she helped me to determine the words were 'transf. to Fourth'—meaning 'transferred to the Fourth Infantry.'"

The Braithwaite family members all looked at each other in shock.

Helen switched to the next photo, a company muster roll for the Fifth Infantry that, in a firm, clear hand, listed Charles Braithwaite as *Deserted*.

"So, you have to remember these abstracts are only as complete as what the War Department had to work with," I said. "Also, it was often the case that if a soldier had been captured or if he were ill, he was often listed as absent without leave, or even dead. Sometimes this was because the soldier was injured in battle and was left behind, and, thus, wouldn't be able to catch up with his regiment for days or weeks. Then, later, you might find this soldier listed back with his regiment again. The point here is, there could have been other information available on Charles—such as why he was transferred, if he indeed was, or why he deserted, if that happened to be the truth. Or maybe it was possible he was simply in the hospital or temporarily in enemy hands. However, those records for Charles were lost along the way." I smiled at the crowd. "So I had to start digging in other places."

As Helen slowly cued up the corresponding photos, I explained how I researched Charles's journal for evidence of where he'd been and found several references. I then cross-checked them against various other reports, anecdotes, and records, some of which I found through the letters, journals, and other documents digitized and kept by Daughters of the American Revolution. Helen brought up a photo of one of Charles's journal entries, where he mentioned losing his horse to a bullet at Gettysburg, Pennsylvania, and that his comrade had lost his horse as well. This was backed up by a mention from his comrade's diary, which I'd found in the Texas State Archives.

"While Charles never applied for a pension after the war because, one, he didn't marry until after he came home, and two, he managed to thrive after the war, some of his fellow soldiers did indeed apply for one. Pension files often contain soldiers' testimonies of where and with whom they fought, in the hopes of proving their right to a pension—so that was one place I looked."

I then explained that I'd found two pension requests that mentioned Charles, though one slightly misspelled his surname, and both spoke of battles at Wilderness, Virginia, and Chickamauga, Georgia, each of which happened well after the Second Battle of Bull Run.

I showed the family small bits of proof after small bits of proof until they added up to an undeniable case that proved what Charles had written and said his whole life was true.

"I also found strong evidence to suggest that even if he were with the Fourth Infantry for a while, he transferred back to the Fifth at some point well before Appomattox, though no muster roll cards exist to prove this. However, if this were indeed the case, it would give a good reason why he presented himself as being with the Fifth Texas Infantry and didn't really mention the Fourth in his journal, except as part of the proud fighting group known as Hood's Brigade."

Nodding to Helen, I said to the crowd of Charles's descendants, "I have two more things to show you before we all go to lunch."

Helen then brought up a photo of a single cursive letter, and I asked the crowd what they saw.

"It's the letter P!" Tor called out, and everyone except for Jensen Hocknell agreed. She merely narrowed her eyes, but didn't say anything.

"Actually, it's the capital letter S. And if you recall, in the *Chronology* article, Charles's accounts in his handwritten journal are instantly put into doubt when he mentions seeing a seventeen-year-old boy—someone he knew from home—being killed in action. He called that boy 'young Powers.' Yet there were no soldiers from the four regiments within Hood's Brigade named Powers."

I then explained that after realizing how hard it was to read flowery cursive writing sometimes, I had thought it might be possible that the name wasn't "Powers" at all.

Helen slowly flipped through another three slides, which showed a weathered headstone, a letter with a very familiar signature, and a blog post titled "Farewell, Young Sowers."

I said, "And sure enough, in the Fifth Texas was a young man killed early on in action named Oliver Sowers. Because he died in battle, no CMSR in his name exists. However, I found his record in the National Archives at Fort Worth. I also discovered his body was shipped home to Houston, and he was buried with a headstone bearing his name, rank, and regiment."

I used the laser pointer to indicate the screen. "Here we have a blog post written five years ago by a descendant of Oliver's younger brother, referencing not only Oliver's regiment, but also that Oliver's rucksack was delivered home to his parents, along with an accompanying letter telling his parents how and when their son died." Using the pointer, I indicated the photo of the carefully preserved letter that had accompanied the blog post. "It was written and signed by Charles Braithwaite himself, and dated June fifth, 1862, just after the Battle of Seven Pines." I used the pointer to highlight three scrawled letters before Charles's name. "And if you notice, Charles signed the letter with his new rank . . ." My grin went wider. This was the best part. "C-p-l—short for corporal."

The audible gasps of happy relief from the family members made me realize that thinking Charles had invented the contents of his journal and life had bothered them more than the possibility of his actually being a deserter.

Turning off the laser pointer and clasping my hands in front of me, I said, "And as the very last piece of my investigation into your ancestor, I contacted the editor of *Chronology* and explained my findings. He has assured me a retraction will be up on the website by this time tomorrow, and that a new article will be written—and approved by Camilla before it runs—on Charles, his life and legacy, and his amazing triptych painting."

With that, Helen and I pulled back the curtains hiding the Braithwaite exhibit to show that it had been updated with a beautiful photographic rendering of both Charles's Texas Emancipation Day drawing and his panoramic triptych. The title of the three-paneled battle scene was *The Battle at Lawson's Bridge*. The title had been found, written in Charles's own hand, on the back of Charlie Braithwaite's recovered panel.

Then I blushed nine full shades of red as the whole Braithwaite family, led by Camilla and her aunt Jensen, stood and applauded me.

Later that night gave us an extra-happy surprise.

I had reserved Flaco's new private chef's table for a dinner with Serena, Josephine, Helen, all their boyfriends, Ben, and me. Then, learning Camilla's family had all gone home, I invited her as well. For the first time ever, Camilla seemed shy around me, but my friends and I all worked to make her feel comfortable, and she was soon laughing and enjoying herself.

Just as the subject of the painting came up, I had gotten a Face-Time call from Grandpa. He'd merely called to check on me and make sure Ben and I would still be coming to Wimberley over the weekend. However, once my girlfriends knew it was Grandpa, my phone was passed around so that Serena and Josephine could shamelessly flirt with him as they always did, making him laugh.

A few minutes later, as Grandpa was chatting with Ben about the best fishing spots near Wimberley, he overheard Helen say to Camilla, "You know, I'm just dying to know how that other painting came to be on the outside in the first place. I mean, who put it there? Who painted it? It's still a mystery, and it's making me crazy."

"Me too," Camilla said. She gave me a wry grin. "Maybe I'll have to hire you and Lucy to team up again just to find out."

Helen and I looked at each other, then said to Camilla in unison, "Yes, *please.*"

Everyone laughed, but Grandpa's voice silenced us.

"I just might be able to help with that, actually," he said.

I leaned in so Ben and I could both see Grandpa's face. "How do you mean?"

On the screen, Grandpa, relaxing in his favorite chair in his living room, said, "Well, as you know, this latest adventure undertaken by you three has been all over the news."

Camilla, Helen, and I looked at each other with embarrassed grins. This time, the press had gotten ahold of my name, but sharing the unwanted spotlight with my two accomplices hadn't been so bad. Plus, the good press that came out of it was nice for both the Braithwaite family and Helen's business.

"So, this morning," Grandpa continued, "I was enjoying my breakfast at the diner, and the ladies who've been teaching me mah-jongg at the senior center came in and insisted I join them."

"*Yeah* they did, George! You're hot stuff," Serena catcalled, with Josephine adding, "Should we be jealous, George, darling?"

Grandpa, turning pink around the ears and grinning, said, "You two beauties say such tosh. Anyhow, the ladies primed me for information, knowing I'm Lucy's grandfather and how proud I am." Now *I* blushed as he went on. "Eventually, though, the subject of the outer painting came up, and one of the ladies, Patsy, told us her childhood best friend had been a Dolly Braithwaite. Patsy apparently spent a lot of time at the Braithwaite house growing up, and she has a fairly strong memory of hearing a story about how the painting came to be." Grandpa chuckled. "Only she can't recall the exact details."

I looked up at Camilla, who was still watching Grandpa over my shoulder. "I've heard Dolly's name, but I don't know who she is in relation to me."

I was already handing my phone to Ben and pulling my iPad out to look in my Braithwaite files for Dolly. "She was one of your uncle Charlie's first cousins," I said. "Born in 1933. Passed away ten years ago."

"Darn it. I was hoping I could contact her," Camilla said.

I looked at my phone to see Grandpa smiling. "Yes, but as I understand it, Dolly had several children . . ."

Picking up on his thread, I added, "And if the story was one that Patsy, a mere friend, heard, then it's possible Dolly's children heard it as well."

Grandpa looked at me with pride. "Do your thing, Lucy, my love."

I soon found that Dolly had five children, all of whom were still alive, though only one still lived in Texas. Three of them had active Facebook accounts.

I met Camilla's eyes. "Want to message them?"

"Are you kidding?" she said. She'd already found her cell phone and was soon messaging her distant cousins.

Grandpa, grinning after Camilla thanked him profusely, signed off, and our little group went back to eating as Flaco passed through a round of insanely good fish tacos as our next course. We didn't expect to hear back from the children of Dolly Braithwaite anytime soon, so we all just stared in surprise when, over coffees, churros with Mexican chocolate dipping sauce, and tres leches cake at the end of our amazing meal, Camilla grabbed her phone and said, "One wrote back!"

We all waited with bated breath as she silently read the message.

"Well?" Serena said finally. "Tell us the scoop."

Camilla began, "Apparently, it was Dolly's father, Harold Braithwaite, who was the culprit."

I checked for Harold's name. "He was born in 1910," I told her. "One of Nathaniel's grandsons."

"Thanks," she said. "So, it seems that, one day, when he was young boy, Harold's mother found the three panels stored under a bed while staying at Charles and Violet's house. Thinking they were a castoff, she stretched a new canvas over each one of them and let Harold paint his own battle scene on top. When he was done, the three panels were put away and forgotten about. Later, Harold was away at college when Charles, who was by then very old, deaf, and suffering from cataracts, directed that each of the three panels were to be given to a member of the three branches of his family—but Harold heard about it. His mother was too embarrassed to confess what she'd done to the family heirlooms, and Harold didn't want to give her up, so he never mentioned it." Camilla looked up from her phone again, her eyes happy. "It became their family secret, which my cousin says was funny at the time, but she's glad the truth is out now."

"Wow," I said, and everyone nodded.

Even better, Camilla grinned and held out her margarita glass to me in a toast. "To another mystery solved. Cheers, Lucy."

"To another mystery solved," I agreed. We clinked glasses, and soon everyone was following suit, calling out, "Cheers!"

FORTY-ONE

✣

Ten days later, Ben and I were back in Houston. He was in a beautifully cut suit, while I wore a pale yellow strapless minidress embroidered with white vines. We stepped into the foyer of the Museum of Fine Arts, Houston, just two minutes before the presentation was about to start.

"There you are," Mom said, coming up to us. "What took y'all so long?"

"I'm afraid it was my fault, Nita," Grandpa said, coming around to my other side. He, too, looked dashing in a dark suit and a blue tie printed, if you looked closely, with tiny armadillos drinking from bottles of Lone Star beer. "I felt a new tie was in order and asked them to take me shopping before we came here."

I put my hand up to the side of my mouth, but didn't attempt to whisper. "He spent half the time flirting with a very pretty widow named Estelle, that's why it really took so long."

Grandpa winked, tightening the half-Windsor knot. "She thought this one brought out my eyes."

"George, you old so-and-so," Mom said with a laugh. "Did you get her number, at least?"

Grandpa unfurled his hand and a piece of flowered notepaper

appeared out of nowhere. "I may have," he said with a cheeky grin. With another wave of his hand, the paper was gone, and Grandpa offered his arm to my mother. "May I escort you to our seats for this incredible evening? You look lovely as always, Nita."

Mom giggled and tucked her hand into the crook of his arm, and they moved off to the second row of seats, passing a large banner that read *The Treasure Beneath: The Wondrous Story Behind the Lost Civil War Triptych of Charles Braithwaite.*

The words were printed over a close-up of the part of Camilla's painting that included the incredibly moving view of the terrified soldier looking back over his shoulder with widened blue eyes. The gloriousness of Charles's true painting had blown the minds of many an art appraiser—or so said Helen, at least. And I figured she would know.

Standing and looking at the banner, I saw the figure of Neil Gaynor and the younger woman I recognized from his Instagram photos as his sister, Dina. They were both smiling, and Neil looked relaxed. Before Camilla went back to Houston, I'd told her about overhearing Neil telling his sister that he planned to drop the lawsuit against the Braithwaites, and that he was giving up school to take a job so he could afford his aunt's caregiver bills. I added that Ben had helped me verify that what Neil had said was true. Camilla had then spoken to her family, and while I didn't know the details, I knew Neil and Dina were both able to remain in school, and they no longer had to worry about affording to keep on their aunt's caregiver.

Camilla seemed to have been watching anxiously for us, and when I waved at her, she gave me an exasperated smile—but it was one you give a friend, so I just grinned and blew her a kiss for good luck. This was witnessed by both Roxie and Patrice, and while Roxie looked like she'd just eaten a handful of sour grapes, Patrice merely smiled and waved at me.

Camilla wouldn't have to deal with either of them for too much longer, though, as she was moving to Austin to help oversee both the running of Charlie's wine merchant business and the distribution and sale of his photographs, which had been appraised at a very nice price. With Camilla giving us a steep discount, Ben and I had bought three apiece, including the photo of the smiling, windswept woman on the streets of Paris. It now sat on the windowsill of my office, next to my desk.

I caught sight of Helen and waved, as Ben and I made our way to the front row, which had been roped off for special guests of Camilla's, including Ben and me, Helen, Cisco, and, sitting in the last seat in the row, Elaine Trudeau. There was still a great sadness in her eyes, but she held herself with grace and smiled as I said hello to her and introduced her to Ben.

As we took our seats, Ben said under his breath, "Okay, you're going to have to explain that. I thought she was Enemy Number One."

There was so much talking around us that no one heard as I said in his ear, "So, Charlie lost all his money to a crooked business partner, right? Well, just before that, back in 1982, that business partner brought his new girlfriend—Elaine, who was going by her middle name at the time—to meet Charlie at the Kentucky Derby. Elaine and Charlie fell in love that day, but she was dating the business partner, so . . . Anyway, she broke up with him after finding out he'd stolen Charlie's money, but she was too afraid to contact Charlie after that, fearing that he would somehow blame her or think she was part of it. She married someone else, had kids, and never saw Charlie again, until she got divorced and moved to Austin last year as a grandmother."

"Did Elaine know Charlie was in Austin?" Ben asked.

"Apparently, yes, but she didn't know where he lived. She was looking at several houses in the area and saw him gardening in his front yard one day. The house next door had a for-sale sign, and she bought it, sight unseen."

Ben merely raised his eyebrows but didn't comment.

"Anyhow, remember me telling you that she seemed obsessed with Charlie's photos, and Helen had seen her holding one the night Charlie died?" Ben nodded, and I said, "Well, Elaine believed that Charlie wouldn't remember her after four decades. Still, she feared that, if he did figure out who she was, he would never give her another chance with her connection to the business partner. So, she was trying to find the photo that proved they'd met and who she'd been dating so she could get rid of it. However, between the fact that Charlie usually came to her house and that he or Camilla changed up the photos so often—not to mention that there were so many of them—it took her a while. She finally found it and took it the night he died."

"I wonder if he knew," Ben mused.

"Turns out, he did," I replied. "The four photos he left Elaine were all of that day they met at the Kentucky Derby. On the back of one, he'd written, 'The girl I love.'"

Ben looked at me, and I had a feeling we were thinking the same thing, about all the time Elaine had wasted trying to conceal her secret and what she must be feeling at the moment. Leaning in closer, he whispered in my ear, "Our situation is different, of course, but I'm really glad you gave me a second chance. I would have hated to lose out on you because of assumptions and off timing."

I smiled, taking his hand and whispering back, "That sentiment goes both ways, believe me."

There was a tap on the microphone and the museum curator took the podium, launching into the history of Charles Braithwaite and the Braithwaite family, deftly glossing over the current troubles within the family stemming from Savannah

Lundstrom's and Trent Marins's greediness. He explained my role, making me stand and blushingly accept more applause, then did the same for both Cisco and Helen.

The curator then explained that beyond the extraordinary triptych that had survived unscathed all these years and depicted such incredible human emotions regarding war and suffering, the three scenes were also the only known rendering of the Battle at Lawson's Bridge, which took place in March of 1865 near Richmond, Virginia.

"Though it's a less famous battle, it was still an instrumental one," the curator explained. "There's a thought that Lawson's Bridge set in motion events that paved the way to the Battle of Appomattox Court House, thus beginning the end of the war. Plus, not only is this the sole painting created of the Battle at Lawson's Bridge, it's also by an artist who was actually there." He moved to stand by the right panel—Camilla's piece of the triptych. "In fact," he said, pointing toward the golden-haired soldier with a cleft chin, whose face I'd watched Helen clean so many days ago, "we believe this soldier might be Charles Braithwaite himself." After the murmurs of excitement from the crowd had faded away, the curator beamed at the restored triptych, displayed in pride of place, the three paintings once more together, side by side. "They simply take your breath away."

"I have to agree," I said, and Ben nodded.

"It's truly an incredible painting. The man had talent for sure."

The curator continued, satisfaction filling his voice.

"On behalf of Ms. Camilla Braithwaite and the entire Braithwaite family, all of whom agreed with Camilla's request, this triptych will not be sold on the open market, as they believe it should be in a museum." He gave the crowd a smile, adding, "Even though the painting could fetch a truly outstanding price. Regardless—and I am so honored to announce this—it has been given jointly in the name of Camilla's beloved great-uncle, the late Charlie Braithwaite, to the Museum of Fine Arts, Houston, and the Smithsonian National Museum of American History. It will be displayed on even-numbered years here in its hometown of Houston, and on odd-numbered years in the venerable Smithsonian museum in Washington, DC."

The clapping was thunderous, and Camilla looked like she couldn't be more proud of her family, her ancestor, and herself.

She came over to me, taking my hands in hers and looking me in the eyes with a smile. Then she wrapped me in a big hug.

"Thank you, Lucy," she said in my ear as I hugged her back. "Thank you for giving my ancestor and me both a second chance."

Well, what do you know? I thought. Mom was right again. Wonders will never cease.

ACKNOWLEDGMENTS

I'm incredibly grateful to my wonderful team at Minotaur Books, including my editor, Hannah O'Grady; my copyeditor, Ivy McFadden; my proofreaders; and the incredible marketing and publicity stars who do such a great job in helping get both my name and Lucy's adventures out in the world. And, of course, another big shout-out goes to David Rotstein for this seriously stunning cover.

My agents, too, are just the best. Christina Hogrebe and Jess Errera of Jane Rotrosen Agency—thank you so much for everything you do, as always.

Once again, I'm truly thankful to Alice Braud-Jones for reading my book for genealogy accuracy, for allowing me to pepper her with questions, and for giving me so many extra details that show the unique magic of Lucy's profession.

Much appreciation also goes to Sergeant Doug Thomas of the Harris County Sheriff's Office and all his great law-enforcement facts and lingo, and for cheerfully always letting me interview him.

I'm also grateful to Luci Hansson Zahray, aka "The Poison Lady," for talking about arsenic being used as a preservative in the bodies of Civil War soldiers back at a Malice Domestic convention, for letting me ask her a bunch of questions about it, and, again, for reading Lucy's first adventure (three books ago now!) and seeing so much potential in her and me.

A second helping of thanks goes to Catherine B. Custalow, MD, PhD (and fellow writer to boot), for being my awesome and kind go-to person for medical questions.

Also, thank you so very much to Athena L. Lark, MFA, MEd, for reading my manuscript and for her thoughtful and informative responses.

Last, but certainly not least, I had so much fun writing about the art in this book, but the learning about it from three wonderful ladies was almost more fun. I'm hugely grateful to Marigold A. Lamb, MS, Life Certified Member, ISA CAPP; Laura Pate, art conservator and owner of Brown Mountain Art Restoration; and Brenda Simonson-Mohle, ISA CAPP, for all their time and patience in explaining art terms to me and helping me hone my art-related scenarios to make them as believable and interesting as possible (and for understanding that I might use artistic license here and there, too). Extra thanks go to Marigold for reading over the art sections of my first draft and to Laura for both introducing me to Marigold and for finding the article that helped inspire how the triptych panels came to have paintings hidden underneath.

As always, if there are any errors or inaccuracies in my book, they are most certainly mine and mine alone. (Though one of these inaccuracies—the Battle at Lawson's Bridge—was deliberate as I decided creating a fictional battle would be the best way to ensure Charles had the lock on painting it!)

And as for family ties, I've got the best ones. Thank you to all my family, and especially my incredible and loving parents.